RAISING STEAM

A Discworld® Novel

For more information about Terry Pratchett and his books, please visit www.terrypratchett.co.uk

BOOKS BY TERRY PRATCHETT

The Discworld® series

1. THE COLOUR OF MAGIC

2. THE LIGHT FANTASTIC

3. EQUAL RITES

4. MORT

5. SOURCERY

6. WYRD SISTERS

7. PYRAMIDS

8. GUARDS! GUARDS!

9. ERIC
(illustrated by Josh Kirby)

10. MOVING PICTURES

11. REAPER MAN

12. WITCHES ABROAD

13. SMALL GODS

14. LORDS AND LADIES

15. MEN AT ARMS

16. SOUL MUSIC

17. INTERESTING TIMES

18. MASKERADE

19. FEET OF CLAY

20. HOGFATHER

21. JINGO

22. THE LAST CONTINENT

23. CARPE JUGULUM

24. THE FIFTH ELEPHANT

25. THE TRUTH

26. THIEF OF TIME

27. THE LAST HERO
(illustrated by Paul Kidby)

28. THE AMAZING MAURICE &
HIS EDUCATED RODENTS (for young adults)

Other books about Discworld

THE FOLKLORE OF DISCWORLD
(with Jacqueline Simpson)

THE WORLD OF POO
(with the Discworld Emporium)

THE COMPLEAT ANKH-MORPORK
(with the Discworld Emporium)

THE STREETS OF ANKH-MORPORK
(with Stephen Briggs, painted by Stephen Player)

THE DISCWORLD MAPP
(with Stephen Briggs, painted by Stephen Player)

A TOURIST GUIDE TO LANCRE – A DISCWORLD MAPP
(with Stephen Briggs, illustrated by Paul Kidby)

DEATH'S DOMAIN (with Paul Kidby)

A complete list of Terry Pratchett ebooks and audio books as well as other
books based on the Discworld series – illustrated screenplays, graphic
novels, comics and plays – can be found on **www.terrypratchett.co.uk**

──────────────── **Shorter Writing** ────────────────

A BLINK OF THE SCREEN

──────────────── **Non-Discworld books** ────────────────

THE DARK SIDE OF THE SUN

STRATA

THE UNADULTERATED CAT (illustrated by Gray Jolliffe)

GOOD OMENS (with Neil Gaiman)

THE LONG EARTH (with Stephen Baxter)

THE LONG WAR (with Stephen Baxter)

──────────── **Non-Discworld novels for young adults** ────────────

THE CARPET PEOPLE

TRUCKERS

DIGGERS

WINGS

ONLY YOU CAN SAVE MANKIND

JOHNNY AND THE DEAD

JOHNNY AND THE BOMB

NATION

DODGER

RAISING STEAM

Terry Pratchett

Doubleday

LONDON · TORONTO · SYDNEY · AUCKLAND · JOHANNESBURG

TRANSWORLD PUBLISHERS
61–63 Uxbridge Road, London W5 5SA
A Random House Group Company
www.transworldbooks.co.uk

First published in Great Britain
in 2013 by Doubleday
an imprint of Transworld Publishers

A CIP catalogue record for this book
is available from the British Library.

ISBN 9780857522276

Addresses for Random House Group Ltd companies outside the UK
can be found at: www.randomhouse.co.uk
The Random House Group Ltd Reg. No. 954009

The Random House Group Limited supports the Forest Stewardship Council® (FSC®),
the leading international forest-certification organisation. Our books carrying the FSC
label are printed on FSC®-certified paper. FSC is the only forest-certification scheme
supported by the leading environmental organisations, including Greenpeace.
Our paper procurement policy can be found at
www.randomhouse.co.uk/environment

Typeset in 11.75/15.25pt Minion by Falcon Oast Graphic Art Ltd.
Printed and bound in Great Britain by
CPI Group (UK) Ltd, Croydon, CR0 4YY

2 4 6 8 10 9 7 5 3 1

MIX
Paper from
responsible sources
FSC® C016897

To David Pratchett and Jim Wilkins, both fine engineers
who taught their sons to be curious.

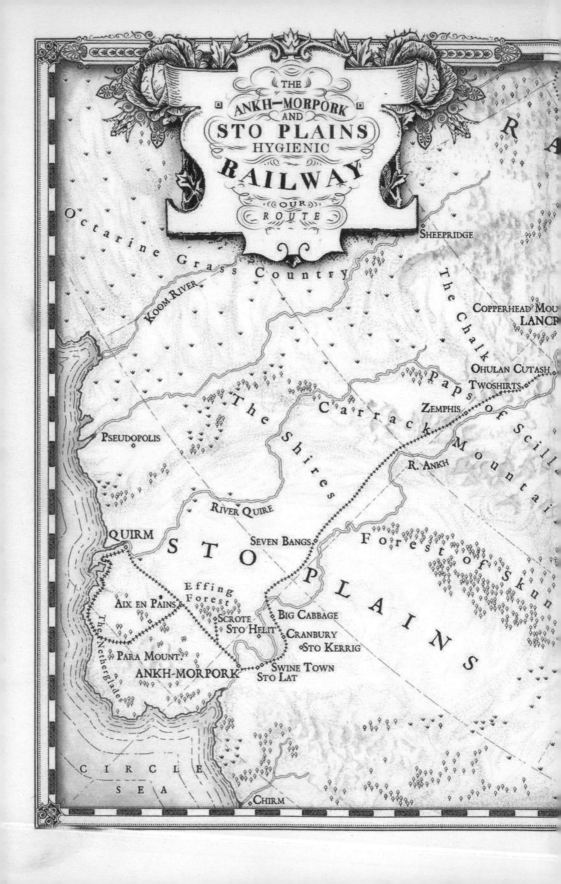

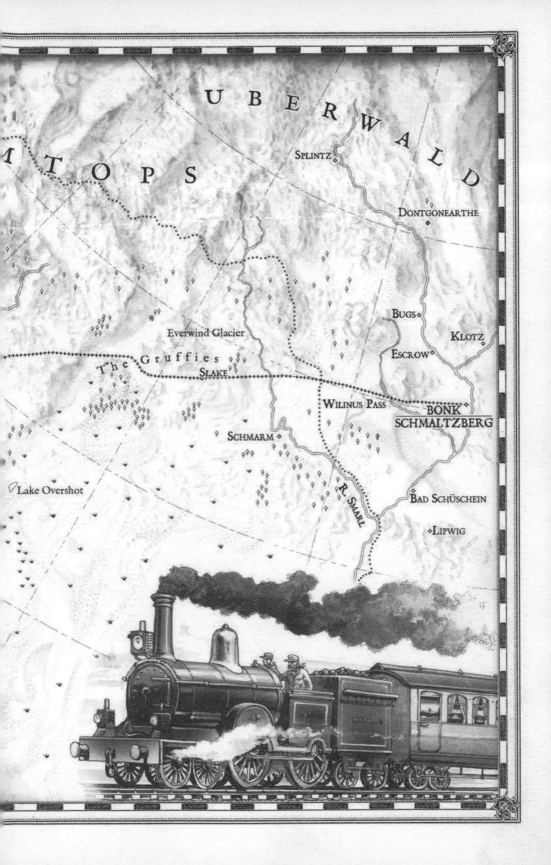

UBERWALD

TOPS

SPLINTZ

DONTGONEARTHE

Everwind Glacier

BUGS

KLOTZ

ESCROW

The Gruffies

SLAKE

WILINUS PASS

BONK

SCHMALTZBERG

SCHMARM

R. SMARL

Lake Overshot

BAD SCHÜSCHEIN

LIPWIG

It is hard to understand nothing, but the multiverse is full of it. Nothing travels everywhere, always ahead of something, and in the great cloud of unknowing nothing yearns to become something, to break out, to move, to feel, to change, to dance and to experience – in short, to *be* something.

And now it found its chance as it drifted in the ether. Nothing, of course, knew about something, but this something was different, oh yes, and so nothing slid silently into something and floated down with everything in mind and, fortunately, landed on the back of a turtle, a very large one, and hurried to become something even faster. It was elemental and nothing was better than that and suddenly the elemental was captured! The bait had worked.

*

Anyone who has ever seen the River Ankh sliding along its bed of miscellaneous nastiness would understand why so much of the piscine food for the people of Ankh-Morpork has to be supplied by the fishing fleets of Quirm. In order to prevent terrible gastric trouble for the citizenry, Ankh-Morpork fishmongers have to ensure that their suppliers make their catches a long, long way from the city.

For Bowden Jeffries, purveyor of the very best in seafood, the two hundred miles or more which lay between the fish docks at Quirm and the customers in Ankh-Morpork was a regrettably long distance throughout the winter, autumn and spring and a sheer penance in the summertime, because the highway, such as it was, became a linear furnace all the way to the Big City. Once you had had to deal with a ton of overheated octopus, you never forgot it; the smell lasted for days, and followed you around and almost into your bedroom. You could never get it out of your clothes.

People were so demanding, but the elite of Ankh-Morpork and, indeed, everyone else wanted their fish, even in the hottest part of the season. Even with an icehouse built by his own two hands and, by arrangement, a second icehouse halfway along the journey, it made you want to cry, it really did.

And he said as much to his cousin, Relief Jeffries, a market gardener, who looked at his beer and said, 'It's always the same. Nobody wants to help the small entrepreneur. Can you imagine how quickly strawberries turn into little balls of mush in the heat? Well, I'll tell you: no time at all. Blink and you miss 'em, just when everybody wants their strawberries. And you ask the watercress people how difficult it is to get the damn stuff to the city before it's as limp as a second-day sermon. We should petition the government!'

'No,' said his cousin. 'I've had enough of this. Let's write to the newspapers! That's the way to get things done. Everyone's complaining about the fruit and vegetables and the seafood. Vetinari should be made to understand the plight of the small-time entrepreneur. After all, what do we occasionally pay our taxes for?'

Dick Simnel was ten years old when, back at the family smithy in Sheepridge, his father simply disappeared in a cloud of furnace parts and flying metal, all enveloped in a pink steam. He was never found in the terrible haze of scorching dampness, but on that very day young Dick Simnel vowed to whatever was left of his father in that boiling steam that he would make steam his servant.

His mother had other ideas. She was a midwife, and as she said to her neighbours, 'Babbies are born everywhere. I'll never be without a customer.' So, against her son's wishes, Elsie Simnel decided to take him away from what she now considered to be a haunted place. She packed up their belongings and together they returned to her family home near Sto Lat, where people didn't inexplicably disappear in a hot pink cloud.

Soon after they arrived something important happened to her boy. One day while waiting for his mother to return from a difficult delivery, Dick walked into a building that looked interesting, and which turned out to be a library. At first he thought it was full of poncy stuff, all kings and poets and lovers and battles, but in one crucial book he found something called mathematics and the world of numbers.

And that was why, one day some ten years later, he pulled together every fibre of his being and said, 'Mother, you know last year when I said I were going 'iking in the mountains of Uberwald with me mates, well, it were kind of . . . sort of . . . a kind of lie, only very small, mind you.' Dick blushed. 'You see, I found t'keys to Dad's old shed and, well, I went back to Sheepridge and did some experimenting and . . .' he looked at his mother anxiously, 'I think I know what 'e were doing wrong.'

Dick was braced for stiff objections, but he hadn't reckoned on tears – so many tears – and as he tried to console her he added, 'You, Mother, and Uncle Flavius got me an education, you got me the knowing of the numbers, including the arithmetic and weird stuff dreamed up by the philosophers in Ephebe where even camels can do logarithms on their toes. Dad didn't know this stuff. He had the right ideas but he didn't have the . . . *tech-nol-ogy* right.'

At this point, Dick allowed his mother to talk, and she said, 'I know there's no stopping you, our Dick, you're just like your stubborn father were, pigheaded. Is that what you've been doin' in the barn? Teck-ology?' She looked at him accusingly, then sighed. 'I can see I can't tell you what to do, but you tell me: how can your "logger-reasons" stop you goin' the way of your poor old dad?' She started sobbing again.

Dick pulled out of his jacket something that looked like a small wand, which might have been made for a miniature wizard, and said, 'This'll keep me safe, Mother! I've the knowing of the sliding rule! I can tell the sine what to do, and the cosine likewise and work out the tangent of t'quaderatics! Come on, Mother, stop fretting and come wi' me now to t'barn. You must see 'er!'

Mrs Simnel, reluctant, was dragged by her son to the great open barn he had kitted out like the workshop back at Sheepridge, hoping against hope that her son had accidentally found himself a girl. Inside the barn she looked helplessly at a large circle of metal which covered most of the floor. Something metallic whizzed round and round on the metal, sounding like a squirrel in a cage, giving off a smell much like camphor.

'Here she is, Mother. Ain't she champion?' Dick said happily. 'I call her Iron Girder!'

'But what is it, son?'

He grinned hugely and said, 'It's what they call a pro-to-type, Mother. You've got to 'ave a pro-to-type if you're going to be an engineer.'

His mother smiled wanly but there was no stopping Dick. The words just tumbled out.

'The thing is, Mother, before you attempt owt you've got to 'ave some idea of what it is you want to do. One of the books I found in the library was about being an architect. And in that book, the man who wrote it said before he built his next big 'ouse he always made quite tiny models to get an idea of how it would all work out. He said it sounds fiddly and stuff, but going slowly and being thorough is the only way forward. And so I'm testing 'er out slowly, seeing what works and what doesn't. And actually, I'm quite proud of me'sen. In the beginning I made t'track wooden, but I reckoned that the engine I wanted would be very 'eavy, so I chopped up t'wooden circle for firewood and went back to t'forge.'

Mrs Simnel looked at the little mechanism running round and round on the barn floor and said, in the voice of someone really trying to understand, 'Eee, lad, but what does it *do*?'

'Well, I remembered what Dad said about t'time he were watching t'kettle boiling and noticed t'lid going up and down with the pressure, and he told me that one day someone would build a bigger kettle that would lift more than a kettle lid. And I believe I have the knowing of the way to build a proper kettle, Mother.'

'And what good would that do, my boy?' said his mother sternly. And she watched the glow in her son's eyes as he said, 'Everything, Mother. *Everything*.'

Still in a haze of slight misunderstanding, Mrs Simnel watched him unroll a large and rather grubby piece of paper.

'It's called a blueprint, Mother. You've got to have a blueprint. It shows you how everything fits together.'

'Is this part of the pro-to-type?'

The boy looked at his doting mother's face and realized that a little more exposition should be forthcoming. He took her by the hand and said, 'Mother, I know they're all lines and circles to you, but once you have the knowing of the circles and the lines and all, you know that this is a picture of an engine.'

Mrs Simnel gripped his hand and said, 'What do you think you're going to do with it, our Dick?'

And young Simnel grinned and said happily, 'Change things as needs changing, Mother.'

Mrs Simnel gave her son a curious look for a moment or two, then appeared to reach a grudging conclusion and said, 'Just you come with me, my lad.'

She led him back into the house, where they climbed up the ladder into the attic. She pointed out to her son a sturdy seaman's chest covered in dust.

'Your granddad gave me this to give to you, when I thought you needed it. Here's the key.'

She was gratified that he didn't grab it and indeed looked carefully at the trunk before opening it. As he pushed up the lid, suddenly the air was filled with the glimmer of gold.

'Your granddad were slightly a bit of a pirate and then he got religion and were a bit afeared, and the last words he said to me on his deathbed were, "That young lad'll do something one day, you mark my words, our Elsie, but I'm damned if I know what it's going to be." '

The people of the town were quite accustomed to the clangings and bangings emanating every day from the various blacksmith forges for which the area was famous. It seemed that, even though he had set up a forge of his own, young Simnel had decided not to enter the blacksmithing trade, possibly due to the dreadful business of Mr Simnel Senior's leaving the world so abruptly. The local blacksmiths soon got used to making mysterious items that young Mr Simnel had sketched out meticulously. He never told them what he was constructing, but since they were earning a lot of money they didn't mind.

The news of his legacy got around, of course – gold always finds its way out somehow – and there was a scratching of heads among the population exemplified by the oldest inhabitant, who, sitting on the bench outside the tavern, said, 'Well, bugger me! Lad were blessed wi' an inherited fortune in gold and turned it into a load of old iron!'

He laughed, and so did everybody else, but nevertheless they continued to watch young Dick Simnel slip in and out of the wicket gate of his old and almost derelict barn, double-padlocked at all times.

Simnel had found a couple of local likely lads who helped him make things and move things around. Over time, the barn was augmented by a host of other sheds. More lads were taken on and the hammers were heard all day every day and, a bit at a time, information trickled into what might be called the local consciousness.

Apparently the lad had made a pump, an interesting pump that pumped water very high. And then he'd thrown everything away and said things like, 'We need more steel than iron.'

There were tales of great reams of paper laid out on desks as young Simnel worked out a wonderful 'undertaking', as he called it. Admittedly there had been the occasional explosion, and then people heard about what the lads called 'The Bunker', which had been useful to jump into on several occasions when there had been a little . . . incident. And then there was the unfamiliar but somehow homely and rhythmic 'chuffing' noise. Really quite a pleasant noise, almost hypnotic, which was strange because the mechanical creature that was making the noise sounded more alive than you would have expected.

It was noticed in the locality that the two main co-workers of Mr Simnel, or 'Mad Iron' Simnel as some were now calling him, seemed somewhat changed, more grown-up and aware of themselves; young men, acolytes of the mysterious thing behind the doors. And no amount of bribery by beer or by women in the pub would make them give up the precious secrets of the barn.* They conducted themselves now as befitted the masters of the fiery furnace.

And then, of course, there were the sunny days when young Simnel and his cohorts dug long lines in the field next to the barn and filled them with metal while the furnace glowed day and night and everyone shook their heads and said, 'Madness.' And this went on, it seemed for ever, until ever was finished and the banging and

---

* There were some salacious comments about this, but it appeared, alas, to the local and as yet unmarried girls that Mad Iron Simnel and his men had found something more interesting than women and apparently it was made of steel.

clanging and smelting had stopped. Then Mr Simnel's lieutenants pulled aside the double doors of the big barn and filled the world with smoke.

Very little happened in this part of Sto Lat and this was enough to bring people running. Most of them arrived in time to see *something* heading out towards them, panting and steaming, with fast-spinning wheels and oscillating rods eerily appearing and disappearing in the smoke and the haze, and on top of it all, like a sort of king of smoke and fire, Dick Simnel, his face contorted with the effort of concentration. It was faintly reassuring that this *something* was apparently under the control of somebody human – although the more thoughtful of the onlookers might have added 'So what? So's a spoon,' and got ready to run away as the steaming, dancing, spinning, reciprocating engine cleared the barn and plunged on down the tracks laid in the field. And the bystanders, most of whom were now byrunners, and in certain instances bystampeders, fled and complained, except, of course, for every little boy of any age who followed it with eyes open wide, vowing there and then that one day *he* would be the captain of the terrible noxious engine, oh yes indeed. A prince of the steam! A master of the sparks! A coachman of the Thunderbolts!

And outside, freed at last, the smoke drifted purposefully away from the shed in the direction of the largest city in the world. It drifted slowly at first, but gathered speed.

Later that day, and after several triumphant turns around the short track in the field, Simnel sat down with his helpers.

'Wally, Dave, I'm running out of brass, lads,' he said. 'Get your mothers to get your stuff together, make us some butties, bring out the 'orses. We're taking Iron Girder to Ankh-Morpork. I 'ear it's the place where things 'appen.'

Of course Lord Vetinari, Tyrant of Ankh-Morpork, would occasionally meet Lady Margolotta, Governess of Uberwald. Why shouldn't he? After all, he also occasionally had meetings with Diamond King of Trolls up near Koom Valley, and indeed with the Low King of the Dwarfs, Rhys Rhysson, in his caverns *under* Uberwald. This, as everybody knew, was politics.

Yes, politics. The secret glue that stopped the world falling into warfare. In the past there had been so much war, far too much, but as every schoolboy knew, or at least knew in those days when schoolboys actually read anything more demanding than a crisp packet, not so long ago a truly terrible war, the last war of Koom Valley, had *almost* happened, out of which the dwarfs and trolls had managed to achieve not exactly peace, but an understanding from which, hopefully, peace might evolve. There had been the shaking of hands, *important* hands, shaken fervently, and so there was hope, hope as fragile as a thought.

Indeed, thought Lord Vetinari as his coach rattled along towards Uberwald, in the rosy afterglow that had followed the famous Koom Valley Accord even goblins had finally been recognized as sapient creatures, to be metaphorically treated as brothers, although not necessarily as brothers-in-law. He reflected that, from a distance, the world might conceivably look to be at peace, a state of affairs that always ends in war, eventually.

He winced as his coach hit another most egregious bump on the road. He'd had the seats supplemented with extra mattress padding but simply nothing could turn the journey to Uberwald into anything other than a penance at every pothole, leading to fundamental discomfort. Progress had been very slow, although stops at clacks towers along the route had allowed his secretary, Drumknott, to collect the daily crossword puzzle without which Lord Vetinari considered the day incomplete.

There was a bang from outside.

'Good grief! Must we hit every pothole on the road, Drumknott?'

'I'm sorry, sir, but it appears that her ladyship cannot even now control the bandits around the Wilinus Pass. She has a culling every so often, but I'm afraid this is the least dangerous route.'

There was a shout outside, followed by more banging. Vetinari blew out his reading lamp moments before a ferocious-looking individual pushed the point of a crossbow bolt to the glass of the carriage, which was now in darkness, and said, 'Just you come out here with all your valuables or it'll be the worse for you, okay! No tricks now! We're assassins!'

Lord Vetinari calmly put down the book he had been reading, sighed and said to Drumknott, 'It appears, Drumknott, that we have been hijacked by *assassins*. Isn't that . . . nice.'

And now Drumknott had a little smile. 'Oh, yes, how nice, sir. You always like meeting assassins. I won't get in your way, sir.'

Vetinari pulled his cloak around him as he stepped out of the coach and said, 'There is no reason for violence, gentlemen. I will give you everything I have . . .'

And it was no more than two minutes later that his lordship climbed back up into the coach and signalled for the driver to carry on as if nothing had happened.

After a while, and out of sheer curiosity, Drumknott said, 'What happened this time, my lord? I didn't hear anything.'

Beside him, Lord Vetinari said, 'Neither did they, Drumknott. Dear me, it's such a waste. One wonders why they don't learn to read. Then they'd recognize the crest on my coach, which would have enlightened them!'

As the coach got up to what might be considered an *erratic* kind of speed, and after some thought, Drumknott said, 'But your crest, sir, is black on a black background and it's a very dark night.'

'Ah, yes, Drumknott,' Lord Vetinari replied, with what passed as a smile. 'Do you know, I hadn't thought of that.'

*

There was something inevitable about Lady Margolotta's castle. As the great wooden doors slowly opened, every door hinge creaked. After all, there was such a thing as socially acceptable ambience. Indeed, what kind of vampire would live in a castle that didn't creak and groan on cue? The Igors wouldn't have it any other way, and now the resident Igor welcomed Lord Vetinari and his secretary into a cavernous hall with spiders' webs hanging pendulously from the ceiling. And there was a sense, only a sense, that down in the basement somewhere, something was screaming.

But of course, Vetinari reflected, here was a wonderful lady, who had made vampires understand that returning from the grave so often that you got dizzy was rather stupid and who somehow had persuaded them to at least tone down their nocturnal activities. Besides which, she had introduced coffee to Uberwald, apparently exchanging one terrifying craving for another.

Lady Margolotta was always short and to the point, as was the nature of the conversation that followed a splendid dinner a few days later. 'It is the grags. The grags again, yes, Havelock? After all this time! My vord, even vorse, just as you, my dear, prophesied. How could you have foreseen it?'

'Well, madam, Diamond King of Trolls asked me the very same thing, but all I can say is that it lies in the indefatigable nature of sapient creatures. In short, they can't all be satisfied at the same time. You thought the bunting and fireworks and handshakes and pledges after Koom Valley was signed and sealed was the end of it, yes? Personally, I have always considered this a mere interlude. In short, Margolotta, peace is what you have while incubating the next war. It is impossible to accommodate *everyone* and twice as impossible to please all the dwarfs. You see, when I'm talking to Diamond King of Trolls he is the mouthpiece of the trolls, he speaks for *all* the trolls. Sensible as they are, they leave it all to him when it comes to the politics.

'And then, on the other hand, we have yourself, dear lady: you

21

speak for all your . . . folk in Bonk* and most agreements made with you are, well, quite agreeable . . . But the dwarfs, what a calamity. Just when you think you're talking to the leader of the dwarfs, some wild-eyed grag will pop out on the landscape and suddenly all bets are off, all treaties instantly become null and void, and there is no possibility of trust! As you know, there is a "king" – a *dezka-knik*†, as they call him – in every mine on the Disc. How does one do business with people like this? Every dwarf his own inner tyrant.'

'Vell,' said Lady Margolotta, 'Rhys Rhysson is managing quite vell in the circumstances and ve in higher Uberwald . . .' now her lady-ship almost whispered, 'are *very* much on the side of progress. But, yes, how can vun vin vunce and for all, that is vhat I vould like to know.'

His lordship set down his glass carefully and said, 'That, alas, is never totally possible. The stars change, people change, and all we can do is assist the future with care and thoughtful determination to see the world at peace, even if it means ushering some of its worst threats to an early grave.

'Although I'm bound to say that subtlety and careful interrogation of the things the world puts in front of us suggest to me that the Low King – whom, as protocol dictates, I called upon before coming here to meet you – is forming a plan right now; and when he makes his play we will throw everything in to support him. He is taking a very big gamble on the future. He believes that the time is right, especially since Ankh-Morpork is now well known to have the largest dwarf community in the world.'

'But I believe his people don't like too much modernity. I must admit, I can see vhy. Progress is such a vorrisome thing when one is trying to maintain peace in the vorld. So . . . unpredictable. Can

* Correctly pronounced Beyonk.
† Literal translation: 'chief mining engineer'.

I remind you, Havelock, that many, many years ago, an Ephebian philosopher built an engine that vas very powerful, scarily so. If those people had persevered with the engine powered by steam the nature of life now might have been very much different. Don't you find that vorryink? How can ve guide the future when von idiot can make a mechanism that might change *everything*?'

Lord Vetinari dribbled a last drop of brandy into his glass and said cheerfully, 'Madam, only a fool would try to stop the progress of the multitude. *Vox populi, vox deorum*, carefully shepherded by a thoughtful prince, of course. And so I take the view that when it's steam engine time steam engines will come.'

'And what do you think you're doing, dwarf?'

Young Magnus Magnusson didn't pay much attention at first to the senior dwarf whose face, in so far as it could be seen, was definitely grumpy, the kind of dwarf that had apparently never himself been young, and so he shrugged and said, 'No offence, O venerable one, but what I think I'm doing is walking along minding my own business in the hope that others would be minding their own. I hope you have no rat with that?'*

It is said that a soft answer turneth away wrath, but this assertion has a lot to do with hope and was now turning out to be patently inaccurate, since even a well-spoken and thoughtful soft answer could actually drive the wrong kind of person into a state of fury if wrath was what they had in mind, and that was the state the elderly dwarf was now enjoying.

'Why are you wearing your helmet backwards, young dwarf?'

Magnus was an easy-going dwarf and did the wrong thing, which was to be logical.

'Well, O venerable one, it's got my Scouting badge on it, you

---

* Humans might have said 'beef' at this point, but not many dwarfs have a taste for cow, whereas rat is perennially dependable.

know. Scouting? Out in the fresh air? Not getting up to mischief and serving my community well?'

This litany of good intentions didn't seem to get Magnus any friends and his sense of peril began belatedly to function much faster. The old dwarf was really, really unhappy about him, and during this short exchange a few other dwarfs had sauntered over to them, looking at Magnus as if weighing him up for the fight.

It was Magnus's first time alone in the twin cities of Bonk and Schmaltzberg and he hadn't expected to be greeted like this. These dwarfs didn't look like the ones he had grown up with in Treacle Mine Road and he began to back away, saying hurriedly, 'I'm here to see my granny, right, if you don't mind, she's not very well and I've come all the way from Ankh-Morpork, hitching rides on carts and sleeping out every night in haystacks and barns. It's a long, long way—'

And then it all happened.

Magnus was a speedy runner, as befitted the Ankh-Morpork Rat Pack,* and as he ran he tried to figure out what it was that he had done wrong. After all, it had taken him for ever by various means to get to Uberwald, and he was a dwarf, and they were dwarfs and . . .

It dawned on him that there had been something in the newspapers back home saying that there were still a few dwarf societies that would have nothing to do with any organization that included trolls, the traditional and visceral enemy. Well, there were certainly trolls in the pack back home and they were good sports, all of them,

* Scouting for trolls, dwarfs and humans was brought in shortly after the Koom Valley Accord had been signed, on the suggestion of Lord Vetinari, to allow the young of the three dominant species to meet and hopefully get along together. Naturally the young of all species, when thrown together, instead of turning against one another would join forces against the real enemy, that is to say their parents, teachers and miscellaneous authority which was *so* old-fashioned. And up to a point, and amazingly, it had worked and that was Ankh-Morpork, wasn't it? Mostly, nobody cared what shape you were, although they might be very interested in how much money you had.

a bit slow mind you, but he had occasionally gone to tea with some of them and vice versa. Only now he remembered how occasionally old trolls and older dwarfs were upset for no other reason than that after hundreds of years of trying to kill one another they, by means of one handshake, were supposed to have become friends.

Magnus had always understood that the Low City of the Low King was a dark place, and that was okay for dwarfs as dwarfs and darkness always got on well together, but here he sensed a deeper darkness. In this trying moment it seemed that here he had no friends apart from his grandmother, and it looked as though there was going to be a lot of trouble between him and the other side of town where she lived.

He was panting now but he could still hear the sounds of pursuit, even though he was leaving the deeper corridors and tunnels behind him and heading out of the underground city of Schmaltzberg, realizing he would have to come back another day . . . or another way.

As he stopped briefly to get his breath back, a guard on the city gate stepped into his path with a certain greedy expression.

'And where do you think you're going in a hurry, Mister Ankh-Morpork? Back to the light with your troll friends, eh?'

The guard's spontoon knocked Magnus's feet from under him and then the kicking started in earnest. Magnus rolled to get out of the way and as a kind of reflex shouted, 'Tak does not want us to think of him, but he does want us to think!'

He groaned and spat out a tooth as he saw another dwarf coming towards him. To his dismay the newcomer looked middle-aged and well-to-do, which certainly meant that there would be no friendship here. But instead of administering a kicking, the older dwarf shouted in a voice like hammers, 'Listen to me, young dwarf, you must never let your guard down like this . . .'

The newcomer smacked his original assailant to the ground with commendable ferocity and a gloriously unnecessary display of violence and as the guard lay groaning he pulled Magnus upright.

'Well, you can run, kid, much better than most dwarfs I know, but a boy like you should know that Ankh-Morpork dwarfs are not in favour at the moment, at least not around these parts. To tell you the truth, I'm not that happy about them myself, but if there's a fight it must be a fair one.'

At that he kicked the stricken guard very hard and said, 'My name is Bashfull Bashfullsson. You, lad, better get yourself some micromail if you're going to come calling on your granny looking all Ankh-Morpork. And it is ashamed I am that my fellow dwarfs treat a young dwarf so badly just because of what he wears.' And the full stop to that rant was yet another blow to the recumbent guard.

'I'll hand it to you, lad, I really have never seen a dwarf that can run as fast as you were doing! My word, you can run, but it might now be time to learn how to hide.'

Magnus brushed himself down and stared at his saviour, saying, 'Bashfull Bashfullsson! But you're a legend!' And he took a step backwards saying, 'I've read all about you! You became a grag because you don't like Ankh-Morpork!'

'I may not, young dwarf, but I don't hold with killing in the darkness like those bastard deep-downers and delvers. I like a stand-up fight, me.'

Saying this, Bashfull Bashfullsson kicked the fallen guard heavily yet one more time with his enormous iron-clad boot.

And one of the most well-known and well-respected dwarfs in the world held out his hand to young Magnus, and said, 'Now let your talent take you to safety. As you said, Tak does not require us to think of him, but remember that he does require us to think and you might want a thought or two about adjusting your attire when you come back to visit your granny again. Besides, she might not appreciate Ankh-Morpork fashions. Nice to have met you, Mister Speedy, and now get your sorry arse out of here – I might not be around next time.'

Far away and turnwise of Uberwald, Sir Harry King was pondering on the business of the day. He was widely known as the King of the Golden River because of the fortune he had made minding other people's business.

Harry was normally a cheerful man with a good digestion, but not today. He was also a loving husband, doting on Euphemia, his wife of many years, but alas, not today. And Harry was a good employer, but also not today, because today his stomach was giving him gyp by means of the halibut to which the phrase *long time no see* could not happily be applied. He hadn't liked the look of it when it was on his plate, halibut being a fish which tends to look back at you reproachfully, and for the last few hours he had envisaged the damn thing looking at the insides of his stomach.

The problem was, he thought, that Euphemia still remembered the good old days when they were poor as church mice and therefore necessarily frugal with their money, and such habits bite to the bone, very much like the inadvisably digested fish which had been swimming somewhere in the vicinity of Harry's bowels and threatening to swim a lot further.

Regrettably, Harry was a man brought up to eat everything that was put in front of him and that meant *everything* eaten up. When he had finally exited from the privy, where he fancied the damn fish had been watching him from the bowl, he had pulled the chain with such vehemence that it broke, causing the woman whom he sometimes called the Duchess to have words with him. And since words tend to lead to more words, nasty, spiteful little words flew on both sides, words that if Harry could help it would be flung back to the wretched fish which had started it all. But instead he and his wife had had what they had known all of their lives as an up-and-downer. And, of course, Effie, born in the next-door gutter to Harry, could give at least as good as she got in such situations, especially when armed with a quite valuable and decorative jug.

Effie had a voice on her that at times could make a barrow boy blush, and she had called Harry the 'King of Shit', causing him to do what he never, ever wanted to do, which was to raise his hand in anger, especially since the jug with which his wife was now armed was also quite a heavy one.*

Of course it would blow over, it always did, and genuine marital harmony would drift into its accustomed place in the household. But nevertheless, all afternoon Sir Harry prowled around his compound like an old lion. *King of Shit*, well, yes, and because of him the streets were clean, or at least considerably cleaner than they had been before what might be called the Harry King dynasty. He mused, as he wandered, that his work was all about those unimaginable things that people wanted to leave behind them. And therefore there wasn't much for him on the top table of society. Oh, yes, he was *Sir* Harry, but he knew that Effie really wished they could leave behind the whole stinking business.

'After all,' she said, 'you're as rich as Creosote as it is. Can't you find something else to do – something that people actually *want* rather than need?'

Generally speaking, Harry was not very good at philosophy. He was proud of what he had achieved, but a tiny part of him was agreeing with Effie that surely there was something better for him than chasing the pure† and making certain the unreliable septic tanks of the city didn't overflow. Somebody had to do it, of course – and it wasn't as if it was actually Harry himself, not for many years, since he paid the gongfermors, dunnykin divers and now a whole army of goblins as well to do the dirty work. Still, what he needed now, he thought, was an occupation that was manly without being despicable.

Absent-mindedly, he sacked his latest lawyer, a dwarf who had been

* Besides being from the McSweeney dynasty and therefore frighteningly expensive. Although, he thought, when he looked at the porcelain shards on the floor, they didn't look *that* expensive.

† A term, technically speaking, for dog muck, much prized by the tanneries.

caught with his nasty little fingers in the till, and managed to do it without actually throwing the little bugger all the way down the stairs.

Unusually despondent, Harry prowled on, seeking to calm his nerves. At the edge of his compound he sniffed the air, so far as he dared. There was a wind blowing from the hub and he turned to face it and caught a tantalizing smell: a manly smell, a smell with a purpose, a smell that wanted to take him places, and it said *promise*.

The relationship between Moist von Lipwig and Adora Belle Dearheart was firm and happy, quite possibly because they didn't see each other for substantial periods of time, since she was immersed in the running of the Grand Trunk and he was dealing with the Bank, the Post Office and the Mint. Despite what Lord Vetinari *thought*, Moist *did* have proper work to do at these institutions and that was, in his own mind, called holding it all together. Things worked, in fact they worked very well, but they worked, Moist thought, because he was always seen in the Bank or the Mint or the Post Office being Mister Bank, Mister Post Office and Mister Mint.

He chatted to people, talked to them about their work, asked how their wives and husbands were, having memorized the names of all the family members of the person he was talking to. It was a knack, a wonderful knack, and it worked a treat. You took an interest in everybody and they took an interest in their work and it was vitally important that he was always around to keep the magic flowing.

As for Adora Belle, the clacks were in her bones, it was her legacy and woe betide anyone who got between it and her,* even if that anyone *was* her husband.

---

* Unless they were a golem. During the dark days when the family clacks company had been usurped by *businessmen*, Adora Belle had diverted her energies into golem emancipation. She was still involved with the Golem Trust, but the pace of change in Ankh-Morpork, she was pleased to notice, meant that the golems were quite happily trusting themselves.

Somehow the system worked as hard as they did and so they could afford Crossly, the butler, and Mrs Crossly too.* Their house in Scoone Avenue had a gardener too, who appeared to come with the territory. Crisp† was also a decent handyman and quite talkative, although Moist never understood a word he said. He came from somewhere in the Shires and spoke using a vocabulary that was theoretically Morporkian, but in reality had lots of straw in it with the syllable 'ahh' working hard in every conversation. He made cider in his shed at the bottom of the garden, utilizing the apple trees that the previous owner had carefully cherished. He also, as a matter of course, cleaned the windows, and with the help of an enormous box full of every type of hammer, saw, drill, screwdriver and chisel, bags of nails and a number of other items that Moist could not recognize, and moreover did not wish to, made Moist's life easy whilst making Crisp possibly the richest handyman in the neighbourhood.

Moist von Lipwig had done some heavy work once and couldn't see any future in it, but he could look at it for hours, provided other people were doing it, of course, and clearly some of them liked what they were doing, and so he shrugged and felt happy that Crisp was happy being a handyman whilst Moist was happy not picking up anything that was heavier than a glass. After all, his work was unseen and depended on words, which were fortunately not very heavy and didn't need grease. In his career as a crook they had served him well and now he felt somewhat smug at using them to the benefit of the citizenry.

There was a difference between a banker and a crook, there really was, and although it was very, very teeny Moist felt that he should

---

* Adora Belle was, as even she knew, a creatively bad cook, mostly because she thought cookery a waste of time for a woman with even half a mind; and since Moist took pretty much the same stance when it came to manual labour, the arrangement seemed to suit all parties.

† Which was his *only* name.

point out that it did exist and, besides, Lord Vetinari always had his eye on him.

So everybody was happy and Moist went to work in very clean clothes and with a very clean conscience.

Having washed and dressed in said clothes in his private bathroom,* Moist went to see his wife, practising his smile on the way and endeavouring to look cheerful. You never knew with Adora Belle.† She could be quite acerbic. After all, she ran the whole clacks system these days.

She also liked goblins, which was why there were some living behind the wainscoting of the house and others in the roof. They smelled, but the smell wasn't, once you got over the shock, all that bad. The compensation was that the goblins had taken the clacks into their scrawny hearts, one and all. The wheels and levers fascinated them. Moist knew that generally goblins hid out in caves and insalubrious places that humans didn't bother about, but now, when suddenly they were being treated as people, they had found their element which was generally the sky. They could scramble up a clacks tower faster than any man could run, and the rattling, back-and-forth clanking and relentlessly busy machinery of the clacks had them in its grip.

Already, after only a few months in the city, the goblins had improved the efficiency of the clacks across the Sto Plains threefold. They were creatures of darkness, but their perception of light was remarkable. There was a whole malignity‡ of goblins up on the roof, but if you wanted your clacks to fly fast, you didn't use the term out loud. The villains of the storybooks had found their place in society, at last. All it needed was technology.

*

* Separate bathrooms of course being the key to any happy marriage.
† 'Spike' to her fond husband. Her brother had called her Killer, but he meant it in a nice way.
‡ The official collective noun for a bunch of goblins.

When Dick Simnel walked into Sir Harry King's compound he wasn't at all certain how you spoke to grand folk. Nevertheless, he managed to talk his way through the people in the front office, who had a rather jaundiced look and appeared to consider it their duty to ensure that no one should ever get to see Sir Harry King, especially greasy-looking young men with wild eyes trying hard to look respectable despite their extremely old clothing which, these gatekeepers thought, needed something, possibly a bonfire. However, Dick had the persistence of a wasp and the sharpness of a razor blade, and so eventually he ended up deposited in front of the big man's desk like a supplicant.

Harry, red-faced and impatient, looked over his desk and said to him, 'Lad, time is money and I'm a busy man. You told Nancy down on Reception that you've got something I might like. Now stop fidgeting and look me in the face square like. If you're another chancer wanting to bamboozle me I'll have you down the Effing stairs* before you know it.'

Dick stared soundlessly at Harry for a moment, then said, 'Mister Sir King, I've made a machine that can carry people and goods just about everywhere and it don't need 'orses and it's run on water 'n' coal. It's my machine, I built it and I can make it even better if you can see your way clear to advance me some investment.'

Harry King reached into his pocket and pulled out a heavy gold watch. Dick couldn't help but notice the famous gold rings that he had been told Sir Harry always wore, possibly as an ensemble of socially acceptable and extremely valuable knuckledusters.

'Did I hear you right? It's Mister Simnel, isn't it? I'll give you five minutes to catch my fancy and if I think you're just another thimblerigger on the slant you'll go out of here rather more quickly than you came in.'

* The wonderfully colourful oak wood of the Effing Forest was much in demand for high-class joinery.

'My old mother always said seeing is believing, Mister King, and so I've come prepared. If you can give me some time to get t'lads and t' 'orses . . .' Dick coughed and continued, 'I have to tell you, Mister Sir Harry, I took the liberty of parking them right outside your compound, 'cos I talked to people and they said that if Harry King wants something to start happening it 'as to 'appen fast.' He hesitated. Was that a glint in Harry's eye?

'Well,' the magnate grumbled rather theatrically. 'Young man, even though time is money, talk is cheap. I'll come out in five minutes and you'd better have something solid to show me.'

'Thank you, Sir King, that's very kind of you, sir, but we'll have to get t'boiler warmed up first, sir, and so we'll have 'er throbbing in no more than two hours, sir.'

Harry King took his cigar out of his mouth and said, 'What?! Throbbing?'

Dick smiled nervously. 'You'll see, sir, you'll see.'

Very shortly afterwards, and just in time, smoke and steam enveloped the compound and Harry King saw and, indeed, was amazed.

And Harry King really *was* amazed. There was something insect-like about the metallic contraption, bits of which were spinning incessantly while the whole thing was shrouded in a cloud of smoke and steam of its own making. Harry King saw purpose personified. Purpose, moreover, that would be unlikely ever to ask for a day off for its granny's funeral.

Over the noise he shouted, 'What did you say this thing is called, my lad?'

'Iron Girder, sir. An engine that uses the expansion or rapid condensation of steam to generate power. Power for locomotion – that is to say, movement, sir. And if you'd allow us to lay down her rails, sir, we can really show you what she can do.'

'Rails?'

'Aye, sir. She runs on an iron road, you'll see.'

Suddenly there was the sound of a banshee on heat as Wally moved a lever.

'Sorry, sir, you 'ave to let t'steam out. It's all about 'arnessing t'steam. You heard her singing, sir, she wants motion, power is going to waste while she's just sitting here. Give me time and allow me to put a test track around your compound. We'll have 'er running very soon, I promise you.'

Harry was uncharacteristically silent. The thrumming of the machine was like a kind of spell. Again, the metal voice of steam rang out over the compound like a lost soul and he found himself unable to leave. Harry wasn't a man for introspection and all that rubbish, but he thought that this, well, *this* was something worth a closer look. And then he noticed the faces of the crowd around the compound, the goblins climbing up to gawp at this new raging devil which was nevertheless under the control of two lads in flat caps and very little to speak of in regard to teeth.

Getting his thoughts lined up properly, Harry turned to Dick Simnel and said, 'Mister Simnel, I'll give you two days, no more. You have your chance, mister, don't waste it. I am, as I say, a busy man. Two days to show me something that astounds me. Go on.'

Dwarfs and men sat and listened intently to the old boy sitting in the corner of the Treacle Miner*, human, possibly, but with a beard any respectable dwarf would have coveted, who had decided to share with them his knowledge of the treacle-mining world.

'Gather round, lads, fill my pot and I'll tell you a tale that's dark and sticky.' He looked meaningfully at his empty tankard and there was laughter as it was replaced by some well-wisher and, as he sipped his ale, he began his tale.

Years back, unexpected deep treacle reserves had been

---

* Known by habitués as the Sticky Head.

discovered under Ankh-Morpork, fathoms down, and as every treacle miner knew, the lower the treacle, the better the texture and therefore the better the taste. In truth, and in Ankh-Morpork at least, there was very little friction between dwarf clans on this matter, and the question of who would be allowed to mine the discovery was amiably dealt with by the old boys, dwarf and human.

Everyone conceded that when it came to working underground there was nothing like the dwarfs, but, to the dismay of the older miners, very few of the dwarf youngsters of Ankh-Morpork were at all interested in mining under any circumstances. And so the grizzled old boys welcomed any local miners of any species to work under the venerable streets of Ankh-Morpork, for the sheer pleasure of seeing treacle being properly produced again, and the miners, whoever they were, went about their sticky business in the search for the deep shimmering treacle.

And something happened, somewhere up near the Shires, where the dwarf miners had been working a reasonable seam, part of which was under land which at that time belonged to the Low King of the Dwarfs. In those not too distant days political relationships between human and dwarf were somewhat nervy.

On the day when things came to a head there had been a sudden fall of dark toffee, extremely precious and very unusual, but feared by every treacle miner because of its tendency to spontaneously collapse into the tunnels. According to the eyewitnesses, both humans and dwarfs were mining underground while politicians argued on both sides of the political divide. And this fall was mostly on the human side of the seam, with many men trapped in a deluge of unrelenting stickiness.

He hesitated for a moment and said, 'Or it might have been the dwarf side, now I come to think about it . . .' He looked embarrassed, but continued. 'Well, it doesn't really matter now who they were, it was a long time ago anyway. The miners working the seam from the other side of the fall heard that there were many miners down there, trapped and drowning in refined sugar derivatives, and said, "Come on, lads, get the gear together and let's get them out of there."'

The old boy hesitated a further moment, possibly for effect, and said, 'But of course that meant that they had to enter territory that required going through two bloody security barriers manned by armed guards. Guards, moreover, who were not that bothered about miners and were certainly not going to let any of the enemy down into *their* sovereign soil.'

Another significant pause, then the tale raced on. All the miners had piled up against the barriers. Someone said, 'We can't tackle them, they've got weapons!' and they looked at one another in what is known as wild surmise, and then another voice yelled, 'But so have we, when you look at it the right way, and ours are bigger!' And the speaker waved his enormous fist and said, 'And we're mining every day, not standing around and looking smart.'

And so as one dwarf, or possibly human, they rushed the barricade and the guards, realizing they were failing to frighten people, ran for cover as the miners with the picks and shovels came down on them at speed and sixty miners were saved from a very sticky situation on both sides of the seam.

Nothing official happened afterwards because officialdom didn't want any part of the shame of it.

The old boy looked around and glowed as if he himself had been one of those miners and, quite possibly, he might have been, and his tankard was topped up once again and he said wistfully, 'Of course, that was the old days. I wish it still was.'

It was just short of the end of the second day when Simnel and his lads had Iron Girder chuffing slowly and purposefully along a short circular track in Harry's compound.

And Harry couldn't help noticing that the look of the engine had changed and it now seemed somehow . . . smoother than before. In fact, he thought, he had been ready to say *sleek*, though it was hard to think of what looked like fifty tons of steel as sleek, but yes, he thought, why not? It shouldn't be beautiful, but *she* was. Stuttering, stinking, growling, smoking, but so very beautiful.

Dick said cheerfully, 'We're taking it slow, Mister Harry. We need to put down some *real* ballast before we can let 'er rip, but she grows on yer, don't you think? And when we've built 'er up, and added on wagons and suchlike there'll be no stoppin' 'er.'

And there it was again. It really ought to be a he, Harry mused, but somehow the 'she' stuck relentlessly.

And then Harry's rather crumpled brow furrowed even further. This young lad clearly knows his stuff, he thought, and he said his machine could carry people and goods . . . but who'd want to ride on this clanking great monster?

On the other hand, the compound smelled of steam and coal and hot grease – manly, healthy smells . . . Yes, he'd give them that little bit longer. Perhaps another week. After all, coal wasn't expensive and he wasn't paying them anything. Harry King realized he was feeling unusually happy. Yes, they could have a little more time. And the smell was good, unlike those he and Effie had put up with over the years. Oh, yes, they could definitely have their time, though he'd need to keep the lads on their toes. He looked up and the clacks towers blinked relentlessly and Harry King saw the future.

The wind above the clacks towers was blowing from the hub, cool and purposeful, and Adora Belle Dearheart fancied she could see the edge of the world from here. She cherished moments like this. They reminded her of when she was young, really young, when her mother would hang her cradle from the top of a tower while she was coding, leaving her daughter cheerfully making baby noises several hundred feet above the ground. In fact, her mother said her very first word was 'checksum'.

And now she could see, clearly out of its mists, the mountain Cori Celesti glittering like a great green icicle. She sang as she tightened up the spinners on the upper gallery. She was out of the office, as far from it as was possible, and it felt good. After all, she could even see the office from up here. In fact, she could probably see *everybody's* office from here, but right now she sorted out the delicate little mechanisms and savoured a world where she could reach out and touch the sun, well, metaphorically at least. This reverie was broken by one of the tower's goblins.

'I am bringing twenty spinners and a flask of coffee, very hygienic, I cleaned the mug myself with my own hand. Me. Of the Twilight the Darkness,' he said proudly.

Adora Belle looked down at a face that would take a frantic battalion of mothers to love, but nevertheless she smiled and said, 'Thanks, mister. I must say you've really got acclimatized for some-body who has spent most of their life in a cave. I can't believe you don't even worry about heights, that never ceases to amaze me. And thanks again, it really is good coffee and still warm, too.'

Of the Twilight the Darkness shrugged as only a goblin could shrug. The effect was rather like a parcel of snakes dancing.

'Missus Boss, goblins no stranger to acclimatize. Don't acclima-tize, don't live! And anyway, things going well down there, no problems. Goblins got respeck! And how is Mister Slightly Damp?'

'*Moist* is fine, my friend, and surely you know my husband doesn't like the name you goblins have given him. He thinks you're doing it on purpose.'

'You want that we stop doing it?'

'Oh, no! It teaches him a lesson in humility. I think he needs to go to university on that score.'

The goblin grinned in the way of a conspirator, and he could see Adora Belle trying not to laugh, while overhead the clacks con-tinued sending its messages to the world.

Adora Belle could *almost* read the messages simply by watching the towers, but you had to be very, very fast; and the goblins were even faster than that. And who ever would have thought their eyesight was so discerning? Using the new augmented colour shutter boxes after dark, most human clacks spotters could separate about four or five or maybe even six colours on a very good clear night, but who could have imagined that goblins, fresh out of their caves, would be uncannily able even to identify puce as opposed to pink, while most humans didn't have a clue what a damn puce was if they saw it?

Adora Belle glanced at Of the Twilight the Darkness and once again acknowledged to herself that goblins were the reason why clacks traffic was so much faster, more accurate and stream-lined than ever before. And yet how could she reward them for the increased efficiency? Sometimes the goblins never even bothered to take their pay. They liked rats, of which there was never a shortage, but because she was indeed the boss* she felt it incumbent on her to persuade the little nerds that there were, indeed, many other things you could be doing apart from coding and deciphering clacks messages. She almost shivered. They actively, obsessively liked to work, all day and all night if possible.

She knew if the name on the door said 'Boss' then in theory she had to think about their welfare, but they weren't interested in their own welfare. What they wanted to do was code and decipher, paus-ing only when the lady troll with the rat trolley came round. Honestly! They liked their work and not just liked it, but lived it. How many bosses had had to go all around the workplace telling people they really had to stop working now and go home? But then they didn't go home, they wanted to stay up in their clacks towers, and in the small hours of the night chat by clacks to goblins else-where. They would rather chatter than eat, it seemed, and even

* If you could give that name to somebody who had to deal every day with forms to sign, go to far too many meetings *about* meetings and handle the most petty of correspondence.

slept on the tower, dragging in little straw beds for when they were forced by nature to take a nap.

Adora Belle had insisted to the trustees that there should be a foundation set up, against the day when goblins and their children might want to move further into society. So a scant while after the remarkable musical talents of Tears of the Mushroom had been so spectacularly unveiled to Ankh-Morpork high society, the goblins had become people, strange people, yes, but people nevertheless. Of course, there was the smell, but you couldn't have everything.

Novelty went around Ankh-Morpork just like an embarrassing disease, thought Sir Harry King the following afternoon as he looked down on to the compound where people were peering through the gates and fencing in a great susurration of speculation. Harry knew his fellow citizens from the bottom up, as it were, willing slaves to novelty and the exotic, rubberneckers all of them. The whole crowd were turning their heads as one to keep track of Iron Girder, like a flock of starlings, and all the time Iron Girder was chuffing away with Dick waving from the footplate, the air still full of the smuts and smells. And yet, he thought, it's all approval. No one's disagreeing, no one's frightened. A beast from nowhere. A fiery dragon, all smoke and cinders, has appeared among them and they hold up their children to look at it, waving as it goes past.

What strange magic—? He corrected himself; what strange *mechanics* could have achieved this? There was the beast and they were loving it.

I'll have to get familiar with these words, Harry thought as he left his office: 'footplate', 'boiler', 'reciprocal', 'molybdenum disulphide',* and all the tiresome but fascinating language of steam.

---

* This black crystalline compound was widely used by troll women as an anti-ageing cream. Dick Simnel had been thorough in his research and it was, apparently, a very efficient lubricant.

Having noticed that Harry was watching them, Dick Simnel allowed Iron Girder to slow down gently until, with an almost imperceptible bump, she came to a halt. Dick jumped off the footplate and strolled towards him, and Harry saw a triumphant look in his eye.

Harry said, 'Well done, lad, but be careful, be very, *very* careful. Be careful of everything right now. I've been watching the faces of them people with their noses pressed up against my fence, their little faces all corrugated, as it were. They're fascinated, and fascinated people spend money.

'The most important thing in business is to work out who gets that cash and it's like this, my boy, it's a jungle out there and I'm more than a multi-millionaire, much more. I know that while happy handshakes are very pleasing and friendly, when it comes to business you can't do without bloody lawyers because in this jungle I'm a gorilla! It's best you tell me the name of yours and I'll get my lawyer to get in touch so they can talk all lawyer-to-lawyer while totting up their dollars. I don't want no one to say that Harry King fleeced the lad who tamed the steam.

'For what it's worth I'll fund you up to a certain point, no doubt about that, because I think this engine of yours has real possibilities, huge possibilities. So now you've got my interest and by the time the papers find out about this you'll have *everyone's* interest.'

Dick shrugged and said, 'Well, Sir Harry, it's great that you're giving me a chance, so anything you suggest'll be okay by me.'

Harry King almost screamed, 'No, no, no! I like you, I like you a lot, but business is, well, *business is business*!' Harry's face was now puce with anger. 'You don't go and tell anyone that you'll take whatever they want to give you! You bargain, lad. Don't get starry-eyed! You bargain. You bargain hard.'

There was silence and then the lad said, 'Mister King, before I decided to come to Ankh-Morpork I talked about things with me mother, a very shrewd lady – she 'ad to be, what with me dad being somewhere out there in the ether, if you catch my drift. And she said if someone wants to do business in the big city, Dick, make out that you're simple and see 'ow they treat you. If they treats you properly, simple as you are, then it's likely you can trust them. And then you can show them how smart you really are. And well, sir, it seems to me you're as straight as lunchtime. I'll go and find a lawyer right now.' He hesitated. 'Er, where can I find a lawyer I can trust? I might not be as clever as I think I am.'

Sir Harry laughed heartily. 'It's a tough call, lad, and a question I've lately needed to ask myself, as it happens. My friend Mustrum Ridcully over at the University told me about one only yesterday: a lawyer so straight he could be used as a crowbar. Why not let your lads go on showing Iron Girder to the crowd, and come with me in my carriage, although it's not a patch on the one you brought here, eh? Eh! Come on, lad, let's go, shall we?'

At his office in the Lawyers' Guild building, Harry King and Dick Simnel met Mr Thunderbolt, surprisingly large and, surprisingly, a troll. A troll with a voice like gently flowing lava.

'You will wish to know my credentials, gentlemen. I am a member of the Ankh-Morpork Guild of Lawyers and served my articles here under Mister Slant,' said Mr Thunderbolt. 'As well as my Ankh-Morpork practice I am the only troll to have, moreover, accreditation as a lawyer in the realm of the Low King. Apropos of nothing, Sir Harry, I am also the nephew of Diamond King of Trolls, although, of course, I must add that the nature of troll families is such that the mere word "nephew" does not do the situation justice.'

The voice was the voice of a professor, but one who had chosen to speak in an echoing cave. The features were more or less like those of all trolls, unless you looked for the giveaway signs and recognized the careful masonry work, the richness of the plant life in

42

the visible cavities and, not least, that elusive shine, and possibly shimmer, which caught the light so delicately; not boldly in your face, but irresistibly there.

'And yes, I am diamond through and through and therefore I cannot tell lies for fear of shattering. Furthermore, I have no intention of trying to do so. It appears to me, gentlemen, from what you tell me, that the two of you are in accord, neither wishing to play unfairly and both of you wishing to act decently with one another and so, on this occasion, much as my Guild colleagues might disapprove, I suggest I act as mediator and lawyer for both of you. Troll justice is remarkably straightforward – I only wish that this could be the case everywhere else. However, should you fall out then I would not undertake work from either of you subsequently.'

Thunderbolt smiled and little sparkles flashed around the room like a firework display.

'I will put together a short document which might, in other places, be called an agreement to agree. And I am the judge not on the side of you individually but on the side of you both. I am diamond and I cannot allow injustice to happen. I suggest, gentlemen, that you continue with your project, which seems to me remarkable, and leave the paperwork to me. I look forward to seeing you at the compound tomorrow.'

Harry and Dick were silent in the coach until Dick said, 'Weren't he nice? For a lawyer.'

By the time they got back to the compound the goblin Billy Slick, who had worked for Harry for many years, was in a tizzy – although he didn't know that, not knowing the word existed – and he was at the gate waiting for them when the carriage drew up.

Frantically, he said, 'I closed the gate, Sir Harry, but it looks like they'll climb over anything to see this . . . this . . . this *thing*! I keep telling 'em we ain't running no fun house here.'

The light was fading and yet still the eyes of the onlookers were following Iron Girder as she travelled around the track while Simnel's team put her through her paces, throwing off sparks in the twilight like signals to the universe that steam was here to stay. And when most of the sightseers had reluctantly left to go home for their supper, some of Harry's goblins slunk into the compound to see the marvel of the age. They did indeed slink, Harry thought, not exactly like a burglar, but simply because the average goblin carcass was born slinking, except that right now they were dancing around Iron Girder, and the lads had their work cut out to keep skinny little goblin fingers out of dangerous places.

Iron Girder sat and occasionally gave out a puff of steam or smoke while all the time, in the twilight, Harry heard tiny staccato voices interrogating the engineers: 'What does this one do, mister?', 'What happens if I push this, mister?', 'I see, mister, that this one connects to the blastpipey armature.'

Harry and Dick joined Dave and Wally as they stood by Iron Girder answering the barrage of questions. To Harry's surprise, instead of the complaints he was expecting to be issuing from the lads' mouths, he saw they were smiling happily.

'They seem to get it, sir! Oh, aye!' said Wally. 'They're into everything! We're 'aving to keep an eye on them, but they seem to understand without being told, can you believe that?'

And Harry marvelled. He quite liked the little buggers, as any employer would quite like somebody who worked hard, but how does a goblin get the understanding of steam engines? It must be something in their nature. Their scruffy little faces were wreathed in smiles at the sight of something metallic and complicated. It was a sign of the times, he thought, and it looks like time for the goblins.

Simnel was silent for a moment as if waking up the internal steam for the next thought, then said, in a careful kind of voice, 'You really would think they were born to it!'

'I can't say I'm surprised, Dick,' said Harry. 'The clacks people say the same thing. It's uncanny but it seems that they automatically understand mechanisms, so be careful as they like to take things apart on the fly just to see what they do. But once they understand how whatever it is works they seem to put it all back together again. There's no malice, they just like to tinker with the best and, you know what, sometimes they improve things. How can you explain that? But if I was you I'd have one of you three sleeping under Iron Girder of a night just so they don't get creative.'

The following day Moist von Lipwig was gently awakened by Crossly, who as yet had failed to grasp his master's attitude to sleep, a fact which was reinforced by Moist turning over in bed and saying, 'Mumble mumble grunt mumble groan mumble off!' The sequence was repeated three minutes later, with the same response, this time with the emphasis on the last syllable, uttered three times with increasing volume.

Subsequently – in fact and to be precise, fifteen minutes later – Moist von Lipwig was pulled out of the arms of Morpheus by the none too gentle prodding of a blade belonging to one of the Ankh-Morpork palace guards, a species he didn't like very much in any case because they were stolid and dumb. Admittedly, so were the majority of the City Watch, in Moist's opinion, but at least *they* were *by and large* creatively and, at least, humorously dumb, which made them a lot more interesting. After all, you could talk to them and therefore confuse them, whereas with the palace guards, well, all they knew was how to prod, and they were quite good at it. It was wise not to put them to any trouble, and so Moist, fully conversant with how this sort of thing worked, dressed grumpily and followed them to the palace, and undoubtedly an audience with Lord Vetinari.

The Patrician was, unusually, not at his desk, but paying attention to something on the large polished table that filled one half of the Oblong Office. He was, in fact, playing. It seemed ridiculous, but there was no denying it: he was watching a children's toy quite intently, a little cart, or trolley of some sort, on a little metal rail, which allowed it to scuttle continuously in a circle for no readily apparent reason. He straightened up after Moist coughed loudly and said, 'Ah, Mister Lipwig. It's so kind of you to come . . . *eventually*. Tell me, what do you make of *this*?'

Somewhat perplexed, Moist said, 'It looks like a children's plaything, sir.'

'In fact it is a very well crafted model of something much bigger and far more dangerous.' Lord Vetinari raised his voice and said, as if talking not only to Moist but to the world in general, 'Some might say that it would have been easy for me to prevent this happening. A stiletto sliding quietly here, a potion dropped into a wine glass there, many problems solved at one stroke. Diplomacy, as it were, on the sharp end, regrettably unfortunate, of course, but not subject to argument.

'People *might* say that I wasn't paying attention and through neglect of my duties allowed the poison to seep into the imagination of the world and change it irrevocably. Perhaps I could have taken some action when I first saw Leonard of Quirm doodle something very much like this little toy in the margins of his drawing of the "Countess Quatro Fromaggio at her Toilette", but of course I would rather shatter the most priceless antique vase than see any harm come to one hair on that most useful and venerable head. I thought it would go the way of his flying machines, nothing more than a toy.

'And now it has come to this. One simply cannot trust the artificers; they design some terrible things for the sheer love of doing so, without wisdom, foresight or responsibility, and frankly, I would like to see them chained up where they can do no harm.'

And here Lord Vetinari paused and added, 'And I could have made that happen in an instant were it not for the fact, Mr Lipwig, that the wretches are so damn useful.'

He sighed, causing Moist to worry. Moist had never seen his lordship so discomfited, staring intently at the little truck as it went round and round on its little rails and filled the room with a smell of methylated spirits. There was something hypnotic about it, for Lord Vetinari, at least.

A silent hand dropped lightly, and eerily, on to Moist's shoulder. He turned around quickly and behind him was Drumknott, smiling gently.

'I suggest you pretend you didn't hear anything, Mister Lipwig,' he whispered. 'It's the best way, especially when he has one of his, er, sombre moments . . .' Still whispering, Drumknott continued, 'A lot of this is to do with the crossword, of course. You know how he is about that. I intend personally to write to the editor. His lordship considers elegant completion to be a test of his integrity. A crossword is meant to be an engaging and educational puzzle.'

And then, his normally pink face reddening, Drumknott added, 'I'm sure it's not intended to be a form of torture, and I'm certain that there is no such word as *lagniappe*. However, his lordship has terrific powers of recovery, and if you care to wait while I make you some coffee I'd wager he'll be his old self again before you can say "death warrant".'

In fact, Lord Vetinari stared at the wall for only eight minutes more before he appeared to shake himself down. He beamed at Drumknott and, less warmly, acknowledged the presence of Moist, who had been surreptitiously looking at the unfinished crossword lying prominently across the table.

Moist said, brightly but with the best of intentions, 'My lord, I'm sure you know that *lagniappe* is spelled differently than it sounds. Just a thought, of course, only trying to be helpful, sir.'

'Yes. I know,' said Lord Vetinari, in dark tones.

'Can I be of any *other* assistance, my lord?' said Moist, reckoning that he hadn't been prodded out of his bed for an undone crossword, or to admire a child's toy.

Lord Vetinari looked down his nose at Moist momentarily and said icily, 'Since you have *finally* decided to join us at this difficult time, Mister Lipwig, I will tell you that there was once a man called Ned Simnel who made a mechanical device, propelled in some arcane way, for taking in the harvest. The present difficulties might have begun there, but fortuitously his device didn't work, tending, apparently, to explode and burst into flames, and so the balance of the world was maintained. But, of course, the men who are drawn to tinkering continue to tinker in their little sheds! And not only that, they find ladies, good sensible ladies, who inexplicably agree to marry them, thus breeding a race of little tinkerers.

'One of them, a scion of the aforesaid Simnel, has apparently been scratching about in his father's shed and most certainly wondered if *he*, with his infinite curiosity, could achieve what his father, alas, had not. And now this young man has created a machine which devours wood and coal and spews out flames, polluting the sky, undoubtedly scaring every living creature for miles around, and making the gods' own noise. Or so I am told.

'Finally, young Mister Simnel has found his way to our good friend Sir Harry King. And apparently the two of them are now dreaming up an enterprise, which I believe is called . . . the rail way.'

Vetinari paused only briefly before continuing. 'Mister Lipwig, I feel the pressure of the future and in this turning world must either kill it or become its master. I have a nose for these things, just as I had for you, Mister Lipwig. And so I intend to be like the people of Fourecks and surf the future. Giving it a little tweak here and there has always worked for me and my instincts are telling me that this wretched rail way, which appears to be a problem, might just prove to be a remarkable solution.'

Moist looked at the Patrician's grey expression. He had articulated the term 'rail way' in something like the voice of an elderly duchess finding something unmentionable in her soup. It had total disdain floating in the air around it. But if you watched the weather of Lord Vetinari, and Moist was an expert in the Patrician's meteorology, you would notice that sometimes a metaphysical cloudburst might very shortly turn into a lovely day in the park. He could almost smell his lordship coming to terms with the reality in front of him: tiny movements of the face, changes of posture and the whole litany of Havelock Vetinari thinking suddenly delivered one of those smiles which Moist knew suggested that the game was afoot, and the mind of Lord Vetinari was running and well oiled.

Vetinari said, getting more cheerful at every word, 'My coach is waiting downstairs, Mister Lipwig. Come.'

Moist knew that any kind of argument was useless, and he also knew that Lord Vetinari most definitely knew that too; but there was such a thing as pride, and so he said, 'My lord, I must protest! I have a lot of work to be done. Surely you are aware?'

Lord Vetinari, his robe fluttering behind him like a banner, was already halfway to the door. He was a long-boned man and Moist had to run to keep up, occasionally hopping down the stairs two at a time, with Drumknott in pursuit.

Ahead of him his lordship said, over his shoulder, 'Mister Lipwig, you *don't* in fact have a great deal of work to do. In fact, as Postmaster General, Deputy Chairman of the Royal Bank of Ankh-Morpork* and, of course, Master of the Royal Mint, you employ on *our* behalf a great many extremely clever people, who work very hard, that is true. Your strange camaraderie, your skill at getting people to like you against all the evidence and amazingly *continue* to like you, makes you a very good boss, it must be said, with staff who are very loyal to you. But ultimately all *you* really need to do in the way of desk work is a little light auditing every so often.'

* The actual chairman being, in point of fact, Mr Fusspot, chairdog.

Lord Vetinari stepped up his pace and continued, 'And what is it that we can take away from all this, I fail to hear you ask? Well, I shall tell you. What the wise man will take away is a certainty that any favour is worth doing for a good boss, and I, Mister Lipwig, am a most exemplary and forbearing employer. This is apparent from the circumstance that *your* head is still clearly resting on *your* shoulders despite the fact that it might possibly be in, oh, so many other places, as it were.'

The country of Llamedos prided itself on being *sensibly* dwarfish. In truth, there were as many humans as dwarfs who called Llamedos home but since most of them were miners, and, as a rule, were either small or almost permanently concussed, you really would have to look carefully to tell the species apart. Therefore, given that practically no one was bigger than anybody else, there was a general amiability in the area, especially since, although this wasn't generally talked about, the Goddess of Love saw to it that her spell covered all alike. And because nobody talked about it, well, nobody talked about it, and so life moved on with the mining for gold – what little there was of it by now – iron ore, such zinc and arsenic as could be teased out of the unforgiving rock and, of course, coal. All this was supplemented with fishing on the coast. The outside world was involved only occasionally, when something of *real* importance happened.

That was yesterday. Today, it happened.

The ship arrived at the dock in Pantygirdl, the largest town in Llamedos, just after lunch. The arrival of the grags on board, who had come to preach the truth of pure dwarfishness to the people of the town, would have been welcomed had they not come with delvers, the shock troops of the grags, who had never before been seen above ground. Until then, the people of Llamedos were quite happy that the grags were doing whatever it was they did in the realm of the spirit and the observances thereof, keeping things done properly so that everybody else could get on with the unimportant things like the mining and the fishing and the stonework up in the hills.

But today it all went horribly wrong, because Blodwen Footcracker was getting married to Davy Counter, an excellent miner and fisherman and, importantly, a human, although the importance of this fact did not seem to most people locally to be, well, important. Just about everybody in Pantygirdl knew them both and considered them a sensible match, especially as they had known one another since they were toddlers. And while they were growing up people wondered, as people did, about the chances of a dwarf and a human conceiving a child and considered it a long shot to say the least, but then they satisfied themselves by telling one another that, after all, love was certainly there in abundance and, besides, whose business was it anyway? He and she were compatible and loving and, as the mines and the boats took their toll of miner and fisherman alike, there were always plenty of orphans anxious for a new home in their own country. And everybody in Pantygirdl agreed that the situation, while not as it might have been, was nevertheless satisfactory to the kind of people who minded their own business, and they wished the happy couple, who were, it must be said, very nearly the same size, all the very best.

Alas, the grags and the delvers must have thought otherwise, and they broke down the doors of the chapel, and since people in Llamedos didn't go armed to their weddings the grags had it all their own way. And it might have been a complete massacre were it not for old Fflergant sitting hitherto unnoticed in the corner, who, as everyone ran for shelter, threw off his cloak and turned out to be exactly the kind of dwarf who *would* take heavy weaponry to a wedding.

He swung a heavy sword and axe together in a wonderful destructive unison, a whirlwind of fighting, and in the end there were only two casualties among the wedding party. Unfortunately one of those was Blodwen, killed by a grag whilst clinging on to her husband's arm.

Covered in blood, Fflergant looked around at the shocked wedding guests and said, 'You all know me. I don't like mixed marriages, but like you I can't abide those bloody grags, the bastards! May the Gap take them!'

Lord Vetinari's coach spun through the streets of Ankh-Morpork, and Moist watched the traffic scatter around them until they reached the River Gate and were out of the city proper. The coach bowled quickly along the road as it followed the Ankh downstream, towards Harry King's Industrial Estate, a world of smokes, steams and, most of all, undesirable odours.

Ankh-Morpork was cleaning up its act. It had been a good act, full of spices, plagues, floods and other entertainments. But now the Ankh-Morpork dollar was rising high, and so was the price of property. Amazingly, a great many people wanted to live in Ankh-Morpork, as opposed to somewhere else (or quite possibly as opposed to being *dead* in Ankh-Morpork, which was always an optional extra). But, as everybody knew, the city was gripped in its ancient stone corsetry, and nobody wanted to be there, metaphorically speaking, when the stays burst.

There was overspill, and my, how it was spilling. Farming land around the city state, always at a premium, was now full of speculative building.* It was a wonderful game, and Moist, in a

---

* A term meaning that the builder speculates about how far away he can be, and with how much money, before the buyer finds that the footings have, in fact, no feet, the septic tank is one foot deep with a tendency to flow backwards, and the bricks owe a lot to that most organic and venerable of all building materials, cow shit. The whole business traditionally begins with a plot, in every sense of the word. Entire suburbs were being built with such beguiling names as Nightingale Valley and Sunflower Gardens which had never heard a nightingale or seen a sunflower in bloom, but nevertheless were on the market with CMOT Dibbler Practically Real Estate and Associates, currently doing a roaring trade.

previous life, would undoubtedly have joined in and made a fortune, several fortunes in fact. And indeed, while Lord Vetinari was looking out of the window, Moist listened to the sirens and their beguiling songs of money to be made by the right man in this right place and the entrancing vision hung in the air for a tantalizing moment.

Ankh-Morpork was surrounded by clay, easily dug up, so if the cow shit ran out there was the material for your bricks, right there in front of you, with timber easily available from the dwarfs, delivered to your site by water. Soon you'd have a terrace of bright new homes available to the rising and aspirational population anxious to buy, and then all you needed was a shiny billboard, and, most definitely, an exit strategy.

The coach passed by many buildings of this sort, which would no doubt be little palaces to the occupants, who had escaped from Cockbill Street and Pigsty Hill and all the other neighbourhoods where people still dreamed that they could 'better themselves', an achievement that might be attained, oh happy day, when they had 'a little place of their own'. It was an inspiring dream, if you didn't look too deeply into words like mortgage and repayments and repossession and bankruptcy, and the lower middle classes of Ankh-Morpork, who saw themselves as being trodden on by the class above and illegally robbed by the one below, lined up with borrowed money to purchase, by instalments, their own little Oi Dong*. As the coach rumbled past the settlements, known together as New Ankh, Moist wondered whether this time Vetinari, in allowing all these lands to be colonized in such a way, had been very stupid or indeed very, *very* clever. He plumped for 'clever'. It was a good bet.

Eventually they arrived at the first outpost of the complicated, stinking, but ultimately most profitable, wire-netting-fenced

* Oi Dong being not dissimilar to Shangri-La.

compound of Sir Harry King, sometime tosher and rag-and-bone man, now believed to be the richest man in the city.

Moist liked Sir Harry, he liked him a lot, and occasionally they shared the wink of men who had made it the hard way. Harry King had indeed come up the hard way and those who got in his way went down the hard way too.

Most of the area before them was full of the products of Harry King's noisome profession, conveyor belts coming and going from who knows where, being loaded and unloaded and sorted by goblins and free golems. Horses and carts went past loaded with even more grist for that particular mill. At the far end of the compound was a collection of large sheds, and in front of them a stretch of surprisingly clear space. Moist suddenly noticed the crowd outside the compound fence, pressing up against every inch of wire netting, and felt their expectancy.

As the coach stopped, he smelled the acrid scent of coal smoke cutting through the general fetor, and heard what sounded like a dragon having difficulty sleeping, a kind of chuffing noise, very repetitive, and then suddenly there was a scream, as if the biggest kettle in the world had got very, very angry.

Lord Vetinari tapped Moist on the shoulder and said, 'Sir Harry tells me that the thing is quite docile if handled with care. Shall we go and have a look? You first, of course, Mister Lipwig.'

He pointed to the sheds, and as they got nearer the smell of coal smoke got thicker, and the almost liquid chuffing noise got louder. Moist thought, well it was a mechanism, that's what it was, wasn't it? Merely a thing like a clock, yes, just a mechanism, and so he straightened up and walked fearlessly, on the outside at least, towards the door where a young man with a greasy hat and an even more greasy overall was beckoning with a greasy grin like a fox looking speculatively at some chickens. It seemed they were expected.

Harry came bustling out and said, 'Greetings, my lord . . . Mister

Lipwig. Please come and meet my new associate, Mister Dick Simnel.'

Behind them, inside the shed, was the shuddering metallic monster, and it was alive. It really was alive! The thought lodged instantly in Moist's brain. He smelled its breath and heard its voice. Yes, life; strange life but nonetheless life of a sort. Every part of it was subtly shaking and moving, almost dancing by itself, a thing alive, and waiting.

Behind the beast, in the shed, he saw wagons, presumably ready to be towed, and he thought, yes, it's an iron horse. All around it were acolytes: men working on lathes, hammering on metal, running backwards and forwards with buckets of grease and cans of oil and occasionally pieces of wood which, right now, looked out of place amongst all the iron. And there was a strong sense of purpose that meant *we want something done and we want it done fast.*

Dick Simnel smiled broadly from behind a mask of grease and said, ''ow do you do, sirs. Well, 'ere she is! Nowt to be afraid of! Her name, technically, is Number One, but I call 'er Iron Girder! She's my machine. I made her, every little bit: nuts, bolts, flanges and not to forget each and every rivet. Thousands of 'em! And all the glasswork too. Very important, your sight glasses and gauges. Had to design everything meself because no one has ever done it before.'

'And when you give her rails she'll move more freight than a battalion of trolls, and get there much faster to boot,' said Sir Harry, standing behind Moist. And he added, 'It's true. I swear that young Simnel tinkers with Iron Girder all the time: tinker, tinker, tinker. An overhaul every day.' He laughed and said, 'I wouldn't be surprised if he eventually got her to fly.'

Mr Simnel wiped his hands on his greasy rag, causing them to get even more greasy, and then proffered one to Lord Vetinari, who gently waved it away, saying, 'I would prefer it if you dealt with Mister Lipwig, Mister Simnel. If I decide to allow you your fascinating . . . experiment, it will be to him that you answer, in the first part. Personally, I treasure my ignorance of how machinery works, although I am well aware that this is something of great interest to some people,' he added, in a tone of voice that suggested he meant strange and secret people . . . busy people, excitable people, fiddling people, tinkering and volatile people. A kind, alas, who would say something as innocent as, let's give it a try, it can't hurt, surely? We can always hide under the coffee table.

'*My* interest,' continued Lord Vetinari, 'lies in ways and means, opportunity, danger and consequences, do you see? I am given to believe that your remarkable engine is propelled by steam, heated until the boiler almost, but doesn't quite burst. Is that not the case?'

Mr Simnel gave the Patrician a cheerful smile and said, 'That's about it, gaffer, and I've blown up one or three in testing, I don't mind telling thee! But now, sir, we've got it right, sir. Safety valves! That's the ticket! Safety valves made out of lead, bungs that melt if the fire box gets too hot so the water comes down and extinguishes the fire before the boiler blows.'

Simnel carried on, 'Live steam is *very* dangerous, of course, to them that don't have the knowing of it, but to me, well, gaffer, it's as playful as a puppy. Sir Harry has allowed me to build a demon-stration track, sir,' and he gestured to the rails that led out of the shed and wound round the perimeter of the compound. 'May I ask if you gentlemen would care to come for a little spin?'

Moist turned to Vetinari and said, with a flat face, 'Yes, how about it . . . gaffer?' And got a look like a stiletto. A look that said, we'll have words about this later.

Vetinari turned to Simnel and said, 'Thank you, Mister Simnel. I think on this occasion I will give that honour to Mister Lipwig. And I dare say Drumknott will be eager to accompany *him*.'

This was said brightly, but Drumknott looked anything but delighted at the opportunity, and frankly neither was Moist over-joyed, remembering too late that he had put on an expensive new jacket.

Moist asked, 'Mister Simnel, why does your contraption need to run on rails, please?'

Dick Simnel smiled the expansive smile of a man who really, really wants to talk about his wonderful pet project and is now keen to illuminate every bystander to the point of boredom, and in the worst cases suicide. Moist recognized the type; they were invariably useful and in themselves amiable and quite without malice of any sort, but nevertheless they were implicitly dangerous.

And right now, Mr Simnel, happy as a clam and greasy as a kebab, said, speaking earnestly, 'Well, sir, steam likes it smooth, sir, and the countryside is full of ups and downs, and steam and iron are heavy, and so putting all this together back at Swine Town we found it much more sensible to lay down what we call t'*permanent way*, it's a kind of road wi' tracks, or rails, just for the engine to run on, as it were.'

'*Railway*'ll do fine for the punters, though,' said Harry. 'I keep telling the lad – short and snappy, that's the kind of name people remember. Can't expect them to ride on something they can't spell.'

Simnel beamed, and suddenly his genial face seemed to fill the world. 'Now then, Iron Girder is greased, in steam and all fired up for you, gentlemen. Who's ready for a little ride?'

Drumknott had not uttered a word, and remained staring at the dribbling engine like a man looking at his doom. Moist, taking pity on the little clerk for once, half pulled him, half helped him up into the small open cabin of the metal beast, while Mr Simnel fussed around, tapping mysterious brass and glass items, and the fire in the belly of the beast burned hotly, and filled the place with yet more smoke.

And suddenly there was a shovel in Moist's hand, put there by Simnel so fast that Moist couldn't avoid it. The engineer smiled and said, 'You can be t'stoker, Mister Lipwig. If she needs stoking you'll need to open up t'fire box when I tell you. Ee, we'll 'ave some fun.'

Simnel looked down at the stunned Drumknott and said, 'Er, as for you, sir, well, I'll tell you what. You, sir, you can blow t'whistle, by means of this chain here. And as you see, gentlemen, this is by way of being a working prototype, with not very much of the comforts of home, but 'old on and you'll be fine, so long as you don't stick your head *too* far out. We'll be pulling a fair few ton today. Sir Harry were interested to see what she were made of, and so, er, Mister Drumknott, blow the whistle, if you please!'

Speechlessly, Drumknott yanked on the chain, and shuddered as a banshee scream came from the engine. And then, well, thought Moist, there was not very much, just one chuff, a jerk, another couple of chuffs, and another jerk, another chuff, and suddenly they were moving, not only moving but accelerating as if the end of Iron Girder was trying to be out in front.

Through roiling clouds of steam Moist looked behind at the loads they were towing in the creaking carts, and he could *feel* the weight, and yet still the engine with its train was gathering speed and momentum. Mr Simnel was placidly tapping his dials and shifting levers, and now here came a curve, and the train chuffed, and every truck followed the curve like ducklings following their dear old mum, rattling a little, certainly creaking, but nevertheless being one big moving *thing*.

Moist had travelled fast before. Indeed, a golem horse, that rare creation, could have easily outpaced them. But this, well, this was machinery, handmade by men: wheels, bolts, brass knobs, dials, gauges, steam and the grunting sizzling fire box, beside which Drumknott was standing now, hypnotized and pulling the chain that blew the whistle as if performing a holy duty, and everything shook and continued to shake like a red-hot madhouse.

Lord Vetinari and Harry came into view as the train raced towards them on its first lap. And they disappeared behind Moist into the cloud of smoke and steam left hanging in the air. Then, as Iron Girder plunged on, it broke through into Moist's consciousness that this wasn't magic, neither was it brute strength, it was, in fact, *ingenuity*. Coal and metal and water and steam and smoke, in one glorious harmony. He stood in the fierce heat of the cabin, shovel in hand, watching and wondering about the future, as the train of carriages bumped round once more, screeching slightly on the second curve. Then, with the sound of tortured metal, it slid to a stop a few feet away from the watchers in front of Iron Girder's shed.

Now Mr Simnel was all arms and business, shutting things down and turning things off as the wonderful engine died. Moist corrected himself: not died — she was sleeping but still dribbling water and hissing steam and, inexplicably, she was very much alive.

Simnel dropped down from the cab on to a makeshift wooden platform and looked at his enormous stopwatch, glanced at the dial and said, 'Not bad, but I couldn't really open 'er up round here. On the test track over at Swine Town I got her going at almost seventeen miles an hour, and I can swear that she could go *much* faster if I could lay down a longer track! And she moved reet wonderfully, didn't she, gentlemen? With all that load, tons of it.' This was said to his fellow engineers.

'Aye, what is it?' And this, in fact, was directed to a small wide-eyed urchin, who seemed to have miraculously appeared by the side of the track. Simnel looked on gravely as the urchin took out a very small notebook from his jacket pocket and meticulously wrote down the numeral *1* as if it were a command.

And Moist, for some reason, couldn't help himself from saying, 'Well spotted, young man, and you know what? I rather feel that you're going to need a much bigger book before long.' And the certainty hit him that, although Lord Vetinari's face was as impassive as ever, those of Harry King and some of the other onlookers were gleaming in the smoky light of the future to come. Given the numbers already lining the fence, straining to watch the train on its circuits of the compound, the news was out and flying.

Harry King said, 'Well, gents, is this iron horse not amazing? She seems to be able to move *anything*, I assure you. Now, there's a nice lunch awaiting us in my boardroom, gentlemen. Shall we go up there? . . . There's some cracking good beef.'

Lord Vetinari broke his silence. 'Certainly, Sir Harry, and perhaps in the meantime someone could locate my secretary?'

They turned to look at the engine, which had come to a stop in a kind of human way, not all at once, but settling down like an old lady making herself comfortable in a favourite armchair, except that at that moment Iron Girder blew out a hissing stream of shining water vapour, which does not normally happen with old ladies, at least not in public.

Drumknott, up in the cabin, was still desperately pulling the chain for the next whistle, and he seemed to be weeping like a toddler bereft of a favourite toy as the sizzling got fainter. He caught their gaze, carefully relinquished the chain, climbed down from the footplate and almost tiptoed through the sizzling steam and the occasional unexpected mechanical creak, as the metal cooled. He walked gingerly over to Dick Simnel and said, hoarsely, 'Could we do that again, please?'

Moist watched the Patrician's face. Vetinari seemed to be deep in thought, then he said breezily, 'Very well done, Mister Simnel, an excellent demonstration! Am I to believe that many passengers and tons of freight could be carried by means of this . . . thing?'

'Well, yes sir, I see no reason why not, sir, although of course there would have to be some additional work, decent suspension, and properly upholstered seats. I'm sure we could outdo the stage coaches, which are a right pain in the arse, sir, and no mistake . . . if you would excuse my Klatchian.'

'Indeed I will, Mister Simnel. The state of our roads and therefore of our horse-drawn carriages leaves much to be desired. A journey to Uberwald is a penance without a cause and no amount of cushions seem to help.'

'Yes, my lord, and riding on sleek steel rails in a well-sprung carriage would be the height of comfort. So smooth!' said Moist. 'Perhaps people could even sleep in a suitable carriage, if there was such a thing?' he added. He was surprised that he'd said this out loud, but, after all, he was a man who saw possibilities, and now he was seeing them in spades. And he saw the face of Lord Vetinari brighten considerably. Iron Girder had ridden her tracks much better than the post horses managed with the flints and potholes of the high roads. No horses, thought Moist, nothing to get tired, nothing that needs feeding, just coal and water, and Iron Girder had pulled tons of weight without a groan.

And as Harry led the Patrician towards his office, Moist ran his hand over the warm living metal of Iron Girder. *This* is going to be the wonder of the age, he thought. I can smell it! Earth, air, fire and water. All of the elements. Here is magic, without wizards! I must have done something good to be in this place, here today, at this time. Iron Girder gave a final hiss, and Moist hurried after the others heading for their lunch and the future of steam.

In the plush comfort of Harry King's boardroom, all mahogany and brass and extremely attentive waiters, Lord Vetinari said, 'Tell me, Mister Simnel, could your engine go all the way to, let us say, somewhere like Uberwald?'

Simnel appeared to cogitate for a moment and then said, 'I don't see why not, your worship. It might get tricky round about Skund and, of course, it gets a bit steeper further on, but I'd say the dwarfs know how to knock damn great 'oles in t'scenery when they want to. So yes, sir, I'm certain it's possible, in time, with a big enough engine.' He beamed and said, 'If we have t'coal and t'water, and t'tracks, a locomotive engine could take you anywhere you wanted.'

'And is it open to anyone to build an engine?' said Vetinari suspiciously.

Simnel brightened up and said, 'Oh, aye sir, they can try, but they ain't had none of my secrets, and we Simnels've been working on steam for years. We've learned by our mistakes. *They* can learn by theirs.'

The Patrician smiled faintly. 'A man after my own heart, though laminating oneself to the roof of one's workshop is such a finite lesson!'

'Yes, I know, but if I might be so bold, sir,' Simnel continued, 'I'd like to bid for t'Post Office work, right here and now. Strike while t'iron's hot, that's always been the Simnel motto. I know the clacks can send a message as fast as lightning, but it can't do parcels and it can't do people.'

Lord Vetinari's face gave nothing away, and then he said, 'Oh really? *I* strike when I like, but never mind, Mister Simnel. I will not stand in the way of your exploring possibilities with Mister Lipwig, but I suggest we must also consider the position of the coachmen and farriers in this time of change.'

Yes, Moist thought, there would be changes. You'd still find horses in town and Iron Girder couldn't plough, although for a certainty Mr Simnel could make her do so. 'Some people will lose out and others will benefit, but hasn't that been happening since the dawn of time?' he said out loud. 'After all, at the beginning there was the man who could make stone tools, and then along came the man who made bronze and so the first man had to either learn to make bronze too, or get into a different line of work completely. And the man who could work bronze would be put out of work by the man who could work iron. And just as that man was congratulating himself for being a smarty-pants, along came the man who made steel. It's like a sort of dance, where no one dares stop because if you did stop you'd be left behind. But isn't that just the world in a nutshell?'

Vetinari turned to Simnel. 'Young man, I must ask you, what do you intend to do next?'

'There's that many people wanting to see Iron Girder up close like, I thought mebbe I'd hitch up t'wagons and put in some little seats, and offer them all the chance of a ride behind her. If Sir Harry's agreeable, that is.'

'There is of course the question of public safety,' said Vetinari. 'Did I hear you say earlier you have blown up . . . "one or three" I think was the phrase?'

'I made those explode a-purpose, to see exactly how it 'appened. That's the way to get the knowledge, you see, sir.'

'You take your work very seriously, Mister Simnel. And have any other engineers evaluated your findings? What I'm asking, Mister Simnel, is what is the judgement of your peers?'

Simnel brightened up. 'Oh aye, sir, if you mean Lord Runcible, sir, he's our landlord over at Sto Lat, but when I asked him, he laughed a lot and said it were amazing what people got up to and told me just not to run Iron Girder in the pheasant season while they were mating.'

'Indeed,' said Vetinari. 'If I might rephrase my question, what is the verdict of other engineers who have seen your wonderful machine working?'

'Oh, I don't think *anyone* calling 'imself an engineer, except me and my lads, has ever seen Iron Girder, although I've heard that over in Nothingfjord a couple of lads've made a damn good steam pump for getting groundwater out of mines and suchlike. All very interesting, but not as interesting as Iron Girder herself. I'd like to go visit them for a pint and a chat one day, but as you can see I'm busy, busy, busy all the time.'

'Your lordship,' said Harry, 'I respect Mister Simnel because I've seen that he's one of those men who tuck their shirt into their trousers and that says *dependable* to me. Now, there's a line of people out there who really want to whizz about behind the lad's . . . er . . . locomotive. I reckon they'll pay top dollar for taking a ride on the very first one of its kind. And the people of Ankh-Morpork are so thirsty for novelty that the whole city is, you might say, hurrying the future along for the sheer joy of watching its progress. So I'm thinking that every man and boy and possibly even their ladies would like to have a ride on this wonderful machine.'

'And should we count the risk, whcn simply to live in Ankh-Morpork is to shake hands with risk every day of the week?' murmured his lordship. 'Mister Simnel, you have my goodwill, such as it is, and I can see a twinkle in the eye of Sir Harry, a man who, if I may say so, looks like someone who intends to be an investor, although, of course, that is entirely up to him and you. I am no tyrant . . .'

There was a moment of hushed silence around the table and Lord Vetinari continued, 'That is to say I am not a tyrant stupid enough to take a stand against the zeitgeist, but, as you know, I am the man who can steer it with care and consideration. That is why I intend to speak to the editor of the *Times* this very evening to leave him, as he would say, in the loop. He always likes to be consulted, it makes him feel important.'

His lordship smiled and said, 'Amazing, how *do* we think up these things? I wonder, indeed, what will come next.'

The atrocity of the attack on the clacks tower at Sto Kerrig, which had so recently been a lifeline to the world for the people in the town, shocked everyone. As Adora Belle Dearheart looked at the wreckage in the gathering dusk, she was not surprised to see a very large and handsome wolf approaching at speed and, unlike most wolves, carrying a package between its jaws. The wolf disappeared behind a haystack, and shortly afterwards out of the haystack came a handsome female, only marginally dishevelled, wearing the uniform of the Ankh-Morpork City Watch.

Captain Angua, the most notable werewolf in the Watch, said, 'Oh my, they've certainly made a mess, haven't they? And are you sure that only one of your people was hurt?'

'Two goblins, captain, but they bounce well. Quick-witted, too. Can you imagine, they managed to send out a final message saying that their tower was under fire from dwarfs before they legged it. Very conscientious, the goblins, when it comes to machinery. They are always better on the night shift. Can I say, captain, when you find out who did this I'll press charges and press them very hard indeed, to a point when a police officer like yourself would have to look away for fear of seeing something they didn't want to.'

'I wouldn't worry about that, Miss Dearheart. His lordship takes the view that to interfere with the clacks is to interfere with the proper running of the world. Treason not only to one's own state, but to all.'

'At the moment, my friend Shatter of the Icicle, the lead goblin on this tower, has a bit of a battered arm, but he'll certainly assist in finding the dwarfs who did this. However, I don't know where Shine on the Moon has got to.'

'I'll prowl the area until my back-up gets here. I'm expecting the cart and Igorina for the forensics,' said Angua. 'If you hear something screaming it might be me, but don't worry. Commander Vimes has no time for senseless saboteurs.'

There was a pause, and Adora Belle said gravely, 'There's something I think you ought to see. Look under this pile of timber: this dwarf looks very, very dead and horribly mutilated. I assume he probably tripped and fell when he was setting fire to the tower. What do you think, captain?'

Carefully, Captain Angua looked at the corpse and said, 'He's lost an ear.'

Adora Belle said, 'Well, apropos of nothing at all, I understand that when goblins get truly riled up they go all frisky and look for souvenirs.'

'But I'm quite certain, of course, that none of your clacks goblins would be getting up to anything like that, right?' Angua asked.

Distantly, Adora Belle replied, 'Yes, having been almost burned alive by dwarf extremists would be shrugged off as another day in the office and not something to get very excited about.'

She looked at the captain quizzically, who said, 'Quite so. Undoubtedly any injuries were caused by the incompetence of the terrorists themselves.'

'Why, yes, indeed, yes,' said Adora Belle.

'Wasn't it amazing how one of them managed to chew his own ear off?' Angua observed.

'So, can Shine on the Moon come out of hiding now?'

'I'm sorry,' said Angua carefully, 'I didn't hear what you said over the cracking of the tower.'

The silence in Lord Vetinari's study was absolute. Nevertheless, the tread of Drumknott's approach contrived to make it even more silent as the secretary handed his lordship a little slip of paper and told him that a second clacks tower had been torched by people calling themselves, in translation, 'The Only True Dwarfs'.

Drumknott waited while not a muscle moved in Lord Vetinari's face before he said, 'Let it be known that enemy action on the clacks system will be followed by the death of not only those who did it but also those who ordered it to be done, whoever they are. Send this to every embassy, consulate and head of state. Action this night, please.'

Still speaking calmly, Lord Vetinari continued, 'It is also time, I think, to let the dark clerks deal with the more unusual suspects. I'm sure your concludium has given you some clues, Drumknott, and of course we will assist in any way possible. The Low King must be . . . unhappy about this. Although the stricken clacks tower was ours, we know that the impact of this problem falls in the last event on the King himself. Therefore, send him a message on the black clacks and let him know that I myself and, undoubtedly, Lady Margolotta will support any new plan he chooses to make. The grags have once again broken a solemn accord and *that*, Drumknott, batters the pillars of the world and not inconsiderably. After all, if you can't trust governments, whom can you trust?'

There was a subtle cough from Drumknott and his smile at that point was more like a grimace. Before the secretary was released to his private office and its other intrigues, Lord Vetinari continued fishing in his own stream of consciousness, and said, 'I seldom get angry, Drumknott, as you know, but I am angry now. I should be grateful if you would send for Commander Vimes in his other incarnation as Blackboard Monitor Vimes. I require his assistance and I don't think he will be a happy man – which, from my point of view, has no downside in these circumstances. Please put the message out to Mister Trooper that this is not the time to be a nice person.'

He went on, 'This isn't war. This is a crime. There will be a punishment.'

Rhys Rhysson, Low King of the dwarfs, was a dwarf of keen intelligence, but he sometimes wondered why someone with that intelligence would go into dwarfish politics, let alone be King of the Dwarfs. Lord Vetinari had it so easy he must hardly know he was born! The King thought humans were, well, reasonably sensible, whereas there was an old dwarf proverb which, translated, said, 'Any three dwarfs having a sensible conversation will always end up having four points of view'.

It wasn't quite as bad as all that, but it was near enough these days, he told himself, as he looked over at the assembled members of his council in which, according to the rules, he was the first among equals. He had read somewhere in the scrolls that they owed him fealty, whatever that was. It sounded like a kind of porridge.

When his secretary, Aeron, had returned from a recent visit to Ankh-Morpork, he had described a foot-the-ball game he witnessed, which had, at its centre, a referee. Right now, Rhys was feeling something of what the referee had to go through since all the balls were kicked right at him. How could you be the Low King in a realm where even the factions had factions and those factions had microscopic factions? He envied, oh how he envied, Diamond King of Trolls who, apparently, gave instruction and advice to his myriad subjects. After which they said *thank you*, something that the Low King didn't hear very often. Diamond King spoke for *all* trolls *everywhere*. The dwarfish race, however, had fractured now almost to the point of disarray and all of this ended up as a problem the Low King had to deal with.

There was today, obviously, an agenda or, rather, a regrettably large number of agendas, one for every faction. Glumly, Rhys wondered what the word was for a large number of agendas, and decided that the term should be a *living death of agendaritis*. It was the deep-down grags that gave him nightmares because, well, there was something offensive about those thick leather clothes and conical hats. After all, he thought, we're all dwarfs together, are we not? Tak never mentioned that dwarfs should cover their faces in the society of their friends. It struck Rhys that this practice was deliberately provocative and, of course, disdainful.

Now, on the everlasting agenda, dwarfs from every mine were grumbling about the exodus of the young to the big cities. And, of course, they all had reasons for why this might be the case, all of them wrong. Anyone who wasn't a dwarf who preferred to live in darkness, in every meaning of the word, knew that the reason the younger generation was now overwhelming Ankh-Morpork, for example, was simply down to those very same grumblers and their activities. On the other hand, those he thought of as progressive dwarfs, the type who would quite happily have a troll as a friend, were bearing down on *him*, the King, about their race's tendency to drive itself into a kind of purdah.

There was a great cloud of misunderstanding in the Low King's hall, which on every side appeared almost wilful, as if any dispute, however insignificant, had to be thrashed through to the bitter end. It was something in the dwarf psyche. We spend too much time indoors, Rhys thought. He sighed when he realized that Ardent, whose voice had become unbearably loud, now had the floor.

Ardent was a dwarf that the King would have liked to see present at a mine disaster, preferably underneath it. However, Ardent had followers, stupid followers, and he also had powerful friends. And that was it. Politics. Politics was like those little wooden sliding-picture games for children: you had to move all of the pieces in the hope of finding a place where the whole picture slotted together.

At the moment Ardent was insinuating that, in truth, the mining of fat in the Schmaltzberg fat mines was not truly dwarfish, a comment which led an elderly dwarf, whom the King recognized as Sulien Heddwyn, to get to his feet.

Heddwyn put his hands on his axe and said, 'My father was a fat miner. My grandfather was a fat miner. And so was my grandmother, she was a *very* fat miner and I was a miner when I was a minor. My mother gave me a tiny pick as soon as I was old enough to hold it. Every one of my relatives back to the dive of the Fifth Elephant was a fat miner and I'll tell you, the export income from the Plains for our purest fats is what keeps this town running. So I won't take an insult like this from a *b'zugda-hiara** too afraid to look at the sunshine.'

The sound of metal on metal echoed around the hall, followed by silence, with everyone waiting to see what was going to happen

* 'lawn ornament'

next. And that meant Rhys Rhysson had to break that silence. After all, he was, was he not, the Low King, the Low King of all the dwarfs?

He smiled, well aware that one wrong word from him would send shock-waves around the cavern and the result, whatever it was, would be his fault. Such is the fate of those who work only for the propagation of peace over warfare, and the way of the conscientious facilitator is a path strewn with thorns.

He looked at the angry councillors brandishing weapons around the huge table. It was as if being a dwarf meant that you lived in a permanent state that the term 'grumpiness' simply couldn't convey. A conference of dwarfs was, in their language, a confusion of dwarfs.

His voice low, Rhys spoke. 'For what purpose am I King? I will tell you. In a world where we formally recognize trolls, humans and, these days, all manner of species, even goblins, un-reconstructed elements of dwarfdom persist in their campaign to keep the grags auditing all that is dwarfish.'

He looked sternly at Ardent as he continued, 'Dwarfs from every area where dwarfs live in sufficient numbers have tried to modernize, but to no avail apart from those in Ankh-Morpork, and the shame of it is that often those determined to keep dwarfkind in the darkness have somehow inculcated their flocks into believing that change of any sort is a blasphemy, no specific blasphemy, just a blasphemy all by itself, spinning through the cosmos as sour as an ocean of vinegar. This cannot be!'

His voice rose and his fist crashed down on the table. 'I am here to tell you, my friends and, indeed, my smiling enemies, that if we do not band together against the forces that wish to keep us in darkness dwarfkind will be diminished. We need to work together, talk to one another, deal properly with one another and not spend all our time in one enormous grump that the world isn't entirely ours any more and, at the finish, ruin it for everyone.

After all, who would deal with such as us in a world of new choices? In truth, we should act as sapient creatures should! If we don't move with the future, the future will twist and roll right over us.'

Rhys paused to accommodate the inevitable outburst of *Shame!* and *Not so!* and all the other detritus of rotted debate, and then spoke again. 'Yes, I recognize you, Albrecht Albrechtson. The floor is yours.'

The elderly dwarf, who had once been favourite to win the last election for Low King, said courteously, 'Your majesty, you know I have no particular liking for the way that the world is going, nor some of your more modern ideas, but I have been shocked to discover that some of the more headstrong grags are still orchestrating attacks on the clacks system.'

The King said, 'Are they mad?! We made it clear to this council and all dwarfs, after the message we received from Ankh-Morpork about their clacks being attacked, that this stupidity must cease at once. It's even worse than the Nugganites,* who were, to be sensible about this, totally and absolutely bloody insane.'

Albrecht coughed and said, 'Your majesty, in this instance I find myself standing shoulder to shoulder with you. I am appalled to see things go this far. What are we but creatures of communication and communication accurately communicated is a benison to be cherished by all species everywhere. I never thought I would say this, but the news I am hearing lately, and am expected to delight in, makes me ashamed to call myself a dwarf. We have our differences and it's right and proper that we should have them, and discourse and compromise are cornerstones in the proper world of politics, but here and now, your majesty, you have my full and

---

* Not to be confused with the fabled Nougat Knights, famed in dwarfish mythology as the ancestors who, at the beginning of the world, created the treacle mines and other subterranean sweets.

unequivocal support. And as for those who stand in our way, I call down a murrain on them. I say, a murrain!'

There are uproars and there are uproars and this uproar stayed up for a very long time.

Eventually Albrecht Albrechtson brought his axe down on to the table, splitting the wood from top to bottom, bringing terrified silence across the gathered dwarfs, and said, 'I support my King. That is what a King is for. A murrain, I said. A murrain. And a Ginnungagap for those that say different.'

Rhys Rhysson bowed in the direction of the old dwarf. 'I thank you, my old friend, for your support. You have my undying gratitude and you leave me in your debt.'

Then, to some onlookers, the Low King might have looked a little taller. Over the hubbub, and there is no hubbub as bubbling as a dwarf hubbub, the King felt strangely buoyant, lifted, like the strange gases found around the crater of the Fifth Elephant. It seemed to the King that some of his councillors were suddenly thinking, actually thinking, and they had listened, actually listened. And now they were trying to think creatively.

Rhys continued, 'Not for nothing is Ankh-Morpork the residence of even more dwarfs than live here in Uberwald; and we now know that quite a large number of our dwarfs are emigrating to the lands of Diamond King of Trolls. So it is that our traditional enemy is now a friend to the many fleeing from the agents of the grags.'

As he expected, the hubbub bubbled even more: wilful bubbled hatred, bubbled misunderstanding, bubbled spitefulness.

He said, 'I tell you now that history will run straight over us squabbling dwarfs and I will not stand by and allow that history to end with our race brought down to the status of angry *b'zugda-hiara*! I am the King, by right, duly elected with all the proper observances. I was anointed on the Scone of Stone in accordance with traditions going back to the time of B'hrian

Bloodaxe and I will serve the sacred duty by all means necessary. I declare these grags and their puppets are *d'hrarak* and I will not suffer their pernicious doctrines any more. I am the King, and I will be King!'

The uproar returned, as it always did, but Rhys thought he could see some comfort in the faces around the table and then his gaze ran into Ardent and triumph wobbled a little and he thought softly: sooner or later, my friend Mister Ardent, I will have to deal with you.

Lord Vetinari's expression did not alter as he read the headline in the *Ankh-Morpork Times*: 'LOCOMOTIVE PROJECT DANGEROUS FOR HEALTH' followed in a much smaller font by 'SO IT IS CLAIMED'. And it wouldn't alter until he had had a word with the editor. Of course, the Patrician knew that any change was an affront to somebody, and quite clearly the proposed locomotive undertaking couldn't hope to be anything other than a target.

'Apparently,' Vetinari remarked to Drumknott, 'the pounding rhythm of the railway wagons will lead to immorality. This from a Mister Reginald Stibbings of Dolly Sisters.' He signalled to one of the dark clerks. 'Geoffrey, what do we know about this Mister Stibbings? Does he have a particular *expertise* in immorality?'

'The one at Loose Chippings, my lord? I am informed that he has a very young mistress, sir. A young lady formerly employed at the Pink PussyCat, and very highly thought of there, I believe.'

'Does he? An expert indeed, then.' Vetinari sighed and continued, 'Though of course I do not imagine it is in my remit to monitor the private doings of my people.'

'My lord,' interjected Drumknott. 'As a tyrant that is, in fact, exactly what you do.'

Vetinari gave him a look that did not actually employ a raised eyebrow but which implied that one might be forthcoming if the recipient of the look pushed his luck. He shook the paper in front of him and continued. 'A Mrs Baskerville from Peach Pie Street says that young ladies travelling on the train might find any kind of gentlemen sitting next to them.' He thought for a moment and said, 'In this city, expecting to encounter any kind of gentleman seems somewhat optimistic. But perhaps she has a point. It might be prudent to have compartments for ladies only. I rather think that Effie King would approve that.'

'Excellent idea as always, sir.'

'And what do we have here? A Captain Slope is very concerned about noxious gases around the lines of the railway.'

Lord Vetinari snapped his paper shut and exclaimed, 'The people of Ankh-Morpork are already at home to noxious gases. It's their birthright. Not only are they at home with them, they quietly persist in making more. It seems that Captain Slope is one of those people who won't like the railway at any price. Suggesting that sheep will miscarry and horses will run until they die of exhaustion . . . Indeed, it seems that Captain Slope thinks the railway will be the end of the world. Well, Drumknott, you know my motto: *vox populi, vox deorum.*'

Curious, the Patrician thought, as Drumknott hurried away to dispatch a clacks to the editor of the *Times*, that people in Ankh-Morpork professed not to like change while at the same time fixating on every new entertainment and diversion that came their way. There was nothing the mob liked better than novelty. Lord Vetinari sighed again. Did they actually think? These days *everybody* used the clacks, even little old ladies who used it to send him clacks messages complaining about all these new-fangled ideas, totally missing the irony. And in this doleful mood he ventured to wonder if they ever thought back to when things were just old-fangled or not fangled at all as against the modern day when fangled had reached its apogee. Fangling was indeed, he thought, here to stay. Then he wondered: had anyone ever thought of themselves as a fangler?

However, on the other hand, his lordship quite saw the point of the coach drivers and the others who even now, according to the *Times*, could see their business falling away if the railway were to be introduced, and he pondered, in such circumstances, what is the careful prince to do?

He thought, how many lives had been saved by the clacks, and not just lives: marriages and reputations and possibly thrones? The clacks towers now spanned the continent this side of the Hub and Adora Belle Dearheart had provided evidence that the clacksmen had several times spotted nascent fires, and on one occasion, outside Quirm, a shipwreck a little way out to sea – when they had clacksed that information to the nearest harbour master, saving all hands.

There was nothing for it but to follow the wave. New things, new ideas arrived and strutted their stuff and were vilified by some and then lo! that which had been a monster was suddenly totally important to the world. All the time the fanglers and artificers were coming up with even more useful things that hadn't been foreseen and suddenly became essential. And the pillars of the world remained unshaken.

As a responsible tyrant, Lord Vetinari regularly audited his actions fearsomely and without favour. Trolls in Ankh-Morpork were rarely talked about these days because, amazingly, people barely thought of them as trolls any more, just as, well, large people. Much the same, although different. And then there was the position of the dwarfs, the Ankh-Morpork dwarfs. Dwarfish? Yes, but now on their own terms. The Low King was certainly aware that in Ankh-Morpork there was a large population of dwarfs that had taken a look at the future and decided to grab a slice of it. Tradition? they had thought. Well, if it suits us then every so often we'll have a parade of all things dwarfish. Sons and daughters of our parents but, as it were, augmented. We have seen the city. The city where almost anything is plausible, if not possible, including, for the ladies, a better class of lingerie.

Far away in a small mine at Copperhead, Maelog Cheerysson the cobbler put down his hammer and tacks.

'Look here, my boy,' he said to his son, who was leaning on his work bench. 'I've heard what you said about the grags being the salvation of dwarfs, and this morning I found this: it's an iconograph of me in Koom Valley. The last time. Oh, yes, I was there, nearly everybody was there. We'd been told by the grags that the trolls were our enemies and I thought of them as nothing more than nasty big lumps of rock out to crush us! Well, we were all lined up facing the buggers, and then somebody shouted, "Trolls, put down your weapons! Dwarfs, put down your weapons! Humans, put down your weapons!"

'And there we stood and we could all hear other voices in different languages and right in front of me there was this bloody big troll, oh my! He had his great big hammer ready to pulverize me. That was not to say that my axe wasn't about to take his bloody knees off at the same time, but the voices were so loud that everybody stopped and looked around and he looked at me and I looked at him and he said, "What's happening here, mister?" and I said, "I'm damned if I know!"

'But I could see the other side of the valley and there was a great big kerfuffle between the top brass, all screaming about dropping our weapons, and I looked at the troll and he looked at me, and he said, "Are we going to have a war, or what?" and I said, "Oh, and I'm pleased to meet you, my name is Maelog Cheerysson," and he sort of grinned and said, "They call me Smack, and I'm pleased to meet you."

'And all around us people were wandering around and asking one another what the hell was going on and were we fighting or were we not fighting and if we were fighting what were we fighting for? So some of the lads sat down and lit a fire for a brew-up, while at the other end of the valley the flags were fluttering and everybody was walking around like it was a holiday or something.

'And then a dwarf came up to us and said, "Good fortune, lads, you're going to see something that no one else has seen for millions of years," and we did, I reckon. We were some way away from the front of the queue because trolls and humans and dwarfs were coming back out of the cavern, and every single one of them going past us looked as if he'd been hypnotized.

'Now, I've told you about the miracle of Koom Valley before, my lad, but you haven't seen this iconograph of me and Smack. It was took at the time just after we realized we weren't going to be fighting that day and we all went in ones and twos into that cavern and saw the two kings: the king of the dwarfs and the king of the trolls, entombed in shining rock, playing Thud! And we saw it! And it was true! They'd been friends in death. And that gave us the signal that we needn't be enemies in life.

'And that was it until later Smack and me tried to find something both of us could drink. A lot of the people were doing the same thing, but the potion he gave me nearly blew my bloody head off. It certainly made my boots burn. Smack has got two kids now, you see, doing all right, working in Ankh-Morpork. Trolls ain't all that good at writing, but I think of him and I think of Koom Valley every day.'

The old cobbler looked sideways at his son's face and said, 'You're a smart boy. Smarter than your brother was . . . and I reckon you've got a question to ask me.'

The boy coughed and said, 'If you saw them playing Thud, Dad, can you remember which one was about to win?'

The old dwarf laughed. 'I asked that when I met Commander Vimes, and he wouldn't tell me. We reckoned he probably broke a few pieces off so no one knew who the winner would be so some curious little fellow like you wouldn't go off and try to start the whole damn war again.'

'Commander Vimes? The Blackboard Monitor?'

'Yes, it was him all right. Shook my hand. Shook both our hands.'

The boy's tone was suddenly reverential. 'You actually shook hands with the actual Commander Vimes!'

'Oh, yes,' said his father nonchalantly, as if meeting the famed Blackboard Monitor was all in a day's work. 'I suspect you have another question, my lad.'

And the boy frowned. 'So, Dad, what's going to happen to my brother?'

'I'm sorry, I don't know. I sent a petition to Lord Vetinari, saying that Llevelys is a good lad who got into bad company. And I received a reply, and his lordship said that a young dwarf set fire to a clacks tower while people were working on it. And his punishment will be at his lordship's leisure. And so I sent him another letter, saying that I had fought at Koom Valley. And I received another reply, and his lordship said that he understood that I *didn't* fight at Koom Valley because fortunately nobody did, but he understood that I must do what I can for my eldest son, and as his lordship said, he will cogitate.'

The old dwarf sighed. 'I'm still waiting, but as your mother says, while we're not hearing anything, then he's still alive. Now don't tell me, my lad, that the grag extremists are on our side, because they ain't. They're the ones that'll tell you that the dead kings have been made up in Ankh-Morpork and were dummies and so were we if we thought they were real. And, my boy, the dumb believe it! But I was there. What I touched I felt, and so did everybody else on that day and that's why I get angry when the grags start preaching about the horrible humans and the terrible trolls.

'They want us to be frightened of one another, thinking there must be an enemy, but the only enemy now is the grags and those poor fools like your brother, who set fire to a clacks tower and got badly burned for his trouble. They are the victims of the sneaking bastards in the darkness.'

*

Far away in the Oblong Office Drumknott put the midday edition of the *Times* in front of Lord Vetinari and looked down at Mr Cheerysson's latest frantic petition, saying, 'They've torched two more clacks towers, my lord, but so far no one has died. Except on their side, of course. Young dwarfs, badly advised. They should have known better.'

The silence enveloped Lord Vetinari. 'Indeed,' said his lordship, 'but it is easy to be an idiot when you are seventeen and I would warrant that the grags who put them up to it are much older. There is no sense in breaking the arrow if, by acting sensibly, you may capture the archer. I'll leave the Cheerysson boy thinking about his fortune in the Tanty for a while and will make a note to have him brought over to talk to me in a month or two. If he's clever, his parents won't be grieving, and I'll have a number of names and, above all, the goodwill of his parents. Always worth thinking about, don't you agree, Drumknott?'

'Damage to property,' said Drumknott speculatively.

'Yes,' said Lord Vetinari. 'That's it.'

A few days later, Crossly quietly entered the master bedroom of the house in Scoone Avenue, nudged Moist, and, when that had no effect, finally pinched his ear in order to get his attention.

He whispered, 'Excuse me, sir, but his lordship requires your presence at the palace *immediately*, and I am sure that neither of us would like to see the mistress troubled at this time, yes?'

At home and, for once, in bed at the same time as Moist, Adora Belle Dearheart was gently snoring, although she was certain that she did not.

Moist groaned. It was the crack of seven and he was allergic to the concept of two seven o'clocks in one day. Nevertheless he dressed with a speed and silence trained by experience, walked noiselessly downstairs, left the house and got a trolley bus to the palace. He ran up the steps to the Oblong Office, reflecting that, day or night, he had never seen it empty. This time Lord Vetinari was at his desk, looking, if the word could be applied to Lord Vetinari, chipper.

'Good morning, good morning, Mister Lipwig! Rather speedier than last time, yes? I imagine you haven't had time to look at your newspaper today? Something rather droll has happened.'

'Is it something interesting to do with the railway, perhaps, my lord?'

Lord Vetinari looked puzzled for a moment and then said, 'Well, there is something, yes, since you ask.'

He sniffed as if what he was dealing with was not in the great scheme of things all that important and continued, 'I am being told that everybody is going to Harry King's compound to see the marvel of the steaming train, which seems to have caught the public fancy. I understand that Sir Harry, with his usual business acumen, is already turning this into a commercial enterprise.

'Of course, that is news, but when you do indeed get hold of a newspaper you might notice a small apology from the editor of the *Times* to the effect that the crossword has been removed, as the compiler is stepping down for a while owing to the pressures of keeping up the standard of achievable games that are nevertheless sufficiently taxing. Of course, as a rule I do not gloat, but I fear she has met her match. I shall ask Drumknott to arrange for a box of chocolates to be sent to her, from a secret admirer. After all, I am generous in victory!'

Lord Vetinari cleared his throat again and said solemnly, 'Alas, Drumknott has taken the morning off to go and have another look at the engine. A morning off. Whoever heard of such a thing? I have to say that I'm somewhat surprised, as the only other time he has ever requested time away from my service was to attend the paperclip, stapler and desktop aids symposium three years ago. He got very excited about that one, too. One wonders what the attraction of this engine can be. Does it not seem rather strange to you?'

Moist was a little nervous of the use of 'strange' and 'Drumknott' in the same sentence, and instead volunteered to visit the site of the train to escort Drumknott back to the palace.

'Since you will be there, Mister Lipwig, I shall be pleased to hear your . . . impressions on the economic opportunities for my city.'

Ah-ha, thought Moist, so that's why he's dragged me out of bed . . . again. Nothing to do with the crossword, nothing to do with Drumknott, but *everything* to do with *his* city getting an interest in the railway.

His lordship gave Moist a brisk nod and waved the paper, suggesting that it was time for him to be on his way.

It took Moist a long time to push his way through the throng anxious to see the modern miracle of the age. Harry King's business compound was at the very end of the queue that seemed to straggle halfway back to the city. There was no sign of Drumknott but Moist wasn't surprised. When Drumknott was standing in front of you, he was so retiring as not to be there.

There were guards on the gates all round the compound, Harry's own and City Watch, watching like hawks as one by one the citizens queueing up parted with a whole dollar a time to ride behind the locomotive. And a dollar was a dollar, possibly a day's food for a family, and yet, as far as Moist could ascertain, flying over the rails on the wonderful train was worth tightening your belt for. It was better than the circus, better than everything, to be speeding along with the wind in your face and black smuts that made the eyes water, but were, well, the badge of the train riders, who nevertheless didn't seem to notice it, given the amount of unpleasantness that could slap, splat, spit or fly into your face when you stepped into the street, or even when you walked into your own house, if you lived anywhere near the Shades.

Moist was well versed in the people of Ankh-Morpork's love of novelty, and, he had to admit it, Iron Girder, pulling her train like the queen she was, was novelty in the extreme. She came trundling around the corner with people in the carts behind screaming and waving to friends still waiting in the queue. And as a connoisseur of the madness of crowds he watched carefully, and noted that some passengers disembarked and scuttled away to the man who was handing out little tokens in exchange for another dollar, and then ran all the way to the back of the very, very long queue for another go.

There was a click near by and then a flash, and he turned to see the perennially cheerful face of Otto Chriek, lead iconographer of the *Ankh-Morpork Times*, who gave him a friendly wave.

'Vell now, Mister Lipvig, surely you're behind zis in your cheeky little vay?'

Moist laughed and said, 'No, not me, Otto, but it's *very* popular, isn't it!' And I want to be at the very centre of it all, he said to himself.

He noticed that periodically the man collecting the money hurried away carrying huge leather pouches, with a troll bodyguard fore and aft, and was instantly replaced with another showman ready for the moneys of the mob. And so Moist, as he told himself in his own cheeky vay, followed the money. He followed it in between the great noisome heaps and stinking lagoons of Harry's empire until the man with the large pouches of coin walked into a large shed. He followed him inside and froze, because he was immediately surrounded by the kind of men who have their noses splashed against one side of their face, little in the way of conversation and, he noticed now, very bad halitosis.

Fortunately, the shed also contained Sir Harry, who was bright enough to wave a hand in the air and say, 'Okay, boys, loosen those sphincters. It's only Mister von Lipwig, my old chum and bank manager. He's practically one of us, ain't you, Moist?'

Moist grinned, thankful that sphincters were, right now, not in play, and said, 'Well now, Harry, you know, as your bank manager I of course make it my duty to look after your interests, and I gather that you're looking after the interests of Mister Simnel too?'

That hung in the air like a sickle, a sharp one at that, and he watched Harry's face, which hadn't moved one single muscle. And then, abruptly, Harry burst out laughing and said, 'Oh my, Mister Lipwig, I always said you was a sharp card and, if it comes to that, a card sharp!'

He nodded to his bodyguards and said, 'Go and have a little break, lads. Me and my old friend here'll be having a little chinwag, such as old friends do. Go on, bugger off, the lot of you.'

And indeed they did, all except one, the very largest, a troll who glittered strangely and was watching Moist most intently, but not as intently as Moist watched him. And, Moist thought, the troll was . . . a gentleman. He couldn't think of him in any other way; he was well dressed, which was remarkable in itself as most trolls viewed clothes as optional.

Somewhat embarrassed at this interest, Moist felt rude enough to say, 'Okay, Harry, but there's one bodyguard still here. D'you think I'm going to try anything?'

Harry King guffawed. 'That, Mister Lipwig, is my lawyer. His name is Mister Thunderbolt, got the letters after his name and everything, ain't you, Thunderbolt?'

Lawyer! Bingo!

Harry was laughing all the way from his belly now and said, 'Mister Lipwig, the look on your face! Don't worry, though. Mister Thunderbolt takes everybody that way. That isn't to say I ain't glad to see you, but you could be of service to both me and our friend the engineer. Shall we go somewhere a bit more private? Coffee?'

Harry waved at a clerk, who bustled away swiftly, and then ushered Moist and Thunderbolt up to his office overlooking the compound. Harry sat down and beckoned to Thunderbolt and Moist to do the same.

'Now then, you know me, Mister Lipwig, like I know you. We're a pair, eh? Not exactly crooks, not exactly, well, not now anyway, 'cos we've grown up and know how to do business properly, don't we?' He concluded with a wink. 'And we both know a once-in-a-lifetime deal when we see it, I'm sure. Tell me if I'm wrong, yes?'

There was somebody who was a lawyer in the room, moreover a lawyer who could presumably kill you with one punch, and it was always worth thinking about anything that you were going to say in front of a lawyer because you never knew if you really could trust the weasels, but Moist nodded at Mr Thunderbolt and said, with careful diction, 'Sir Harry, Lord Vetinari has set me the task of assessing this wonderful new invention on behalf of the city.'

Harry King opened a box of big cigars, sniffed them and chose one before proffering the box to Moist and Thunderbolt. The troll declined, of course, but Moist was never one to turn down one of Harry King's finest cigars. They came from far-off places and were truly excellent. Harry puffed out a big cloud of smoke, leaving him for a moment looking just like Iron Girder, and it occurred to Moist that Harry, who knew that symbols were important, was definitely hoping to be the first railway baron.

'Mister Lipwig, Iron Girder is peacefully, for want of a better word, transporting eager citizens around the track regular as clockwork. Round and round they go, happy as you like, you must agree? Mister Simnel says he built her as a proof of concept and he needs a lot of money to build a full-size version that can pull even more people and, above all, freight, because he reckons that's where the money is to be made, although looking out of the window at all those smiling faces I'm not so sure of that.'

Sir Harry sent another plume of smoke into the air and looked smug, which, Moist considered, was probably the case, before adding, 'Since I know you, Mister Lipwig, and I know that you can read me, yes, I'm prepared to bankroll the lad in exchange for a slice of the profits, a *big and fair* slice. I understand that he's now all but skint, totally boracic, with the arse nearly out of his trousers, and if he's ever going to get his ambition to run bigger trains to here, there and bloody everywhere then he needs a partner with experience of the world, and I have that experience from the bottom up, as it were.

'But, you know how it is, gents . . . when a man gets older and he's made his pile he starts caring a bit more about what people think about him, so I ain't no dwarf, I won't steal an advantage on a young man with prospects. That's why I'm happy to say that with the help of Mister Thunderbolt here I've struck a fair deal with the young lad. Ain't that so, Mister Thunderbolt?'

The air seemed to glitter as the troll stood up, shimmering as he spoke. His voice appeared to come from twilight canyons far away. It wasn't just sound, it had a presence in its own right.

'Yes, that is so. Sir Harry, I suggest now that even though you have a handshake deal with Mister Simnel, there should be three shares in this enterprise, to avoid deadlock, with the third and very small share in the hands of the city, to wit, Lord Vetinari. The purpose of the arrangement is in case Mister Simnel and you, Sir Harry, are unable to agree on a matter connected with what we are all calling the "railway". Lord Vetinari will have the casting vote to end that deadlock. But the city will not take any dividends; its income will come, as always, from straightforward taxation, which I am sure Lord Vetinari will consider an important part of this enterprise.

'The small print will be a little more complicated, and of course if Mister Simnel's locomotives catch on there will be opportunities to sell extra shares in the future. If you both agree, gentlemen, I will deal with that aspect and you may be certain that in compliance with Sir Harry's instructions Mister Simnel and his family will have a significant share in the business.'

As slowly as he had stood up, Mr Thunderbolt sat down again, and Moist von Lipwig and Sir Harry King looked at one another.

Harry, beaming, said, 'I suppose I'd better get the lad in, then,' and nodded to Thunderbolt to open the door.

A few minutes later Dick Simnel sat uncomfortably in his seat, trying not to make anything greasy, without much hope and even less success.

Harry appeared not to notice and said cheerfully, 'Now then, lad, it's like this. You reckon that with enough money you could make engines larger and more powerful than Iron Girder, right? And with long enough, er, rails, you could get to all the other cities? Well, lad, I'll bankroll you in this enterprise until you're in a position to prove that this is possible.'

He stopped talking for a moment, looked at the ceiling and said, 'Tell me: how long d'you think that'll be?'

The engineer looked thoughtful and somewhat baffled and said, 'I couldn't rightly say, sir, but the more the money jingles the faster the wheels'll turn. I mean, if I can hire the best skilled workers and, well, sir, I've made my calculations, done a lot of testing and I reckon I could have a new engine ready for . . .'

Moist held his breath.

'One thousand dollars.'

Moist glanced at the face of Harry King, who flicked the ash from his cigar and said, in a deadpan way, 'A thousand dollars? And how soon can you have it on the rails, lad?'

Simnel took his small sliding device out of his pocket, played with it for a minute or so and said, 'How about two months?' He fiddled with the device again and added, 'Around teatime.'

Moist was fidgeting at this point, and he chimed in with, 'Excuse me, I know you said that Simnels have been working on steam for years and that other people might have been too, but do you know if anybody else has anything like this? Might they steal a march on you even if they don't have your secrets?'

To his surprise Simnel said cheerfully, 'Oh yes, sir, about four or five of them, but none of them have yet produced even a working concept like Iron Girder. They're making all t'mistakes my dad did, and making a few others of their own an' all, from what I hear. Superheated steam doesn't give you a chance. Get it wrong and it'll tek t'flesh off your bones. Now me, sir, well, I'm a stickler for measurements, tiny teeny weeny measurements. They ain't very exciting but that's the soul and centre of being an engineering artificer.

'Unfortunately, my granddad and my dad were a bit slapdash about them, seeing as they didn't have the proper knowing of them, but measurements is your saving grace if you want to raise steam. Me mum paid for me to get a better learning, being as 'er side of the family had money from . . .' he paused, 'fishing, and one of my uncles made theodolites and other delicate instruments, and I thought to meself, well, this is very helpful, especially when he taught me 'ow to blow glass, and what I need glass for is my own little secret . . .'

Simnel looked anxious for a moment and said, 'I'll need a shedload of iron, especially for t'tracks themselves. And, of course, then there's the question of laying t'tracks through people's land . . . someone'll have to talk to the landowners. I'm an engineer, always will be, and I'm not sure I know how to 'aggle with the big nobs.'

'Ah, as it happens we have a born haggler with us right now,' said Harry. 'What do you say, Mister Lipwig? Do you want to be a part of it?'

Moist opened his mouth to speak.

'There you are, then, young Dick. We'll use Mister Lipwig for any negotiations. He's the kind of man who'd follow you into a revolving door and still come out in front. And he speaks posh, when necessary. Of course, he's a bit of a scoundrel, but aren't we all in this business?'

'I don't think I am, sir,' said Simnel cautiously, 'but I know what you mean. If you don't mind, I'd like to suggest that my first track is laid all the way back to Sto Lat. Well, not exactly Sto Lat, it's a place on the outskirts called Swine Town, there being so many pigs in the area. That's where the rest of my gear and machinery is stored.'

Simnel looked nervously at Sir Harry, who was pursing his lips. 'It's a long way, lad, must be twenty-five miles or more, and you'd be right out in the sticks there.'

Moist couldn't hold his tongue. 'Yes! But they wouldn't be the sticks for long, would they? Try and get fresh milk in the city . . . it's always bad cheese by the time it gets to you, and then there are things like strawberries, watercress, lettuce, you know, everything with a limited shelf life! The areas that have the railways'll be more prosperous than those that don't! It was the same at first with the clacks. Everybody said they didn't want the towers, and now anybody who's anybody wants one at the bottom of their garden. The Post Office'll be on your side too, moving the mails faster and all that, and I can assure you that the Royal Bank will be right behind you, and indeed, Mister Simnel, I'll invite you to join me in my office as soon as possible to discuss our *special* banking facilities . . .'

Harry King slapped his thigh and said, 'Mister Lipwig, didn't I say it: you're a man who sees an opportunity when it's in front of him!'

Moist smiled. 'Well, Harry, I think it's in front of all of us now.'

In fact, in his mind's eye Moist could see *lots* of opportunities and plenty of room for problems, and here right in the middle of it all was Moist von Lipwig. It couldn't get better than this! His smile widened, inside and out.

It wasn't about the money. It had never been about the money. Even when it was about the money, it wasn't entirely about the money. Well, it was *slightly* about the money, but most of all it was about what the dwarfs called the *craic*. The sheer pleasure about what you were doing and where you were doing it. He could feel the future catching him up. He could see it beckoning. But, of course, sooner or later someone would try to kill him. That usually happened, but you had to take the chance. It seemed to be a necessary part of the whole thing, whatever the whole thing actually was. You *always* had to take the chance. Any chance.

Harry gave Moist a sideways glance and said, over his shoulder, 'Mister Simnel, if you've got a lot of your valuable stuff in a shed up there in Pig City or wherever, would you mind me sending a couple of my . . .' Harry paused, seeking for a genteel wording, '. . . my *useful* gentlemen to keep an eye on the place for you?'

Simnel looked puzzled and said, 'It's really a quiet old place, sir.'

Harry moved into what might be called his avuncular persona and said, 'That might very well be so, my lad, but I think that you and me are going to a place where there'll be a lot of money, and where there's a lot of money there are a lot of people trying to take it off you. I'd like to think that if anyone broke into your big shed to fossick around for any interesting bits of machinery or clues as to how you build your engines, they might find themselves having to explain their interest to Snatcher, Stiletto Dave and Grinder Bob. They're all good lads, kind to their old mums and wouldn't hurt a fly. Call it, well, call it . . . *insurance.* And if you can be good enough to let them have a key, I'll send them up there right now. Mind you, if you can't find a key I'm sure they'll find their way in. They're very versatile in that respect.'

Young Simnel smiled and said, 'That's very thoughtful of you, Sir Harry. Perhaps I should give them a message to take to my mother. She'll show them where everything is. My dad said always put a few nasty little booby traps around the place before you lock up and then after that owt they can steal from you they're welcome to, if they've still got their arms to carry it away, that is.'

Harry laughed out loud and said, 'Sounds to me like your old dad looked at things just the way I do. What's mine is mine and what is mine is me own.'

When Moist and Mr Thunderbolt stepped out into the compound Moist saw that people were *still* queueing up for a ride on the train, which was waiting like a queen while Mr Simnel's lads filled her bunker full of coal, and oiled and greased everything again, including themselves. They tapped her wheels and polished everything that could be polished, once again including themselves, while just about every little boy in the city, and, amazingly, most of the girls, stared at her in awe, worshipping at her shrine. And then it came back to him: earth, air, fire and water, the sum of everything! The goddess had found her worshippers.

There was a sound like thunder, but it was only Mr Thunderbolt clearing his throat to say, 'Remarkable, isn't it, Mister Lipwig? There appears to be what one can only call a *presence* of sorts, a hint, as it were, that life turns up in many different guises, perhaps? Just a passing thought.'

Moist had never heard such clear diction from a troll, and it must have shown, because Thunderbolt laughed, saying, 'A touch of diamond does the trick, Mister Lipwig, and I will endeavour to draw up contracts that suit all parties, you need not worry.'

Just then Moist beheld Drumknott, greasy and cheerful and covered with smuts, stepping off the engine and regretfully handing a hat and a very grubby jacket to one of Mr Simnel's lads. Moist grabbed the little secretary by one arm.

'Where did you get to, Mister Drumknott? I've been looking for you *everywhere*,' he lied. 'His lordship is expecting you back any time now.'

Moist wasn't sure he liked Drumknott, but it wouldn't do to have him as an enemy, being so close as he was to the engine that drove Ankh-Morpork, and so he cleaned up the little man as best he could and flagged a coach back into the city, noticing, as they travelled along the busy towpath, that the major traffic was still going the other way.

Moist knew about the zeitgeist, he tasted it in the wind, and sometimes it allowed him to play with it. He understood it, and now it hinted at speed, escape, something wonderfully new, the very bones of the land awakening, and suddenly it seemed to cry out for motion, new horizons, faraway places, *anywhere that is not here*! No doubt about it, the railway was going to turn coal into gold.

'Excuse me, young man.'

Sergeant Colon and Corporal Nobby Nobbs, who had taken it upon themselves to patrol the line of expectant sightseers queueing for a ride on the train, looked around uncertainly. It had been a long time since Sergeant Colon had been a young man, and as for Nobby Nobbs, although it was generally agreed that he was the younger of the two, there was some doubt about whether the term *Homo sapiens* could be applied to him; the jury of Ankh-Morpork was out. Colon and Nobby were supposed to have been on the beat in the Shades, but Colon had delegated that task to a couple of new recruits. 'Good experience for 'em, Nobby. And it's likely to be a dangerous business, this streaming engine. Needs someone to have a look-see – a couple of experienced coppers, let's say, prepared to put therselves in harm's way for the public good.'

'Young man . . . excuse me,' came the voice again. The speaker was a harassed-looking lady with two boys at heel, who weren't at all at heel and were expressing their frustration at having to wait for the promised ride on the train in the supremely annoying ways that only small children can manage. In a desperate attempt to distract them from their contest to inconvenience as many people in the queue in front of them as possible, their mother had seized on the first official-looking people who might be able to entertain her offspring with some interesting facts.

'We were just wondering if you could tell us how this locomotive goes?' she asked.

Fred Colon took a deep breath. 'Well, missus, there's the boiler, you see. It's like a kettle.'

This was not enough for the smaller child, who said, 'Mum's got a kettle. That doesn't go anywhere.'

His mother tried again. 'And how does this "boiler" work?'

'Well, you see, it sends the hot water to the engine,' said Nobby hurriedly.

'Right,' said the lady, 'and then what happens?'

'And then all the hot water goes into the wheels.'

The elder boy looked sceptical. 'Really? How's that done?'

Nobby, cornered, said, 'I think the sergeant can tell you that.'

A little bead of sweat appeared on Colon's face and he was aware that the two children were looking at him as if he were some kind of exhibit. 'Ah, well, the water is magnetic, right, because of all that spinning,' he said.

The elder boy said, 'I don't think it works like that.'

But Colon was on a roll and ignored him. 'The spinning causes the magnetism and that's what makes the water stick in there. Lots of iron in train wheels, stands to reason. And that's what keeps the train on the iron road, magnetism.'

The smaller boy changed tack. 'Why does the engine go *chuff*?'

'That's because it's chuffed,' said Colon with a sudden flash of inspiration. 'See, you've heard of "*chuffed*". That's where it comes from.'

Nobby looked at his friend in admiration. 'Is that why, sarge? I never thought of that!'

'And when it's had enough of a chuffing, there's enough magnetism to hold the train on the iron road, see?'

The last phrase was delivered in a rush in the hope that no more questions would be forthcoming. But it doesn't work like that with children. The elder boy had had enough and decided to show off the knowledge gleaned from friends who had been there earlier in

92

the day. 'Isn't it to do with reciprocating motions?' he said, with a glint in his eye.

'Ah, well, yes,' blustered Colon helplessly. 'You've got to have your recip-roca-tory motions to get the right *kind* of chuff. And when everything is chuffing and reciprocatoring, away we go.'

The smaller child was still puzzled, as well he might be. 'I still don't understand, mister.'

'Well, perhaps you're too young to know,' said Colon, taking refuge in the excuse used by exasperated adults through the millennia. 'Very technical stuff, your chuffing. Probably shouldn't even be trying to explain it to children.'

'I don't think I understand either,' said the mother.

'You know clockwork?' said Nobby, coming to the rescue again. 'It pretty much goes like clockwork, only bigger and faster.'

'How's it wound up?' asked the boy.

'Ah yes,' said Colon, 'that chuffing noise, of course, is the winding up. And when it's wound up, then off it chuffing goes.'

The smaller boy held up a clockwork engine and said, 'He's right, Mum, you wind them up and away they go.'

Bemused, the lady said, 'Right . . . well, thank you, gentlemen, for a comprehensive little talk. I'm sure the boys were fascinated.' And she handed Colon several coins.

Colon and Nobby watched the happy family as they climbed on to the cart behind Iron Girder. And Nobby said, 'It's a nice feeling, isn't it, sarge? Being helpful to people.'

Moist's cab halted at the palace, and he helped an exhausted Drumknott up the stairs. Amazingly he was beginning to feel sorry for the little chap, who was looking like a lotus eater who had run out of lotuses.*

Moist very carefully knocked on the door of the Patrician's

---

* Moist wondered whether it should be loti, but thought, well, what the hell.

office, which was opened by one of the dark clerks. The clerk stared at Drumknott and looked askance at Moist, as Lord Vetinari himself stood up in surprise, leaving Moist impaled between two askances. So he saluted smartly and said, 'I beg to report, sir, that Mister Drumknott very gallantly and fearlessly and at some personal cost has helped me form an opinion as to the practical aspects of the new-fangled train, risking his life *repeatedly* in so doing, and for my part I have seen to it that your government has a suitable measure of control over the railways. Sir Harry King is funding further research and trials, but personally, my lord, I believe the new railway will be a winner. I'm convinced that this prototype can pull more stock than dozens of horses. Mister Simnel seems to be very thorough in his work, extremely meticulous and, above all, the people appear to have taken the train to their hearts.'

Moist waited. Lord Vetinari could outstare a statue and make even a statue start to feel nervous and confess. Moist's counter was a fetching grin, which he knew annoyed Vetinari beyond measure, and there was absolute silence in the Oblong Office while blank stare and cheery grin battled it out for supremacy in some other dimension, which ended when his lordship, still staring fixedly at Moist, said to the nearest dark clerk, 'Mister Ward, please take Mister Drumknott to his rooms and clean him up, if you would be so kind.'

When they had departed, Lord Vetinari sat down and drummed his fingers on his desk. 'So, Mister Lipwig, you believe in the train, do you? It certainly appears that my secretary is impressed. I have never seen him so excited by something that wasn't written on paper, and the afternoon edition of the *Times* seems to be in agreement with him.'

Vetinari walked over to the window and stared down at the city in silence for a moment and continued, 'What can a mere jobbing tyrant achieve in the face of the even greater, multi-headed tyrant of public opinion and a *regrettably* free press?'

'Excuse me, sir, but if you wanted to you could shut down the papers, couldn't you? And forbid the train and put anyone you like in prison, yes?'

Still staring down at the city, Lord Vetinari said, 'My dear Mister Lipwig, you are clever and certainly smart but you have yet to find the virtue of wisdom, and wisdom tells a powerful prince that firstly he shouldn't put just anyone he likes in prison, because that is where he puts the people he *doesn't* like, and secondly that mere unthinking dislike of something, someone, or some situation is no mandate for drastic action. Therefore, while I have given you permission to continue, the train does not have my whole-hearted approval. Neither does it have my curse.' The Patrician seemed to consider for a moment and added, 'Yet.'

He walked up and down again for a second or two and then, as if the thought had only just struck him, said, 'Mister Lipwig, do you think it a possibility that a train *could* in fact get all the way to, say, Uberwald? That journey is not only extremely slow, tedious and uncomfortable by coach, but it is fraught with many . . . ah, perils . . . and traps for the unwary traveller.' He paused and added, 'And indeed the unlucky bandit.'

'Oh, yes, that's where Lady Margolotta lives, isn't it, sir?' said Moist breezily. 'But it would mean negotiating the Wilinus Pass, sir. Very dangerous up there! Bandits have been known to knock out coaches by throwing down rocks from the crags.'

'But there is no other way without a very lengthy detour, Mister Lipwig, as you probably know.'

'In that case, my lord . . . I think it might be possible to construct such a thing as an armoured train,' said Moist, inventing furiously. He was gratified to see that Lord Vetinari brightened when he heard that, repeating the words 'armoured train' once or twice more.

Then his lordship said, 'Can it *really* be possible?'

And in the squirrel cage of Moist's mind, he thought, Can it? Can it really? It must be more than twelve hundred miles! It takes

95

well over two weeks by coach and that's if you don't get hijacked, but who was going to try to hijack an armoured train? The engine would be wanting water frequently and is it possible that it could carry enough coal for the whole journey? The numbers rolled in his head. Stopping places, troughs for water, mountains, gorges, bridges, marsh land . . . So many things, any one of which could scupper the project . . .

But going to Uberwald would mean passing through so many other places on the way and all of them could be opportunities to make money. The demons of critical path analysis swarmed around his brain. There was always something that you had to do before you could do the thing you wanted to do and even then you might get it wrong.

To Vetinari he said cheerily, 'Well, sir, I don't see why not. And, of course, for such a long journey it should be possible to sleep on the train and for heads of state to occupy a complete suite of carriages, if not the whole train. Surely that could be arranged?' Moist held his breath.

After a few seconds his lordship said, 'That would be appropriate, but, Mister Lipwig, I am not *entirely* bribed. The train must prove itself both financially *and* mechanically. However, I look forward to its success. It seems, Mister Lipwig, that you are using your extra-cheery voice and so once again you find yourself in your own chosen environment, that being the centre of everything. But tell me: where do you think will be the destination of the first commercial train? Quirm?'

'Actually, sir, that has been discussed and it looks as if it's going to be Sto Lat, because that's where Mister Simnel has his machine tools and a large stock of materials that he would need to transport to Ankh-Morpork. Besides, that place is a nexus for the Sto Plains, and nexus means—'

Lord Vetinari raised a hand and said, 'Thank you, Mister Lipwig. I do know what a nexus is.'

96

Moist smiled and headed for the door, showing his panic only on the inside, and as his hand reached the doorknob Vetinari's voice behind him said, 'Mister Lipwig, you surely realize that a thoughtful prince, a prince who wishes to keep his throne for some time and is shrewd in the ways of people, would not travel in a thrilling armoured train . . . He would put somebody *else* on that train, somebody expendable, having himself travelled the previous day in a suitable disguise. After all, there are such things as very, very large boulders, and most definitely there are a great many spies. But I shall consider your idea. It has a beguiling ring to it.'

Over the next few weeks more and more people heard about Iron Girder and even larger crowds passed through Ankh-Morpork to see the new marvel of the age, including delegates, ambassadors and representatives from most of the towns across the Sto Plains. And, of course, there were the *other* artificers and freelance tinkerers, inspecting everything they could see and trying to find out everything they could about what it was they weren't being allowed to see.

Every night Iron Girder was driven along a set of rails into a locked shed on the compound where she would be safe from interference due to the presence of Harry's most fearsome attack dogs and also two golems, brought in by Harry because, unlike dogs, they couldn't be killed by a meal laced with poison poked under the door. They patrolled the huge shed, sometimes with members of the City Watch just for the look of the thing.

Moist spent a lot of time in and around the compound in his not very official but somehow understood role as the grease in the outfit's management, as essential as the buckets of the stuff that seemed to be required in everything to do with the railway. He had, after all, a stake in the railway's fortunes as head of the Royal Bank of Ankh-Morpork, where money was starting to go in and out faster than a revolving door as Harry wrote cheques for iron shipments, timber and extra metalworkers, many of whom were from the company of Free Golems: every one of them his own man, albeit one made of clay.

And grease was definitely needed here. There was a mountain of paperwork already being generated by the railway, which Moist skilfully passed along to Drumknott, whose passion for paperwork was not quite yet eclipsed by his new passion for the railway. The little pink man was in hog heaven.

Surveyors had been called in to work on a route. They were everywhere with their little theodolites. They treated Dick Simnel as one of them, only different. Moist was pleased about that. Dick had friends now, and if they didn't understand all of his language they did indeed recognize it as bona fide language somewhat similar to their own and therefore they gave him respect. After all, these other people, in a way, did what he did only in different shapes, stresses, curves, loads, tolerances and substances, and thus where it counted were brothers under the skin. And like Dick, they worked by numbers and knew the absolute necessity of getting them right, and especially they knew the absolute requirement for precision.

In the compound the sound of metal on metal filled the air, and on every flat surface in Harry King's offices maps were laid out, and they were good maps.

'Lads,' Dick Simnel had said to the theodolite men, 'Harry King is a good gaffer who pays top dollar for a top-rate service. He's chancing everything to get the locomotives running, so I want you to make it easier for him. Iron Girder can take some slopes, and by 'eck she'll take more before I'm through, but for now, what I'm telling thee is to keep t'permanent way as level as possible. And I know that there are such things as tunnels and bridges, but they take a lot of time and are flippin' expensive! Occasionally a little detour might save us a lot of money, which is to say your wages. But think on, and I know it's obvious, but do not go anywhere near swamps and other shaky ground. A locomotive with its coal tenders, carriages and crew is reet, *reet* 'eavy and the last thing we want to be learning is 'ow to pull a bogged-down locomotive out of t'quicksand.'

And off they'd gone. The men with clean shirts every day. The men of the sliding rule. Moist liked them because they were everything he wasn't. But maybe he should teach them about being a scoundrel. Oh, not about taking money from widows and orphans, but about being aware that many people weren't as straight as a theodolite.

The surveyors proved only too happy to agree that the area around Sto Lat was the gateway to the Sto Plains, so now all they needed to do was get the people with, as it were, the keys to the gate to understand this, a job that everybody was extremely happy to turn over to Mr Moist von Lipwig.

As it turned out, there were a great many landowners between Ankh-Morpork and Sto Lat, and any number of tenants. Nobody minded a clacks tower near by. Indeed, often these days they demanded one, but, well, a mechanical thing chuffing through your cornfields and cabbage plantations spewing out smoke and cinders, well, *that* was a different matter, which would be the kind of problem that could be settled only by the application of that wonderful lubricant known to every negotiator as warm specie.*

The aristocrats, if such they could be called, generally hated the whole concept of the train on the basis that it would encourage the lower classes to move about and not always be available. On the other hand, some were of a type that Moist recognized: shrewd old buffers who'd lead you to believe they were harmless and possibly slightly gaga and then, with a little twinkle in their eye – BANG! – squeeze more money out of you than a snake, twinkling all the way.

* The term 'specie' requires the person asking for it to rub their thumb and forefinger together in a *knowing* way, if you know what I mean, guvnor?

Lord Underdale, one such gentleman, had plied Moist with an indecent amount of gin and brandy while naming his terms: 'Now see here, young man – *twinkle, twinkle* – you can take your tracks across my land if we can agree a route and it won't cost you a penny if you will firstly carry my freight for nothing and secondly put a loading station just where I want it so that I can also travel anywhere I want merely by flagging down one of your locomotives. Do you see, young man – *twinkle, twinkle* – I go free and my freight goes free. Do we have an accord?'

Moist looked out of the wonderful mullioned windows at the smoke beyond the ancient trees and said, 'What exactly *is* your freight, sir?'

The old man, all beautiful long white hair and ditto beard, said, 'Well, now, since you ask, it's iron ore with a certain amount of lead and zinc. Oh dear, I see your glass is empty again. I must insist you have another brandy – it's such a cold day, is it not? *Twinkle, twinkle.*'

Moist smiled and said, 'Well, your lordship, you are a tough bargainer and no mistaking – *twinkle, twinkle, TWINKLE.* Since our project is *very* heavy when it comes to metals, we could perhaps do business? That is to say if our surveyors don't come up with any problems, such as swampy ground and suchlike.'

'Well, Mister Moist, since you have drunk every last drop of brandy I have pressed on you without appearing to be the least bit intoxicated, I must consider you a man after my own heart – *twinkle, twinkle.*'

And here Moist definitely detected the subtle signs of intoxication as the old man said, 'I have to tell you that yesterday I was contacted by a man who said he represented the up-and-coming Big Cabbage Railway Company.'

Moist knew about them, yes, they were a company all right, but they didn't yet have a single engine or anybody as skilful as Simnel to tame the raw steam. He rather suspected that a lot of money would go their way from the gullible and then, when there was enough, the bright office would be empty and the gentlemen concerned, with different moustaches, would be legging it somewhere else to start up *another* railway company. Part of him longed to be one of them and then he thought, I *am* one of them, only this one has to work.

'Apparently,' continued Lord Underdale, 'they are going to build a far superior engine to the one being demonstrated in Ankh-Morpork.' The old man laughed at Moist's almost total lack of expression and said, 'You told me that you represented a railway company, Mister Lipwig. Well, now your company has . . . *company*!'

Moist belched forensically, very carefully choosing his time. 'This may be the case, sir, but we have – *hic!* – a working engine, which is . . . the toast of Ankh-Morpork!' And here Moist allowed a certain slur to enter his voice and continued, 'And now, why don't we, as gentlemen, cut a deal and shake hands on it like gentlemen so we both know where we stand?' He stood up and stumbled a little, saw the extra *twinkle* in the old man's face, and rejoiced.

Later, in the stables, as he saddled up to go home, Moist audited his afternoon's work. This was a game he knew all too well. He had seen the trap and had been prepared, and thus the side deal for iron-ore shipments and railway access was a sensible one but slightly more beneficial for the railway, in recognition of the fact that elderly gentlemen shouldn't try to get impressionable young men drunk, especially when they own more land than any reasonable person could ever need. Yes, Moist thought, moral compass? He smiled.

Before he mounted up, Moist carefully removed from about his person two hot-water bottles and a rubber pipe. He very carefully stowed both bottles in a large padded saddlebag, smiling as he did so. The old boy really shouldn't have tried to make him drunk. It was so . . . unethical.

When Moist eventually got back to the city, he went straight to the centre of Harry King's compound, ran up the stairs to Sir Harry's great big office, and dropped yet another portfolio, prepared by Mr Drumknott, of all the contacts he had dealt with, the rents, the routes agreed.

'These are for your lads, Harry, and this is for you.' He set down very carefully a large crate containing a number of bottles.

Harry stared at him and said, 'What the hell are these for!'

Moist shrugged and tapped his nose. 'Well, Harry, it's like this. A lot of the people I have to deal with are elderly men who think they're cunning and try to fill me with expensive alcohol in the belief that they can get the better of the deal and no mistake. Of course, I drink every drink put in front of me! No! Don't look like that! I really can hold my drink. In fact I can hold a great deal of drink, and I'm pleased to report that rubber doesn't detract from the taste of whisky, very fine brandy or Jimkin Bearhugger's best gin.'

'Well done, Mister Lipwig. I've always known you're a man to watch *extremely* carefully and I do so like to see a master at . . . *work*. Now follow me, Mister Lipwig, and try not to slosh, will you?'

In a few weeks the compound had changed beyond recognition: the big drop forges that used to thud behind Quarry Lane had been moved wholesale out of the centre of the city and enormously augmented their rate of hammering with the rhythms of the rail-way factory.

Harry seemed very proud of it, considering that if muck was brass, a thump of the hammer was pennies from heaven. As they walked through the cacophony he shouted, 'Great lads, the golems! They're always punctual, and they don't get ill. Most of all, they just *like* working! And I like anyone who likes to work: goblins, golems, I don't care what you are if you're a good worker.' He thought for a moment and added, 'As long as you don't dribble too much. Just look at the way those lads hammer things with their fists. I wish I could get more of them, but you know how it is.'

Moist looked around the fiery hellhole that was the ironworks. In the satanic air he could just about tell the golems from the human workers in their leather overalls, because the golems were the ones walking around holding pieces of red-hot iron in their bare hands. The furnaces illuminated the grey sky, and always and forever the clanging went on. And the pile of fresh new rails got bigger and bigger.

He nodded, since normal speech was clearly out of the question among the clanging and the banging. Indeed, he knew how it was. In short, the citizens of Ankh-Morpork who might be expected to fill the heavy-lifting trades, such as the golems and the trolls, were increasingly realizing that just because they were big and tough did not mean they had to do a big tough job if they didn't want to. This was, after all, Ankh-Morpork, where a man walked free even if he was not, strictly speaking, a man.

The problem, if you could call it that, had been building up for some time. Moist had first noticed what was happening when Adora Belle said that her new hair stylist was a troll, Mr Teasy-Weasy Fornacite*, and, as it turned out, a pretty good hairdresser, according to Adora Belle and her friends. And there it was: the new reality. If all sapient species were equal, that's what you got: golem housekeepers and goblin maids and, he thought, troll lawyers.

Harry King was rumbling on as they emerged back into the open: 'It's a bugger! Now they're free, you can't get the golems! Ask your missus! They're all off doing landscape gardening and suchlike daisy rubbish, and I reckon I'm paying every human ironworker in

---

* The moment Moist heard the name he went for the dictionary and was relieved to find that fornacite was a rare lead, copper chromate arsenate hydroxide mineral. The troll was a lovely bluey green colour.

the damn city double the odds, and only twenty-one of them heavy boys. It's such a shame, such a shame.'

'I don't know, Harry, you seem to be moving phenomenally fast.'

Harry nudged Moist and said, in a conspiratorial tone, 'I'll have you dumped in the river if you tell anybody this, but I'm loving it! I mean, most of my life has been, not to put too much of a fine point on it, shit, honest to goodness shit, not to mention of course piss, which has also been a very good friend to me, but you see all *that* is just moving stuff about, not actually *making* something. And it gets better because, you see, it's something me and the Duchess can talk about in polite company. Oh, of course, I'll still be maintaining the night-soil business and all of that . . . it is, after all, my bread and butter, so to speak, which, to tell you the truth, is more like steak and all the trimmings nowadays, but right now my heart is in the iron. And who can say that ain't beautiful, Mister Lipwig? I mean, daffodils, well, I quite like them, but look at the sheen on the steel, the sweat on the men; the future being made one hammer blow at a time. Even the slag is beautiful in a way.'

Iron Girder passed by on her everlasting journey around the compound and Harry said, 'What we need is the right class of poet.' He flung out a hand towards the admirers with their notebooks and all the others who clung to the railings. 'Look at them all! They're looking for miracles. And you know what? They'll get them.'

It started to rain, but the onlookers, especially the train spotters, with their very useful clothing, just stood there, watching Iron Girder kick up a mist into the air.

It seemed to Moist that for a moment Harry King was somehow different, even more alive than usual, and Harry, it had to be said, was pretty vital in any case. And now Harry King, Cess Pit Man, was metamorphosing into a National Treasure.

Bedwyr Beddsson tried to get his boots off. After a night in the mines it was amazing what you found in your boots, some of it alive. When the boots were off, not without a struggle, he took the harness off Daisy the pit pony and watched her sniff the clean air and canter into the little field near the entrance to the mine. It did your heart good to see her. There were times when Bedwyr would have liked to do the same thing. His mother had told him, you can't change your stars, meaning, presumably, this is your life and you have to live it. Now, as he stepped inside his living quarters, he wondered if Tak might let him try again.

He loved Bleddyn, his wife of many years, and his children were doing just fine in the school in Lancre, but today he was troubled. The grags had called and were quite polite this time, although neither he nor Bleddyn really cared for politics. How could they mean anything when you've spent your life sweating down in the mines? His pony was now free, but he was at the end of his tether. He just wanted to provide for his family as best he could. What was a dwarf to do?

Bedwyr wanted his children to do better than him, and it looked as though they would. His father had been annoyed about this. Bedwyr was sorry that the old boy was dead, but the world kept turning and the Turtle moved. New things were being done in new ways. And it wasn't that the grags were holding hard to yesterday; they hadn't even got as far as this century.

Bleddyn had cooked a good rat supper and was upset when she saw his face and said, 'Those damn grags again! Why don't you tell them to put their nonsense where the light shines too much!'*

Bleddyn didn't usually swear, so that surprised him, and she continued, 'They had a point once. They said that we were being swallowed up by the humans and the trolls, and you know it's true, except that it's the wrong kind of truth. The kids've got human friends and one or two trolls as well and nobody notices, nobody thinks about it. Everyone is just people.'

* Humans would have said, 'Put it where the sun don't shine.'

He looked at her face and said, 'But we're diminished, less important!'

But Bleddyn was emphatic and said, 'You silly old dwarf. Don't you think the trolls consider themselves diminished too? People mingle and mingling is good! You're a dwarf, with big dwarf hobnail boots and everything else it takes to be a dwarf. And remember, it wasn't so long ago that dwarfs were very scarce outside of Uberwald. You must know your history? Nobody can take that away, and who knows, maybe some trolls are saying right now, "Oh dear, my little pebbles is being influenced by the dwarfs! It's a sin!" The Turtle moves for *everybody* all the time, and those grags schism so often that they consider everyone is a schism out there on their own. Look it up. I've cooked you a lovely rat – nice and tender – so why not eat it up and get out into the sunshine? I know it isn't dwarfish, but it's good for getting your clothes dried.'

When he laughed she smiled and said, 'All that's wrong in the world is that it's spilling over us as if we're stones in a stream, and it'll leave us eventually. Remember your old granddad telling you about going to fight the trolls in Koom Valley, yes? And then you told your son how *you* went back to Koom Valley and found out the whole damn business was a misunderstanding. And because of all this, our Brynmor won't even have to fight unless someone is extremely stupid. Say no to the grags. Really, they're bogeymen. I've spoken to all the women round here and they say exactly the same thing. You're a dwarf. You won't stop being a dwarf until you die. And you could be a clever dwarf or you could be a stupid dwarf, like the ones who knock down clacks towers.'

Bedwyr very much enjoyed the rat, which had been nicely seasoned, and, as a wise husband does, he thought about things.

Two days later, coming back from Blackglass, where he had gone to buy a load of candles, Bedwyr found two dark dwarfs setting fire to the base of a clacks tower. All he had on him were his tools

106

and it was amazing how useful a simple miner's tools could be. A number of clacksmen and goblins joined him hastily in putting out the fire, and they had to stop Bedwyr from using his heavy boots to show his disdain for those who resort to arson. He told them, 'My brother's daughter, our Berwyn, she works on the clacks down in Quirm . . . All this stuff you don't notice until it's on your doorstep, and now I think I've woken up.'

Bedwyr didn't kill the delvers, he just, as it were, disabled them. But when he left hurriedly to go home, he noticed that the goblins were . . . busy. From the point of view of people working in an undefended clacks tower in the wilderness, the world was seen as black and white, and for these delvers it went black.

Railway fever, already red-hot, was becoming incandescent, at least across the Sto Plains. Would-be investors clamoured for a stake in the Ankh-Morpork and Sto Plains Hygienic Railway.* There were swamps to drain, bridges to reinforce and so theodolites twinkled in the sunshine.

But even with Vetinari's support and Harry's millions, it was a slow business. Every piece of track had to be laid with care and tested before anything could be run along it – let alone a train. Moist had expected that Harry would want to get things done fast at any cost with little thought of safety all round. Oh yes, he shouted a bit when the surveyors took up too much time, but the grumble remained a grumble. The same picture kept coming back into Moist's mind: Harry King already had the money, lots of it, but the railways were going to be his legacy. No more the King of the Midden. A Lord of the Smoke was better any day and so while he screamed that he was being sent to the poorhouse he nevertheless signed the paperwork promptly.

* There had been some discussion about the word 'hygienic', and Moist had lost. Hygienic, everyone else thought, gave the project a certain tone, a sort of *je ne sais quoi*. Lady King said this herself and who was going to argue with the Duchess?

To Effie, now definitely a Lady,* her husband the railway entrepreneur at last had a job that his wife liked to talk about. And Effie didn't just like to talk about it, she got involved with it and increasingly often was to be found in Harry's office. As it happened, it was Effie who came up with the idea of the moving gangs. And so trail after trail of wagons were working their way through the countryside, in which working men and surveyors could sleep and take their meals anywhere the railway wanted them to go rather than wasting time going home at night.

The track-laying was now pressing hard at Moist's heels as he dealt with the multiplicity of landowners along the route. And that was a painfully slow business too, every one of them exercised by the internal conundrum: if you held out for too much then there might just be somebody reasonably close by who would welcome the train for a pittance, if he was stupid enough, but then of course he might be clever and he would get his perishable produce to market before you could, and there you would be: with all the dust and all the noise and all the smoke and *none* of the money.

In the interests of keeping things moving as quickly as possible, the Patrician had allowed Moist to requisition one of the city's few golem horses. The horses were notable for their indefatigable galloping and also for turning your pelvis into jelly if you didn't pad up extremely well, but even with all the multiple layers Moist was just about rattling when he got back to the city after weeks of negotiations.

Exhausted, and in defiance of custom and practice, health and safety – but, on the other hand, with all the glory of the gods of style – to the dismay of the palace guards he rode the golem horse all the way up the steps to the door of the Oblong Office. There he

* Although in the eyes of her spouse she had always been the Duchess, a pet name he reserved for just her.

was pleased to see Drumknott, who deftly opened the door and stepped backwards so quickly that Moist, by ducking, managed to trot neatly to within a foot of Lord Vetinari's desk.

Unruffled, the Patrician lowered his coffee mug and said, 'Mister Lipwig. It is customary to knock before entering my office. Even, and especially, when entering on horseback. You may thank the gods that Drumknott had the presence of mind to disable our . . . little alarm system. How many times must I tell you?'

'Every time, sir, I'm sorry to say, because you see, sir,' said Moist, 'if I'm to be of any use to you I have to be Moist von Lipwig, sir, and that means, I'm afraid, sir, that I have to find the edge of the envelope and put my stamp on it, sir, otherwise life wouldn't be worth dying for.'

Moist could see Drumknott wincing at the concept of anyone stamping on any stationery whatsoever and continued, 'It's in my blood and frankly, sir, I'm fed up with dealing with old codgers who think they can get the better of Moist von Lipwig, and the cunning and the unpleasant and the stupid and the clever and the greedy . . . sometimes all wrapped up in one man. After all this, I think my soul needs a bit of a wash and brush-up, sir.'

'Ah, soul!' said Lord Vetinari. 'I didn't think you had one, Mister Lipwig. Well, I live and learn.' He steepled his fingers. 'Mister Lipwig, Mister Simnel's activities have drawn the eyes of the world. Of course one could not expect that every country, sizeable town and great city would *not* start thinking about the railway. It is a weapon, Mister Lipwig, a mercantile weapon. You may not know this because you don't live in *my* world. Young Mister Simnel came to Ankh-Morpork because this dirty old town, for all its faults, is the very place upon which this world spins, the place where history is changed, where because of an enlightened and caring government – which is to say *me* – every man, child, dwarf, troll, werewolf, vampire and even zombie and yes, goblin, can call themselves free; free of any master, save the law, which applies to everybody equally whatever their species and status in life: *Civis Ankhmorporkianus sum!*'

There was a thump as Lord Vetinari banged his fist on the table. 'Ankh-Morpork, Mister Lipwig, is not to be outdone! Now, I know you have been spending a lot of your time these days in making sure that the first fully commercial and grown-up train will indeed have a railway upon which it can run, and when it does it will be the wonder of the world. But all things move on, and it is for us to keep our city in the forefront of that movement.

'No doubt you, Mister Lipwig, Sir Harry and Mister Simnel are already thinking ahead. May I suggest that a daily railway service to and from Quirm could only set the seal on the usefulness of the railways. While a more efficient way to get to Uberwald is eminently desirable, alas I fear it must wait. I am naturally being badgered by all the other governments to bring the railway to them, but Quirm is our neighbour and an important trading partner and' – he lowered his voice – 'perhaps we could get our fresh seafood before it walks to Ankh-Morpork on its own. Agreed?

'You may leave the final details of the negotiations for the line to Sto Lat to Drumknott,' Vetinari continued. 'He has my permission to call upon the services of one of the dark clerks . . . The talents of Mister Smith would be eminently suitable for sorting out any . . . recalcitrant landowners, I think.'

Moist noticed that Drumknott's eyes had an unusual gleam in them, although the little secretary said nothing.

'You may go, Mister Lipwig, and may I counsel you that riding a golem horse in here again will be a *very* dangerous errand and may result in you having kittens.' His lordship smiled nastily and continued, 'Cedric is always waiting – *twinkle, twinkle.*'*

---

* The feared kitten torture was actually one dreamed up by Moist, and Vetinari had been impressed. In the dungeons of the palace there was a large iron maiden, seldom used. In these modern times the kitten torture regime was the punishment that would cause the miscreant to pause before doing anything that would place them in the

Leading the golem horse from the office, Moist thought, '*Twinkle, twinkle?* Oh, gods, it's catching.'

Mustrum Ridcully, Archchancellor of Unseen University, was held up on his walk across the University's Great Hall by Barnstable, one of the Bledlows.

The man touched the brim of his bowler hat in traditional salute, coughed politely and said, 'Mister Archchancellor, sir, there's a . . . person who wants to see you, and he won't take no for an answer. A very sorry-looking cove, sir, looks like he never had a decent meal in his life, sir. And personally, sir, I reckon he's just after a handout. Bit of an undesirable, sir, and he's wearing a kind of a dress. Shall I show him the door, sir?'

The Archchancellor thought for a moment and said, 'This man, does he smell like a badger?'

'Oh yes, sir, you got it in one!'

Ridcully smiled. 'Mister Barnstable, the old man to whom you refer is a master of every martial art ever conceived. In fact he conceived most of them himself and he is the only known master of déjà fu*. He can throw a punch into the air and it'll follow you home and smack you in the face when you open your own front door. He is known as Lu-Tze, a name that strikes fear in those who

dungeon again. The mechanism and the kittens were presided over by Cedric: not clever, but grateful for the pay packet every month, and he was very fond of kittens, with which the streets of Ankh Morpork were overflowing. The kittens would be placed in the iron maiden in large numbers, along with the miscreant who could just about sit. At the bottom was a little hatch, large enough to push through a sizeable saucer of milk. Every time a kitten was in distress and made its distress noticeable, Cedric would open up the maiden and give the victim a whack with his cudgel, the amount of cudgelling being contingent on the state of upset of said kitten. There were some idiots who thought this laughable, but it worked, and after a certain amount of cudgelling visitors were said to be amazed at the general atmosphere of happiness inside the iron maiden, where the purring was so loud it resonated throughout the dungeon.
* A discipline where the hands move in time as well as in space, the exponent twisting space behind his own back whilst doing so.

don't know how to pronounce it, let alone spell it. My advice is to smile at him and, with great care, deliver him to my office.'

Lu-Tze looked carefully at the range of brandies on the Archchancellor's heaving, creaking drinks trolley and sat back. Ridcully, his pipe smoking like the funnel of Iron Girder, said, 'How nice to see you, my old friend. It's all about the locomotion, yes?'

'Of course, Mustrum – is there anything else to talk about? The Procrastinators are grinding and everybody in Oi Dong is fearful of the Ginnungagap . . . the darkness at the end of the world before the new world takes its place, hmm? Although personally, I think it's a jolly good idea, what with this one being all battered about and unkempt and uncared for. The only problem I have yet to solve is how to get from the dying world into the new world. *That* is a bit of a puzzle. But even the Abbot is disturbed about the arrival of steam engines when it isn't steam-engine time.'

Ridcully poked at his pipe with a pipe cleaner and said, 'Ye-es, that is a conundrum. Surely the steam engine *cannot* happen before it is steam-engine time? If you saw a pig, you would, I think, say to yourself, well, here's a pig, so it must be time for pigs. You wouldn't question its right to be there, would you?'

'Certainly not,' said Lu-Tze. 'In any case, pork gives me the wind something dreadful. What we know is that the universe is a never-ending story that, happily, writes itself continuously. The trouble with my brethren in Oi Dong is that they are fixated on the belief that the universe can be totally understood, in every particular jot and tittle.'

Ridcully burst out laughing. 'Oh, my word! You know, my wonderful associate Mister Ponder Stibbons appears to have fallen into the same misapprehension. It seems that even the very wise have neglected to take notice of one rather important goddess . . . Pippina, the lady with the Apple of Discord. She knows that the

112

universe, while it requires rules and stability, also needs just a tincture of chaos, the unexpected, the surprising. Otherwise it would be a mechanism – a wonderful mechanism, ticking away the centuries, but with nothing *different* happening. And so we may assume that the loss of balance will be allowed this time and the beneficent lady will decree that this mechanism might yield wonderful things, given a chance.'

'For my part, I would like to give it a chance,' said Lu-Tze. 'Serendipity is no stranger to me. I know the monks have been carefully shepherding the world, but I rather think they don't realize that the sheep sometimes have better ideas. Uncertainty is always uncertain, but the difficulty with people who rely on systems is that they begin to believe that nearly everything is in some way a system and therefore, sooner or later, they become bureaucrats.

'And so, my friend, I think we say hail Pippina and the occasional discord. I'm sure the rest of the circle will be of the same mind, to judge by their activities. After all, it's as clear as the nose on your face: here is a steam engine. Ergo, it *is* steam-engine time.'

'Hurrah!' said Ridcully. 'I'll drink to that.'

'Why, thank you. I'll have a tincture of brandy with my tea, to keep out the cold, if you don't mind,' said Lu-Tze.

Moist sat at his desk, his mind churning over how best to introduce the matter of Quirm to Sir Harry. He blankly registered a . . . substantial . . . gentleman in front of him saying, 'Mister Lipwig? I have a proposition to—'

Moist laughed. 'Sir, anybody who has a proposition for me these days will get a maximum of five minutes, one of which has already passed. What is it?'

'I'm not just anybody, Mister Lipwig,' said the man, drawing himself up to his full height, which was in fact slightly less than his full girth. 'I am a chef. Perhaps you've heard of me – All Jolson. I understand from certain sources* that any day now your wonderful locomotives will be going to and from Sto Lat. I wonder, have you thought about what the people on board will eat? I'd like to bid for the franchise to sell food on the trains and possibly in the waiting rooms as well. Small snacks, and more substantial servings for the long-distance passenger. There's nothing like a pot of my slumpie to lift the spirits of a weary traveller. Or Primal Soup – very warming, that. I've been experimenting with serving it in cups, with little lids on, 'cos there are things in that soup that, to be honest, you wouldn't want to spill on yourself.'

Moist caught the essential words like a trout catching a newborn mayfly. Food on the trains! Waiting rooms, yes! Places where people would want to spend their money. Once again he remembered that the railway was not just about the rails or the steam.

And as Jolson handed over a slightly lard-stained calling card Moist let his mind fill with ancillary possibilities. Yes, you would definitely need a place to stay while you were waiting for your train, somewhere dry and warm with something to drink and even, heaven forfend, a sausage inna bun that actually had seen a pig. And yes, since Dick had said he'd be quite happy for a locomotive to travel at night, then at the destination there might be railway hotels, as swish as the railway carriages and sprightly, because people would be coming and going at all times of the day or night. It would seem as if the whole world were on the move.

Restless himself, he went out into the compound and crossed to the great shed. Having thought that young Simnel was happily living every dream he had ever had, he was surprised to come across the engineer sitting beside the throbbing Iron Girder, alone and, there was no other word for it, glum.

Moist automatically stepped into his position as the oil that

---

* All's mastery of artery-clogging cuisine had made him a number of friends in interesting places – trading sources for sauces had turned out to be very good business practice.

greased the wheels of progress and said, 'Something wrong, Dick?'

As if beset by unseen demons, Simnel said sombrely, 'Well, it's like this, Mister Lipwig. I were invited along to t'Guild of Cunning Artificers last week, to see Mister Pony, and do you know what? He told me I should get apprenticed to somebody! Me! The lads are coming on fine and should be *my* apprentices, but it turns out that I'm not a master and so 'ave to be indentured for four years to a *real* master and then I might just about make a journeyman after a little while. But I told them, I never had indentures, never 'ad a master, because, d'you know for why? I haven't been an apprentice because there were no one to teach me all the stuff I know. I 'ad to work it out for meself!

'And then I read about those old guys in Ephebe who once built a little steam engine which worked . . . and then exploded all over them, although nobody got 'urt, and any road, they were saved because their steam engine were a kind of boat and they all ended up in the water wi' soggy togas. And then I thought to meself, well, those old guys must've known a trick or two and so I got another book about them from t'library in Sto Lat, and you know what, Mister Lipwig? All those old boys wi' their togas and sandals, they also invented the sine and cosine, not to mention your tangent! All that mathematics, which I love. And then there's your quaderatics. Can't get anywhere without quaderatics, can you?

'And any road, they looked like a bunch of old guys who you'd think would do nowt more than lie about arguing about philosophy and then it turns out that all along they knew just about everything about, well, everything and just wrote it all down. Can you believe it? They 'ad it in their 'ands. They could've built a proper steam engine, and steam boats that didn't explode. That's academics for you. All that knowing and they went back to discussing t'beauty and truth of numbers and missed the fact that they'd discovered summat reet important. Me? If I want beauty and truth I look at Iron Girder.'

Dick slapped his fist down on the metal carapace and said, 'There's beauty. There's truth, right there. And they had all that knowing 'iding away. Look at 'er! My machine! I built her! Me! And I'm not even good enough to be an apprentice.'

He paused for breath and continued, 'Now don't get me wrong, Mister Moist, I know it's just words but, you see, it's come home to me that, since I've never done me indentures, I can never be a *master* because there's nobody who knows more about what I'm doing than, well, me. I've looked in all t'manuals and read all t'books and you can't be a master until all the other masters say you are a master.'

Simnel looked even more haunted while Moist stood with his mouth metaphorically open and listened to the meticulous Mr Simnel blaming himself for being a genius.

He continued, 'The lads, as I call 'em, could never 'ope to be masters neither because they won't have been taught engineering by a master! It's flaming ridiculous!'

Moist burst out laughing and put his hands on Dick's greasy forehead, carefully turning the lad's head around to face the length of the compound and the huge ever-present queues for the train ride, and he said quietly, '*They* all know you're a master and Iron Girder is your masterpiece. What boy would not wish to be you, Mister Simnel, a manmade masterpiece yourself. Do you understand?'

Simnel looked doubtful, possibly still hankering after letters after his name and a certificate for his old mother to hang on her wall.

'Yes, but with all due respect, the people aren't authorities on the taming of steam. I mean no offence, like, but what do they know?'

Moist snapped and said, 'Dick, in some respects down there somewhere is the soul of the world, and they know everything. You'll have heard of Leonard of Quirm. There are some masters who make themselves and you have, you've made yourself an engineer and *everybody* knows it.'

Simnel brightened and said, 'I don't intend on starting me own guild, if that's what you're thinking, but if some young lad comes to see me and wants to learn the way of the sliding rule then I'll do him right. I'll make 'im an apprentice the old-fashioned way and his hands'll never be clean again. And I'll give him indentures until they're coming out of his flaming teeth, all writ down on vellum, if I can find any. That's how it should go, and he'll work for me until I reckon he's done enough to be a journeyman. That's how you do it. That's how you make your trade.

'When I saw you first, Mister Lipwig, I reckoned you were all mouth and no trousers. And I've watched you running around hither and yon and being the grease for the engine of the railway. You ain't so bad, Mister Lipwig, ain't so bad at all, but you'd look better with a flatter cap.'

Iron Girder let out a sudden hiss of steam, and the two men, laughing, turned to look at her. There was something new about the engine. Hang on, Moist thought, her shape has changed, hasn't it? She looks . . . bigger. I know she's the prototype and Simnel is forever tweaking things, but somehow I don't think I ever see the same engine twice. She's always bigger, better, sleeker.

As Moist was pondering the question he became aware of Simnel beside him shifting from foot to foot. At last Dick said hesitantly, 'Mister Lipwig, you know that girl with the long blonde hair and pretty smile who sometimes comes into the compound? Who is she? She acts as if she owns the place.'

'That,' said Moist, 'is Emily, Harry King's favourite niece, not married yet.'

'Oh,' said Simnel. 'The other day she brought me out tea – and a bun!'

Moist looked at the worried face of Dick Simnel, who was suddenly in a place where the sliding rule couldn't go. No, this was a different kind of rule, and so he said, 'Would you care to take a walk with her, Dick?'

Simnel blushed, if a blush could actually be seen under all the grease. 'Aye, I really would, but she's all smart and dandy as a daisy and I'm—'

'Stop right there!' said Moist. 'If you're going to say that you're just a bloke in greasy dungarees I'd like to draw your attention to the fact that you own a very big slice of all the revenue the railway is ever going to make. So don't go around saying "Oh dear me I'm too poor to even think about making advances to a nice young lady," because you're the best catch that any young lady in Ankh-Morpork could ever find, and I imagine that even Harry, in the circumstances, wouldn't throw you down the stairs as he did with the swains who were the suitors of his daughters. If you'd like to go walking out with Emily I'd say go to it and I'm sure her uncle and parents will be overjoyed.'

To himself, Moist thought: in fact, Harry would love it because it'd keep the money in the family. I know Harry King, oh, yes. 'What's more,' he added, 'she's a lawyer in the making: understands the legalities of running a business. You should get on like a house on fire.'

In the voice of a man encountering new territory, Dick said carefully, 'Thank you for the information and advice, Mister Lipwig. Mebbe one day when I've got meself clean I might get meself the courage to knock on 'er door.'

'Well, don't wait too long, Dick. There's more to life than the sliding rule.'

The Grand Opening of the Ankh-Morpork and Sto Plains Hygienic Railway brought the international press out in droves.

Dick Simnel had always intended that the first *serious* public railway journey would start from Sto Lat, putting the old town on the map as it were. Sir Harry was somewhat dismayed by this:* a

---

* A dismay shared by many of the journalists, who worried they would get mud on their new shoes and be attacked by pheasants.

true denizen of Ankh-Morpork, he tended to get a little disorientated when outside the city. Still, as Moist had pointed out, after an outward journey by road the guests would find the return rail trip with refreshments all the more impressive.

When their coaches eventually arrived at what the gold-edged invitation had described as the 'Sto Lat terminus', the journalists and other invited guests discovered that terminus apparently meant a work in progress: which is to say most of it wasn't there yet (being full of workmen, human, troll and goblin, labouring at cross purposes just like on every big construction site anywhere) but nevertheless a sympathetic eye could arrive at the conclusion that something rather good was being built here.

The guests were ushered on to a long raised platform, standing above gleaming steel rails that ran off into the distance, the tracksides crowded with onlookers. In the other direction the rails led to a very large barn, where Dick's apprentices, recently scrubbed, were lined up on either side of the closed doors, along with a brass band that could hardly be heard above the noise of the workmen.

Moist von Lipwig was, of course, master of ceremonies, there to welcome them with Harry King and Effie by his side. Lord Vetinari too was there, as holder of Ankh-Morpork's guardian share in the railway, accompanied by Drumknott, who wouldn't have missed the occasion for a big clock. And Queen Keli of Sto Lat* was present to give the occasion the royal seal of approval, with the Mayor by her side looking stunned by the circus that appeared to have taken over his town.

As always in these matters, everything had to wait until everything else was ready. That seemed to have been anticipated,

* Proctector of the Eight Protectorates and Empress of the Long Thin Debated Piece Hubwards of Sto Kerrig.

judging by the door with a neat label WAITING ROOM, alongside the entrance to the platform.*

And then the waiting was over. At Moist's invitation Queen Keli stepped forward to drive in the golden spike, the last one on the line, signifying it was now open for business. The chuffing sound that was the signature tune of the railway got louder and more expansive, the crowd of bystanders thronging the sides of the track waved their colourful little flags and cheered with increased enthusiasm, and two apprentices opened the gates of the barn. To a metaphorical drumroll Moist announced: 'Ladies and gentlemen, Mister Dick Simnel and Iron Girder!'

Leading the dream of steam, Dick Simnel, in pride of place on the footplate, beamed an unmissable look of *I told thee so*.

Behind the engine ten carriages bumped along and, glory be, some of them even had a roof! The iconographers' flashes popped and, very gently, Iron Girder moved along the track and stopped beside the platform.

Moist waited until the applause faded away and said, 'Ladies and gentlemen, you may safely climb aboard. There will be refreshments, but first may I invite you to inspect the carriages.'

Now Moist needed to be everywhere at once. Anything to do with steam and locomotives was news and news could be good news or news could be bad news, or occasionally news could be malicious news. Dick just loved talking about Iron Girder and everything else to do with locomotion, but he was a straightforward man and the press of the Sto Plains could eat up for lunch a straightforward man if he wasn't careful. Moist, on the other hand, in the vicinity of the press, was as straightforward as a sackful of kaleidoscopes. While the chattering was going on,

---

* There were in fact two waiting rooms, one for men and families and the other for single ladies; as predicted, Effie was very firm that all aspects of the railway should be clean and wholesome, indeed hygienic, something she was very keen on.

he did his best to hover around Dick Simnel like a wet-nurse.

The *Ankh-Morpork Times* wasn't bad, and the *Tanty Bugle* was mostly interested in 'orrible murder and the more salacious aspects of the human condition, but Moist's heart sank as he realized that Dick, temporarily off the reins, was now talking to Hardwick of the *Pseudopolis Daily Press*, who was adept at getting the wrong end of the stick very much on purpose and then hitting people over the head with it. And Pseudopolis disliked Ankh-Morpork with a sullen and jealous vengeance.

As Moist executed the world's fastest nonchalant walk, he heard Hardwick saying, 'What do you say, Mister Simnel, to people who are upset because the noise and the smoke will cause their horses to bolt and their cows and sheep to miscarry?'

'I don't rightly know,' said Simnel. 'Never had a problem here on the Plains. When I were doing me tests the horses in the next field would try to outpace Iron Girder, racing her, as it were, and I reckoned they thought it was fun!'

But Hardwick wasn't to be thrown off. 'You must admit, Mister Simnel, that the train is inherently dangerous? Some people have said that your face melts if you reach speeds greater than thirty miles an hour!'

It seemed to Moist that everyone else who had been chattering away in the vicinity went silent to listen as one person, and he knew that if he intervened at this point things would get worse, and so all he could do was hold his breath, just like everybody else, to see what the solemn country boy would say.

'Well now, Mister 'ardwick,' said Simnel, sticking his thumbs into his belt as he always did when broaching long sentences. 'I think many things are inherently dangerous: such as wizards, and trees. Dangerous things, trees, they could fall down and drop straight on your 'ead without you knowing it. And boats are dangerous an' all, and other people might be dangerous and you, Mister 'ardwick, you've been talking to me for five minutes now, 'oping that a

121

country lad like me might be tempted into saying summat I shouldn't.

'So I'll tell you this: Iron Girder is my machine, I made her, every single bit of her. I tested her and every time I find a way to make her better and safer, I do it. But, oh aye, *you*, Mister 'ardwick, you might be dangerous! Power is dangerous, all power, yours included, Mister 'ardwick, and the difference is that the power of Iron Girder is controllable whereas you can write whatever you damn well like. Do you think I don't read? I've read the rubbish you spout in your paper and, Mister 'ardwick, a lot of what you write is flamin' gristle, Mister 'ardwick, total stinking made-up gristle, meant to frighten people who don't know owt about steam and power and the cosines and the quaderatics and tangents and even the sliding rule ... but I hope you enjoy your journey anyway, Mister 'ardwick. Now, if you don't mind, I've got to get in t'cab. Oh, and I've had Iron Girder up to more than thirty mile an hour and all I got were sunburn. Good day to you, Mister 'ardwick. Enjoy your ride.'

And then, reddening as he registered the hush all around him, Simnel said, 'Apologies to all the ladies here for my straight language. I do beg your pardon.'

'No apologies necessary, Mister Simnel,' called out Sacharissa Cripslock, reporter for the *Times*. 'I believe I speak for all the ladies present when I say that we appreciate your candour.' And since Sacharissa was not only respectable in the same way that other people are religious, but was also invariably armed with highly sharpened pencils, the rest of the crowd suddenly found that they too had the greatest admiration for Mr Simnel and his plain talking.

On board, there were many marvels to show off, including the lavish lavatories, apparently another brainchild of Effie, which came as a surprise even to Moist. He wondered what the press would make of Effie's gift to railway travel. Sometimes the art editor of the *Ankh-Morpork Times* could be quite creative.*

'This is as good as those they have in the poshest hotels,' Moist said privately to Sir Harry, who emerged from the cubicle flushed with pride.

Harry beamed. 'You should look in the ladies, Mister Lipwig! Scent, cushions and real cut flowers. It's like a boudoir in there!'

'I suppose the, er, waste can be dropped straight down on to the tracks, eh, Harry?'

Harry looked shocked. 'Oh, some people would do that, but not Harry King! Where there's muck there's money, lad, but don't tell the Duchess. There's a big cistern under one of the carriages. Waste not, want not . . .'

Questions were coming thick and fast from all sides. For those people who hadn't already taken a ride behind Iron Girder in Harry King's compound, the matter of railway etiquette loomed: could you stick your head out of the window? Could you bring your pet swamp dragon if it sat on your knee? Could you go and talk to the driver? On this occasion, Moist was pleased to say yes; the editor of the *Ankh-Morpork Times* being selected for this accolade. The smile Mr de Worde gave as he stepped from the platform on to the footplate cemented this moment on to the front page, assuming this journey was a success – although you had to be aware that it would also make the front page if the engine blew up. Journalism was, well, after all, journalism.

The train pulled away with a whistle and a cloud of smoke and everything was moving along nicely, especially when the trolley with the refreshments rattled through the carriages. Harry and All Jolson were in complete agreement about what made a good meal – namely, calories – and had not stinted. There was enough butter on the slumpie to regrease Iron Girder from top to bottom. The

---

* The caption as it turned out was '*Let the train take the strain*'. It appeared that Mr de Worde and his wife were very impressed with the toilet facilities.

scenery flew past, to the guests' well-oiled admiration and gasps of awe, until the train approached the first bridge.

Moist held his breath as the train slowed down almost to a halt. There was a troll and he waved a big red flag and cheerfully announced* that he and his gang had worked on this bridge and were so pleased to see it being used and thank you for coming ladies and gentlemen. There was laughter, assisted most certainly with alcohol, but nevertheless there was laughter and it was genuine. Moist let the breath go. He supposed few of the passengers could remember the days when to see a troll was to be frightened (or, if you were a dwarf, want to kick his ankles in). Now here they were, building the railway, quite at home.

Moist looked across the First Class carriage to where Lord Vetinari was seated. He had openly commended Effie on her part in the planning and design, and given his usual urbane, anodyne answers to journalists looking for a quote, but Moist couldn't help but notice that the Patrician was smiling, like a granddad at a new-born grandchild. Moist caught his eye and thought he saw his lordship wink with the speed of a cyclone. Moist nodded and that was that, but he hoped that it might be at least one sin forgiven. Three deaths in one lifetime would definitely be over-egging it.

But it was a nice day, the sun was shining, and as Iron Girder raced along the track a couple of horses in the field alongside tried to catch up with her. So much for Mr Hardwick, and poo to him again because Iron Girder chugged her way down through gentle slopes to the township of Upunder where they stopped to allow the passengers to enjoy the very best of brassica hospitality.

After that it was a short run down to Ankh-Morpork itself, which was beckoning with long smoky fingers. They crossed the new iron bridge over the Ankh and wheezed on to Harry King's compound, where a brass band was playing the national anthem,

* And when a troll announces, you really are announced at.

'We Can Rule You Wholesale', to the cheers of the waiting crowd.

At the banquet that evening the rail travellers were joined by other Ankh-Morporkian and Sto Plains dignitaries. And in the peroration of his address Sir Harry announced that the next city to receive the magnificent railway would be Quirm, it was hoped very shortly. In the thunder of applause, Harry toasted the Quirmian ambassador, Monsieur Cravat, and this was followed by more toasts, including one to Iron Girder herself. Lord Vetinari opined that it had been a very helpful day; and the unknown quantity of sphincters that had been tightened once again relaxed somewhat.

When the party broke up, some of the guests were walking sideways or hardly at all. Dick, seeing a familiar face swim into his happy world of coloured lights, said, 'Ee, that were champion, Mister Lipwig! All those tiny places in the distance all along t'track . . . I were thinking that the railway could be like a tree: you know, one big trunk and then all branches . . . You'd make 'em cheap and small but I reckon people'd like 'em . . . Make folks' lives easier if they could get a train from *anywhere*—'

Moist, resolutely ignoring the beckoning possibilities, cut him short. 'Steady on, Dick. First we have to get to Quirm.' And then drive that express train route to Uberwald, he added to himself . . . His lordship was so very keen on international relations.

Later that night, Fred Colon and Nobby Nobbs proceeded in a policeman-like fashion around the railway compound. After all, they bore the Majesty of the Force and therefore had a right to be absolutely anywhere they liked, looking at anything they wanted to.

And as their boots swung in unison, Fred Colon said, 'I hear they're taking the railway all the way to Quirm. My old woman's always going on at me about us taking a holiday down there. You'll know about that, Nobby, now you're practically married and got responsibilities. But you know me, I'm allergic to all that avec, and I hear you can't get a good pint there for love nor money.'

'Actually,' said Nobby, 'it ain't all that bad. When I was working the rota last week on the goods yard there were a load of cheeses that got broken open by accident, as it were. Of course, they couldn't be sent back and it's amazing what Shine of the Rainbow can do with cheese. It's good stuff, especially with snails.' Nobby realized he was talking treason and so hurriedly added, 'Their beer is still like piss, though.'

Fred Colon nodded. All was what it should be. He glanced back at his friend and said, 'If the railway works properly, things are going to be quite different. I hear telling the train'll be going very fast and that means if a bloke does a robbery and then goes and catches the train, he could be away on his toes long before we could ever catch up with him. Maybe the railway will need policemen. You never know! It's like old Stoneface said, wherever you get people, you'll get crime and then you'll get policemen.'

Nobby Nobbs considered this information like a goat chewing the cud, and said, 'Well, you go and tell old Vimesy that you want to be the first railway policeman, eh? I'd love to see his face!'

Billy Slick surveyed the very large person at the front of the queue and sighed.

'Look,' he said, 'you can't all be train drivers. We've got lots of train drivers right now and it takes time to work your way up to being a driver. Ain't there anything else you can do?'

'Well,' said the crestfallen lad in front of him, 'my mum says I'll make a very good cook one day.'

Billy smiled and said, 'Might have something for you then, we need cooks.' He pointed out another recruiting table a bit further along and said, 'Get yourself over to Mabel. She's looking for catering staff and that sorta thing.'

The young man's face lit up with excitement and he hurried off to a future which almost certainly included unsociable hours and hard labour in cramped conditions but, most importantly, unlimited free rides on the wonder of the age.

'I'm a painter, mister,' said the next man in Billy's line.

'Excellent! Sure you don't fancy being a train driver?'

'No, not really. I've always been a good painter and I expect the locomotives need painting.'

'Great!' said Billy. 'You're hired. Next!'

When Billy looked up from his clipboard he found the craggy figure of a young troll looming over him.

'Man said der's a job wiv a shovel and tons of coal. Could do dat,' the troll said, adding a hopeful 'Please?'

'A stoker?' Billy guessed. 'Blimey, you're a bit big for the footplate, but we could use you around the place and no mistake. Put your mark here.'

The table shook as the troll's thumb hit the form and cracked his clipboard.

'Good man – I mean, troll,' Billy said.

'Nuffin' to worry about. Get dat all der time.'

The troll rumbled away in the direction of the coal store and his place in front of Billy was taken by a smartly dressed young lady with an air of authority.

'Sir, I think the railway is going to need a translator. I know every language and dialect on the Disc.' Her voice was firm but there was a glint of excitement in her eyes as she looked at Iron Girder and the other engines in the compound and Billy knew she was hooked. He also knew that 'translator' was not on his list of vacancies and sent her off to Sir Harry's office, while he returned to his search for shunters, tappers and other workers. And so the line moved on again. It seemed everybody wanted to be part of the railway.

It felt to Moist, bumping in the saddle as the golem horse bore him back towards Ankh-Morpork, that he had been talking for years with greedy landowners who were asking for enormous rents even if it was achingly obvious that the railway would benefit the whole area, and this time, to reach Quirm, there was going to be more than eight times the length of route to cover. And when he wasn't talking to landowners, he was talking again to the surveyors, who were not greedy but were definitely horribly *precise*. They rejected proposed routes as too steep, too waterlogged, crumbling, or occasionally flooded and, in one case, full of zombies. Acceptable routes might just as well have been drawn by a snake snaking around the landscape from suitable ground to suitable ground. And everybody wanted the railway close, oh yes please, but not so close that they could hear it or smell it.

And that was the Sto Plains in a nutshell, or, if you like, a cabbage bucket. Everybody everywhere wanted the benefits of steam but not the drawbacks. And no city on the Plains wanted the Big Wahoonie to get more than its fair share.

It took the diplomatic genius of the Patrician to set the record straight, reminding them that although the railway was being built initially in Ankh-Morpork, if other cities and towns wanted to partake of its usefulness, well, yes, in a sense it would be theirs because what goes down on the up line must go up on the down line.

Politics? Vetinari loved it. This was the ocean in which he swam. But assuredly you never crowed, just showed the world the tired visage of a conscientious civil servant, doing things cheaply and with the minimum of fuss. He had long ago perfected the art of giving way with a smile when engaged in complex negotiations, but Lord Vetinari's smile was that of a man who knows that his opponents have yet to find, metaphorically speaking, and despite their cleverness, that their underpants are now down around their ankles and their backside on show for all to see.

Ankh-Morpork to Sto Lat was becoming a regular journey, and it was *working* now. Moist had written the slogan, '*You don't have to live in Ankh-Morpork to work in Ankh-Morpork'* and properties in Sto Lat were becoming quite sought after. The idea of a little place in the country away from the big city, but with acceptable communications to Ankh-Morpork, suddenly looked *very* inviting.

The hours of travel on the golem horse were proving altogether conducive to creative thought. His mind was filling up with the world of locomotive possibilities at the speed of a hamster *really* at odds with its treadmill. Another synapse in Moist's head flashed; the trains were just the start! The railway now, he knew, was something in the ether, floating over the whole world. An *idée fixe*, if he would excuse his own Quirmian.

Nevertheless, the engines remained important. Dick Simnel's workshops at Swine Town had been turning out many marvels, carefully placed on wagons behind the never-tiring Iron Girder. She now shared the big shed with two newcomers that Simnel had called the Flyers, which made the regular run to Sto Lat and back, while Iron Girder herself had gone back to giving rides around the Ankh-Morpork compound, extended with a short loop along the river to show off the new bridge. The small but growing band of patient train spotters had written down a number two in their little books, then a number three.

Within minutes of his arriving back in Ankh-Morpork, Moist was borne off by an ebullient Harry to see the latest development. Dodging sparks, they arrived at the doorway of the monstrous engine shed guarded by one of Harry's heavies, who glared even at his employer. He looked human, or at least humanoid, and Harry introduced him merely as 'Trouble'. Trouble, glaring at Moist, moved away from the door so that Moist and Sir Harry could go inside.

Moist could feel Trouble's glare on the back of his neck as he walked through, and asked, 'Harry, does Trouble have an official Watch record?'

Harry King stared for a moment at Moist and said, 'Of course he's got a Watch record! He's a *security guard*! And I need him. People have been hanging around, trying to break in, especially at night, and the *official* security – the Watch, the golems and guard dogs – generates a whole lot of paperwork whereas Trouble deals with trouble. Don't trouble Trouble and Trouble won't trouble you, as .my granny always said.' Harry chuckled and added, 'Don't you worry, Mister Lipwig, I've expressly told him not to kill you . . . today.'

Moist took this under advisement and turned for a last brief look at Trouble, who made up a new scowl just for him, a reminder that there were oh so many painful things you could do to a person without actually killing them.

Harry nodded to the giant, who began to pull at a large tarpaulin in the middle of the floor – and clearly when Trouble pulled something it definitely remained pulled – to reveal an engine much larger than Iron Girder or any of Simnel's creations Moist had so far seen.

Harry slapped Moist on the back and said, 'Well now, Mister Lipwig, while you've been wining and dining with the nobs and diddling them out of their fortunes, I, and of course Mister Simnel, have been very busy boys, oh yes indeedy! The lad is up finishing off in the drawing office right now, but this new engine is the bee's knees, I don't mind telling you.'

'It's not exactly fun, what I've been doing—' began Moist indignantly, but Harry cut in.

'Yes, I know, we're all doing our bit towards Vetinari's dash for Quirm, although personally I don't have much time for the lobsters; but I can see it's showing the flag of Ankh-Morpork and all that, and of course, if we can get really fresh fish and seafood into the city, then we'll be on the hog's back or, as they'd say, "the snail's shell". And Dick says this new baby,' he slapped the gleaming sides of the new engine as though it were a prize racehorse, 'will haul more freight and get there more quickly than any of the others!'

Moist thought about this and said, 'You know what, I bet you that as soon as our boy Simnel finishes this new Flyer he'll make sure that Iron Girder goes just that little bit faster. Harry, he's not going to let her be eclipsed even if it means constant tinkering until she's up to scratch. There's so many workers on the job these days, he spends most of his time on her in any case. She's the prototype of all of them, and he keeps changing the prototype.'

'And he wants to walk out with our Emily! Well, he's a smart lad and she'll always know where he is.'

The thought flitted across Moist's mind *I wonder what Iron Girder thinks about that.* And even as he dismissed the ridiculous notion he fancied he could hear a slight hiss.

Harry was still admiring the latest locomotive. 'I reckon the lobsters will be like chiens with deux tails to be the first real foreigners to have the famous railway. And our Emily tells me that the Quirmian for "railway" means "card game" so that would be right up your ruelle, yes? Make sure you keep an ace up your manche, Mister Lipwig, okay?'

'Manche?'

'Effie is learning me to talk lobster, she thinks it's a lovely and romantic language.'

Moist was moved to point out that he had hardly seen his own wife in the last month and had completed over fifty complex negotiations just to get to the border with Quirm.

'Capital, so you've really got your eye in now, yes? Anyway, Quirm ain't so far away and you'll enjoy the sunshine when you get there. And I tell you what! Before you go you can have a day off in lieu! And I don't say that to many people.'

Moist cleared his throat. 'Actually, er, Harry, you don't in fact employ me. The city does.'

'Does that mean I can't sack you?'

'I'm afraid so, Harry.'

Harry snorted with laughter. 'I hate having people around I can't sack. It's unnatural.'

It had been a long day after some long weeks and even longer months and that evening Moist was grateful to step into his own house, looking forward to his big four-poster bed which had a mattress that wasn't stuffed with straw, and pillows – actual pillows! Very few of the hostelries that Moist had stayed at during his travels considered pillows necessary or useful. Right now, metaphorically singing, he let himself in before Crossly could get there, and went not into the main part of the house but into the little corridor that led to Adora Belle's study, where his beloved was talking to Of the Twilight the Darkness.

The clacks was an equal opportunities employer, especially when it came to people who could swarm their way up the skeletal ribs of a clacks tower *and* once at the top sit down in a little chair and code like a demon, without actually being one, despite their appearance.

Adora Belle was going through clacks reports with a suspicious eye while the goblin crouched like a nightmare on the end of her desk. She waved her fingers to indicate that she couldn't afford to let go her concentration, then rolled up a script, handed it to the goblin and snapped, 'Get that out *now*, please, to tower ninety-seven. Someone there isn't coding accurately. Might be a trainee. I want to know, okay?'

The goblin snatched the scroll in a claw, sprang off the desk like a frog, headed for a little door near the floor and disappeared through it. Moist could hear rattling all the way up the wall as the goblin clambered up the panelling and scuttled to the private clacks tower on the roof. He shuddered, but before he could say anything Adora Belle looked up and said, 'Look, he's punctual, fast, reliable and codes more accurately even than me and all he wants from us is to be allowed to live with his family on the roof. Now don't you give me all that again about being traumatized by seeing the picture of a grinning goblin in that children's book when you were little, okay? Get over it, Moist. The goblins are the best thing that has happened to the clacks since, well, you know – us! They *love* running it and, what's more, with them around the place we don't have those nasty rat and mouse infestations that we used to have.'

Adora Belle stood up, walked around the desk to Moist and gave him a big kiss, and said, 'How was your latest marathon, mister? I got reports of your progress throughout, of course, as you may imagine.'

Moist took a step back. 'Reports? How?'

Adora Belle laughed. 'What is a clacks tower but an enormous watchtower? And every clacksman has a very expensive pair of Herr Fleiss's binoculars, made using the very best in Uberwald technology. There are lots of towers, so I made certain they kept a friendly eye on you – well, a lot of friendly eyes on you. After all, every clacksman knows your face and even the top of your head, and I thought it was my duty as a wife . . .'

'What, spying on your husband! Supposing I was messing about with other women?'

'That's all right, I know you weren't and if you had been I'd have had you killed – no offence meant – but you didn't and so I didn't and so everything is all right, yes? Mrs Crossly is doing a wonderful beef and oyster pie. See? Aren't you glad I knew exactly when you were coming home?'

Moist smiled, and then the smile broadened as he realized what it was he had been told, and he added thoughtfully, 'Are you telling me, my love, that you could spot and follow *anybody*?'

'Oh yes, probably, if they walk around a lot. The lads and lasses often peek when they have some down time. They just do it, there's no harm in it. The other day when you were heading home I was at the Grand Trunk office and was privileged to get a report of you bobbing up and down on your golem horse . . . *very* fetching, they said.'

Adora Belle stared at her husband and added, 'Do you know that when you've found out something amazingly interesting and useful your eyes light up like a Hogswatch decoration? So stop glittering right now and go and smarten yourself up before we sit down to a proper dinner.'

It was a rule of Moist and Adora Belle's household that the evening meal, if at all possible, was sacrosanct. No eating at their desks, no rush, but candles, and silverware, as if it were always a special occasion. And a special occasion it was: the only time they could sit down face to face and just, well, be at least moderately married to each other.

However, Adora Belle couldn't conceal her dismay about losing her husband again for yet another prolonged absence in a foreign country.

'Quirm isn't that far away,' Moist soothed. 'And once I get the local lads on side it won't be too bad.'

Adora Belle cleared her throat. 'Garçons. If they're lobsters, your lads will be known as garçons.'

'What?'

'Garçons. It's Quirmian, but don't worry, most of them speak Morporkian. And you know why? Because none of us can be bothered to learn Quirmian.'

'Well, no matter what they're called. Once the railway line's built I'll probably be able to come home more often.' He paused to take another mouthful of pie. 'By the way, Harry's just had a clacks from the King of Lancre asking if we could eventually run a line all the way to his kingdom so that, and I quote, "Lancre can take its rightful place on the world stage".'

'Don't underestimate that place,' said Adora Belle. 'They've got witches up there. They fly up to the clacks towers and scrounge coffee off the lads – well, at least one of them does, especially when the lads are young and the goblins aren't on shift. And then there

134

are all the dwarf mines up at Copperhead. I'm sure they could find a use for the railway.'

Moist made a face. 'The lads say no way. It's too steep, and anyway, the Lancre bridge wouldn't take the weight of the engine. Sorry. But I suppose we could tell his majesty that we'll send surveyors to take a look once the Quirm line's complete.' Moist put down his fork. 'But here we are, and it looks like for the first time in ages we have an evening free. What shall we do? Perhaps it might be a good idea to give the staff the rest of the evening off . . .'

And Adora Belle replied with a smile, 'Yes . . . What shall we do?'

'It's simply mechanical,' said Ponder Stibbons over tea in the Uncommon Room at Unseen University. 'It just *looks* magical.'

'Shouldn't be allowed, then,' said the Senior Wrangler, spearing a whole pie with his fork. 'Looking magical is our business.'

'Well,' said Mustrum Ridcully, pointedly ignoring him, 'you can't stand in the way of progress, so why don't you hitch a ride on it? Does anyone else want a train ride? It gets so stuffy in here and I'm sure we don't want people thinking of us as being stick-in-the-muds.'

'But we are stick-in-the-muds,' said the Lecturer in Recent Runes. 'I treasure the fact.'

'Nevertheless, it's time we looked the railway in the face. Mister Stibbons will lead the way.'

The wizards left the University in a small fleet of coaches which caused quite a stir when they appeared at the Ankh-Morpork terminus. Stibbons, knowing his fellow wizards, had made arrangements beforehand and a special train had been laid on for the occasion, with particularly well cushioned seats.

'You will of course travel First Class, gentlemen,' said the station master, who had been well primed by Stibbons. 'But if you wish, some of you might be able to ride on the footplate.' He hesitated and said, 'Although I'm not sure those robes would be safe.'

The Archchancellor burst out laughing. 'Young man, a wizard's robe is impervious to fire. Good grief, if they weren't we'd be burned alive every day before elevenses!'

Stibbons, who had already had several rides with Iron Girder over the previous weeks followed by some intense conversations with Dick Simnel, had got the hang of the business and took some pleasure in seeing the best minds in the University coming to terms with their first railway ride.

It was a short journey to Upunder and back, including a dinner at the halfway mark which lasted longer than the train ride itself. On the homeward stretch, the Chair of Indefinite Studies was allowed to operate the emergency brake to the envy of the rest of the wizards, and there was a certain amount of waving of flags, blowing of whistles, and slamming of doors at each stop for the wizards to try their hands at. Iron Girder was in full steam and the fireproof wizards taking their turn on the footplate stared into the fire box and approved.*

Replete and tired on their way back to Ankh-Morpork, they considered this new form of locomotion as a phenomenon. The Senior Wrangler thought about objecting again, but was too full.

'Amazing, people waving at you as you go past,' said Ridcully. 'I've never seen that before. Who'd have thought it? Machinery making people smile. What are you writing down, Mister Stibbons?'

Blushing, Stibbons said, 'I like to spot an occasional train, you know . . . I'm just interested in them . . . It's like watching the future go past.'

The Archchancellor smiled and said, 'Then perhaps we should be the ones who are minding the doors, not to mention the gap, because the future is coming down the track fast. And who knows what is going to arrive next.'

---

* Even Professor Rincewind, who spent most of the journey hiding under his seat in the firm belief that locomotion was exactly the kind of thing that usually led to certain death, conceded that trains could come in very handy when one wanted to get somewhere, or, more importantly, *away* from somewhere, quickly.

It was a wonderful sunny day. Skylarks sang in the deep blue sky. It was a great day to be alive. Moist, needing a change of air, walked away from the compound with a spring in his step, a little way along the railway track.

And right there on this perfect day . . . yes, there out of sight of anyone excepting, of course, the ambling Moist himself, on the rail that Iron Girder would have to travel along as soon as she came around the bend on to the little incline leading to the station, were two small . . . creatures. Rabbits, his common sense tried to tell him, plenty of them around here . . . even the compound was riddled with them. And, for a moment, the whole world stopped right in his face, leaving him spinning slowly in a little world of his own, looking out on to the real one.

There were the main engine sheds, over there was the crowd queueing for their rides, and there on the track was the future of the railway. It was one perfect moment where time stretched out, and Moist the only witness to this terrible tableau. It was like a strange game of high-speed chess unfolding before his eyes.

And then, suddenly, his legs took off from under him and he ran and ran, too breathless to shout, towards the two children who had hunkered down with their ears pressed against the rails, giggling because the vibrations were at times funny and bouncy and loud and . . .

RIGHT HERE, RIGHT NOW!

And . . . gone . . .

Moist woke up, which could be interpreted as a good thing. First time round, Iron Girder was over him and he was dead, but his next careful waking was in a white room that smelled of camphor wood and other disinfectants, sharp and reassuring smells: tangible proof that he had a nose at least, because he couldn't really feel anything else.

After a while subtle little noises grew into louder ones, coming closer and forming words, loudly reassuring and somewhat hearty words that crystallized into an individual in a white coat saying, 'Well, madam, he keeps going up and down, but with fewer downs and a welcoming parade of ups. He's getting more stable all the time and nothing's broken, although he's ruined a decent pair of boots – and, may I say, madam, that even here in the hospital there are already people organizing a whipround to replace them.'

Moist made a mighty heave, fought his way out of unconsciousness and arrived back in the here and now – a place where *everything* hurt. On the plus side, Adora Belle was looking at him, while looming behind her, in a white coat, was a large and expansive man of a sort that had played many rough competitive games when he was younger and wished he could do so now, if only the belly were smaller and the limbs willing.

Moist's wife was regarding her husband carefully, as if checking that all the bits were there in their rightful places, at which point the doctor grabbed his hand and boomed, 'Somebody up there must be watching over you, Mister Lipwig. How do you feel? As your physician I must tell you that jumping in front of railway trains is not recommended by medical practitioners, but acts of mindlessly idiotic bravery most certainly are, and can be applauded!'

Dr Lawn looked carefully down at Moist and said, 'You don't know what you did, do you, Mister Lipwig? Just you come along and we'll see if you can walk.'

Moist could walk and wished he couldn't. The whole of him felt as if it had been smacked very hard, but the nurses helped him upright and led him carefully to the ward next door, which contained, as it turned out, among the noise, two families; and there were small children and parents weeping. Bits of the past slammed into place in Moist's memory and got bigger and more horrible as once again he felt the breath of the engine as it sailed over the top of him, a toddler under each arm. No, it couldn't have happened like that – could it?

But clamouring voices were telling him otherwise, with women trying to kiss him and holding up their offspring to do likewise, their husbands at the same time trying to shake his hand. Bafflement filled him up like smoke and now in front of him Adora Belle was looking at him with a funny little smile, such as only husbands know of.

When they were at last able to disembogue themselves of the crowd of happy parents and somewhat sticky children, Adora Belle still had her faint smile. 'Well now, my dear, didn't you once say that a life without danger is a life not worth living?'

Moist patted her hand and said, 'Well, Spike, I married you, didn't I?'

'You couldn't resist it, could you? It's like a drug. You're not happy unless someone is trying to kill you, or you're in the centre of some other kind of drama, out of which, of course, the famous Moist von Lipwig will jump to safety at the very last moment. Is it a disease? Some kind of syndrome?'

Moist put on his meek face as only husbands and puppies can do and said, 'Would you like me to stop? I will if you say so.'

There was silence until Adora Belle said, 'You bastard, you know I can't do that. If you stopped all of that you wouldn't be Moist von Lipwig!'

He opened his mouth to protest just as the door opened and in came the press: William de Worde, editor of the *Ankh-Morpork Times*, followed by a porter and the ubiquitous Otto Chriek, the iconographer.

And, because Moist would never stop being Moist von Lipwig until he died, he smiled for the iconograph.

He reminded himself that this was only the start. All the rest would be along soon ... but no matter, he had danced this fandango many times before, and so he maintained his best boy scout face and smiled at Mr de Worde, who started off by saying, 'It appears that you are a hero *again*, Mister Lipwig. The driver and the stoker say that you ran faster than they could brake the train, picked up the children and jumped to safety just in time. Safety, at that precise moment, being *under* your Iron Girder. It was a miracle that you were there, wasn't it?'

And so the dance began.

'Not at all. We make a point of keeping an eye on the visitors at all times, of course. The children were outside the compound and, strictly speaking, the responsibility of their parents, but we'll be putting up barriers along that stretch of the line immediately. You have to understand, people are flocking here. They seem to be irresistibly drawn by the novelty of live steam and speed.'

'And a very dangerous novelty, would you not say, Mister Lipwig?'

'Well now, Mister de Worde, everything old was once new and until explored was unfamiliar and dangerous, and then, as sure as night follows day they become just part of the scenery. Believe me, sir, that'll happen here with the railway, too.'

Moist watched the journalist painstakingly taking down his words and was ready when the man said, 'I've heard from elderly people all across the Sto Plains who're frightened of the noise and speed. And the trains leave smoke and cinders . . . Surely that's dangerous for our fine city?'

Moist flashed his grin once more, thinking, here we go again.

'This place you choose to call "our fine city" is almost all smoke and cinders, and a lot else besides. The trials of Iron Girder have impressed everybody with her ability to carry heavy loads safely and at speed. Let's not forget that speed is essential when dealing with certain goods: your newspaper for one – no one wants to get their news late – and there's my Post Office parcels for another. We can get your first printing on the breakfast tables at Sto Lat. And as for scaring the elderly, well, one old lady recently told me that we should have waited until all the old people were dead before start-ing up with the railway, and I think you'd agree that that might be a very long time!'

Moist saw the journalist's face break into a smile, and knew he had a result. He continued, 'People often use the excuse that old people won't understand something when, in fact, they simply don't want it or understand it themselves. Actually, old people can be quite gung-ho about risk, and very proud of it.'

And here, for dramatic effect, he looked serious. 'Regrettably, prototype work cannot provide guaranteed safety; it's hard to make things safe until you know they're dangerous. Do you understand? I'm absolutely certain that one day the train will save many, many lives. In fact, I guarantee it.'

As soon as the excited press had got its quotes and pictures of the hero of the hour, and Moist had submitted to a final check by Dr Lawn, he said goodbye to Adora Belle and caught a cab to the compound. Once there, he barged into Harry King's office without even knocking.

'There should have been someone else on duty, Harry!' he shouted, banging a fist on the desk. 'If you have any sense, you'll put proper guards around the track close to the compound to keep an eye on people when the trains are running! I pulled your chestnuts out of the fire this time!' he screamed. 'But I'll tell you this, Harry. A couple of dead toddlers in a front-page story would've shut the railway down before we've hardly got started! Vetinari would do it, believe me. You know his distrust of mechanisms, and I doubt he'd lose much in the way of popularity if he told Mister Simnel to put his toys back in the box. It'd be a great shame, but people mustn't die just because of a bloody engine!'

Moist stopped. He was panting and out of breath, and Sir Harry King, whose expression had hardly changed during the diatribe, now had a face of flaming red.

In the silence Moist thought he heard a curious sizzle, like the sound made by Iron Girder when she was relaxing after a heavy day on the straight and curves. You could perhaps call it a kind of metal purring, but it had now gone, leaving doubts that it had ever been there.

Harry looked Moist up and down and said gravely, 'They said you flew under the train, holding two little kiddies in your arms. Did you?'

'You know, I have absolutely no idea. I *did* see the kids with their heads on the tracks, listening to the funny noises on the rails, and I distinctly remember myself saying Oh bugger! Then something whacked me on the side of the head and I don't remember a thing until I woke up in the Lady Sybil, on a bed, and that's the truth. I *am* a liar for the purposes of amusement, publicity, trivial one-upmanship, personal profit and the gaiety of nations, but I'm not lying to you now.'

There was silence, broken when Harry said hoarsely, 'You know I'm a granddad, don't you? A little boy and a little girl, courtesy of my eldest, and I don't often shiver, my friend, but I'm shivering now.' Harry stood up, with eyes running tears, and said, 'You're the man for this, Mister Lipwig, so you tell me what I should do, please.'

Moist hadn't expected this, but he managed to catch the metaphorical ball. 'Clean up your act, Harry,' he said. 'Engineers and suchlike know all about hot steel, high speeds and wheels spinning fast, right! For most people, exhilarating speed is a run-away horse. Many people get hurt in this city every year when dear old Dobbin the dray horse suddenly feels his oats and heads for pastures new down the middle of the road.

'My advice is to shut down the Iron Girder rides for a week, for "maintenance". Tidy up, keep all the sharp stuff out of the way, stick up some barriers and have a few lads wandering around in uniform looking like they mean business. You know the kind of thing. Make a show of being safe.'

And now Moist heard the little sizzle again, and it seemed to sizzle in his soul, filling him with ideas, and in the theatre of his head he sat up in the gods, watching the stage of his imagination, agog to see what he came up with next.

'It's not just around the compound that there could be incidents like this, Harry – we need to keep an eye on the whole line. Someone to spot if there are kids on the track, or cows, or a train going the wrong way.' He saw Harry blanch at the thought of all the things that could go wrong, but he was in full flow now. 'They'll need a good view – some kind of watchtower would do the trick, with a clacks attached to signal to the drivers . . . Ask Dick – that brain of his is coming up with new designs faster than his hand can get them down on paper.

'And here's a tip: do something about those greasy old cattle wagons you're running behind Iron Girder. They're okay for a circus ride, maybe, but all of your rolling stock should be as good as the special ones we're using on the Sto Lat line.' *Sizzle*. 'Yes! More posh carriages for the nobs, and . . .' here Moist saw the money smile and continued, 'here's a thought, for those who aren't quite nobs but aspire to be like them, well, why not give them carriages that are not *quite* so plush, but visibly better than the very cheapest coaches which are, perhaps, open to the weather. That would give them something else to yearn for, and you'll have made yet another money pump.'

Moist now found himself caught in the glare of one of Harry King's most dangerous expressions.

'Mister Lipwig, damn me if you ain't a most dangerous man, yes indeed! You're inciting people to have ideas above their station, and that sort of thing makes people suspicious and anxious and, above all, very, *very* nervous.'

To Harry's surprise, Moist almost sprang into the air, spinning. 'Yes! Yes! That's the way! Lord Vetinari's way, too. He believes that people should strive to be better in every respect. I can see it now, Harry. Picture a young man taking his young lady on the train and hazarding an extra sixpence to go in the better-class seats. Well, he's no end of a swell, and he'll look around him and think, This suits me down to the ground and no mistake, I could do with more of this.

'And when he goes back to work he'll strive, yes, strive, to become a better, that's to say, *richer* person to the benefit of both his employer and himself, and not, of course, neglecting to thank the owner of the railway, to wit, your good self, who allowed him to have ideas above his railway station. Everybody wins, nobody loses. Please, please, Harry, allow people to aspire. I mean who knows, they might have been in the wrong class all this time. Your railway, my friend, will allow them to dream, and once you have a dream you've got somewhere closer to a reality.'

Throughout all this Harry stared at Moist as if he'd just seen a giant tarantula, but he managed to say, 'Mister Lipwig, a little while ago you were under a railway engine with fifty tons of rolling stock going past your ears and now you spring up like a jack-in-the-box, full of vim and vigour and schemes! What is it you've got? And how can I get some of it?'

'I don't know, Harry, it's just me being normal. You just keep going, whatever happens, and you never stop. It works for me. And remember: clean up your act – our act – to make sure that the public don't get caught up in the mechanisms.'

The sister state of Quirm comprised, like Ankh-Morpork, a major city, several theoretically autonomous satellites each vying with all the others for advancement, any number of squabbling townships, all bloated with self-importance, and a vast number of homesteads, parishes, farms, vineries, mines, hamlets, bends in the road that someone had named after their dog, and so on, and indeed, so on again.

Around the edges of the Ankh-Morpork hegemony* it was quite possible these days for a small farmer on the hypothetical outskirts

---

* Which, it has to be noted, included a certain amount of hinterland, as with most city states.

of all that could be called Ankh-Morpork to lean over his own hedge and chat with a Quirmian farmer who was most definitely in Quirm at the time, without in any way considering that this was a political matter. The conversation would generally be about the weather, the abundance or otherwise of water and the uselessness of the government, never mind which kind, and then happily they would shake hands, or give a little nod, and one would go home to drink a pint of home-made beer after such a busy day, while the other would do likewise with a decent home-made wine.

Occasionally the son of one farmer would go to the hedge and see the daughter of the other one, and vice versa and that was why, in a few – but very interesting – places along the boundary, there were people who spoke in both tongues. This sort of thing is something that governments *really* hate, which is a very good thing.

Technically speaking, Quirm and Ankh-Morpork were bosom friends, after centuries of conflict mostly about things that turned out to be inessential, inconsequential, untrue or downright lies. Yes, you used to need a passport to travel in either direction, but since Lord Vetinari had taken office nobody really looked at them any more. Moist had been there many times in his younger days and in different guises and under different names and, on one very memorable occasion, a different sex.*

Moist mused for a moment as that triumph came back to him. It had been one of the all-time great scams, and, although there had been a large number of other fruitful escapades, he had never dared try it again. The nuns would have got him for sure.

But now, as the coach to Quirm finally reached the border, the only obstacle was a gate, theoretically locked and manned by a couple of officers, one on each side. However, such was the nature of inter-state relations that they were quite often asleep or, if not

---

* The jailers couldn't understand how he'd escaped until they realized they weren't getting their washing back.

sleeping, were happily cultivating their little gardens on either side of the border. Some might ask what was the point? Everybody smuggled and, after all, the smuggling went both ways, and so a pragmatic approach was floating in the zeitgeist.

And today Moist had a list of people to see, oh yes, he always had a list. He knew that Quirm itself desperately needed the railway as it had lots of produce to sell or be left with heaps of stinking fish, and so Moist was expecting a happy week dealing with the lobsters,* but right now he was dealing with people far from the coast who considered their tiny patches of ground to be sacred. Yes, they wanted the railway, but if it went across *their* land they wouldn't have any land left that wasn't railway.

Moist was assisted in his negotiations in Quirm by Acting Captain Haddock of the Ankh-Morpork City Watch, presently seconded to the Quirmian force, who had learned the lingo, in an Ankh-Morpork kind of way. Acting Captain Haddock explained the dilemma created by Quirmian traditions of landownership over a pint of very weak beer.

'It's all to do with something they call *le patrimony*. It means that all the kids have to get something when mum and dad pass over. A big farm might have to be split into two or even three or more so everyone can get their share. Even the government knows this is stupid, but no one in Quirm takes any notice of what the government says. So it's up to you, Mister Lipwig, to get them to understand, but that's it, I'm afraid.'

Well, Moist tried, he really did, and after a frustrating fortnight haggling over every handkerchief-sized plot, he was ready to give up and head back to Ankh-Morpork. Harry wasn't going to like this, he thought, and, worse still, neither was Vetinari, but he could probably talk his way out of it, possibly.

---

* He knew he couldn't use that colloquial term around there, of course, but after all, the people of Quirm called the people of Ankh-Morpork *sphincters*, mostly in fun. Mostly.

His gloomy mood was lightened when he reached a small but prosperous estate belonging to the Marquis des Aix en Pains, a well-known wine grower. The Marquis was one of the last landowners on Moist's list. He had married a girl from Ankh-Morpork and was apparently extremely keen to have his very fine wines conveyed to customers as soon as possible with a minimum of jolting, which had a deleterious effect on the wine. Currently the coach journey, littered with potholes, required the wines to lie down in a dark cool cellar to settle for months afterwards.

The Marquis had invited Moist for lunch, which turned out to be something he called *fusion cuisine*, with pâté devoid of avec, a main course of lobster and mash, followed by a most excellent spotted dick, a combination of dishes that you would expect to live long in the annals of gastronomic infamy but which wasn't too bad, especially when consumed in conjunction with the remarkably good house wines.

The Marquis was young and forward-looking and clearly taken with the idea of the railway, not only for the wine trade but also as a means of bringing people together. He winked at his wife as he said so, with the definite implication that getting people together was something very close to his heart; and he believed that the more people knew about one another, the better they got along. His views on Quirm's curious and slightly bucolic attitude to the division of wealth after the death of the parents were of great interest to Moist.

'Everyone wants to sell their wine and cheese and fish to Ankh-Morpork, zat is certain, but *nobody* wants to lose land. We all like our slice of Quirm: it's *real* real estate, something you can pick up and crumble in your fingers, something zat you can fight for. It's old-fashioned, I know, and of course its continued existence leaves the government exasperated, which, as a true son of Quirm, I consider perfectly acceptable.

147

'However, for you, my friend, zis is difficult because we don't sell our birthright unless, that is, the price is extremely 'igh. And, when the news gets out about the railway the price will be *extremely* 'igh: you will, as my wife says, 'ave to pay "*dans le nez*". I think, my friend, you will 'ave to find another route from here to Quirm City if you want to get ze job done before *les poules auront des dents*.'

He hesitated for a moment and said, 'Come with me to ze library. I want to show you some maps.'

In a large and ornate room, filled with the heads of many stuffed animals – or at least *probably* stuffed – and a stench of old formaldehyde, Moist pored over a large map which the Marquis had pulled out of an old chest.

Pointing to what seemed to be a rather empty part of the map, the Marquis said, 'Most country *'ere* is worthless land, maquis all the way, nothing to mine except ochre, and precious little of zat too. It's more or less a wasteland, covered in scrub zat would tear your boots off and with nothing to induce people to be zere. Badlands, you might say, 'ome to rogues on the run, highwaymen, bandits and occasionally smugglers, all of them extremely nasty and armed to ze teeth. Oh, the government makes a play of getting rid of them every so often, but that isn't all. There are goblins and zey know nothing about land rights.'

'We've now come to terms with goblins in Ankh-Morpork,' said Moist quickly. 'It's a matter of finding something for them to do that they really like doing and are good at and, of course, after that it's just a case of remembering their names and refraining from kicking them. They can be extremely helpful if unkicked, although not necessarily likeable.'

'I wish *we* could get on decent terms with zem,' said the Marquis wistfully, 'but these, you must understand, are *Quirm* goblins, and therefore extremely argumentative and intractable and on top of it, often drunk. They brew their own wine for 'eavens' sake.' He thought for a moment and then corrected himself, 'Or, rather, a wine-like substance.'

'That doesn't sound so bad, does it?' said Moist.

'Really? They brew ze wine from snails. From the fruit of the wall, as you call it in Ankh-Morpork. It makes zem *extremely* rowdy, but zey would probably be okay if it wasn't for the bandits, who 'unt them for fun.'

'So do the *bandits* own the maquis?' said Moist.

The Marquis hesitated. 'No, it is indeed no man's land. I suppose if we talk to lawyers, they will say it's owned literally by ze state of Quirm in its entirety.'

'Well, sir, since it appears that the state of Quirm is gagging to have the railway, even if the landowners aren't, and if you can assure me of the land rights issue, I'll be very happy to do them a favour.'

The Marquis grimaced. 'Unfortunately, it's not as simple as zat. We are not difficult people, but the government drags its feet when it comes to cleaning out ze bandits, because, as you understand, bandits and governments 'ave so much in common that they might be interchangeable anywhere in the world . . . I see you smiling, Mister Lipwig. Is something amusing?'

'Many bandits?'

'A considerable amount. This whole area is rather spoiled by them – unpleasant bandits who would cheerfully commit murder if and when zey think zey can get away with it. I 'ave to tell you that if you are in a 'urry to clear the maquis of bandits, I'm afraid, Mister Ankh-Morpork, you might 'ave to do it yourself. And I see you are *still* smiling! Will you be so good as to share ze joke? The well-known so-called Ankh-Morpork sense of 'umour does not translate very well here, I'm afraid.'

'Don't be,' said Moist. 'When the humours were handed out, Ankh-Morpork got the one for joking and Quirm had to make do with their expertise in fine dining and love-making.'

He held a beat and said, 'Would you fancy a trade?'

The Marquise giggled into her wine, smiled at Moist and winked, while her husband grinned and said solemnly, 'I think, monsieur, we prefer the status quo.'

And Moist, who had almost but not totally embarrassed himself, said, 'Sir, apart from the goblins, do *any* decent people live in those badlands?'

The Marquis shook his head. 'No, certainly not, they're as dry as dust.'

Moist looked thoughtful for a while, then stood up, bowed to both of them, kissed the hand of the Marquise and said, 'Thank you so much for your hospitality and your help and information. I should get away now if I'm to make the overnight coach back to Ankh-Morpork, but I have a funny feeling that happier circumstances will soon prevail. In fact, I can feel them just floating in the air.'

Ankh-Morpork was full of dwarf bars, big and small, accommodating all comers. The gloom of the Dirty Rat was particularly popular with those who preferred a traditional style of establishment and a definite lack of umbrellas in their drinks.

'Knocking down clacks towers. What good does that do us? My old granny lives under a clacks tower and the lads let her send clackses for nothing.'

In the shadows somebody said, 'You shouldn't allow her to do that. The clacks is for humans.'

And then the quarrel began.

'You've got to admit the clacks is useful sometimes. It'd save a ship at sea, I heard. And anyway it helps you keep in touch with your friends.'

The voice from the dark corner said again, 'Don't touch the clacks towers, then. There are other ways. I've seen the locomotives. It should be easy enough to turn one over on the rails.'

'Oh yeah? And why d'you want to do that?'

'It'll show that us dwarfs are not to be trifled with and anyway, I'm hearing that dwarfs aren't being allowed to work on the railway.'

'I hadn't heard that. That's discrimination.'

'No, that's because silly buggers have been chopping up clacks towers, isn't it? It's what you get if you go around doing things like that. No wonder at all.'

'That's as may be, but the railway employs lots of trolls and even goblins . . . I mean, goblins! Filth! We're being pushed aside. The Low King has sold his soul to bloody Vetinari and the next thing you know they'll have built a railway line to Uberwald and all our mines will be full of stinking goblins . . . unless we stand up for ourselves now!'

'Yeah! Bloody goblins. All over the place!'

The conversation was punctuated by the sound of much quaffing and the subsequent cleaning of the tables.

'Not that a true dwarf would *want* to work on the railway, mind you,' said the soft voice that hadn't yet identified itself.

'No! You're right. I'd never work on the railway. It's an abomination! It should be stopped!'

'They're laying tracks to Quirm from Ankh-Morpork. It would make a statement if we got in the way,' the voice from the shadows continued.

Someone thumped a hand on the bar and said, 'We must show them that dwarfs are not going to be pushed around any longer!'

'We could smash up those bloody water towers and steal the coal,' another suggested. 'That wouldn't hurt anyone but it would mean they'd have to walk.'

'That's not big enough. They'd just rebuild and carry on, like they've done with the clacks. We'd need to do something really big. Something that would make people pay attention.'

There was the sound of people thinking who didn't think very much. Somebody said, 'You mean killing people?'

'Well, you know, you have to make a stand. And later on, when people find out, we'll be the heroes.'

And then the barman, who had been keeping an eye on the group, said pointedly, 'It's closing time, gentlemen, ain't you got no holes to go to?' And shooed them out on to the street.

Ardent walked confidently away. After all, there was another dwarf bar a few streets away and the poison could drip so gently. Amazing how simple people could be manipulated by the right voice at the right time. And after that they did it for themselves with vocabulary like 'stands to reason' and 'they're up to something', little caltrops on the road to interspecies misunderstanding.

When Moist finally arrived back in Ankh-Morpork around breakfast time, he hurried to Harry King's house. It was unusual to see Harry being, as it were, just Harry King, family man. He was even wearing carpet slippers. Effie fussed about with the servants for more coffee while Moist made his report to her husband.

'Sir, we have a little problem down in Quirm. To put it bluntly, some unpleasant gentlemen are getting in the way of the success of our railway.'

Moist explained the land-rights situation to Harry and proposed that since the rolling acres of maquis didn't belong to anybody it belonged to everybody and he could put the railway line straight through. There was just the little matter of the bandits to be dealt with. The look on Harry's face would have warmed the cockles of any heart, especially if it was the heart of a shark, and really Moist didn't need to say much more, but did so anyway.

'It would be very helpful, Harry, if I could go back there one night soon with some of your golems and possibly some of your . . . security men, your *specialist technicians*, as it were. The kind of gentlemen who are adept at resolving conflict. Of course, I'll need to commandeer a coach.'

The expression on Harry's face changed like a kaleidoscope until at last he said, 'Do you mind if I come too?'

And Effie shrieked, 'Harry King! At your age you're going to be doing nothing more than stopping home!'

'Oh, come on, my love, the man said these are bandits. It's my duty as an honest citizen. After all, I'm Harry King, the man who does business, and *this*, well, this is my business and I'm going to take care of it.'

'Harry, please! Remember your position in life!'

'A man makes his own position in life, Duchess, and this is business and I'm going to sort it and it will be the last time, okay?'

'Oh, all right . . . but you mind and take notice, Mister Lipwig. And Harry, you do what Mister Lipwig tells you, he's a very sensible young man,' said Effie. 'And there's to be no alcohol and, Mister Lipwig, make certain he's wrapped up nice and warm because of his bladder, er, thing, you know. He's not as young as he thinks he is.'

And Harry roared. 'Yes, Effie! But right now I reckon I'm ready for anything. I'll get the word out to my lads and my golems, Mister Lipwig, and I'll see you back here tomorrow morning. Seven o'clock sharp.'

At home, Adora Belle said, 'It's a harebrained idea, of course, otherwise *you* wouldn't have had it, would you?'

'Actually, my sweetness, the raid was Harry's idea,' Moist lied. 'I think he thinks of it as his last grand hurrah, but he really had to twist my arm, I promise you, or my name isn't Moist Lipwig. You should have seen the look on his face!'

'Yes, you *are* Moist von Lipwig and you are really looking forward to this, aren't you? You have that look about you.'

153

'Not exactly,' said Moist. 'But it'll be a moonless night, and it might be instructive to see Harry and his chums having one of their little parties. Of course, *you* don't know anything about this, okay?'

Adora Belle's face went delightfully blank. 'This what? But just you remember, Moist, if it's going to be a mêlée do try to come back with all your bits in their rightful place.'

The following morning, two large coaches were waiting outside Harry King's house with a crew of Harry's chums on board. Moist wondered how Harry could gather them together so quickly and then thought about all the things Harry used to do back in the bad old days that he now fondly remembered as being so good. Actually, it was no surprise that the man could assemble an army to settle a little dispute about who owned the streets.

They were all on their best behaviour now and almost all of them didn't spit and there was no cursing, because the Duchess was looking out of the window, ready to wave them off.

Before the coaches departed, Harry addressed his team. 'It's like this, lads: this isn't exactly a killing job, unless they tries to kill you first. These ain't our streets, but they're bandits all the same. You could say we're making the world better for decent people, like what we are, and we're cleaning up the mess like we've always done.'

Moist looked at the faces of Harry's associates. Some had gold teeth and some had no teeth, but all of them had the surreptitious look of gentlemen that mostly go abroad after dark. And if you looked with an experienced eye, bits of them bulged, indeed one of them was holding a toolbox and an eager expression, clearly a man who wasn't for half measures.

Harry had made it clear that there was to be no alcohol, at least until the homeward stage, and so it was a subdued journey through the day. By mid-afternoon they came to the edge of the maquis. The country that lay before them was clearly no place for coaches, with the road petering out into a vague track amid the scrub. Harry ordered the drivers to halt at a spot that offered some grazing and water for the horses, where the coaches would be screened from view, and sent his associates to scout the maquis ahead.

Moist had never before travelled with such silent men; they seemed to absorb all noise and as they jumped down from the coaches with flannel feet they melted instantly into the landscape. Content to leave this part to the specialists, Harry and Moist settled back to wait.

It was a black night, and the whole party had made its stealthy way to the edge of the bandits' camp. They were now in the depths of the wretched wilderness of the Quirmian maquis, a nightmare of dense blackthorn that could strip the skin from your bone. It was a garden from hell, especially in the darkness. They could see the fitful flames of the cooking fires and hear the unmistakable sound of alcohol-assisted snoring. These outlaws ought to be ashamed, Moist thought, not one single lookout!

With his associates strategically deployed around the perimeter, Harry made his way quietly into the centre of the camp.

'Good morning, gentlemen! We are the Goblin Preservation Society and all of yous has got two minutes to get up and be out of here. Got it? Nice and smart, chums!'

A bandit stumbled out of his tent and sneered, 'We don't care who you are, and you can shove all of that right up your jacksie, monsieur.'

And Harry said, 'Good! We like shoving it anywhere! Go on, lads, but no goblins get hurt, okay?'

Moist took a careful step backwards and watched. Harry had stipulated that murdering people wasn't really on the cards tonight, but most of the bandits were either lying on the ground or running away within a couple of minutes of Harry's chums being unleashed. It was gang warfare, but one gang had no sense of strategy. Harry's men were surgical and methodical and very, very professional, even somewhat sombre. This was a job of work and they did it with care and precision. It was what you did, didn't you, and they were flattering themselves that for once they were the good guys, an experience, Moist thought, that they seldom ever had.

Harry took a look around the battleground to assure himself that nothing more than a little concussion and the occasional broken leg had been achieved and was satisfied on all points.

'What do you plan to do with them?' Moist asked.

'Deliver them to the local justice, like the honest citizens we are. I suppose that'll be your Marquis.'

'Very good, but can I suggest we leave one or two behind, to make sure the rest of the bandit population get to hear what happens if they make honest citizens upset?'

'Suppose so,' Harry grunted. 'But I'll get the lads to do a few further ... excursions in the area first, see if we can't mop up some more of 'em. Actions speak louder than words, Mister Lipwig.'

At the chateau later that night the Marquis emerged in his dressing gown to receive them, accompanied by two servants.

'Monsieur Lipwig, *mon ami*, what an unexpected pleasure to see you again so soon. And with companions.'

Harry stepped forward before Moist could speak and said, 'We've a parcel of miscreants here we've brought to you, my lord, since I reckoned you were the closest figure of authority in these parts.'

The Marquis cast a bright eye over the prisoners. 'I see at least two appear to 'ave "'ARRY KING" stamped across the temples. Can it be I 'ave the 'onour to address Sir 'arry King in person? Don't be surprised. My wife has told me much about ze King of ze Golden River, including his famous rings. You are most welcome, monsieur, and I 'ope we will be doing much business together. May I offer you some refreshment?'

''scuse me, sir, but what d'you want done with this lot?' said the toolbox-holding associate.

'Put them in the oubliette, if you would be so kind, we'll fish them out sooner or later.'

'What's an oubliette, sir? Is it like a privy?'

'Yes,' the Marquis laughed, 'I suppose it is in this instance! These garçons 'ave been a thorn in our side for quite a while, but I don't think we'll be getting any further trouble from *them*.'

When Moist, Harry and associates reboarded the coaches in the small hours and started on the long journey home, this time the crates of beer were brought out for the victors.

'Well done, lads,' Harry boomed as he cracked the top off a bottle. 'You did all I expected and more, gentlemen. And you know Harry King is a generous man and so I look forward to working with you again soon. You can rely upon it.'

He lay back on the seat and starting smoking one of his cigars, every so often chatting to one or other of his chums about the escapades they had had long ago when the Watch was a laughing stock.

Adora Belle eventually woke Moist with a cup of tea around about four o'clock in the afternoon. As he supped the tea his wife puffed up his pillows and said, 'Come on, then, tell me, how did it go? I wasn't woken by any big bangs last night, which I consider a result, don't you?'

'Well, it wasn't a massacre and it wasn't a lot of smacked bottoms, as far as I could tell, but the good guys won, well, to a given value of good guy. Harry King's cronies are very sprightly for old guys, and devious as well.'

Placing a tray of food on his knees she said, 'I suppose breakfast in bed just can't present the same frisson for Mister A Life Without Danger Is A Life Not Worth Living, yes?'

Puncturing a sausage, Moist said, 'How well you know me, Spike. Now listen, it seems there are a lot of goblins in the maquis and the people of Quirm haven't found out yet how useful they can be even though they apparently do a good line in wine made from snails.' Moist grimaced and continued, 'Do you mind if I take Of the Twilight the Darkness to Quirm with me?'

His wife looked astonished. 'I didn't think you liked him?'

'Well, he grows on you, you know, like a fungus, and there's going to be a lot of puzzled goblins around now so they might like to see a friendly face.' He hesitated. 'If you can call it that.'

In darkness far from Moist in just about every sense that could be imagined, including the metaphysical, deliberations were taking place in a cavern that was paradoxically glittering and dark when tested by a different eye. It *was* illuminated, in so far as there was illumination, by one solitary candle, whose light was, as the saying goes, just there to show you the darkness. Nevertheless, its trembling little light was refracted in a veritable hoard of gems, the like of which, if you added up the sad little glimmerings, gave off entirely less light than could be delivered by a humble tallow candle.

It was, in short, a light that hid from light, and it had a reason to hide. Just as the unfortunate dwarf now sitting uncomfortably in the centre of the cavern had reason to wish to be elsewhere. Elsewhere, he thought, was the operative word; anywhere would surely be a better place than here.

On the other hand, he was under a religious obligation. He had first heard it on his father's knee, or possibly his mother's, because he had never seen or heard either of them clearly and their voices were always muffled, because silence was as much of a virtue as darkness among the grags, and as he recalled the

158

undeniable fact, he almost tried to cut and run, stopping himself in a nanosecond because there was nowhere to hide. He was in it too high!* Never a good place to be for a dwarf, and the grags had the measure of him.

It was said that they had many ways of killing in the darkness and even had ways of moving from darkness to darkness without being apprehended by the intervening light. Oh, so much was said of them, although generally it was whispered. And he had done *so many* bad things, like eating beef and buying his wife colourful earrings and, worst of all, he had become friends with Rocky Debris who was, horror of horrors, a troll, and also quite a decent bloke, who he quite often sat next to when they were going to work and who, like him, was a supporter of Dolly Sisters United and generally went with him when there was a match on, and surely anyone who cheered for your side was a friend, wasn't he?

And yes, he was, but down in the base of his brain was the bogey-man of his childhood, and subtle whisperings, curdled fragments of old songs sung on special occasions, little observances made holy by repetition with the right people sitting at the same fireside, in those cosy days when you were not really old enough to understand and didn't have your wretched brain stuffed full of ideas that part of you thought you shouldn't *ever* obey, like not shaking hands with a troll *and now he had been seen* and now they had him and now they stood between him and his chances of a new life after death. They held the keys to the next world and, on a whim, could have him floating in the ultimate darkness of the Ginnungagap where there were . . . things, tormentors, creatures of indefinite invention and patience.

He shifted because of the cramp in his legs, and said, 'Please, I know I've got into bad ways and I've strayed from the path and indeed may be unworthy to call myself a dwarf, but if you allow me

---

* For humans he would have been in too deep. Way too deep.

I can make recompense. Please, I'm begging you, remove my shackles and I promise to do whatever you ask.'

The silence in the room grew thicker, more dense, as if it was pulling itself together. How long had he been in here now? It might as well have been years, or merely seconds ... That was the difficulty about darkness; it encompassed everything, turning it into an amorphous substance in which everything got twisted, and remembered and then lost.

'Very well,' said the voice. 'We have looked into your wretched soul and are minded to give you one last chance. Be aware there will be no other.' The voice softened a little and said, 'Tak is watching you. Now you can eat your meal, which is right in front of you, and go from this place and be assured that Tak will be with you. Remember, for those who turn away there is no redemption. And when Tak needs you, you will be contacted again.'

After a rare, well-earned evening with his wife, Moist set off the next day on the golem horse with Of the Twilight the Darkness clinging on behind him.

As they galloped along, there was something about the golem horse that was troubling Moist von Lipwig. A golem horse was incredibly useful if you needed to get somewhere fast, that is if you liked a ride where you spent a lot of the time finding that stirrups just didn't do the job. You merely hung on until you got there, it was as simple as that. No need to steer, NagNav did the trick: if you told it where you wanted to go it took you there. The creature made no sound, required no water or oats and simply stood patiently when it wasn't in use.

And then it dawned on Moist what the problem was. It was all give and no take. Generally speaking, he didn't have much to do with the concept of karma, but he had heard of it and felt that a ton of it was dropping on him right now. The horse was all give and he was all take ... But that was nuts, he told himself. A spoon doesn't want you to say please and thank you, does it? Ah yes, he thought, but a spoon is a piece of metal and the golem horse is a horse. He hesitated, pondering. And thought, *I wonder . . .*

Shortly before the border crossing they reached the head of the finished railway track. He and the goblin thankfully slid off the horse and a sudden impulse prompted Moist to ask the creature a question.

'Can you speak?' he asked, feeling more than faintly ridiculous.

And the answer came back out of the air rather than from the horse's mouth, as it were.

'Yes, if we want to.'

The goblin sniggered. Moist ignored him and pressed on with his line of inquiry.

'Ah, we're getting somewhere. Would you like to run around in meadows and generally cavort in pastures and so on?'

Out of nowhere came, 'Yes, if you wish.'

Moist said, 'But what do *you* wish?'

'I don't understand the concept.'

Moist breathed in and said, 'I saw a little stream not far back, and some green pastures and, for the sake of my soul, I would like you to go over there and gallop in the meadows and enjoy yourself.'

'Yes, enjoy myself, if you want me to.'

'For heavens' sake, this is manumission we're talking about here!'

'That would be horseumission, sir. And I must point out that I don't need to enjoy myself.'

'Well, do so for my sake, will you, please? Roll around on the flowers and neigh a bit and gallop about and have some kind of fun. If not for your own pleasure, then for my sanity, please.'

He watched the horse disappear into the meadow.

Behind him Of the Twilight the Darkness cackled. 'What a piece of work you are, Mister Slightly Damp, freeing the slaves and all. What you think his lordship will say about that?'

Moist shrugged. 'He might be acerbic, but a little acerbic isn't all

161

that bad. He's quite a one for freedom is Vetinari, though not necessarily mine.'

Turning his attention to the railway, Moist was pleased to see that the work gangs, under the tutelage of Mr Simnel's young men, were evidently making steady progress laying down the next stage of track towards Quirm.

To travel onwards, Moist and Of the Twilight the Darkness hitched a ride on a handcar operated with gusto by two young railway workers, a curiously amusing contraption whose wheels ran along the newly laid rails still waiting to be fully bedded in.

They passed the border with only a brief stop to deal with the formalities which were, in fact, nothing more than nodding at the guards and saying, 'Is it okay if we cross, lads?' Whereupon they briefly stopped digging their respective allotments and waved him through.

Where the handcar ran out of track, they found an old man with a horse and cart waiting, as arranged, to take them the rest of the distance to the chateau. He was clearly very sniffy about having a goblin in his nice clean vehicle, even though it was only a cart.

The Marquis was waiting for them at the chateau and beamed at Moist. His nose wrinkled at the sight of Moist's companion.

'Who is this?' he asked in a tone a society lady might take upon finding half of something bristling in her soup.

'This is Of the Twilight the Darkness.'

Of the Twilight the Darkness gave the Marquis a smart salute. 'Of the Twilight the Darkness, Mister Mar-keee. Nice place you got here. Veeery nice. Don't worry about smell. I'll get used to it.'

After an awkward silence, the Marquis said, '*Mon Dieu.*'

'Not a god, Mister Mar-keee,' said Of the Twilight the Darkness, 'just goblin, best there is, oh yes. Very useful, you know.' The goblin continued in ringing sarcasm, 'And not only that, Mister Mar-keee, I'm real. If you cut me, do I not bleed? And if you do, I bleeding well cuts you too, no offence meant.'

162

The Marquis's laughter bounced off the scenery. There was no doubt about it. The goblin knew how to break the ice. Even an iceberg.

The Marquis held out a hand and said, '*Enchanté*, Monsieur Of the Twilight the Darkness. Do you drink wine?'

The goblin hesitated. 'Are there snails in it?'

As they climbed the wide stone steps up to the terrace, the Marquis said, 'Regrettably we don't include snail. I know your people like snail wine but I'm afraid I 'ave none to offer you.'

'Never mind, squire, will have it as it comes, please. And for record, Mister Mar-keee, they ain't my people, they your people. I'm an Ankh-Morpork lad. Have seen the big horse* and all that stuff.'

The view in the late afternoon sun over the maquis from the terrace was wonderful.

'You have many goblins in Ankh-Morpork, Mister Lipwig?' the Marquis asked as he poured Moist a glass of chilled wine. 'I've 'eard, of course, of Milord Vetinari's famous melting pot. And yet I am informed zat many people in Ankh-Morpork still feel very unsure about them and think that getting involved with goblins shows that ze owner is dirty! So much for the prejudices of your countrymen who are, one 'as to say, a fairly dirty lot in any case. Whereas 'ere in Quirm *notre logique* points out that we are cleaner. After all, Quirm is the 'ome of Monsieur Bidet! Yet another apparatus for keeping clean and yet *you* in Ankh-Morpork sneer at *us* for being dirty.'

'Yes, I know, it's deplorable,' said Moist. 'I did meet Monsieur Bidet, although regrettably I didn't shake him by the hand. Excuse me? Is something wrong?'

---

* An Ankh-Morpork citizen will never yield to the idea that there are other cities at least as good as their own and treat the concept that there could be with humorous disdain. The phrase originated when an Ankh-Morpork citizen was shown an equestrian statue in Pseudopolis and when faced with the beast, said, 'Maybe it's a Big Horse I'm Morporkian', an incident that gave rise to a popular bar room song.

The Marquis suddenly looked preoccupied. 'Someone was watching us from the tree over zere. I must 'ave spoken too loudly because 'oever it is has made 'aste to get down to the cover of the ground. He's small, but larger than a goblin; you 'ardly ever see *zem* in ze trees.'

There was a movement in the air as Of the Twilight the Darkness vaulted over the parapet and disappeared into the landscape below. He reappeared almost as quickly, saying, 'Dwarf bugger. Have it away on toes. I spit me of him!'

The Marquis topped up Moist's glass and said, 'A dwarf? Something to do with you, Mister Lipwig? Industrial espionage? One would expect the dwarfs to be keen on something like a railway . . . they are, after all, metalworkers and traders in ore.'

'I don't think so,' said Moist. 'The clacks saw a bit of trouble a few months ago with extremist factions knocking down some of their towers, but that seems to have died down now. And there don't seem to be many dwarfs interested in working on the railway. Something to do with the grags, I expect. The grags don't seem to like anybody of importance in Ankh-Morpork.'

'Oh, yes,' said the Marquis. 'The famous Koom Valley Accord and all zat business. I believed it to be sorted out.'

'So did everybody else. You must know how it is. Can't please absolutely everybody. And you certainly can't please the grags, however hard you try.'

Fully refreshed, Moist and Of the Twilight the Darkness set off into the maquis to find the goblin denizens, who even if they did not, strictly speaking, own the land through which the railway would go, needed to be informed and consulted. As squatters on unclaimed land, Moist thought, they surely must have some claim to it.

As they made their way into the scrubby and thorny landscape, Moist pondered the significance of the dwarf who had been spying on *him*, right here in Quirm, where you didn't normally see dwarfs.

This meant he had been followed, and that almost surely meant more than one person. During his misspent youth and, not to put too fine a point on it, his largely misspent early middle age, he'd reckoned to be conversant with the methodology of spying, and one person alone couldn't ensure reasonable tracking of the target. What was the dwarf doing there? Where had he come from? And, more important, where did he go?

His reverie was interrupted when Of the Twilight the Darkness stopped suddenly by a rocky outcrop which, as far as Moist could tell, was indistinguishable from several other similar outcrops they had passed already. It was hot. Very hot.

'Wait here,' said the goblin. 'Will be back in a shake.'

In fact it was another sweaty hour and the sun was beginning to dip below the horizon before the goblin came back along the track, trailed by a large crowd of Quirmian goblins, their numbers swelling all the time as even more of them emerged from the undergrowth.

When it came to looks the Quirm goblins seemed exactly the same as the ones over the border in Ankh-Morpork. However, unlike the Ankh-Morpork goblins, the Quirmian goblins were dressed in a way that could only be called snazzy. They had a certain panache unavailable to their Ankh-Morpork brethren, and a whiff about them of what was probably eau de snail.* Admittedly, the materials on show were effectively the same – bits of animal skin or indeed the animals themselves, birds, feathers – all embellished with sparkling stones. It was as if goblins had discovered taxidermy, but hadn't *quite* got the important, nay, *essential* point of scooping out the messy bits first. But trust Quirm goblins to make their own *haute couture*.

---

* Which instead of masking the ubiquitous goblin smell merely lent it an extra piquancy.

Moist smiled. He could see that somehow the goblin lads here in Quirm were trying to do it *better*, possibly because they had a better class of shaky swagger and a certain cheerful *up yours* look in their eyes.

Nevertheless, they looked like a people who had been hammered hard on the anvil of fate and had been laminated with a natural bravado, which did not entirely hide their wounds.

Moist was glad he had Of the Twilight the Darkness on his side, because the goblins of this part of the maquis clearly had no liking for humanity. Of the Twilight the Darkness now sidled up to him in his bandy-legged and sneery little way and said, 'These people hurting oh-so bad it is. People gone. Little ones gone. Pots gone. Gone. But put big faces on it, yes. Can no more be truly goblin. Hurt. Hurt. Hurt. Now I give speech.'

Of the Twilight the Darkness turned out to be the goblin equivalent of Moist himself.

Moist wasn't fluent in goblin, but you didn't need to know what was being said as you watched the faces and the way Of the Twilight the Darkness waved his hands. He was, in fact, doing a number.

Moist couldn't make out the words, but assumed it was something like, 'New life in Ankh-Morpork with all the rats you want *and* wages.' For there they were, ideas and promises curving through the air.

And so certain was Moist that he had picked up what was going on that he leaned down and said, 'Don't forget to say that in Ankh-Morpork goblins are now citizens with *rights*.'

Moist was extremely pleased to see the goblin pause and look at him. 'How you know I was talking of Ankh-Morpork, Mister Lipwig?'

'Takes one to know one.'

While Of the Twilight the Darkness delivered his speech, the goblins stared at Moist. As stares went, their eyes were not baleful or angry, they were just . . . hopeful, in the grudging way of people who had had to learn pessimism as a survival tactic.

One of the goblins then stepped forward and beckoned, clearly wanting to show him something. Of the Twilight the Darkness was also nudging him to follow. As Moist gingerly threaded his way through the network of almost invisible paths in the wasteland of thorns, pools of poisonous water and occasional blockages caused by old rock falls, he noticed a crackling underfoot. Bones, he realized – mostly small bones – and in his ear were the words of Of the Twilight the Darkness: 'Young goblins! Veeeeery tasty! A lot of good eating. Bandits thought so. But we hang, Mister Lipwig, we hang. We hang on.'

The horror tripped its way icily over Moist's backbone. Of the Twilight the Darkness continued.

'Those bandits was hungry. Small goblins. Easy to catch.'

'Are you saying they were *eating* the goblins?'

The vehemence of Moist's cry was picked up by Of the Twilight the Darkness immediately.

'Sure. Easy meat. The bandit men eat anything they can catch. Rats. Moles. Shrews. Birds. Even stinky bird like raven. Eat it up. Yum. Yum. Shit out nasty poisonous stuff. Goblin meat like chicken. Miracle of nature may be not, but no use to goblin when bandits around. They don't want much, mister, and good job, 'cos they don't get, but like me will do any job in free air. Place to live not being killed. Yes! Hunky-dory. And no need food in Ankh-Morpork. Big Wahoonie! Rats *everywhere*!'

'Okay, Mister Twilight, where do we go from here?'

The goblin gave Moist a cynical look, something which is very easy to do when you're a goblin, because you learn cynicism early and you learn it fast.

'You give me half name, Mister Damp. I forgive, have mercy. This time. I ask you. *Don't* do again. Is very important. Half name is shame. Challenge to fight. Know you hasty. No understanding. Will

167

forgive you. Will forgive once, *Mister Lipwig*! This by way of friendly information. No charge incurred.'

Whatever Moist von Lipwig was, he knew the use of the right word at the right time.

'Mister Of the Twilight the Darkness, thank you for your forbearance.'

It was beginning to rain. Sticky, lazy rain but the goblins seemed to be oblivious to it. These people are the world's most stoical of stoics, Moist thought, albeit with a sting in their tail. I wonder what they are like when they decide, and they will decide, not to take everything on their greasy chins.

Of the Twilight the Darkness grinned at Moist again and declared, 'Hey you, mister big hero, mighty warrior, except, hah, these dumb buggers really think you is bee's bollocks, think sun percolate out your arse.'

Moist realized that Of the Twilight the Darkness's presentation to the goblins of the delights of Ankh-Morpork and his status in the city might have been somewhat exaggerated.

'What did you say to make them think that?'

'These goblins need hope, Mister Lipwig. You ain't genuine good guy, but you can pretend like no bees' nest. I have already explained to them that you are great citizen of Ankh-Morpork and dreadful fighter.'

'Well,' said Moist, 'at least you got one bit right. But the bandits have surely been scared off now. The goblins can stay here, can't they? There'll be jobs on the railway when it comes through here. They'd like that, wouldn't they?'

'Bandit men come back in time. Always is bandits. These goblins can't fly, Mister Soggy. Long way back to Ankh-Morpork line! Looks for you to get them out of here. Me? I ain't just fallen off Hogswatch tree. You don't carry knife, and now it night-time and you are still in maquis. Worse here than just bandits! Bad worse! Everything bad end up in the maquis and you *still* with no weapon. What are your orders, Mister Big Man?!'

Moist hesitated. He had a feel for this sort of thing, he was sure, and it hardly ever let him down.

'Okay. We'll take them with us. But first you must get us out of here.'

'No, Marvellous von Lipwig is going to take the people out. Plucky goblin sidekick just bring up the rear.'

'Really? Okay, then. Just point me in the right direction.'

There was a track of sorts, and myriad little pathways in every direction. Moist and his unhappy but hopeful band were shepherded surreptitiously from behind by Of the Twilight the Darkness, who was becoming a great lieutenant, despite the fact that he brazenly considered Moist to be a bit of a tit. But a useful tit all the same.

As they struggled back to what, in a fair wind, might have been called a proper track, Moist told himself that while it was true that Commander Vimes was the man who had been most prominent in the manumission of the goblins, he, Moist, could at least give them a job; you couldn't have a profession as *goblin*, now could you? It just made no sense. And yet if there were such a thing as a professional goblin, then it was definitely Of the Twilight the Darkness, who was so goblin that you could imagine that other goblins would tap one another on the shoulder and say, 'Blimey! Look at that goblin! Doesn't he look like a goblin to you?'

But jobs got things going, got *people* going, and raised their self-esteem. After all, goblins, quite apart from now being ubiquitous in the clacks industry, were also doing very well and picking up serious folding money in the ceramics business. Goblin pots were beautiful, extremely fine and as iridescent as a butterfly's wing.*

---

*Unggue pots, as they were called, had a major and sacred part in goblin society. In Ankh-Morpork sensible goblins were making quasi unggue pots for sale, looking like the real thing, Adora Belle said, but with the magic taken out and the wonderful sparkle left in. However, it helped if you didn't pay too much attention to what the pots *traditionally* held . . .

Moist's reverie was broken by Of the Twilight the Darkness. 'These poor herberts behind us think you need to know that dwarfs been asking after you, like sneaky one up tree I saw off. My, can't the greedy buggers shift when need. Don't like good flint edge! But still are some around. Reckon they waiting until we get to railway. Right place for ambush.'

Moist had devoted considerable energies to being a non-combatant, words being his weapon of choice, but when words weren't enough, in extremis he could deliver telling blows with his fists and feet. Right now he was wondering whether to surreptitiously drag said feet a little so that he would be surrounded by the band of goblins if there was an attack. After all, they all had stone weapons, didn't they? And he didn't, did he? Goblins acquired a fighting spirit with their mothers' milk, if indeed their mothers *had* milk.*

They continued cautiously into the ever-deepening dusk, now moving as silently as they could manage. Even the goblin toddlers were quiet as they walked towards the promised land.

They skirted the grounds of the chateau and moved on through the woods in the direction of the railhead. A while later there came a crushed-gravel whisper at Moist's elbow from Of the Twilight the Darkness.

'I sending out some of swifter lads to scout ahead. Something not right at railhead. Couldn't get close enough to see but says at least dozen dwarfs in the woods up there, maybe more. Could hear the buggers clanging. They trying to be surreptitious, but dwarfs has not first idea of surreption. It's all been hammer and tongues to dwarfs. Could try go round 'em – but the buggers might try go round us same time. Best, I say, to deal with bogeys today, right? No worry, some these lobster lads know how to fight and they proud you leading them . . . ain't you!'

---

* There was no point in speculating on what else they could have. Just the thought turned Moist's stomach.

It wasn't a question, it was a demand. Moist was horribly aware of the whole refugee group clustered around him, their unprepossessing faces full of expectation and miscellaneous fragments of food. There were little ones, some no more than babes in arms. Moist could feel the pressure of their hope which, alas, he knew was unfounded and probably misplaced. He was no leader. Not like Commander Vimes. But what would Of the Twilight the Darkness do if he just ran away? He could outrun any dwarf, make it back to the chateau . . . but could he outrun a goblin . . . ?

He shivered and shoved that thought to the very back of his mind just as a small goblin woman came up to him.

'Go into battle with nice cuppa tea!' she said. 'Special goblin tea! Very good for you! Boiled in sheep bladder! Excellent when always having to run! Got herbs! You drink! You drink *now*! Ain't nothing like a nice cuppa tea. Medicinal it is!'

Of the Twilight the Darkness handed Moist a large goblin club.

'Many, many ways to die today,' he said, with devastating humour. 'Trust elderly goblin, this one very much the best, hang! We hang together.'

Moist understood that last rather unfortunate suggestion. It was the traditional goblin-to-goblin greeting, as in, hang together or hang separately. He swigged the cold tea, which had a harmless accent of hazelnuts with a soupçon of wool, expecting at any moment either to be poisoned or to throw up. In fact, it was . . . pleasant and it also felt quite nourishing. If there were snails in it, like the wine, then, well, viva escargot! Although the secret ingredient, he was quite sure, was likely to be avec.

The potion appeared to work because a few moments later he felt ready for *anything*, full of beans, or possibly full of avec. Why, in the face of all the gods, had he been so apprehensive when there was absolutely nothing to be frightened of, oh dear no!

This cheerful state of mind continued right up until the moment they spotted the red lights of the railhead shining out like a beacon through the surrounding woodlands. Leaving the most elderly goblins with the twigs* hiding in the undergrowth as only goblins could hide, Moist and the rest crept forward.

The young men in the travelling work gang had crafted themselves cosy little shacks covered with oilskin. These were extremely portable and always a place where a friendly face could be certain of a hot drink, stirred with a spanner, of course. And if no gamekeepers were known to be about, a wild avec and rabbit stew might also be available for an al fresco meal.

Indeed, the pot of stew still bubbling over the embers of the camp fire smelled as good as any Moist remembered. He had expected to see the young lads he had met only that morning, cheerfully tucking in after a hard day's work. He had not expected to see corpses . . . but corpses were what he found. By the glow of the fire and the pale light of the lanterns, he could see that the workers had many things that could usefully have been employed as a weapon, but they had evidently been taken unawares. It had been a terrible encounter and most certainly they had lost. A quick assay of body parts indicated that there had been nine of them, cut down while having their meal outside their makeshift bothy.

Of the Twilight the Darkness was instantly on the case, sniffing the corpses and the ground.

'The damn dwarfs have been here, oh yes, can smell the naaaasty buggers! But some of them still here,' he added quickly, pointing to a small piece of woodland in the distance and dropping his voice to a whisper. 'Hiding in the wood' – *sniff* – 'over there' – *sniff* – 'several, one injured.' His beady goblin eye was glittering and Moist . . . Moist had a sudden sensation of being on fire.

'Please,' he managed to say, 'please, tell me, what is the goblin for "Charge!"?'

* Any young goblin is thought of as being a twig.

172

Much, much later, Moist remembered that he had heard the goblin say at least the beginning of the word and then the whole world was a crimson haze full of shouting and the dark fog of war. He felt his arms and legs going about their terrible business, especially his arms, and he was aware of noises, *unpleasant* noises, cracking noises, splatting noises, but they came as a kind of incoherent memory, as did the screams ... Little parcels of recollection bobbing up and down like the bubbles in a bottle of home-made ginger beer, coming and going and never staying long enough to mean anything. But the bubbles were gradually drifting away now and, when he came to what was left of his senses, he was lying with his back up against a tree.

The railhead camp fire had been relit and to Moist's bemused amazement there were the signs of dawn on the horizon – but hadn't they been in this place for only a couple of minutes? Of the Twilight the Darkness was sitting on a lump of wood near by, smoking a pipe and occasionally blowing smoke rings into the early blue sky. It was a sight that a painter would love to paint, were it not necessary to paint it in various shades of blood, and, to do justice to the scene, with several tubes of gore and a splash of what-ever colour you needed for guts. Moist's memory of the night before was now strewn with corpses.

'Well now, ain't you a dark horse, Mister Dripping!' grinned the goblin. 'Who ever would thought it? Tell you this: you ain't half going to be sore later. You done a man's job! Almost goblin job! Three! Count 'em! Well, count bits of 'em and work it out, but three dwarf crack fighters smash down like skittles. Two of 'em wearing first-class micromail armour, assassin grade, worth mint. Pillage. Here, take this as souvenir to show Miss Adora Belle. Good on mantelpiece!'

The goblin threw over what Moist had thought was a lump of wood and which he could now see was the head of a dwarf, still inside its helmet.

'That's right! Get it out of system! Throw it up, throw it up and throw it up again. Very good for tubes, does world of good. Better out than in.'

Moist staggered to his feet and said, through the winding mists, 'I couldn't have killed three dwarfs! I'm no fighter! Never! It plays havoc with your shoes.'

'Reckon dwarfs would disagree. Mind you, I show the one over there bit of goblin disapproval, as you may say! Especially when I got him on ground. Most time, everybody keep out of your way, just in case. You was getting a bit . . . *indiscriminate*, oh yeees. Still, no harms done.'

'No harm done?' Moist wailed. 'I just killed three dwarfs! Wouldn't you say that counts as a little harm?'

'Was fair fight, Mister Slightly Damp. One against many, like in best anecdote. Tell you already, most us lads climbing trees to get away from *you*. And you not a fighter. You said this, we all hear.'

'It was that drink! That's what it was! You've filled me full of goblin rot-gut! Who knows what it's done to me!'

'Me?' said Of the Twilight the Darkness, trying to look hurt. 'I keep you alive so you will see your very nice lady, who is always kind to goblins. Take from me, Mister Sopping, that drink just open up what's there already.'

'And what was here, may I ask?'

'Rage, Mister Dripping. You let something off leash. Now you can help us clean bloody mess and get us out of here.'

Moist looked at what remained of the railway workers who had just been doing their job, being no threat to anybody. Simple men who knew nothing whatsoever about politics and had wives and children and were now lying dead for a quarrel they had nothing to do with, and the rage swelled up again, almost lifting him off the ground. They hadn't deserved it, nor had those goblins whose fallen corpses he now saw here and there across the battlefield.

Of the Twilight the Darkness was staring at him and said,

'Amazing, what things we learn, that goblins can be people and you, Mister Damp, has a heart and crying because of death of men you don't know. World is full of miracle. Maybe I will see you singing in choir.'

In the misty light of morning Moist stared at the grinning goblin: as evil-looking as anything in a picture book that was designed to give the little kiddies all the nightmares they would ever need, and yet reading him a lecture on morality.

'What *are* you?' he asked. 'I've been listening to you for days, and you look like a goblin, no doubt about that, but every so often you come out with something I wouldn't expect to hear from a goblin. No offence meant, but you are a smart one.'

The goblin relit his pipe, which made him somehow more human, and said carefully, 'Are you saying goblins not ever clever, Mister Lipwig? Goblins not ever brave? Goblins not ever learn? Me, finest learner. All things to all men and all goblins.'

Moist looked at the little pile of micromail armour. It was treasure and a half. Light and strong. And easy to carry. And worth a fortune, lying there on the damp grass. He looked into the goblin's eyes.

'All yours, Mister Lipwig. To the victor the spoils,' Of the Twilight the Darkness said cheerfully.

'No. They can have it,' said Moist, indicating the Quirmian goblins.

'Don't need it,' said the goblin. 'Take your spoils, Mister Lipwig. You never know when useful.'

Moist looked at what remained of the dwarf fighters and thought, where's Mr Chriek when you need him? And that thought prompted another: a reliable witness was essential. He asked Of the Twilight the Darkness to fetch the Marquis or any of his workers from the chateau, with an iconograph if they had one.

'We need people to know about this.'

*

175

After the Marquis, trailed by goggling servants, had inspected the scene, exclaimed his horror, organized the taking of iconographs, and departed back to the chateau, promising to send the news by clacks at once, the decencies could be attended to.

The corpses of the railway workers and goblins who had fallen in the battle were carefully, even reverentially, placed on to the hand-car. A few of the goblins disappeared into the scenery and returned with wild flowers to put on the bodies. It was one of those little observations that subtly turned Moist's universe around. Goblins believing that those who fell in battle had paid their dues.

After the solemn ceremony was over, the goblins took turns at pumping the lever of the handcar as Moist, the goblin band and their sad cargo headed back slowly along the track to the border, where they stopped to send out their own clacks. Moist arranged with the border guard for the bodies to be shrouded and put in a cold place until someone was sent to pick them up.

One of the guards took umbrage that the dead goblins were being left alongside the bodies of what he called 'real people'. And so Moist had a rather pointed little chat with him, after which the man was much better informed, although bleeding slightly from his nose. The memory of oh so many little bones hadn't had enough time to be forgotten. And perhaps some of the potion was still alive inside Moist. It was that kind of day.

That done, Moist looked at the ribbon of goblins trailing behind him and then looked up at the sign beside the Quirm turnpike which told the world that it was the well-known 'Fat Marie's'.

There could be no mistake about how the proprietor got her name and like so many roadside eateries she sold hot food quickly and served reasonable coffee to travellers and that was that. Her clientele hadn't even heard of cuisine, they just needed surety of carbohydrate and grease. However, she proved somewhat dubious about feeding goblins, and said, 'I might lose my regulars if I let them lot in.'

And once again Moist had to explain the facts of life, making it clear that refusing to serve goblins would very soon lead to her not feeding anyone else at all once Lord Vetinari had been informed. Fat Marie's was on Ankh-Morpork land and Vetinari was strict.

'After all,' Moist said, 'they'll sit outside, they really don't like rooms, and I'm paying, okay?'

Suitably chastened, Fat Marie shovelled out rather bad fish and chips and a fried slice to every goblin and was amazed at how fast they ate, especially the fried slice. That was one thing about the goblins, they weren't fussy.

After their meal, Moist arranged for the goblins to travel on to Harry's compound in the freight trucks of the utility engine that serviced the railhead, went to find the golem horse, still obediently rolling and galloping in the meadow, and headed back towards the city.

Harry King was close to incandescent at the best of times, but the state of mind he was in when he heard the news of the massacre could only be described as volcanic: one of those slumbering volcanoes that suddenly go off pop and the calm sea is instantly awash with dirty pumice and surprised people in togas. Moist tried to calm him down, but that was like trying to put a cap on a geyser, and you can't do that, especially not to a geezer like Harry King. Then the explosion became tears, the bubbling and sticky tears of a hard man who would never want anybody to see him cry.

Learning that Moist himself had got rid of a few of the dwarfs responsible helped, but even so Harry continued to dribble snot on to a very expensive tie while calling down the wrath of the gods on to the remains of the culprits, with a footnote that the gods had better get to them before Harry's curses did.

Moist offered to tell the workers' next of kin, but Harry declared that he would do the job himself. He set off on this doleful task immediately, leaving Moist with nothing to do but collect Of the

177

Twilight the Darkness and the band of Quirmian goblins who had meanwhile arrived at the compound and were being entertained by Billy Slick and his grandmother.

When he arrived home in Scoone Avenue, Adora Belle opened the door herself. Moist, as ever, was impressed by her *sang froid* as she surveyed the motley group of Quirmian goblins he had in his wake. 'So good to see you again, Spike,' he said. 'I've brought you some little presents. Say it with goblins, as you might say.'

'How many are there, do you think?' she enquired.

'Two hundred or more,' said Moist. 'I haven't really been counting.'

'I suggest that Of the Twilight the Darkness takes them over to the Tump Tower where there's enough room in the basement for them to sleep.'

'You don't mind?'

'Of course not. Quite a lot of my best goblins are taking holidays to the Shires and elsewhere. We're very short. Well done, you!'

As soon as Moist had seen the goblins on their way, the Ankh-Morpork Watch metaphorically felt his collar. As collars go, Moist's was expensive, but a little the worse for wear after the fight with the dwarfs.

In this case, the hand doing the feeling belonged to Captain Angua, who asked him to accompany her to the Yard in tones that did not allow for an argument.

Once ensconced in an interview room, she took down his statement about the massacre in a deliberately methodical way, asking pointed questions, which was to say pointed at Moist.

'So you, Mister von Lipwig, took down a bunch of dwarf terrorists with the help of a number of goblins, yes? You must like goblins, then?'

'Yes, and so does Commander Vimes, captain,' Moist snapped. 'Tell me, where is Chuckles today?'

It was worth it to see the captain grimace; if you looked carefully you could see the outline of the fangs. It was a risky move, but he had a reputation to live down and cheeking the Watch was a pastime he cherished and was very good at. They were altogether too stuffy and Captain Angua, try as she might, looked stunning in her uniform, especially when she was angry.

'With the Patrician,' she growled. 'An attack on the railway is an attack on Ankh-Morpork. With delvers involved there is a possible connection with the attacks on the clacks. All of this needs to be investigated and it would have been *helpful* if one of the perpetrators had been left alive and available for interrogation.'

Moist almost choked, saying, 'Captain, when a lot of unpleasant people are trying to kill you, it's hard to remember that leaving one of them alive might be a spiffy idea. You have other things on your mind such as, maybe, not dying yourself. If it's any help, I think you'll find that the Marquis des Aix en Pains will by now have sent iconographs of the dwarfs who did this. The Marquis is a decent bloke and generally helpful and keen to have the railway, so I'm certain that you'll get your evidence.'

And as he thought that, mischief rose in Moist's mind and he said, 'And I know that you yourself can travel very fast, captain. They might still be fresh if you hurry.'

This time it was not a black look that Moist got. It was a look that said patience was about to crack.

Fortunately, the door opened just at the right time and Commander Vimes entered, his expression grim.

'Ah, Mister Lipwig, please follow me to my office, if you'd be so good. I always know when you're in the building.' He nodded at the simmering Angua and said, 'I'll deal with Mister von Lipwig, captain.'

Moist was unsure about how much Commander Vimes actually disliked him. After all, the man was so straight that you could use him as a pencil, whilst Moist, on the other hand, despite the success of the Post Office and the Royal Bank and even the wonderful new Mint, was still seen by Vimes and many others as bent as an old spoon and most certainly up to no good.

'Would you like some coffee?' Commander Vimes asked as they entered his office. 'The pot downstairs is *always* on and it doesn't always taste of mud.' He opened the door again and shouted down, 'Two coffees up here, please, Cheery, one black, and you can empty the sugar bowl into mine.'

Moist was somewhat disorientated, because Vimes was acting in a way that, if looked at forensically, might even have been somewhere within the circumference of friendly, rather like, he supposed, an alligator yawning. The commander was now back in his chair, and, yes, *smiling*.

The truth was that between Moist von Lipwig and Commander Vimes there was a certain . . . what they politely called a difference of opinion. Sam Vimes did *not* live in the same world as Moist von Lipwig. Did the man ever laugh, he wondered – the commander must have done something funny at some time. Probably he'd laughed at somebody falling over a cliff or suchlike.

At which point, to his surprise, Commander Vimes cleared his throat and said slowly, like a man essaying something unfamiliar, 'Mister von Lipwig, it may be the case in recent years that I've given you the opinion that I consider you a cheat and a fraud and no better than a worm. However, the fact that you threw yourself in front of that train to save two kiddies suggests to me that the leopard can change his shorts.

'Theoretically, I'll be dressing you down for sorting out the murderous dwarfs involved in this latest atrocity and telling you that you should leave that sort of thing to the damn Watch. But I'm not stupid and I'm prepared to give credit where credit is due. The delvers are a vicious lot, a type of vermin that I'd very much have liked to see dance to Mister Trooper's tune just to show them how justice should be done. But knowing that at least some of the buggers are out of the way must suffice for now. So, on a personal note, which I'll certainly deny if you repeat this to *anyone*: Well done.'

And at this Vimes waggled, yes, waggled a finger, and in tones of a funeral bell and much louder said, '*Don't do it again!* That was an official reprimand, you understand, Mister Lipwig? And *this* is my hand.'

To Moist's amazement Vimes walked around the table and gave him the hardest handshake he had ever had. It was like shaking hands with a boxing glove full of walnuts. Nothing actually broke and there was no blood and Vimes hadn't even tried to squeeze, so it appeared to Moist that what had just been perpetrated must be Commander Vimes's everyday handshake. He decided it was probably the commander being a man who didn't believe in half measures.

And now the commander looked sombre, saying, 'If I were you, Mister von Lipwig, I'd make certain that my wife spent a lot of time out of the way in clacks towers for a while and I'd ask the Watch to keep an eye on my property. Those wretched delvers will stop at nothing, and I mean no offence when I say I'm surprised that you managed to take the bastards down.' He lowered his voice, almost to a whisper, and said, 'What did it feel like, son?'

There was an expression in Vimes's eyes that told Moist that now, if ever, it was time for the truth and so he too lowered his voice and said, 'To tell you the truth, commander, I had some unexpected back-up. You wouldn't believe it.'

And amazingly, Vimes's smile broadened and he said, 'Actually, Mister Lipwig, I just might. I know a little something of fighting dirty in the dark, don't I just. It was under Koom Valley a few years back and I had some back-up too, and I don't think I want to know where it came from. Just be careful now. The grags clearly have your number. You'd better go and see Vetinari, but I'm very glad we've had this little chat.'

181

'Why d'you think I'm going to see Vetinari next?'

'I *know*, because I've just come from the palace. He was sending for you and I asked his lordship if I could get a crack at you first.'

Moist walked to the door, turned round and said simply, 'Thank you, Commander.'

Outside on Lower Broadway, Moist hailed a one-troll trolley bus* and he was not pleased when a dwarf jumped into the pannier beside him. He braced himself for a blow, but the dwarf just smiled at him.

'Mister Lipwig, how pleased I am to see you. I'd appreciate a moment of your time.'

'Look,' said Moist, 'I'm a *very* busy man with a great deal to do, and I'm expected at the palace.'

'The palace? Allow me.'

And the dwarf flipped the correct fare to said troll and gave him the destination in the troll's own language, much to the amazement of the troll. Oh my, thought Moist. Ankh-Morpork, the melting pot of the world, which occasionally runs foul of lumps that don't melt.

Moist looked down at the dwarf which was, of course, inevitable. He seemed to be more, well, streamlined than your traditional dwarf, although smiling in a confrontational sort of way: not unpleasantly, but with a kind of inner dedication to the smile. He realized that the dwarf reminded him of something . . . oh dear, what was its name? Oh, yes, a gyroscope, which he'd seen demonstrated in Unseen University's High Energy Magic building. In short, and of course this person *was* a dwarf, he did have the feel of a gyroscope about him, something spinning around an undeclared centre. The insight built itself in a matter of seconds, at the end of

* Which consists of a troll with a comfortable pannier on either side that can carry up to four people.

which, instead of insisting that his unwanted fellow passenger got out, Moist was paying a lot of attention to the smart little figure.

'Who are you?' he asked.

'I am merely a messenger,' replied the dwarf. 'I am here to tell you something that you cannot ignore. In a sacred place near Koom Valley your name is on the list of people to be summarily executed, *but* do not fret unduly, because—'

'Er, you mean I should just simply fret in a duly kind of way, then? So what the hell is that supposed to mean?'

The annoyingly grave face of the dwarf, with its curious essence of smile, was irking Moist, and the dwarf said, 'Well, Mister Lipwig, you are in a queue behind Lord Vetinari and Commander Vimes and, of course, so are a very large number of dwarfs considered to be un-dwarfish. It is a tiny war at the moment, it's burning underground like an abandoned coal measure, waiting to break out in unexpected places and soon, I suspect, to a place containing yourself.'

'Look,' said Moist, 'it may have escaped your notice, but I am not and never have been a dwarf, okay? I don't have a beard and I can't walk under a table. Human, you see?'

The composure of the dwarf was unshakeable, just like his smile, which now broadened a little as he said, 'You may not be a dwarf, my friend, but you are considered a vector, a symbol of all that is opposed to real dwarfishness, a carrier, if you like, and also a central figure in a city that some dwarfs would love to see burned to the ground. The clacks were just the start. Your railway will not succeed in tempting dwarfs from the true path of Tak. The commander and Lord Vetinari are surrounded by people who carry a large variety of useful weapons. You don't, though, do you, Mister Lipwig? You are not a warrior, you are a target, admittedly a remarkable and ingenious one. I suggest you remember how Albert Spangler watched his back and, above all, do not go into dark places.'

The dwarf shook his head and added, 'You have been warned, sir. I understand you have been known to say that a life without danger is a life not worth living, and frankly all I can say is, good luck with that. Tak does not require that you think of him, but he does require that you think, and I suspect that Tak will be requiring your services in the near future. There are things happening, political things, that you know nothing of, but Tak knows where to find you when Tak needs you.'

And with that the dwarf smiled, jumped out of the pannier and ran off at speed before Moist could react.

Taken by surprise, Moist continued the journey to the palace with his head in a whirl. Until the massacre at the railhead, he hadn't been doing *anything wrong*! Just trying to help everybody! And now he was apparently a target because he represented the wicked ways of Ankh-Morpork ... which was not only unfair, but also untrue. Well, probably untrue, well, at least a bit. He assumed that the grags were hurt about the fact that he had just killed some of their number, even though it had been a fair fight. Well, probably fair and, anyway, they'd got what they deserved. Moist had hardly done anything actually truly *wicked* in his life* and now his new cleaned-up, hard-working, upstanding citizen persona was at risk.

Moist was seething by the time he arrived at the Oblong Office.

'It seems I'm a damn target,' he began, 'and you knew it, sir!'

In the following silence Lord Vetinari's head did not move until he folded his newspaper. 'I assume the grags found you, yes, Mister Lipwig? I thought you knew that, along with myself, Drumknott,

---

* Apart from occasionally going with a few clients down to the Pink PussyCat Club to *appear* to have a good time and stick money down the garters of the gyrating young ladies, which really was hardly evil at all in the light of early-onset middle age, just rather sad, although extremely enjoyable at the time and a death warrant if Adora Belle ever found out.

Commander Vimes and many others, you are on what I believe is called a hit list drawn up by radical grags. But if I were you I wouldn't worry. After all, a life without danger is a life not worth living, eh, Mister Lipwig?'

And Moist said, 'Well, yes, but what about Adora Belle?'

'Oh yes, Mister Lipwig, I told her last week.'

'What! She didn't tell me!'

'I believe she wanted to surprise you, Mister Lipwig. She knows how much you like surprises and you do enjoy a quantum of frisson, she told me.'

Moist almost squealed, 'But you know I'm no fighter!'

'Really, Mister Lipwig? But I already have reports that say otherwise: thrilling tales of derring-do and, believe me, nothing was said about derring-don't.'

Moist, a long-time student of Vetinari and his moods, knew that you could never be sure of what he was thinking. But now the Patrician seemed carved out of stone, like a statue.

'Mister Lipwig, you know what they say about dwarfs?'

Moist looked blank. 'Very small people?'

'"Two dwarfs is an argument, three dwarfs is a war", Mister Lipwig. It's squabble, squabble, squabble. It's built into their culture. And in the squabbling, the grags hide and poison.

'The Koom Valley Accord, which I helped to broker with the Low King and Diamond King of Trolls, was hailed around the world as a fresh hope for the future. But now some of the senior dwarfs appear to be in thrall to a faction of the grags who are bent on destruction. Differences of opinion are one thing, but this sort of atrocity cannot be borne. Diamond King of Trolls and I are putting pressure on the Low King and we have every expectation he will deal with the matter.

'It has gone too far, Mister Lipwig. Once upon a time the grags were bold dwarfs who checked the mines for firedamp, hence the heavy clothing. Of course that gave them status but, in truth, they were just plucky miners . . . expert at mining, perhaps, but certainly not skilled in politics and thinking. After all, you don't negotiate with a lump of rock. With people, you negotiate all the time. The Low King knows it. The grags know it but don't like it.

'I am a tyrant and, if I say so myself, good at it, but I understand the ways of people and the way of the world. Everything is mutable. Nothing is unchangeable. A little give and a little take and a little negotiation, and suddenly the balance of the world is back on track again; that is what politics is for. But the politics of the grags consists only of "Do what you are told, we know best." And I find that rather tedious.'

'And I find it tedious when your men wake me up by prodding me,' said Moist.

'Really, is that all?' said Vetinari. 'I shall tell them not to prod too much in future.' He smiled and said, 'Mister Lipwig, Commander Vimes is a decent man and he spends much of his time telling people what to do and that is how the Watch works. It's not an area where freelancing is allowed. Things have to be seen to be done, in the proper manner. There is indeed a difference between tyranny and running a police force. There must be rules that everyone understands. Do you understand, Mister Lipwig?'

The Patrician stared at Moist, who said, 'Yes, I understand. The commander is Vetinari's terrier and I—'

'You, Mister Lipwig, are *useful* and a conduit for serendipity. For example, I understand you have just blessed us with more goblins at a time when we need them. Apart from that, I am told by Sydney, the head ostler, that one of our golem horses arrived here declaring "Give me livery or give me death". We had been given to understand that golem horses do not talk, but it would appear, Mister Lipwig, that you have introduced that one to the delights of speech. I am impressed.'

Lord Vetinari's smile was widening. 'What a little bundle of joy you are, Mister Lipwig.' He sighed and continued, 'To think I once fed you to Mister Trooper's capable hands. He often asks after your wellbeing. You know he never forgets a neck. Now off you go, Mister Lipwig . . . your audience needs you.'

The Low King's bellow of rage and betrayal when the news of the massacre at the railhead arrived echoed around the state quarters and into every corner of the great cavern. Bats dropped out of the ceiling, in the bakeries the dough refused to rise, and the silver on the decorative weaponry tarnished.

Rhys Rhysson sat down heavily on the Scone of Stone and waved the clacks flimsy he had just received.

'Dwarfs have killed railway workers!' he shouted. 'Ordinary men, going about their business in an enterprise that would be useful to dwarfs as well as humans.' The King looked almost in tears and thumped a fist into the palm of his hand. 'This after the clacks towers!' he said, with a groan of loss. 'This is a message from Diamond King of Trolls and he is trying not to upset me, but I think he feels sorry for me.'

He raised his voice and shouted, 'And this is the king of the trolls, our one-time arch enemy, but now a personal friend of mine! What will *he* think about the trustworthiness of dwarfs now? Thanks to intelligence gathered by the Ankh-Morpork Watch, including our own Cheery Littlebottom, we have the names of the idiots who did the deed. And now I know exactly who is behind it all.'

He paused and glared at the growing crowd. 'Where is Ardent? Bring him to me at once! I'll show him what his idiotic ranting has caused! I want him brought here in chains if possible. Good heavens, Tak gave us the Koom Valley Accord and now the little blister is trying to break it.'

The crowd was bigger now and the voice of the King was even louder. 'I repeat, I want him here. Now. Today. No excuses. No second chances. No redemption. Let it be known that the King will not let the benefits of the Koom Valley Accord be turned to dust by adventurers who believe that the past is still with us and belongs to them. All I see is its sterile echo.

'And I notice these days talk against goblins who are working in the human industries, such as the new railway and the clacks. I hear a lot of complaints that it is taking work from us dwarfs, but why is that? Because goblins learn quickly, work hard and are glad to be in Ankh-Morpork! And the dwarfs? We have factions that bring us down with every flaming tower . . . Who would trust us after that? Remember, if Tak teaches us anything, he teaches us to be tolerant of all sapient shapes. Let me tell you, the world changes with every generation and if we don't learn to surf on the tide then we will be smashed on the rocks.'

By the Low King's side, Bashfull Bashfullsson picked up the theme. He looked around at the assembled dwarfs and spoke.

'Tak did not expect the stone to have life, but when it did, he smiled upon it, saying "*All Things Strive*".' Glaring at the onlookers, Bashfullsson continued, 'Time and again the last testament of Tak has been stolen in a pathetic attempt to kill the nascent future at birth and this is not only an untruth, it is a blasphemy! Tak even finds it in his heart to suffer the Nac Mac Feegles, possibly for their entertainment value, but I wonder if he will continue to tolerate *us* . . . He must look at us now with sorrow, which I hope will not turn into rage. Surely the patience of Tak must find some limitations somewhere.'

Bashfullsson bowed to the Low King and said, 'I am your servant, your majesty. What would you have of me?'

The King, still red in the face, said, 'I won't have you bow to me, my friend, I rather think I should bow to you. Your words are wise as ever and will be proclaimed in every mine.'

At this point a dwarf arrived in the chamber at a run and whispered something to the Low King's loyal secretary, Aeron, who looked sombre.

'I regret to report, sire, that Ardent and his friends seem to have disappeared.'

'So, the stupid troublemaker has run away,' hissed the Low King in barely suppressed fury. He raised his voice and announced to the crowd, 'They are banished. All of them. No doubt the cowards will find a place to hide, but anyone who helps them will be treated as traitors, not to me but to the Scone.'

In the privacy of the robing room a little while later, the King was pacing up and down when Aeron arrived with the latest report.

'They've caught some of the small fry, but the main players have indeed got away.' As he mentioned a couple of names, Rhys Rhysson's face went as cold as marble. Aeron placed a calming hand on his shoulder and continued, 'Albrecht and the folk of his mines are on your side, though many of the others appear to be wavering.'

'Wavering? That's not good enough. I need their full commitment,' said the King.

His secretary smiled. 'You'll get it, I'm sure. There may be some rogue elements still to be mopped up but we'll get them soon. But do be careful, Rhys, I can see this is taking a lot out of you and that's not good. And you do have another card to play.'

The King shook his head. 'Not yet, but perhaps some time soon, at a point of my choosing. I just have to find the moment.'

Aeron smiled again. And then there was the sound of a kiss.

The dwarf vandal had a stroke of luck. There was Engine One, right below him, the one they called Iron Girder, and there was no time to waste. He was an expert, and cunning, and the grags would pay handsomely if even one wretched locomotive was destroyed.

He dropped down silently from the roof and landed just behind the prestigious engine. It was a good time to throw a monkey wrench in the gears . . . There were guards, he knew, but they were stupid and sluggish and tonight they were on secondment and

189

patrolling a long way away. He had checked and double-checked. And so he soundlessly approached the locomotive, alone in her cavernous shed.

There were so many things you could do to kill a railway engine and he had imagined them all. And so in the dark, ready to climb up again, out of the skylight, he unrolled his bag of implements, all carefully wrapped in hide so they didn't clink or rattle, and stepped up purposefully on to the footplate of Iron Girder . . .

. . . and in the gloom the locomotive spat live steam, instantly filling the air with a pink fog . . .

The dwarf waited, unable to move, and a sombre voice said, PLEASE DO NOT PANIC. YOU ARE MERELY DEAD.

The vandal stared at the skeletal figure, managed to get himself in order and said to Death, 'Oh . . . I don't regret it, you know. I was doing the work of Tak, who will now welcome me into paradise with open arms!'

For a person who didn't have a larynx Death made a good try at clearing his throat. WELL, YOU CAN HOPE, BUT CONSIDERING WHAT YOU INTENDED, IF I WERE YOU I WOULD START HOPING HARDER RIGHT NOW AND, PERHAPS, VERY QUICKLY INDEED. Death continued, in tones as dry as granite, TAK MIGHT INDEED BE GENTLE. STRIVE AS YOU HAVE NEVER STRIVEN. YES, TAK MIGHT BE GENTLE, OR . . .

The vandal listened to the sound of silence, the sound like a bell with, alas, no clapper, but finally the dreadful silence ended in . . . NOT.

Iron Girder had screamed the shrill whistling scream of a lady in distress that had cut through the air like a knife, and by the time Corporal Nobby Nobbs and Sergeant Colon reached the shed, running extremely carefully and precisely,* all they found besides

* Colon and Nobby had lived a long time in a dangerous occupation and they knew how not to be dead. To wit, by arriving when the bad guys had got away.

Iron Girder was some warm dampness, vaguely pink, a tool roll and a few fragments of bone.

'It looks like the locomotive fought back!' said Nobby. 'I know what this is, sarge. It's eldritch – uncanny, you could say.'

Fred Colon stepped forward and said, 'It don't look oblong to me, Nobby. Look at this crowbar and tool roll . . . You can't tell me that the engine lies awake at night like an old biddy keeping a poker beside her bed to fight off burglars. I reckon she was being coy. Live steam! It's a good job me and you were able to scare away all the other assailants!'

'And they was *very* heavily armed,' said Nobby, speaking very deliberately, to make things absolutely clear, 'but they didn't have the spunk to face us, that's what it was.'

Water was dripping from the stout girders high up in the shed. Colon looked around and said, 'Hey, Nobby, what's that white thing up there embedded in the roof?'

Nobby squinted and said, 'Er, it looks like half a skull if you want my opinion, sarge, and it's still steaming.'

In the distance were sounds of thudding feet as the golem guards came at speed and quickly spread out.

Nobby raised his voice and said, 'We'd better tell them that the others'll be ten mile away by now, sarge, at the speed they were going, and I think old Vimesy might give us a day off in lieu for this night's work.'

'But look,' said Colon. 'We've been patrolling past that locomotive time and time again and nothing has happened to us.'

'We weren't proposing to smash her up, now, were we, sarge?'

'What? Are you saying Iron Girder knows who her friends are? Do me a favour . . . she's only a lump of old metal.' And in the silence something made a little clinking noise. Colon and Nobby held their breath.

'Wonderful machine, though, ain't she, Nobby! Look at those beautiful smooth lines!'

There was another pause as breaths continued to be held and Nobby said, 'Well, the golems are here now, sarge, and it's the end of our shift. I'll write a fulsome report as soon as we get back to the yard and that reminds me, you've got to give me my pencil back.'

The two of them perambulated away at impressive speed and for a while Iron Girder was alone; and then there was a very small sound that appeared to be half whistle and half giggle.

Sooner or later everything to do with the railway passed across Moist's desk and generally he hastened it all along its way. Today he was looking across the paperwork at a clearly embarrassed Dick Simnel.

'Now come on, Dick, you tell me what you think happened last night. It seems as if the grags were setting about to put more than a dent in Iron Girder. This could be connected with the attack on the railhead, but there were some . . . significant differences. I expect there are a lot of ways of putting a locomotive out of commission, but the Watch was on the scene within minutes and according to them *she* fought back and got one of the murderous band. I know the two watchmen of old and every fight they have is always against much bigger forces, at least that's what they say if no one else is around, but it does seem that she got her retribution in first, you might say, and boiled him. They're still mopping the floor. How do you think that happened, Dick? Was it magic of some sort?'

Simnel blushed and said, 'Mister Lipwig, I'm an engineer. I don't believe in magic, but I'm wondering right now whether magic believes in Iron Girder. Every day when I come into work there're the train spotters, always there, and now they've got little sheds of their own . . . Have you noticed? They almost know more about 'er than I do, I tell thee, and I look at t'people who're still taking rides, I look at their faces and they're not the faces of engineers, they're more like the faces of people going to church, and so I wonder what's 'appening. No, I can't tell you how Iron Girder killed the dwarf who was trying to kill her and why she's never done it while everyday folk are around. That looks like thinking to me and I don't know how she thinks.'

Dick was glowing red now and Moist felt sorry for the engineer who lived in a world where things did what they were told, all the little numbers adding up, all the calculations dancing to the rattle of the sliding rule just as they should. But now he was in a conceptual world where the authority of that sliding rule held no sway.

Dick looked desperately at Moist and said, 'Do you think it possible that an engine like Iron Girder has a . . . soul?'

Oh, dear, thought Moist, he's really having problems here. Out loud he said, 'Well, I see you move your hands over her once she's stopped and it seems to me that you're petting her, and I notice that all the other drivers do that too, and although the Flyers have numbers I notice that the drivers give them names and even talk to them – in expletives, occasionally, but nevertheless they're talking to a mechanical thing. I do wonder if life is catching somehow, because I also notice that every time people go for joyrides on Iron Girder they pat her too and they would swear they don't know why. But what do *you* think?'

'Ee, I know what you mean. In the early days when I were just getting started I remember I spoke to Iron Girder all t'time and shouted often enough and occasionally swore as well, especially if she were truculent. Aye, you might have a point. There's a lot of me in her; a lot of me blood and buckets of me sweat and many, many tears. I've lost the end of one thumb to her and most of my fingernails are blue and I suppose, when you think about it, there really is a lot of her in me.'

He looked ashamed when he said that and so Moist quickly jumped in with, 'I think you're right, Dick, it's one of those times when you have to stop thinking about how and why and just remember that whatever's happening is working and it just might not work if anyone gets smart and tries to find the soul of what's happening. There are times when a sliding rule just doesn't cut the mustard and if I was you this morning I'd get her all sleek and shiny and let her *see* her worshippers and *feel* their worship. They're yearning for something and I don't know what it is, so drink up the gravy and don't spoil things with too much thinking or too much worrying either. And I promise you I won't mention a word of this conversation to anyone.'

And then he brightened up and said, 'Come on, Dick, life is good! Has your sliding rule allowed you to come to an arrangement with Miss Emily?'

Simnel blushed. 'Aye, we've been doing some talking, mostly about Iron Girder, and her mam's letting me come to tea wi' 'er tomorrow.'

'In that case, I suggest you get yourself a new shirt . . . you know, one that isn't greasy, and clean your boots and your nails and everything else, and now you're getting loaded up with money you must get yourself a sharp new suit. I know a few places that'd give you a good deal.' He sniffed and added, 'And have a bath, why don't you, for the sake of Miss Emily.'

Dick blushed further and grinned. 'Right you are, Mister Lipwig. I wish I could be deb on air like you are.'

'It's easy, Dick, you've just got to be yourself. They can't ever take that away from you.'

And when Moist left his desk for another look at where last night's excitement had taken place, he met Harry King, dressed to the nines and distressed to the maximum.

Harry flourished a bow tie at Moist and said, 'I hate these damn things, I mean, what's the point?' He growled. 'Got another bloody civic thing on tonight, Effie just thrives on them. I told her I'm busy, what with dealing with the railway, but she's determined to make a better man of me. And all this business about what knife and fork you eat from, it's a deliberate puzzle set out to make a simple bloke like me feel like a stranger. Whatever you pick up isn't going to change what the food tastes like, but Effie presses my knee hard if I gets it wrong.

'She wants me to have electrocution lessons, gods be damned, and I'm putting my foot down about that one. Knobs or not, I'm still Harry King and I'm still going to sound like Harry King. And I told Effie that I don't mind giving the money away to orphanages and suchlike – I like to see the faces of the little kiddies light up like daisies – it's the swank I don't like and all the incessant chattering when I could be doing good work in my office. Effie says it's knoblyess obligay, but just because I've got a lot of knobs I don't have to accept it, right? It's a terrible thing when a man can't be himself, knobs or no knobs.'

Fifty miles turnwise of Ankh-Morpork lies the Effing Forest, a source of laughter for some, but nevertheless, throughout the year, full of birdsong and, surprisingly, the occasional logger, as well as the family-run coal mines that are too small for the dwarfs to covet but just about big enough to scratch a living.

On this fine morning in the Wesley family forge, Crucible Wesley was arguing with his brother.

'Okay, you're a blacksmith, granted, but that engine looked complicated to oi. Jed, you're a good smith and a big lad, but I can't see you hammering out a whole locomotive on your own. You need a bit more of the book learning, say oi. You saw those boys at that there compound in the smoke with their sliding rulers, although you couldn't quite work out what them was for.'

The aforesaid Jed, dripping perspiration and stink, looked up from his anvil. 'Look, it's simple, you boils up the water, you boils it up *really* hot, and that drives the pistons and it's them as turns the wheels. There ain't really that much to it, apart from the oiling and the greasing. Oi reckon that stopping it once started'll be the 'ardest thing to do.'

Crucible Wesley, considered by locals as the brains of the outfit, in so far as the outfit had any brains, was nervous about this and went on, 'I know you were Blacksmith of the Year in Scrote three years running and got the silver cup that our mam's so proud of, but oi dunno . . . Oi reckon there's summat more to it'n that. Trade secrets and whatnot.'

Jed appeared to commune with the spirits for a while and then he announced, 'Well, oi've got the boiler half done and that's a fact. And oi reckon that if we takes it slowly there shouldn't be nuffin' to worry about. After all, oi seen steam coming out of Mam's kettle, 'tis only wet air after all.'

He thumped the boiler standing on its makeshift pedestal next to his work bench with one enormous hand.

'Come on, help me outside with this and us'll give it a go . . . We can always shut her down if she looks like she's turning on us and oi reckon oi can outsmart a bloody kettle.'

They carried the huge vessel outside, although, truth to tell, Jed proudly picked up most of the weight on his own. His brother watched in admiration and a certain amount of trepidation, or it would have been trepidation had he known the word existed. As it was he could feel sweat trickling down his back. He started edging away backwards and once again he tried to remonstrate with his elder brother.

'Well, oi dunno, Jed, they was doing all those measurements and things like that with levers and suchlike and when it was hissing, it damn well hissed.'

'Yeah, and it cost we a dollar to see it! Don't 'ee worry about a slipping stick . . . like I said, oi reckon oi got more brains than a boiler! And if it gives oi any problem then I'll hammer it out into horseshoes. Come on, I'll get the fire going and you can help oi pump the bellows.'

After Crucible had managed to help his brother set the boiler up in the clean open air amongst the trees, he had one last stab at trying to crowbar some sense into the dialogue.

'Oi reckon it's too difficult, otherwise us'd hear about other folk doing it as well.'

But to his dismay this suggestion only served to make his brother even more determined to tame the steam, because the man said, tapping the side of his nose, 'That's because oi reckon they weren't as clever as oi!'

There is something vaguely worrying about the word '*reckon*' that leaves the ear, for many hard to understand reasons, wishing it was something else a little more certain and a little less frightening. And as bad luck would have it, some twenty minutes later an ear was exactly what spiralled down out of the settling steaming fog and through mangled trees that looked as if they had been scythed by dragons, and the birds that were coming down cooked . . .

Moist was, by inclination, a stranger to the concept of two in the morning, a time that happened to other people. He didn't object to a certain amount of early alfresco when he was on the road, especially on the rail road, which was more like camping and therefore fun, but to be awakened in his own bed in the small hours was an abomination. That cried to the heavens for justice, although he did not cry at Sir Harry, who had just arrived in Scoone Avenue with all hell following him.

Crossly the butler rushed to get in front of Sir Harry as etiquette required, but Sir Harry swarmed up the stairs waving a clacks flimsy at anyone he could see, and burst into Moist's bedroom, booming, 'Someone has been buggering around with a steam contraption and has managed to kill two people, including himself, down in the Effing Forest. And you know what? Clacksmen on the Scrote tower spotted the explosion then went out and found the carnage, and you know the clacksmen! The news is already all over the bloody place! And so, apparently, are bits of the poor buggers!

Two people dead, Mister Lipwig. The press'll have our guts for garters.'

By this time Moist had managed to get his pants on the right way up. He spluttered, 'But Harry, we aren't doing anything in the Effing Forest at the moment. There's going to be a little branch line that goes to Scrote and that'll be a very good earner, but this is nothing to do with us. Crossly, please get Sir Harry a stiff brandy and a soft chair.'

'Nothing to do with us or not, Moist, you know the press will be round us like flies on a midden.'

Moist said, to the annoyance of Harry, 'Trust me, Harry. Trust me. It wasn't us and I see no reason to worry. I'll deal with the press. I imagine they'll all be going to the Effing place as soon as it gets light, so if you don't mind I'll head there right now and be ahead of the game.'

'It's no bloody game!' Harry boomed.

And over his shoulder, Moist said, 'I'm sorry, but it helps to think of it like that, Harry.'

Just as Moist was heading down the stairs with Harry simmering behind him, Adora Belle arrived home. She sometimes worked nights on the Grand Trunk; she told Moist that it was to keep people on their toes, but he knew that she actually loved the quiet watches of a clear night when messages would twinkle from hill to hill like fireflies.

That was the spell of the clacks, and it wasn't only goblins who felt it. Adora Belle knew and didn't mind that the clacksmen and clackswomen would fraternize along the wonderful scintillating lines of light. After all, quite a few marriages had been brokered through the unsuspecting ether in the small hours of the night and sooner or later little clacksmen and women would be born.

Adora Belle had once told Moist, 'You know that it takes a special kind of person to be a clacksman and especially a clackswoman, and it's important that they marry and have children with the right kind of blood. They're our future, and heaven help them if their spouse doesn't also work on the clacks. Clacks people are a type and like attracts like.'

When Moist told her the news of the accident in the Effing Forest she disappeared into her office, and Moist could hear the goblins stampeding towards it and then a rattle of the clacks on the roof. Before long she sent down another goblin with a flimsy that said, 'News from Scrote. Stop. It's a boiler that burst. Stop. Not a train. Stop. Horrible deaths of two people, but no engine as such. Stop.'

That latest discovery made Moist doubly sure of himself and he clamped his hand on Harry's shoulder and said, 'Please, don't worry, Harry. I know how this one is going to go. All I need is for you and Mister Simnel to meet me in the Effing Forest as quickly as you can. And, oh, I think we might need Thunderbolt.'

It was time to talk to the golem horse once more. Moist was rather concerned about taking it on another long journey so soon, but the horse said, 'Sir, I am a horse. Being a horse is my passion in life, and getting to the Effing Forest will be a breeze. Saddle up, please, and let's be off.'

Moist had found something like a sweet spot in the gait. No muscle and bone horse could possibly gallop at this speed without legs getting tangled, but even so he covered the fifty miles to the Effing Forest by sunrise without much in the way of groinal sprains.

He immediately sought out the nearest pub to the accident, which was the premises of Edward Forefather, purveyor of fine beers, stouts and ales. At least that's what it said on the rather large plaque behind the bar and Moist was not going to argue.

The publican, already up and dressed, looked him up and down and said, 'I've been expecting somebody like you. You're from the city, aren't you? It's about the explosion, isn't it? Are you one of them reporters? Only I wants money if you're a reporter.'

Moist said, 'No, I'm not, I'm with the railway. I heard about the explosion and came to see what had happened.'

Forefather looked him up and down again and said, 'We know all about it. It was them Wesley brothers. How good is your stomach, young man? Of course, I'd leave the bar to help you, but that means I'd have to get my wife up to start on the early shift for the miners. They'll be coming up for their breakfast soonish.'

Moist understood the unspoken request and handed the man a reasonable sum, then followed him outside where he was led along a path into the forest. This part of the forest was quite pleasant, not too dark, the kind of place where people would go for a picnic, but as they got in further, Moist could see that whatever they were going to find next, it wasn't going to be a picnic.

In a clearing just a short walk from the pub the trees were stripped of their leaves, tangled wood was everywhere and the remains of the forge were embedded in various trunks. And there were fragments of the stricken boiler, too, some of them driven so hard into mighty oaks that Moist couldn't pull them out. The haze in the clearing sent a chill down his spine.

He took a deep breath and said, 'What happened to the bodies, Mister Forefather?'

'Oh, yes, sir. I've got them back in my cellar, it being quite cold down there. They're in a bucket. It isn't a big bucket, either. It was two brothers, strapping great lads. Crucible was the brains and Jed was the blacksmith. Although in the bucket I couldn't tell you which bits were whose. Jed was boasting about building a railway engine one day, and to tell you the truth, sir, he was a very good blacksmith, but what he knew about locomotives I wouldn't dare think of. But he thought he could do it and all his mates were egging him on.'

He hesitated for a moment and then said, 'I was the first one to arrive here and mostly all there was was a mist, and I didn't like that at all. It was clammy and hot and made you want to puke. And that's it, sir. Not much more to be said, sir.'

Moist looked up and said, 'Should there really be an anvil up in that tree?'

The publican looked at him and then at the tree and said, 'You're a man with his eye on the business, aren't you? Generally speaking, the anvil has always been on the ground, by and large, but it was a most powerful bang.'

Moist brightened up as best he could and said, 'Thank you, Mister Forefather. Pretty soon there'll be a lot of journalists coming to see all this and I'm sorry about that, but they turn up like flies.'

'That's all right, sir. Good for business. Journalists drink twice as much as anyone else and for twice as long. We had them around when the mine fell in and they really can take their liquor.' Mr Forefather was rubbing his hands in anticipation.

In fact, it was mid-morning before most of the journalists put in an appearance. But well ahead of the pack was Otto Chriek of the *Ankh-Morpork Times*, who was always first on the scene.*

As for the rest of the press gang, they arrived at cross purposes, all of them expecting the others to tell them what was going on.

Mr Forefather was making hay by making bacon butties while his wife was frying eggs and the obligatory slice.

Moist put the word out that, while of course the railway was in no way involved, the owners were coming to see the accident site for themselves and would be happy to answer questions. By the time Harry King, Simnel and Thunderbolt arrived, Moist could see Forefather carefully raising the prices on his beers as, gradually, the pub filled from across the Sto Plains.

*

* It would be impolite to ask Otto how he got around so quickly. Of course, everybody knew that he was a vampire, but he was a fervent black ribboner and so whatever anybody thought they knew about him, they didn't talk about it.

Moist had already gleaned from Mrs Forefather that the brothers' old mum was being comforted by friends back in her own home, a short walk from the pub, and he was careful to see that no mention of this or the current whereabouts of the unfortunate Wesley brothers was made to the gang of journalists. And he surprised himself by realizing that this was a sensible and humanitarian thing to do, some of the press gang being the sort who would most definitely say things like, 'Well now, Mrs Wesley, how did you feel when you found out that both of your sons had been melted?'

As the press seized on the new arrivals, Moist, like a chess grandmaster, tried to keep his king, that would be Sir Harry King, away from the worst questions and instead played his shining knight, Mr Dick Simnel. He was learning a lot from Mr Simnel. They faced him with questions like, 'What do you say to people who think that live steam will kill everybody in the end?'

To which Dick's answer was, 'I don't know, sir, I've never met anyone who thought that. Steam is *very* dangerous if you don't know what you're doing and I feel sorry for them poor boys.'

Hardwick of the *Pseudopolis Daily Press* said, 'I hear your own engine killed someone the night before last. What do you have to say about that, Mister Simnel?'

Before Dick could speak Thunderbolt came down like a judge and said, 'The person in question was clearly trying to sabotage the locomotive and while we naturally regret the fatality he was in a place where he shouldn't have been, doing something that he shouldn't have done. It is evident that he entered the engine shed through a skylight, which seems to show lawful business was not on his mind. His death, alas, was self-inflicted.'

'And what about Mister Simnel senior?' said Hardwick. 'Was *his* death self-inflicted?'

Simnel took the floor once again. 'It just goes to show you have to treat steam with respect, and yes, I learned t'hard way when me

202

dad died and that's why I measure and test and measure again. It's all about t'little numbers. It's all about taking care. It's all about getting the knowledge. Steam has its rules. After all, we call it *live* steam for a reason. It's dangerous in t'wrong hands, but my hands, sir, have spent a long time building boilers and static engines, just to see 'ow far I could go. That generally meant me hiding behind a stone wall while bits of engine whistled over me 'ead. You learn by your mistakes, if you're lucky, and I tried to make mistakes just to see 'ow that could be done, and although this is not the time to say it, you 'ave to be clever and you 'ave to be smart and you 'ave to be 'umble in the face of such power. You have to think of every little detail. You have to make notes and educate yourself and then, only then, steam becomes your friend. Like Iron Girder, you've all seen her. Yes, miss?'

Moist recognized Sacharissa Cripslock. She said, 'You speak so caringly of your locomotive, Mister Simnel, and so I have to ask, do you have a sweetheart?'

There was a certain amount of tittering from the hacks, but Simnel barely blinked. 'Why, thank you for asking and yes, there is indeed a young lady who is looking at me kindly.'

Simnel turned towards another waving notebook and said, 'Yes, sir?'

'Grievous, sir, Grievous Johnson from the *Big Cabbage Gazette*. Is it your intention to share your knowledge with others trying to build their own engines? That might save a lot of lives.'

Simnel glanced at Moist and Moist looked at Harry King, who dropped an eyebrow, which Moist knew he could take as a yes.

Simnel knew it too and had spotted the signal. He said, 'Oh, yes, sir, we will do. At least the basics, safety and so forth. But it'll cost. Research and development has to cost. But I'll tek apprentices, show them t'ropes, and generally make them safer workers. In fact we're planning regular classes, a Railway Academy, you might call it.' His smile dropped as he continued, 'O'course I'm reet sorry about those lads, sir, but learning is hard and failure is sharp. I'd hate that kind of thing to happen again, but it's got to be done proper like. No scrimping. No cutting corners.'

Mr Simnel had won again. The press couldn't deal with a straightforward man. The certainty in his face simply disarmed them and possibly, thought Moist, made them wish they were better people. There wasn't an inch of politics in him and that stunned them.

Simnel was still beaming at them. 'Aye, if any of you'd like to come back to t'works at Ankh-Morpork at any time I'll gladly show you around. I'll show you *everything*.'

Far away from Moist and certainly from common sense, the grags took counsel, if it could be called that. Things in the outside world were changing so fast.

'We are losing, you do know that?' said a voice in the darkness.

'It can't be helped. It's the zeitgeist, it's in the air,' said another voice, sounding somewhat more cracked.

'And what do we care about the air, or any kind of geist? We are the justified, the stalwarts, the kings and servants of the darkness. Our people *will* come back.'

'No, they're leaving! Burning clacks towers was stupid! I say stupid! Everybody wants their news and it makes us look like criminals, which we are. And that's *not* justified.'

A dwarf who had been silent during the conclave in the cavern was remembering the old Djelibeybi legend about the way to get an ass down from the minaret, and of course the answer was you first have to teach it *not* to be an ass. But in what world could that ever happen when you're dealing with grags? It was, she thought, time to see for herself just how life was in the lands of the Troll King. She had been very careful, oh dear, so very careful and so she had survived, she hoped, to be the jackass that got out of the minaret, but alas, the idiots were still encouraging impressionable young dwarfs to attack the clacks towers. Whoever had had that idea had doomed them without dialogue.

Rhys Rhysson was right, she thought. We've lost all balance. We have to get out of here, out of everything that is *here*, out into the light. Surely, she thought, they wouldn't suspect her. She had been forensic in her search for unbelievers.

Nevertheless, when at last she ran the knives got her before she stumbled. And then there were eight left in the cavern and those watching in the darkness watched more closely to see who would be next. The time would be coming when the purity of darkness could not be mocked!

The terrible fact was that when dwarfs schism, they *schism* . . . every deviation from the norm was treated as an attack on all that was truly dwarfish.

Others had already fled and died, and who could say they knew how many more were left, not only in this cavern but in other caverns all the way to Uberwald. And the trouble with madness was that the mad didn't know they were mad. The grags came down heavily on those who did not conform and seemed not to realize that this was like stamping potatoes into the mud to stop them growing.

Everywhere one looked there were committees nowadays, mostly because, by arrangement and with the blessing of Lord Vetinari, other principalities, large towns and city states saw no reason to wait for the completion of *their* slice of the magic of the train, and, seizing these opportunities, new companies were entering the railway business with rather more success than the Wesley brothers. Drumknott was in his element as the paperwork mounted and his files multiplied; he contrived to be everywhere and into everything, ably supported by Mr Thunderbolt.

There were committees discussing industry standards, public safety, passenger welfare, whether one company's freight truck could be hitched to another company's train to complete its journey without need to offload* – and all the knotty financial and legal arrangements that would entail.

The whole proposition of other businessmen launching their own railways had made Harry call for Thunderbolt.

After hearing Harry's complaints, the lawyer said, 'It's a matter of patents, Sir Harry. You know, all that fiddly stuff that you said you paid other people to get their heads around? Well, Mister Simnel and I have filed applications for every one of his innovations. But I am sure there is more than one way of building a machine to run on rails. You cannot patent the idea of a railway as such, and if you take a walk down the Street of Cunning Artificers you will find someone quite bright enough to discover how to make a train that will run on rails without infringing any of the patents I have been able to obtain for you.

'The idea of steam locomotion as such has been there for all to see and we all know that a boiling kettle will try to lift its own lid. Being clever, some young man watching the fire will work out that if he builds a bigger kettle he will be able to lift a bigger kettle lid. Although, as we saw at Effing Forest, he soon learns that it's not as simple as that. They're not all as bright and clever as Dick Simnel.'

Harry snorted. 'Stupid hayseeds. Not a patch on our Dick and his lads. All they've done is leave their old mum bound for the poorhouse.' And Sir Harry harrumphed. A full-blown harrumph.

Unaware that his client was temporarily distracted by the thought of a destitute lady living in the Effing Forest, bereft of her boys, her pride and joy, Thunderbolt continued. 'Take Mister Simnel's pressure gauge. Once the principle is proved and

---

* A development that proved fatal to the Brassica Carriage Company, which had elected to construct its engines and tracks to a gauge based on the horse-drawn cabbage delivery carts.

206

understood, the Cunning Artificers, extremely cunning as they are, might well find some way of achieving the same results without breaching patent. It's what they do. Cunning by name *and* nature.'

Thunderbolt had got Harry's attention now. 'And before you explode, Sir Harry, it is all within the law.'

'What? After all I've done and the money I've put in!' Harry's face was as red as a beacon. He looked as though he needed one of Dick's pressure gauges himself.

Moist decided to intervene. 'Harry, the whole point of trains is that they're universal. Put them on the tracks and away they go.'

In his mellifluous tones, the lawyer continued. 'If I were you, Sir Harry, I would simply leave it to me to keep an eye on such things as patents and licences and regulation whilst you and Mister Simnel fill the world with steam. And remember, Sir Harry, the important thing is that you were the first. Nobody can take that away. You, Sir Harry, are on what I believe is called the hog's back, the top of the heap, the founder of the railway. The Ankh-Morpork and Sto Plains Hygienic Railway Company is as solid as the bank.'

The troll smiled and said, 'Or, indeed, as me – and I am diamond.'

Business for the Hygienic Railway Company was indeed booming, and the workforce ever expanding. The goblins from the Quirmian maquis had passed news back to their friends about the opportunities in the Big Wahoonie, which they seized with alacrity. And once Dick's announcement of his Railway Academy had been splashed across the papers, in the wake of the Effing Forest incident, there were queues of people every day wanting to be taken on as apprentices. Simnel was heavy on the lads he accepted, telling them they had got to let the iron into their soul. And it was not unknown for him to kick someone straight out again if he felt they weren't up to scratch.

Returning from another trip to review progress on the Quirm line, Moist paused to take in the latest changes to the compound. There were the apprentices . . . engrossed in their own little mechanical world with Wally and Dave tutoring them and making sure they had got their caps sufficiently flat. Moist watched them in their blissful mechanical dream and he could not help but notice that they were surrounded by goblins, most definitely paying attention, seriously so, as if their lives depended upon it, and gathering up any discarded greasy rags, which to goblins were like *haute couture*, and the mark of a real swell back in the burrows. And near by the train spotters were comparing numbers. And there was Mr Simnel, equally engrossed in his latest contraption.

As Moist crossed the compound towards him, Mr Simnel, with his greasy hat and his grubby shirt, the sleeves of which were rolled up to his elbows, wiped his grinning face with a rag, leaving a greasy smear on the grease.

'Mister Lipwig! Grand to see you! I have something to show you! We brought this beauty down from Sto Lat yesterday and built it last night!' He was shouting even louder than normal. 'Essential equipment! It's my design! I built it and I call it t'turning table!'

Moist almost had to put his hands over his ears as the engineer stepped closer. It's because he works with the trains all day, he thought, he has to be heard among all the hissing and clanking, but I wonder how he talks to his Emily?

And as for the turning table, it was, well, it was a table and it turned: a huge metal table with a pair of rails running across the centre, which was turned around by means of a large handle attached to a ratchet mechanism being wound by a troll with a look of intense concentration. Moist watched while Dick gave his demonstration.

'Great! That's brilliant, Dick, but . . . for the sake of the hard of thinking, what in hell's name is it for?'

Dick looked at Moist as if he was an infant and said, 'Can't you see it, Mister Lipwig? You drives your engine on to t'turning table and, here's the clever bit, you turn the whole thing around and it's now facing t'other way!'

And then Mr Simnel danced on the circular iron table in his clogs as it slowly revolved, and shouted, 'Grand! Gradely! We're nearly there!'

The triumph was emphasized with a hiss like Iron Girder at the end of a long run, which would have been a fitting end to the experiment, except that it took some time to get the troll to stop turning the handle so that Dick, who was starting to look a little green from the continued revolutions, could get off.

Happy that the tussle of wills between the other companies operating on the Sto Plains was being ably managed by Thunderbolt and Drumknott, no doubt with assistance from the dark clerks, Moist was looking forward to a period of domestic harmony, when he was summoned to the palace.

He was not surprised to see his lordship staring at the day's crossword puzzle. Drumknott whispered from behind Moist, 'There's a new compiler, you know, and I'm sad to say that it looks like an improvement. However, his lordship is doing his best.'

Lord Vetinari looked up and said, 'Mister Lipwig. Can it be that there is a word *quaestuary*?'

Actually, Moist knew exactly what it meant because of his misspent youth and so he girded his metaphorical loins and said, 'I think you might find, sir, that it means someone doing business simply for profit. I remember coming across the word once upon a time and it puzzled me because I thought profit was what business is all about.'

His lordship's face didn't move a muscle until he said, 'Quite so, Mister Lipwig.' And he pushed the paper aside and stood up. 'I hear that the line to Quirm is all but completed . . . If the Quirm Assembly is still dragging its feet I shall have to have a word with Monsieur Jean Némard . . . one of my special words. I have to say, Mister Lipwig, that your contribution to the development of the railway has been most gratifying to observe and I am sure we are all in your debt.'

'Oh,' said Moist. 'Does that mean I can get back to my day job and see my wife more than once every week or so?'

'Of course you may, Mister Lipwig! You have, after all, been acting in an entirely voluntary capacity. However, *my* business now concerns the railway to Uberwald. So I have to ask you, how soon can we have a locomotive run all the way there? Non-stop.'

Moist was taken aback. 'You couldn't do it, sir. Not non-stop. You have to take on water and coal and it must be more than a thousand miles up there!'

'Twelve hundred and twenty-five miles *exactly* from Ankh-Morpork to Bonk by coach, although I am aware that the train would have to take a different route.'

'Yes sir, but non-stop—'

'Mister Lipwig. If you're going to tell me that it's impossible you will be down with the kittens in short order. After all, you are the man who gets things done.'

'What's the hurry, sir? The lads are doing a great job, but it would be a rare day if they could lay more than three miles of track, even with all the money Harry King is throwing at it. And then, of course, there's all the unforeseen obstacles along the way and on top of that you know that every city along the Plains wants to be a part of the network. We're spread wide, sir. Any further and we'd split down the middle.'

Vetinari walked around his desk at speed and said, 'Good, then you could both work more efficiently! It appears, Mister Lipwig, that you do not understand the nature of our relationship. I ask, very politely, for you to achieve something, bearing in mind that there are other ways I could ask, and it is your job to get things done. You are, after all, a man who can apparently do *anything*, the great Mister Lipwig, yes? And my advice to you is to cease all the work that does not assist in getting from here to Uberwald in the quickest possible time. Everything else can, and will, wait.'

He held up his hand. 'Do not tell me what the problems are, just tell me the solutions. Indeed, you do not need to tell me the solutions, you merely have to achieve them.'

Moist said, 'Do you mind if I sit down, sir?'

'By all means, Mister Lipwig. Do get the man a drink, Drumknott. He looks a little hot.'

'I have to ask, sir . . . Why does it have to be done like this?'

Vetinari smiled. 'Can you keep a secret, Mister Lipwig?'

'Oh, yes, sir. I've kept lots.'

'Capital. And the point is, so can I. You do not need to know.'

Moist tried. 'Sir! Even now the trains are part of life to a lot of people, especially to those on the Plains who commute! We can't just drop everything, sir!'

'Mister Lipwig. Is there something in the word "tyrant" you do not understand?'

In desperation Moist said, 'We don't have enough workers, sir! Not enough people to man the foundries! Not enough people to dig the ore! We've probably got enough stock now to get halfway, but it's all about the workers.'

'Yes,' said Lord Vetinari. 'It is. Isn't it. Think on that, Mister Lipwig.'

'What about the wizards? Can't they get up off their fat backsides and help their city?'

'Yes, Mister Lipwig, and you know and I know it will rebound on

211

us. Live steam is friendly compared with magic going wrong. No, Mister Lipwig, we will not look to the wizards. You just need to get the train to run to Uberwald on time.'

'And what time would that be, sir?'

'As I say, Mister Lipwig, any time soon.'

'Then I haven't got a prayer. It's going to take months, a year . . . or more . . .'

And suddenly the atmosphere turned to ice and his lordship said, 'Then I suggest you get going.' Vetinari resumed his seat. 'Mister Lipwig, the world lives between those who say it cannot be done and those who say that it can. And in my experience, those who say that it can be done are usually telling the truth. It's just a matter of thinking creatively. Some people say "Think the unthinkable", but that's nonsense – although in your case, sir, I think you have the nerves for it. Think about it. Now, don't let me detain you.'

The door closed behind Moist and silence enveloped the Oblong Office as the Patrician returned his attention to the crossword. Eventually he frowned, filled in a line and laid down the paper.

'Drumknott,' he said, 'how's Charlie's Punch and Judy business going these days? Is he doing well? I wonder whether he might consider a short holiday. Just a short one, that is.'

'Yes, sir,' said Drumknott. 'I'll go and see him this afternoon.'

'That's the way to do it,' said Lord Vetinari.

While he was still reeling from the Patrician's latest demand, Moist found himself riding back to the Effing Forest on a mission for Harry.

'Go and see the old girl and send her my sympathies,' Harry had said. 'Tell her I was impressed at how her boys tried to harness steam and I salute them as pioneers. Have a look around and see what she's got and since it would seem as if I have got gold coming out of my ears then I reckon we can give her a little pension, though for heavens' sake don't let anyone else know. Oh, and tell her that I'll make it certain that her lads will be up frontline when the history of the railway is written down, and say she can call on me at any time.'

The old homestead in the forest was all that Moist had expected, and Mrs Wesley burst into tears when he told her about Harry's offer. She was determined to think of Sir Harry as a saint or angel and if Moist knew anything about the ways of the world Harry's gesture would be all over the forest within hours; and because news spreads, it would get as far as Ankh-Morpork by the end of the day. Moist knew Harry the man as he was: extremely sharp with a heart of gold and tears of soppy. Harry's gesture was entirely Harry, with no ulterior motive, but nevertheless once the news had got around, he would be in all the papers as a benefactor of the poor and therefore a celebrity. Not for the first time Moist deplored his own tendency to see the angles in whatever happened, good or bad.

'*How much?*'

The simple question sounded like a declaration of war, which it almost was, as Harry was presented with the costings for the express line to Bonk.

Moist stood his ground. 'Dick says there's iron everywhere, Harry, but it needs digging out and then it's the making of the steel that uses up the money,' he put in hastily, before Harry could throw anyone down the stairs.

'You've got to put the gold in to get t'steel out, Harry,' said Simnel calmly. 'We've been getting a good deal from the lads down at the smelters, but it's twelve hundred miles to Uberwald, and that's a *lot* of steel.'

'Harry,' Moist said patiently. 'I know very well that when you and your lady first married you used to cut the matches in half to make them last longer. But you are not that man any more. You *can* afford this.'

They watched Harry's face. In truth, Moist knew Harry had kicked his way up from the gutter and was proud of it, but he had made his money cheaply – since minions, on the whole, don't incur much of an overhead – and looked at every suggestion that he should pay for anything as evidence that something was wrong in the world.

Dick Simnel had got the measure of the man and said, 'If I was you, sir, I'd look at my money box and buy as much steel as I possibly could while I can, not making a big fuss about it, otherwise it'll suddenly get more expensive, if you know what I mean. Supply and demand.'

Harry still looked as if he thought people were trying to get something of a move on him, which was his ground state of being, and Moist thought, well, what *does* Harry spend his mountains of money on?

And so he plunged on. 'Go on, Harry, as a customer in good standing, the Royal Bank'll definitely give you a loan, if indeed you ever need one. Though frankly, I know your balance is more than enough to get rails all the way to the moon and back and that's including a fleet of locomotives as well.'

There was a rumble from Mr Thunderbolt. 'Of course, Sir Harry, you could sell shares: that means you *share* some of the outlays but, alas, you also have to *share* some of the dividends. It's up to you.'

Moist saw his cue right there and said, 'You see, Harry, everybody who buys your railway shares would then be dead keen on *their* railway and on your side. It's what the trolls call a no-brain. When the smoke is making you rich, it's *your* smoke and you don't complain about it. And,' Moist took a deep breath, 'if you share the risks you can afford to build houses for the railway workers, too. That way they'll live close to the railway, right alongside it, so they'll always be ready—'

214

'I don't need any telling on that score, Mister Lipwig. The lads that work for me on the conveyor belts all live on the doorstep. Difference is they built their own.'

'The buildings don't have to be little palaces,' Moist said, 'just comfortable, with a bit of a garden, which is nice for the kiddies, and then everyone is happy and you've got it made. After all, who doesn't like to have a place close to their work? Nice and warm with all the coal you need thrown in.'

Harry King would probably punch anyone who called him a philanthropist, but beneath the grumbling there was an undercurrent of curious softness. Elderly employees, no matter their species, ended up with a pension, a rare beast in Ankh-Morpork as a whole, and Moist, as Harry's bank manager, was aware that expensive hospital bills had a habit of disappearing when he got to hear about them. And most certainly at Hogswatch, Harry, grumbling like an elderly troll with a headache, nevertheless made sure all employees had actual named meat on their tables, and lots of it.*

Moist, who knew his man, continued, 'Look at it like this: I know that as a self-made man, sharing would be anathema to your soul, and so you *could* take all the risk and become as rich as Creosote. However, it seems to me, Harry, that you're already as rich as Creosote and so, as a scoundrel, I'd suggest that another fortune is not exactly what you need right now! As your bank manager I'd like to suggest that sharing both the risks and the profits would be the most prudent and socially acceptable way.'

For a moment Moist saw the psyche of Harry King putting together a retort that social acceptability could go and get its hands dirty by doing a proper day's work rather than interfering with

* And yet Harry was still a Titan, a humorous term meaning deep trousers and short fingers, owing to his tendency to look on the disgorging of money in much the same light as root canal surgery delivered by a troll dentist.

honest entrepreneurs who were working their guts out day and night. But Moist also saw the grin, and realized that Harry knew this was all part of the solution. After all, Lord Vetinari liked the people of Ankh-Morpork to feel they had a stake in *their* city.

'Anyway,' he said, to clinch it, 'Vetinari wants the Uberwald route and he's the ultimate boss. Who knows, the city might be very generous with its level of funding. The trains go round and round and so does the money.'

The main line to Quirm was completed with a ceremony at the Ankh-Morpork terminus in which, regrettably, alcohol played a major role. The new engine was launched and named *Fierté d'Quirm* with an especially good bottle of champagne smashed across its boiler by the Marquis des Aix en Pains and his wife who, Moist noticed, was now very cheerfully, as they say in Quirm, enceinte.

And amid all the celebrations, it seemed that it was only Moist who noticed that Simnel had wandered away from the party to wipe the engine clean of sizzling champagne with his handkerchief, which immediately became a greasy rag. He gave Moist a severe look.

'We can't have this kind of thing going on, Mister Lipwig, interfering with the engine . . . not when I'm determined to get us up to forty miles per hour across the flat of the maquis, just to show those lobsters what we can do.'

On the maiden journey, Moist rode with Simnel and the stoker on the footplate as the maquis passed away behind them at terrible speed, with goblins waving from every rock and ancient tree. He thought at one point that he had spotted Of the Twilight the Darkness, waving, but to his surprise found the egregious goblin waiting when they pulled into the Quirm city terminus. It seemed to Moist that the little bastard had channels through the world that weren't available to humans.

In the carriages behind, a good time was had by all, with avec galore and lashings of the famous entente cordiale. The smart new passenger carriages were much admired. A highlight for many was the dapper gentleman looking after the First Class gentlemen's facilities, who was adept at handling towels and explaining the workings of the glass cistern – which contained goldfish that appeared to revel in the rush of the flush but were, in fact, kept from going with the flow by a concealed sieve of some kind.

There was a big parade to greet them at Quirm Central, heralding another round of civic and political razzmatazz, all punctuated with more alcohol and ending with a huge dinner in the engine shed. And there were yet more toasts before the loco-motive was turned around on the new-fangled turning table to take the Ankh-Morpork contingent home, where they had to be decanted from the train.

And so it was that one fine summer evening shortly afterwards, Moist and Adora Belle sat down to an excellent dinner of fresh lobsters from Quirm brought up on the new *Fruits de Mer* Express. They were good, and cheaper now than he ever remembered, and the dish went very well with the watercress, which burned all the way down as they ate it.

And afterwards there were fresh strawberries and a soft bed with fluffy pillows and somehow it made all the running around worthwhile.

It began in Higher Overhang in the Shires. People locally were saying they could hear noises in the night . . . metallic noises, clanking, and the occasional scream of metal straining in torment. Of course everybody said, Well, goblins, what can you expect?

And all this came to the notice of Chief Constable Feeney Upshot, attached to the Ankh-Morpork constabulary. Feeney liked the attachment. It meant that anyone getting stroppy with him would sooner or later have to deal with Commander Vimes or even Sergeant Detritus, whose appearance in this sleepy hinterland had caused such a big stir a couple of years before. So Feeney got on his horse and headed to the Overhangs, so called because in the flaming distant past the landscape had been twisted all over the place with unfathomable caverns and a jagged unforgiving terrain.

Feeney was a decent and sensible copper and such men made friends because they never knew when they would need one, especially when they were a copper all alone, although in theory Feeney had the support of Special Constable Of the Chimney the Bones. There had to be a law, and law applied to *everyone*, and now the law had decreed that goblins were people and therefore protected by the law in these parts, which, in fact, was made incarnate in Chief Constable Feeney and his constable. Amazingly, the constable allowed his superior officer to call him Boney on the sensible basis that if there was some mêlée or other and you needed help you'd want a simple word to scream.*

Feeney had been to Ankh-Morpork and was proud to have undertaken his basic training in Pseudopolis Yard under Sergeant Detritus. He recognized that Boney was slightly more intelligent than the notorious Corporal Nobby Nobbs and so he didn't grumble. And now he was glad to see his constable waiting for him just outside the main goblin cave where he had an office, regarded by the local goblins as something of a shrine.

These days there was a flourishing colony of goblins in Overhang Minor. The goblins were purveyors of fine pots, and Feeney knew that the production of pots was generally a quiet pastime and didn't involve very much banging. The small cave that passed as an office was, and you have to be careful about this sort of thing,

---

* Feeney was privileged. To a goblin, the name is always the name, untouchable and part of the goblin itself.

definitely not manned but goblined. And the sound coming from the great cavern beyond it was not about pots, that was certain. It was metallic, heavy metal. Well – and Feeney stumbled here slightly, mentally at least – goblins were free, and if people wanted to bang metal around in the privacy of their great caverns, then they could. He blinked. It was the new world. If you didn't get your head around it, it could turn you upside down.

Feeney was polite and had been smart enough to pick up some of the goblin lingo, which really helped. It was a sunny day and it was an easy trip to the Overhangs and, yes, on the hill above the cavern there was a clacks station, goblined by goblins. After delivering his papers and force orders, Feeney sat down for a quiet word with his fellow officer and broached, in a careful way, the subject of the goblins banging things around in a context of dis turbing the peace. Since there were very few humans living anywhere near the goblins' settlement, Chief Constable Feeney put the complaints down to the humans' residual dislike of goblins doing anything whatsoever anywhere, but he did advise that maybe moving whatever it was they were doing further into their caves might be a very good idea.

The crackling voice of Boney said, 'No worries, boss, hang. We are copacetic on this one. No problems here.'

'Well, that's good to know, but why all the banging and clanging, Boney?'

'Chief, you know plenty goblins go to Ankh-Morpork and work for Sir Harry King, the shit magnet, on the railway. Know how it is, yess? Comes back every month with wages. Never had wages before! Sometime they comes with diagrams . . . And ideas and scheming attics.'

Boney watched his superior officer with a certain level of concern, and heard Feeney say, 'They are stealing . . . *ideas*?'

There was silence and Feeney knew he had made a faux pas, but Boney laughed and said, 'Nosir, improving! We like Sir Harry, veeery good employer, but we plan to build own goblin railway. Quick to get around and easy-no-problem – has found best way to build railway is not build. Digging! Dig underground. Underground goblin-size railway, yess? Will bring all goblins together from every caverns. So many caverns in bowels of world. It's no fuss. Goblins needed all over. How would nice Miss Adora Belle Dearheart do, if no goblins on clacks? We can be trusted – well, as muches as we trust you stinking humans. Wonderful railways underground, narrow gauge, of course. You see? We even have lingo! No rain and no snow, no bothering donkeys, no frightening old ladies underground. Hang! At last goblins' own world in tunnels under big-man human world. We goblins up in the light now. No turning back.'

Feeney thought about this on the ride home as his horse trotted gently towards the sunset. He wasn't a philosopher and couldn't even spell the word, but the voice of the goblin officer rang in his head. He thought, what would happen if goblins learned everything about humans and did everything the human way because they thought it was better than the goblin way? How long would it be before they were no longer goblins and left behind everything that was goblin, even their pots? The pots were lovely, he'd bought several for his mum. Goblins took pots seriously now, they sparkled, even at night, but what happens next? Will goblins really stop taking an interest in their pots and will humans learn the serious, valuable and difficult and almost magical skill of pot-making? Or will goblins become, well, just another kind of human? And which would be better?

And then he thought, maybe a policeman should stop thinking about all this because, after all, there was no crime, nothing was wrong . . . and yet in a subtle way, there was. Something was being stolen from the world without anybody noticing or caring. And then he gave up, because he was nearly home and his mum had promised him Man Dog Suck Po with mashed carrots, and it wasn't even a Sunday.

*

Building the longest railway the world had yet seen was a matter of daily grind, and nightly grind too, and each week took Moist further away from the city. Visits home to enjoy the fruits of his labour* became even rarer.

Scattered along the thousand-mile route new railway yards were springing up, each one a constant hive of activity with wagons coming and going all hours of the day and night. And while the company made sure the workforce was well provisioned, since, as Harry King had told the *Ankh-Morpork Times*, railway workers seriously needed a good meal and a good sleep in a comfortable bed after a day of heavy labour, in the end whether or not the bed was warm or comfortable didn't in fact really matter because a lad would sleep the moment he fell into it, just as soon as the former occupant, waving his billy can, had hurried off for *his* shift.

It was all about speed and occasionally pure machismo, or whatever it was called in the languages of trolls, goblins and golems and, of course, the real hard-core steel men from the mountains who fought amongst themselves over nothing.

Where the new line followed the course of the River Ankh as it narrowed towards its source high in the Ramtops, barges came up or down the river with wood for sleepers, iron ore, coal and other supplies. The smelters worked through the night casting rails and if you were lucky enough to be in the right place and sufficiently protected you could see them open their guts and spill the glowing liquid steel: dancing and living like a creature from the underworld. If you were not lucky and stood too close then quite probably you would end up in that underworld facing the deity of your choice.

And all was fuelled by money, money, money, eager investors

* Or indeed, the *fruits de mer* of his labour.

221

turning gold into steel and coal in the hope that it would turn back into even more gold.

The company was building bunkers everywhere along the tracks and it truly came home to Moist that when it came to the railways the engines and carriages and so forth were just the show up front, the iron horse, which needed to be fuelled and watered. And all of this was done by people almost the same colour as the coal, momentarily spotted as you went past, and then forgotten. He knew, because he had attended all the meetings and *listened*, that running a railway was a lot of small puzzles which, if you opened them, presented you with another sequence, full of constraints, and lists of things that definitely had to be done before anything else could happen. In short, the railway was complexity on wheels. It was amazing that Mr Simnel's sliding rule didn't glow as red-hot as the furnaces he worked.

And in Swine Town the workshops were turning out more and more engines: little tank engines that trundled up and down the ever-growing compound, shunting trains and carriages together; night trains, slow and heavy, that picked up wagon after wagon from the watercress farmers and others who needed to get their produce to the cities by dawn; the new Flyer Mark II, which had a roof to the footplate and wonderful new green livery; all now with names such as *Spirit of Scrote* and *King of Pseudopolis**.

The scream of steam was no longer an intrusion, just one of the noises of Ankh-Morpork, like the explosions in the Alchemists' Guild, and, as one old man said to his wife, 'You don't need a clock to tell you the time when you know the sound of the seven o'clock to Quirm.' It seemed only weeks since Iron Girder had first puffed

* Moist suspected Vetinari had had some say in that coinage since Pseudopolis had never had a king and was beset by the curse of democracy, an affliction the Patrician couldn't abide.

gently around Harry King's compound, but now, inside a year, branch lines were springing up all across the Sto Plains, connecting little towns and villages in every direction.

And near these little towns and villages spanking new houses for the new railway staff were beginning to appear. Houses with baths! And hot running water! Admittedly the privies were outside, but nevertheless the plumbing was well maintained.* You could say that for Harry: if something was to be done then it was to be done properly, and doubly so if Effie was around.‡

It was as if there had been a space waiting to be filled. It was steam-engine time, and the steam engine had arrived, like a rain-drop, dripping precisely into its puddle, and Moist and Dick and Harry and Vetinari and the rest of them were simply splashes in the storm.

Then one day at the Ankh-Morpork terminus, as Moist was setting out yet again to the Sto Plains, a lady got into his carriage, intro-duced herself as Mrs Georgina Bradshaw and sat down, gripping her expensive-looking bag with both hands. When Moist got up to offer her his forward-facing seat as railway etiquette apparently demanded, she said, 'Oh, my dear sir, don't worry about me, but thank you. I know a gentleman when I see one.'

'Moist von Lipwig at your service, ma'am.'

'Oh – are you *the* Mister Lipwig? Mister Lipwig the railwayman? I've heard all about you.'

'Yes, I am, I suppose,' said Moist, 'when no other contender is available.'

---

* Around the Sto Plains, as in other places, it took a while for country people to come to terms with indoor . . . facilities. A privy in the garden with fresh air all around was considered much more hygienic and, if you were careful, the tomatoes you grew would be most excellent.†
† If you don't know what this means, your grandparents will tell you.
‡ On the Quirm line Harry had had to stop her from giving them a bidet.

'Isn't this fascinating?' continued Mrs Bradshaw. 'I've never been on a train before. I've taken the precaution of bringing some pills in case I feel nauseous. Has that ever happened to you?'

'No, madam, I quite like the rhythm of the railway,' said Moist. 'But tell me, where did you get those precious pills?'

'It was a gentleman called Professor Dibbler, a purveyor of nostrums against the railway illnesses. He was *quite* persuasive.'

Moist couldn't help his smile and said, 'I imagine he was. Madam, Mister Dibbler is at best nothing more than a charming scamp, I'm afraid. And I'm quite certain his nostrums will be nothing more than expensive sugar and miscellaneous substances. I fear he's in the vanguard of the pedlars of patent medications which tax my patience.'

She laughed. 'Well put, sir. I'll consider that tuppence ha'penny down the drain.'

'So may I ask what is your business on the railway?'

'None, really. I thought, well, you only live once, and when I was a little girl my mother said I was always following carts to see where they were going and now that my husband Archibald has passed on I thought that this should be the time to go and see the world . . . you know, faraway places with strange-sounding names . . . like Twoshirts and Effing Forest and Scrote. One imagines all manner of *exotic* occurrences must take place somewhere with a name like Twoshirts. So many places I've never been to . . . I have a whole world to experience before it's too late, and I'm keeping a journal of it all as I go, so I'll be able to enjoy the world all over again when I get back.'

Something struck in Moist's head, causing him to say, 'May I ask, Mrs Bradshaw, if your handwriting is good?'

She looked down her nose at him and said, 'Indeed yes, Mister Lipwig. I used to write a beautiful cursive script for my dear late husband. He was a lawyer and *they* expect excellence in the writing and use of the language. Mister Slant was always very . . . *particular* about that, and no one appreciates the judicious use of Latatian better than dear Archibald did.

'And, may I add, I was schooled at the Quirm College for Young Ladies, where they are *very* solid on the teaching of foreign tongues, even though Morporkian rather seems to have become the *lingua quirma* of late.' Mrs Bradshaw sniffed. 'And in working for my husband I learned a lot about people and the human condition.'

'Mrs Bradshaw, if you *were* to go everywhere where the trains go and write about all those places, perhaps you could send me a copy of your notes? They could be useful to other intrepid passengers . . . People would know what to expect from the Effing Forest or Twoshirts before they'd even paid a penny for their ticket. Already so many people from Ankh are travelling to Quirm just for the sunshine. It's become our heaviest service! And some of them go just for the day! I'm sure they'd think about going on other trips too if they saw all the little details of every place you visit, and perhaps you could include notes on accommodation as well as other places of interest en route?' he added, on fire with his own imagination. 'All the things that *you* would like to see and would be interested in. Wherever your travels take you, you can address your manuscript to Moist von Lipwig and give it to the nearest station master, and they'll see to it that it gets passed on to me.'

Moist thought about the amount of gold accruing in the coffers of Harry King's accounts and added, 'And I'm sure we could arrange some remuneration . . .'

As Mrs Bradshaw settled into the journey and looked out of the window Moist took out his notebook and scribbled a memo to Harry King: 'Please allow Mrs Georgina Bradshaw to travel anywhere she wants, even those little branch lines we haven't fully opened yet. She went to one of the best girls' schools I know of and understands language, and she is writing notes on all our destinations which may come in very useful. My instincts say that

225

she will do us proud. I have an inkling that she will be either meticulous or humorous or, hopefully, both. And a widow who wears the kind of gold and diamond ring that she is wearing to travel through Ankh-Morpork and is still wearing it when she leaves is not going to be a fool. She speaks as well as Lady Sybil; that's Quirm College for you. Up School! Isn't this what we're after? We want people to widen their horizons on the train, of course, but why not day trips? You know what, there are people in Ankh-Morpork who haven't even got as far as Sto Lat yet. Travel broadens the mind, and also railway revenue.'

A sample of the great work arrived on scented paper one week later.

> *High Mouldering, on the Sto Plains, boasts wonderful salt-water baths from a pleasantly warm spring, and the owner and his wife give hygienic massages to those who would like to enjoy the benefit. Ladies and gentlemen separately, of course; there is nothing here that could be considered insalubrious or that would shock the most delicate of sensibilities.*
>
> *Near by, the Hotel Continental offers accommodation for trolls, humans, dwarfs and goblins; fifty rooms are available at present. People wishing to tour the area may be interested in the Sacred Glade of Shock Knee, which deserves to be noticed for its amazing echoes. A short distance away is a shrine to Anoia, patron goddess for people who have difficulty with things stuck in their drawers.*
>
> *A welcome break for the tired at weekends, with excellent meals. Highly recommended.*

Moist made a note to see Mr Thomas Goatberger when he could next get back to Ankh-Morpork. If he was any judge, the publisher would be ready to bite his hand off to get a share of the railway magic.

*

When Moist did next return to the city, the matter of the railway to Uberwald had to take priority. Pacing up and down in the big room where Harry and Dick Simnel presided over their charts and reports and blueprints, Harry was still clearly worried.

'Now then, Moist, between ourselves and these four walls I've got the heebie-jeebies. We've taken gangs off the other lines, we're putting in more and more work on the long haul to Uberwald. This is a hell of an undertaking. I'm more at home knee-deep in shit, which is what we're going to be in here in this office if this doesn't work, believe you me.'

'Yes,' said Moist, 'but what you have to remember is that getting to Uberwald will mean getting to a whole load of other places on the way, and all of them'll want the railway and that will help cover costs right there. It's the tunnels and bridges that are a problem, but the best of it is that they're old technologies. There are plenty of masons who can build good bridges for us, and as for tunnels, the trolls are just begging to do them if they can dig out a home near by.'

Harry's only response was a grunt.

'And the nice thing about the trolls,' Moist added, 'is that they bring the whole family with them, even their kids. It's their way. If you don't know your rocks, you're no good as a troll. They just love changing the landscape. One of them asked me the other day if he could be a surveyor and I was just opening my mouth to say no when I thought, why not? He seemed like a bright lad, slow, yes, but quite bright. So I've told the boys to give him a bit of tuition, on the job, as it were.'

'Are you going to give him one of Simnel's special sliding slabs?' said Harry, smiling.

Moist laughed and said, 'Why not, Harry? I might just do that! No reason why a surveyor shouldn't be strong enough to lift up a mountain to see what's underneath!'

227

He took advantage of the lightened atmosphere to steer Sir Harry towards happier subjects, asking to be brought up to date on all the latest developments.

Every morning now the desk of Harry King was inundated by letters from people wanting no trains, some trains, or seriously wishing to have trains available right now. And then there were all the other helpful comments and suggestions: a Mr Snori Snorisson had written to say so many other people had arranged to meet under the station clock that his friend had taken four hours to find him . . . Shouldn't the railway provide stepladders for the use of shorter citizens . . . ? Help was requested for passengers with heavy luggage, and for the elderly or undead . . . With all the dangerous machinery involved, shouldn't there be guards – not the City Watch, of course, but somebody with some sense – to act as guardian of the train and its passengers? And that meant uniforms, hats, flags, whistles and other exciting accoutrements.

And this excitement was presumably why the editor of the *Ankh-Morpork Times* had decided to employ a railway correspondent, Mr Raymond Shuttle, who was an unashamed and self-confessed train spotter. The glint in his eyes was unmistakable.

Alongside the main business of the railway, Harry confessed himself delighted to see the enthusiasts spending their dollars on railway souvenirs such as the little clockwork models that were even now being created under licence by those deviously cunning artificers who were making a small fortune from railway memorabilia.* And the cannier artificers, always on the lookout for moneymaking opportunities, were constantly making additions to these playthings for children: a little shed and four tiny figures to wait for the train. A signal box with a waving goblin. And yes, a miniature turning table just like the one in the

---

* This would have been an even bigger fortune had not Thunderbolt carefully made certain that the Hygienic Railway Company took its slice.

compound, and so it went on. A lad with a doting parent could get his own tiny Iron Girder and oval track with straights and curves; and even miniature railway workers including a miniature Harry King.*

And once again, Moist marvelled at the power of the dream.

And then it was out into the grease-filled world of the compound to see the latest engines the lads were testing, and find out what the ingenious Mr Simnel had been up to since Moist had seen him last.

One thing he was sure of: even though Dick Simnel was forever coming up with blueprints for the next locomotive, every day would have seen him still hard at work on Iron Girder, which was probably why on every visit she continued to look a little different: a different boiler here, different wheels there, different paintwork and quite probably a host of integral things that Moist couldn't see. She was Dick's pride and joy, his first locomotive love, thought Moist, taking care not to say it aloud, the first test bed for every new innovation. No locomotive shone as brightly as Iron Girder. No locomotive got the next big improvement before Iron Girder. She was, indeed, the iron stalking horse for the railway and Simnel her willing slave.

Just as Moist was debating where first to look for Simnel, Emily King, in a very fine white cotton dress, came jauntily skipping through the compound towards the sacred engine shed as if completely unaware of the attendant muck and grease. But after all, he thought, she must have grown up with her uncle's *other* business, against which the railway was a fragrant pleasure garden. And here she was, bouncing along cheerfully, and here was Iron

* Harry was thrilled; he'd tried to be nonchalant about it but when he heard the suggestion that he should be part of a toy railroad he grinned from ear to ear, although Effie complained that they had made him look too fat.

Girder, and suddenly Moist's spine went cold, every sinew twanging, and he was near to biting his nails as the girl continued towards the locomotive in her pristine white cotton dress.

Moist moved like lightning across the compound as Emily skipped on and reached Iron Girder. He looked at Simnel, whose face had gone curiously grey even under the grease and grime, and he was ready for anything as Emily patted the engine and said, 'Hello, Iron Girder, how are we today, you lovely girl?' And while Moist was still gawping, Emily took out her handkerchief and buffed Iron Girder's brass nameplate industriously until it sparkled to the heavens. And as Emily was talking to Iron Girder about how good she was looking today, Simnel turned to Moist and said, very quietly, 'She wouldn't have, you know, not Iron Girder.'

'Good,' said Moist. 'And now you have *two* ladies, you lucky man.' But in his head a voice said to him, 'But you more than half expected it, didn't you, Mister Lipwig? Oh, ye of little faith.' And then there was a sigh of steam.

For the next two hours Moist sat at his desk in Harry's compound, feeling as if he were a locomotive speeding along watching the scenery blur past. Every so often a boy came up with another pile of paperwork from some part of Harry King's domain and towards the end of the afternoon he felt himself subtly drifting into a coma, quite a pleasant one at the start: he visualized himself in a pale pink mist and it didn't matter. Nothing mattered. And little by little Moist von Lipwig began to unravel, but just as he was sliding under Of the Twilight the Darkness dropped down in front of him out of the evening glow, though exactly where he had dropped *from* Moist couldn't work out.

'Must go to sleep, Mister Lipwig! Burning candle at both ends means man with egg on face and burning bum. When did Mister Lipwig last eat? Not snack! Serious munch! I have some dried mushrooms if you are feeling peckish. No? Acquired taste . . . more for me, but you must sleep if nothing else. Mister Lipwig can't do everything. If he can't eat, can't do anything. Making money is good, but there is no pockets in a shroud. Give it a rest, Mister Railway! And *this* will help you big time no mistake.'

The goblin handed Moist a little bottle on which a grubby label proclaimed the contents as 'RAT POISON'.

'Label one big lie, Mister Lipwig, bottle cleaned out and rats eaten, yes indeed, and filled with special goblin potion for tired person. Guaranteed no worms and it will give you refreshing sleep and you feel a lot better *if* you wake up in the morning! Guaranteed! Pure quill. None finer!'

It had been a long day and the heat of the smelters had made him as dry as the smelters themselves and so, what the hell, Moist took a long swig.

'Well done, Mister Lipwig!' chuckled the goblin. 'It will make your hairs curl . . . everywhere!'

Later, after Moist had finished talking to the dancing toadstools and Mr Whoopee, the man who could amusingly eat his own face, it must have been Moist's feet alone that found his bed, plodding along like a couple of old donkeys via the good offices of Sergeant Colon and Corporal Nobby Nobbs, who apparently found him just outside his house talking to his knees. And, according to Nobby, listening intently to what they had to say.

He awoke lying on his bedroom floor. Somebody had put blankets over him and even tucked him up nicely. He grasped his head and thought Oh no! I drank *another* goblin concoction! His dismay dwindled when he realized that he felt absolutely fine and not just fine, either, but so full of beans that the world probably had no beans left. When he stepped outside on to the balcony for a breath of fresh air the birds were singing and the sky was a wonderful shade of blue.

231

The door opened behind him and Adora Belle said, 'I know we have what might be called an unconventional marriage, what with our jobs and the pressure of work and so on, but I wouldn't be doing my wifely duty if I didn't ask you whether you have been firkydoodling with fast and loose women? No pressure. Answer in your own time.'

More or less spinning with the ecstasy of being alive and, of course, all those beans, Moist said joyfully, 'Now then, just a minute, bear with me now, tell me, is it *loose* women or is it *fast* women? Is there a spotter's guide or does one, as it were, cancel out the other?'

'Moist von Lipwig, you are rascally drunk. Can you even walk?'

For an answer Moist jumped in the air, clicking his heels, and said, 'Fast or loose, my girl, or why not both at once?'

Dragging him back into their bedroom and closing the door behind them, Adora Belle said, 'Well now, husband of mine, in that case let's find out.'

There was a thunderstorm over Schmaltzberg, but that was ever the case. Thunder rolled around the mountains, like the marbles of the gods. And in the privacy of his office, the Low King was discussing progress with Aeron who was looking more cheerful than usual.

'Things appear to be calming down,' Rhys said. 'They argue and argue and then somebody remembers that he has business to deal with concerning his rat farms, or there's some trouble over in his goldmine, water coming in, pit props buckling and so on and so forth, things they can't leave to underlings, and then everything goes quiet.'

'I know you're worried,' said Aeron, 'but I think . . . no, I believe, that you have more friends than you ever thought possible. Even the goblins know that you were one of the first who signed up for goblin emancipation. They, whether we like it or not, are becoming the future, Rhys. It was the business with the clacks towers that made even traditional dwarfs angry. The clacks is needed: every-body wants news. People are furious everywhere. After all, they say, goblins and trolls are minding their own business, so why not the dwarfs?'

'No more news of Ardent?' asked the King. 'It's been months, hasn't it? No more towers down or idiots trying to destroy the rail-way? Can I believe that his firebrand has burned out?'

Aeron handed the King his coffee and said, 'I believe Lord Vetinari said never do anything until you hear the screams. However, Ardent is not one to come back, helmet in hand, to say "sorry". There is too much pride there by half.'

After a quiet moment while Rhys Rhysson considered the possibilities, Aeron continued.

'So you will accept the invitation to the summit in Quirm? In these circumstances, Rhys, it does seem to me that it is *very* important that you are there and seen to be there.'

'Of course. Diamond King will be chairing proceedings this year and I must mend fences. He's helpful but I'm in no mood to try his patience. He has always been a most understanding ally.'

'And the other . . . thing?'

'The other thing is satisfactory,' said the King. He paused. 'Yes, we should go to Quirm, but I think it would be wise to leave Albrechtson in charge here, just to take care of any business.'

Without his quite knowing how it had come about, and regardless of how little he was actually at the compound, it appeared that Moist was now Mr Railway. If anyone wanted to know anything about it, they asked him. If they'd lost their little child in the queue for Iron Girder, the call went out for Mr Lipwig and if somebody had a new idea for the railway it was sent to Mr Lipwig and after a while it didn't seem to Moist to matter what time it was or, worse, where he was: the claims on his attention were never-ending.

He was pretty certain that he slept quite often, sometimes back at home, if at all possible, or saving that a mattress and blanket somewhere within the warm and ever enlarging foundries along the route to Uberwald, or, if all else failed, snuggled down under the tarpaulins of whatever railway gang was near by, having shared whatever was in the cooking pot. If you were lucky it was pheasant or possibly grouse, and if you weren't so lucky, at least there would be pot luck, which generally meant cabbages and swedes and almost certainly something that was protein, but you wouldn't want to see what it was in daylight. However, to give them their due, the railway gangs, including the vanguard now bearing down on Slake, were resourceful men, especially in the tradition of setting snares to fill their pots along the permanent way.

Slake was one of those places, Moist thought, that you put on the map because it was embarrassing to have a map with holes in it. There was some mining, forestry and fishing and after a while you got the feeling that those people who chose to live in Slake and the surrounding area were people who didn't want other people to know where they were. And when you walked around Slake you were always certain that you were being watched. He put it down as a place to avoid unless you liked bad cooking and banjos. Nevertheless, it had a mayor and was nailed to the map as a coaling and water stop.

No longer did Moist wear the snazzy suits and handmade shoes that, along with his collection of official-looking hats, were his calling card back in the city. They didn't stand up well to the regime of the railway worker and so now he wore the greasy shirt and waistcoat with rough trousers tied at the knee. He loved the huge boots and the flat cap that seemed to go with them, making you feel safe at both ends. But the boots, oh the boots . . . a troll could drop on your head and you'd be dead, but the boots would be still alive and kicking! They had hobnails and were more or less like tiny fortresses. Nothing could get past a railway worker's boots.

Messages found Moist wherever he might be, via train, goblin

234

runner or clacks, since there were very few places these days where their towers hadn't found a niche in the landscape.

In the small hours of one morning in the Plains township of Little Swelling when it was pouring with rain that hammered on the makeshift lodgings, Moist pulled back the tarpaulin and wood door to see the face of Of the Twilight the Darkness, who couldn't be called soaked, because there was really very little of him to soak.* As soon as the goblin got inside the bothy, such water as was on him simply disappeared.

Almost automatically Moist looked up to see the lights of the local clacks tower and as he did so it flashed a familiar code: it was from Adora Belle. He recognized her code as easily as he would recognize his own. 'Quickly!' he said. 'Get up that tower and get that message back to me, *now!*'

He waited, and in the gloom the voice of Of the Twilight the Darkness said, 'Did I hear the magic word, Mister Little Damp?'

Moist was surprised at himself because, even though the goblin had a smell you could almost see, that was no reason for not minding your manners, so he said, '*Please*, Mister Of the Twilight the Darkness. Thank you so very much.'

And thus chastened, Moist kept silent as the little goblin scuttled back out into the rain and scampered towards the tower.

Moist finished his ablutions, gathered his things together – on the assumption that whatever the message it would require him to go somewhere else – and went out to where the golem horse was waiting unregarding of the weather, just in case it needed waking up, because however hard he tried he couldn't think of it as anything other than alive. Admittedly, the horse was giving him incipient piles, no matter how much padding he put between

---

* With all goblins, the male ones especially, you got the impression of sinews but they mostly consisted of sinews tied together with other sinews. Surely, the mind protested, there must be muscles in there somewhere, but quite possibly they had to fight to find some room among all those damn sinews.

himself and it. And although the creature could now speak, Moist still yearned for all those fussing little rituals that defined horsemanship. He was aware that there should be such things as nose bags and adjusting the straps and giving the beast some water. The lack of these rituals slightly unbalanced Moist. It was creepy. In the falling rain it was as if he was in two different worlds.

And while he was wondering whether he should give the horse a name, which somehow would have made things feel better, *Mister Of the Twilight the Darkness* arrived, clutching a damp and smudged pink clacks flimsy.

Vetinari wants to see you immediately. Stop. PS Any chance of bringing home some of that goblin potion with you. Stop. PPS If you pass a bakery we could do with a couple of sliced loaves. Stop. Your loving wife. Stop.

And he thought, well, isn't it nice to be wanted?

No more than a few hours and a bumpy ride through pouring rain later, the door to the anteroom outside the Oblong Office was opened by Drumknott, replete in a very smart engine driver's hat, wiping his greasy hands on an equally greasy piece of ever-present engine driver's rag.

'His lordship will be with you presently, Mister Lipwig. You've been a very busy man lately, haven't you?'

Moist could now see that the little secretary was also looking tanned beneath the smuts and soot, and the hat was, gods forbid, jaunty, a term never before applied to Drumknott.

'Have you spent much time on the railway, Mister Drumknott? It looks like it's doing you some good.'

'Oh, yes, sir! His lordship allows me to take a few turns on the railway late mornings after he's finished the crossword. After all, *everything* is about the train these days, isn't it, and he was gracious enough to say that I'm keeping him in touch.'

At that moment, there was a shrill whistle from the other side of the door and Drumknott pulled it open to reveal Lord Vetinari, to Moist's total surprise, catching one of the new little steam engines just as it was about to plunge off the highly polished desk. The familiar straights and curves were surrounded by little toy people: guards, engine drivers, passengers, the portly controller with a big cigar and various engineers with tiny crafted sliding rulers. And the tyrant caught the falling engine in a gauntlet, leaving water and oil dripping down on to the expensive polished ebony floor tiles.

'Quite amazing, isn't it, Mister Lipwig?' he said cheerfully through the smoke. 'Though isn't it a pity that they can only run on rails? I can't imagine what the world would be like if everyone had their own steam locomotive. Abominable.'

His lordship held out his hand for Drumknott to clean it with a not-so-greasy rag, and said, 'Well, Mister Lipwig is here, Drumknott, and I know you can't wait to get back to your wonderful railway.'

And Drumknott – the Drumknott who thought the finer things of life were stored in manila folders – headed off down the stairs two at a time to get into the cab, shovel the coal, start the engine, blow the whistle and breathe in smuts and soot and be that most wondrous of creatures, an *engine driver*.

'Tell me, Mister Lipwig,' said Vetinari, as the door closed. 'It occurs to me that rocks on the line could easily derail a locomotive . . .'

'Well, my lord, away from Ankh-Morpork we give the engines cow-catchers, a kind of plough, if you will. And remember, sir, a locomotive running free has a considerable weight and the signallers and linesmen keep an eye on the track.'

'So, there has so far been no deliberate sabotage?'

Moist said, 'Not since the attack on Iron Girder months ago,

237

unless you mean the little boys who put their pennies on the track just to get them flattened? That seems to be more of a pastime, and copper bends easily. It's gone quiet, hasn't it, sir? I'm thinking about the grags knocking down clacks towers and generally being difficult. It looks like they've given up.'

Vetinari winced. 'You could be right. Certainly the Low King appears to believe so, and Commander Vimes reports that his agents in Uberwald are not picking up any disturbances. Other sources indicate the same. But . . . I worry that extremists are like perennial weeds. They may disappear for a while but they don't give up. I fear they've gone further underground, waiting for their moment.'

'Which moment would that be, sir?'

'Do you know, Mister Lipwig, I wonder about that every night. I take some pleasure in the fact that the era of the locomotive has begun with care and thought and a scientific outlook instead of a lot of tinkering. Encouraging free-for-all simply encourages more episodes such as we saw in the Effing Forest. So . . .' Vetinari now stared directly at Moist. 'Tell me, how is the railway to Uberwald coming along?'

'Making very good progress, sir, but there is a shortfall . . . as it were. We were expecting to drive the golden spike halfway through next month. There's a lot of work still to do and we're driving the train underground around the Gruffies. We're tunnelling hard, but there are already a lot of cave formations up there.'

And there's the bridges, he thought. You haven't told him about the bridges. 'And, of course, once we get to Uberwald we'll eventually continue on to Genua.'

'Not good enough, Mister Lipwig, not good enough at all. You must speed up. The balance of the world could be at stake.'

'Er . . . with all due respect, my lord, why?'

Vetinari frowned. 'Mister Lipwig. I have given you your orders; how you execute those orders is up to you, but they *must* be obeyed!'

238

Moist's mood was not helped by finding the golem horse had been clamped, apparently by the Watch since he could see a watchman close by, laughing. The horse looked at him, embarrassed, and said, 'I regret this inconvenience, sir, but I must obey the law.'

Seething, Moist said, 'As a golem horse, are you as strong as any other golem?'

'Oh, yes, sir.'

'Very well,' said Moist. 'Then get yourself out of the clamp.'

The clamp cracked and split and the watchman ran towards Moist just as he leapt on to the back of the horse, yelling after him, 'Oi! That's public property, that is!'

And Moist shouted over his shoulder, 'Send the bill to Sir Harry King, if you dare! Tell him it's from Moist von Lipwig!'

Looking back as the horse galloped away down Lower Broadway, to his glee he saw the watchman picking up the pieces of the yellow clamp and he shouted, 'No one interferes with the progress of the Hygienic Railway!'

Moist always preferred to move fast – after all, in his previous businesses a turn of speed was essential – and he arrived at Harry's compound with the horse panting like a celestial runner.* Stepping down and, for nothing more than effect, tying up the horse, he said, 'Why were you panting? Golems don't pant. You don't breathe!'

'Sorry, sir. You wanted me to be a more horse-like horse, so I am doing my best, sir . . . neigh, whinny, whinny.'

---

* It is well known that it is possible to climb Cori Celesti. Many athletes have attempted to climb to the summit and most of them have failed, although history *does* admit that a posse of elderly gentlemen with arthritis and bandy legs did manage this feat but subsequently died like heroes which was, after all, what it was all about. Other aspiring and indeed perspiring athletes have managed to get at least a little way up by using what is known as the Path of Lights, which it has to be said does not favour anyone who is not a *true* hero. Nevertheless many still attempt to run up Cori Celesti or at least break their femur in trying.

Moist burst out laughing and said, 'That'll do, Dobbin . . . No, not Dobbin! How do you fancy Flash?'

Reflectively the horse said, 'I've never had a name before. I've always been "horse". But it's a very nice feeling to know who you are. I wonder how I did without it for these past nine hundred and three years. Thank you, Mister Lipwig.'

Moist made his way to Harry's office and made certain that he spoke directly and in private to Harry, who stared at Moist for an eternity before saying, 'Surely you know that they've hardly started reinforcing the first of the bridges on the Uberwald line? No train can run on thin air!'

'Yes, Harry, I know. Gods bless me, I speak to the surveyors and inspectors all the time. But it's only the beds of the bridges that need lots of work. The uprights have stood the test of time.'

And while Sir Harry was drawing breath to protest, Moist told him what he had in mind if Simnel's engineers weren't ready in time for whatever Vetinari was cooking up.

It took some time for Harry to get to grips with Moist's plan, but finally when he'd heard it all he said, 'You're breaking all the rules, my lad, and you can only do that once to Vetinari. I'm pretty sure about *that*.'

It took all of Moist's guile and self-control in the face of an angry Harry King, but he held his ground and said, 'Harry, in all my time working for Lord Vetinari I've learned to understand the words "plausible deniability".'

'Eh? What does that mean, smart boy?' said Harry.

'It means his lordship chooses to have little idea of what I do and certainly doesn't give me clear instructions, and it also means I have to guess a lot, but I've always been very good at that. Got a lot to do, Sir Harry, or shall I say *my lord* Harry or should I even dare to say *Baron King of Ankh-Morpork* . . . you can fill in that bit for yourself . . . and, if I remember correctly, when Vetinari makes you the first railway baron you'll be entitled to six silver balls on your coronet. A knighthood? Pah! You could be a Baron overnight. I imagine Lady King would be most impressed by a man with six balls.'

Harry snorted. 'That'd give the missus a surprise!' He considered the picture Moist had painted of the future and said, 'Actually, I reckon she'd be swanking like a . . . Duchess!' He sobered up a little and continued, 'Believe me, I thought I was the King of the Shit, but *you* are full of the stuff! Would you damn well tell me how much trouble it's going to get us both into? Baron, my arse. All right, mister, how do we get this thing done, scoundrels that we are?'

Even with the added pressure from the Patrician and with every lad, troll and goblin that Harry could provide, it still took time to build a railway. 'Tsort was not built in a day,' was the mantra when anyone got impatient. Still, day by day the great new railway line to Uberwald got closer to its destination.

If building the railway was one thing, maintaining it was quite another. The railway was out there in the wind and the weather, and, in many cases, far from civilization. Moist looked every week at the complaints, breakdowns and miscellaneous problems book, his instinct always being to start with the miscellaneous and sometimes humorous: intoxicated troll on line, harpies nesting in coal bunker, woman in labour.* And then, of course, there were also the landslides, which played havoc with the schedules. People also didn't appreciate that to leave a huge truck full of pigs on a level crossing was actively to prevent any movement on the railway,

---

* Miss Daisy Snapes was officially the first person to be born on a moving train, thanks to a midwife who rushed the mother to the guard's van. Young Daisy was born at thirty miles an hour and her doting parents named her Locomotion Snapes, until Moist got to hear about it and gave her and her parents a free season ticket on the railway, along with the suggestion that Locomotion might sound better as a middle name.

and as for the people who believed that if they held out their palm to the oncoming locomotive it would stop for them immediately! As, in fact, it might, but a skidding locomotive was a matter of filling up a large number of forms afterwards.

As Moist was all too aware, ever since the maiden voyage the newspaper editors of the Sto Plains had been waiting for the first true railway disaster, which, for preference, would include at least one horrible death.

And they got one, although not on the Hygienic Railway Company's line. Instead, the first casualty happened in the back country of Quirm, where three entrepreneurs, Monsieur Lavasse the winemaker, Monsieur Croque the cheesemonger and Monsieur Lestripe, a purveyor of decorative onion-wreaths, had invested in their own small single-track line between their vineyards and farms.

They had called on Simnel for expert advice, in particular how to avoid a head-on crash between their two locomotives on the single track, a conundrum that Dick had solved with classic Simnel simplicity by providing them with signals that could not be changed without a special brass token, carried by whichever driver had right of way on the line.

Amid press headlines claiming SIMNEL SYSTEM FAILS and ARE PASSENGER LIVES AT RISK? Simnel and Moist were summoned to Quirm to investigate, where they discovered the terrible truth. A middle manager at Chateau Lavasse had looked to speed things up and had duplicated the safety token and explained to the drivers and the signalmen that they just needed to be sensible. Trusting them to get it right had worked well for a while and so everyone relaxed, and then one day Signalman Hugo was preoccupied and forgot a vital safety step, and there were two trains heading for each other at some speed along the single track, with each driver thinking he had the right of way. And they did indeed meet halfway. One driver died, the other was seriously scalded by runaway cheeses which flowed like lava when they reached the heat of the footplate, and there was a great disturbance of foie gras.

And the clerk who had seen fit to order a second token said, 'Well, I thought I would be saving time so I only—'

According to Raymond Shuttle's report in the next day's *Times*: ' "I am very sorry about the gentleman who was killed, and the man who was injured," Mr Lipwig told me. "I'm sure none of us will ever look at fondue the same way again. However, Mister Simnel has made it clear that while it's easy to deal with stupid, bloody stupid is horribly difficult to erase. I wonder how many dreadful crimes have been perpetrated following a well-meaning person saying 'I only . . .?'" '

Damage limitation achieved, Simnel and Moist headed back to Ankh-Morpork. As the slow train on the coastal branch line left the rocky ground which was so good for the famous Quirmian vines and started to skirt the steamy world of the Netherglades,* Simnel slept and Moist pondered the many challenges ahead while staring

---

* The swamps in this part of the world are famous for their birdlife but also notorious, because they move constantly and quickly. Dry land is hard to find. The human inhabitants live on large rafts that serve as both shelters and gardens. The older generations have splayed feet, which they try to encourage in their offspring because the webs show that the owner is a great hunter of the swamps. They have no known enemies, probably because most people don't *want* to step into a swamp. They are in fact helpful to travellers, and they distil extremely useful medications from the floating flora and fauna of the swamps, which include the twisting honeydew and the egregious flytrap, whose venom can be used in the making of delicate ironwork etchings, and which must be approached with extreme caution as the venom can be spat over several yards.

There clearly has been magic at work in the Netherglades and its future as the pharmacopoeia of the world is being tested by Professor Rincewind of Unseen University. A dispatch from him reveals that the juice pressed from a certain little yellow flower induces certainty in the patient for up to fifteen minutes. About what they are certain they cannot specify, but the patient is, in that short time, completely certain about *everything*. And further research has found that a floating water hyacinth yields in its juices total *un*certainty about anything for half an hour. Philosophers are excited about the uses of these potions, and the search continues for a plant that combines the qualities of both, thereby being of great use to theologians.

out of the window at the passing landscape. Watching the swamps roll by, Moist felt faintly relieved that the train didn't stop until back in drier terrain at the small town of Shankydoodle, a great exporter of champion racehorses. That was fine, he thought: there was a long winding footpath from there to the Netherglades and if you couldn't find it you had no business being there.

The rain poured down on the Sto Lat terminus, water gushing off the roof as people scurried to get out of the downpour, seeking a respite from the deluge. The little coffee shop of Marjorie Painsworth was dry and as an extra attraction on this dreadful night she had warm buns on sale. It was a beacon of solace for the young troll lady, who stirred her cup of molten sulphur uncertainly while waiting. She watched people coming in and out, and was surprised when a dwarf gentleman indicated the chair next to her and said, 'Excuse me, is this place taken?'

Crackle had never had much to do with dwarfs, of course, but since the whole Koom Valley business had been sorted out, it was surely in order for her to talk to a dwarf, especially since this one was very well dressed and, well, looked human; an Ankh-Morpork dwarf as they called them. So she smiled and said, 'By all means do take a seat, sir. Isn't the weather inclement for this time of year?'

The dwarf bowed, sat down and said, 'Forgive my intrusion, but I am so happy to hear you use a word like "inclement". The very word itself paints a picture, don't you think? A grey one, but nevertheless . . . Oh, where are my manners? Please let me intro-duce myself: Dopey Docson at your service, madam, and may I say you speak extremely good dwarfish?'

Crackle looked around. People were still coming in out of the rain and leaving as the trains came and went. Sto Lat was, after all, a hub of the railway and almost all traffic passed through there. She had one ear cocked for the porter announcing her own train, but she managed to say, 'Your grasp of troll is likewise also remarkable, if I may say so. May I ask where your travels have taken you?'

The dwarf smiled again and said, 'I'm a librarian in Klatch, but I've recently buried my father in Copperhead.'

And Crackle stifled a laugh and said, 'Do excuse me, I'm very sorry to hear about your father, but that's amazing! I'm also a librarian, in the service of Diamond King of Trolls!'

'Ah, the Diamond Library! Alas not available to us at the moment, even under the famous Accord. I'd give anything just to see it.'

And the two librarians ordered more drinks and talked about books while whistles blew and train after train left the station. Crackle told Dopey that her husband didn't like books and considered that mumbling should be good enough for trolls like it was in the old days, and the dwarf told her about his wife who even after the Koom Valley Accord still thought of trolls as a kind of animal, and they talked and talked and talked about the meaning of words and, indeed, the love of words. And Marjorie recognized the syndrome and kept the hot coffee and sulphur flowing, with the occasional warm rock cake.

Of course, it wasn't her business, she thought, it wasn't up to her how other people led their lives, and she definitely didn't eavesdrop, well, not much, but she couldn't help hearing the dwarf say, 'I've been offered a post as librarian at Brazeneck University and they've already told me I can bring my own assistant.'

And Marjorie was not surprised to find two empty cups and an empty table when she next looked: this sort of thing was bound to happen with the railway. It expanded horizons, inside and out, people went looking to find themselves and what they found was somebody else.

As coups went, the Schmaltzberg coup went slowly, dripping through the tunnels and mines like treacle, and just as sticky. A connoisseur of coups would recognize the form. Two would get up to impress on a third that this was what should be done because this was what everyone else was going to do, and there was no point in being on the losing side, was there? There were always the ones who had misgivings, but the pressure of the tide was strengthening. Underground Schmaltzberg was in many respects a beehive and the swarm was deciding that they needed a new Queen.

Ardent and the banished grags were, of course, at the centre of all this, and now having triumphantly* returned were settling down as if the place was theirs by right . . .

'Nobody has to be hurt,' they said, and it may have been too that people would murmur, 'After all, it's in his own interests,' and there were other little giveaways such as 'It's time for fresh blood,' and such things as 'We must preserve our most hallowed ordinances,' and if you were susceptible to atmospheres, you could see that dwarfs, perfectly sensible dwarfs, dwarfs who would consider themselves dwarfs of repute and fair dealing, were nevertheless slowly betraying allegiances they had formerly undertaken with great solemnity, because the hive was buzzing and they didn't want to be the ones that got stung.

The watchwords were 'restoring order' and 'going back to the basics of true dwarfishness'.

Nevertheless, there is always somebody who will not buzz with the swarm and in this case it was Albrecht Albrechtson, around whom there coalesced the dwarfs who were totally against the takeover and who remained loyal to Rhys Rhysson come what may. The air in the corridors thickened, and the unspoken question was who would be the first to sting?

Albrecht Albrechtson placed his hand on the Scone of Stone.

'My fellow dwarfs, I made an oath, and so did you. And as we all learned on our mother's knees, the Ginnungagap awaits all

---

* In their minds, at least, although it has to be said that they had been too careful to attempt to overthrow the Low King until he was far away in Quirm.

murderers and oath-breakers.' His smile was a grimace. He went on. 'Perhaps I misheard.'

'Circumstances have changed,' said Ardent. 'The King is far too friendly with the trolls and the damn humans and, for goodness' sake, he also signed the declaration that the goblins – goblins, I ask you – should be treated as well as dwarfs! I don't know about you, but I don't see a goblin as being *my* equal.'

In the ringing silence, Albrechtson almost whispered, 'And the Koom Valley Accord? The understanding that would maintain peace in our time? We were all party to it. How easily do we break *our* oaths these days?'

'I never signed,' said Ardent.

'No, you didn't,' said Albrechtson. 'It was signed by Rhys Rhysson on behalf of all dwarfs.'

'Not on my behalf,' Ardent countered. 'And I didn't believe that little tableau of the two kings in the cavern. You know how humans are? I wouldn't put it past someone like Vetinari to have had it placed there.'

This time the silence banged. They had all walked past that strange shining tableau in Koom Valley where the air was so chilly in the cavern and the two dead kings rode into history in a state of intentional stalemate. And perhaps some of them might have wondered what the dead kings would do if their peace were disturbed. The moment was broken by Ardent.

'What we need is stability,' he said. 'No one need come to blows, nobody will be hurt. I give you my oath on that.'

'Excuse me,' said Albrecht. 'Would that go the way of the oath you gave your King, you traitor?'

The clang of weaponry being deployed at speed echoed around the halls, to be followed by the resounding silence of not wanting to be the one to take the first slash. It was a stalemate, so stale as to be stinking.

'I will not rise to idiotic taunts,' said Ardent. 'We must deal with

247

the world as it is. We have to make certain that it becomes the world that we want, where the dwarfs take their rightful place at the table. Times have changed. We need someone ready to defend our interests. Everyone keeps talking about the world changing. I intend to see that it changes to the betterment of dwarfkind.'

He walked over to Albrecht and held out a hand. 'You used to think like this, my friend. Won't you join me?'

The multiple intake of breaths went around the cavern.

Albrecht hesitated for a moment. 'You can stick that right up your jumper.'

There was silence. Apart from some dwarfs saying to each other, 'What does that mean?' and other more travelled dwarfs, who had dealt with humans, coming to the rescue with, 'It's rather like saying "Put it where the sun does not shine", causing those dwarfs who did not know the ways of humanity to say, 'Isn't that the little valley over near Slice, rather nice?' until one of them said, 'As I understand it, it means shove it up your arse.'

'Oh, really?'

'May I suggest a show of hands?' said Ardent. 'All those *not* for me and a proper resolution to dwarf affairs as they have been since time immemorial should raise their hand and make themselves known.'

Albrechtson promptly sat on the Scone of Stone.

'Well,' said Ardent. 'Stay there long enough, my friend, and you will have piles.'

And there was laughter, but worried laughter. And unusually, for dwarfs, people were thinking first. Yes, the goblins were rising and so were the humans and the trolls, and on the playing board of the world the dwarfs surely had to keep some allegiances. So what if a king changes? When the King came back he would find a *fait accompli* and the world would be busy with its own occupations. Politics notoriously change all the time . . . The unseen, unheard point was that everybody knew that if a dwarf-against-dwarf fight happened now it would go the distance, and where would they all be then?

In the highest room in her castle over the deepest canyon in Uberwald Lady Margolotta was awakened by the duty Igor and was not happy about it.

She opened the lid of her casket and said, 'Vhat's this all about? It's not even dusk yet.'

'Theriouth thingth happening, my lady. I heard there'th a coup in Schmaltzberg and Ardent ith in the athendant.'

Igor looked carefully at his mistress, who appeared to be suddenly lost in thought. He stepped back a little in case of an explosion. To his surprise, Lady Margolotta merely said, 'That little veasel? Sometimes the black ribbon is sorely tested. How far has the news got around?'

'Hardly at all, my lady. The clackth ith down, on the orderth of Ardent.'

A sudden syrup in his mistress's tone worried Igor. If silk could speak it would sound like that.

'On his orders? Really? Ve'll see about that. Oh, yes, ve vill.'

Lady Margolotta walked over to the balcony and dropped into the canyon, gathering speed until she glided towards the first clacks tower outside Uberwald and landed softly on the little deck, so close to the superintendent that he nearly lost a year's growth. But he knew the ropes. Lady Margolotta was a black ribboner and generally quite a useful neighbour.

'Oh, it's you, Arthur,' she said. 'How's your vife? Sorry to upset you.'

Rather nervously, the superintendent said, 'Dolores is fine, m'lady, thank you for asking.'

'And the children?'

'Doing very well, thank you, m'lady, and thank you so much for helping with the tuition fees.'

'Not at all. Is your clacks still vorking?'

'Oh yes, m'lady, but something seems to have happened up the line. We've got one hell of a backlog and we don't know what's going on. Looks like the grag militants have been up to their old tricks again.'

'Yes, I know, Arthur. Could you please send a clacks to Lord Vetinari and a copy to Diamond King of Trolls? Also to the major clacks office in Quirm for delivery to Rhys Rhysson. My usual codes, of course, and priority vun.'

She waited while the man set things in motion, tapping her foot on the floor, and was relieved when Arthur had finished.

'Thank you, Arthur. Vould you be so good as to have any messages brought over to me as soon as possible by vun of your goblin couriers, please? And oh, it's your son's birthday, isn't it?'

'Yes, tomorrow!'

A heavy gold coin dropped into the man's hand.

'Tell him not to spend it all at vonce,' said a voice in the distance and suddenly Lady Margolotta was no longer there. The man looked nervously at the shiny coin in his hand. But there, that was the gentry for you. It paid to be in with the gentry. She had been so helpful when his daughter was taken bad, as well. Yes, of course, she was a vampire. But she wasn't a bad person. And he was oh so very glad he could be of use to her.

It had been a long wait to get home, but a wait worth waiting for, and after a pleasant evening with Adora Belle, what could be better than being woken up at 3 a.m. by members of the palace guard? And of course, the answer was absolutely everything, thought Moist.

Crossly was so furious that they were backing away from him across the threshold and Moist heard him say, 'This is insufferable! What about *habeas corpus*?'

250

And the most senior of the guards said, 'What about *habeas corpus?*'

Moist sighed and pulled on his trousers. Nowadays he kept a pair at hand, ready for occasions such as this. He had had enough. And so, stepping into his shoes and buttoning his shirt, he more or less slid down the stairs to where the grinning guards were shouldering aside the still protesting Crossly.

He was aware of Adora Belle, at her spikiest, looking over the banister and he had one of those *to hell with it* moments . . . As the guards strode into the hallway, he walked up to them and said, 'Where's your warrant?'

'What? We don't have to have a warrant.'

'Okay,' said Moist. 'Then you should seriously consider, for your own sake, apologizing to my wife for disturbing us at this time of the morning. She gets very . . . unhappy if her sleep is interrupted.'

At that instant Adora Belle leaned over the banister and said, 'This is a most excellent crossbow, one of Burleigh and Stronginthearm's finest, and I can only fire it once, gentlemen, so which intruder will I hit? Because right now intruders are what you appear to be, and rude intruders at that. After all, a simple "Do you mind coming with us, sir?" would have done the trick.

'Moist?' Raising the loaded crossbow, Adora Belle continued, 'Is this the one with the dodgy hair trigger? I always get them confused.'

Moist held out his hands and said, 'This is how it's going to go. You may think that Vetinari will be on your side, the majesty of the Patrician and what have you. On the other hand, my wife could shoot any one of you if she wanted to and quite possibly might hit me instead. And I suspect Moist von Lipwig is more important to the Patrician than you bunch of herberts.'

'Off you go, gentlemen,' Adora Belle chimed in from her vantage point. 'I'm sure my husband will attend on his lordship around breakfast time. It's always good to do business on a full stomach.'

Moist looked at the guards and said, 'Gentlemen, I have no intention of getting you into trouble, or indeed of allowing my wife to skewer any one or two of you. And so I think I'd like to have an early-morning stroll to the palace. If it so happens that you are walking that way at the same time, well, so be it. Although you might want to make that a brisk walk, because I fear my wife will be watching us go from the upstairs window and that *is* the dodgy crossbow she's holding in her hands.'

And as he sauntered after the suddenly very sprightly guards clanging against each other in their hurry to get away, Moist was surprised to see the impeccably ironed Crossly make a fist and whisper, 'Well *done*, sir! They don't even clean their boots when they step inside.' And the sedate little man's face was fierce and fiery.

Within the palace, Moist found Lord Vetinari in conversation with a stone-faced Commander Vimes. The normal calm of the Oblong Office had been replaced by a low hum of determined-looking clerks arriving with messages to hand over to Drumknott.

Vetinari looked up and said, 'Ah, Mister Lipwig. I'm so glad you could spare us a little time from your early-morning exercise routine.'

'Your guards can't run for toffee. You ought to do something about it, sir, and while we're on the subject, it would be a good idea to teach them some manners.'

The Patrician lifted an eyebrow. 'I understood it was the prodding you objected to, Mister Lipwig. Was there prodding?'

'No, sir, but—'

'I am glad to hear it,' said his lordship. 'So, if we may to business? As I suspected, the apologists for the grags and other dwarf malcontents have merely been lying low, and I believe that in the

252

darkness scandalous undertakings are still sprouting like mushrooms. It appears that there has been a palace coup in Schmaltzberg, only the third one in the history of the dwarfs. Unfortunately, the Low King is, as they say, out of position in Quirm where he has been attending a summit with Diamond King of Trolls. Rhys Rhysson is a notable negotiator, as we all know well from the Koom Valley Accord, and he has held the fractious coalition of dwarf chief mining engineers together for many years. And he is no mean practitioner with the axe, I believe, but he needs to be back in Uberwald with his inner council if this . . . unfortunate turn of events is not to spread underground to other mines.

'Having considered the options,' continued the Patrician, 'it would seem that the railway route to Uberwald, presently under construction, would provide the swiftest and safest and most comfortable method for transporting the Low King, his retinue and war councillors. Time is, as they say, of the essence. You, Mister Lipwig, will travel with all speed to Quirm and take charge of arrangements. Commander Vimes will provide watchmen as an escort and will join you himself as you pass back through Ankh-Morpork, with reinforcements as he sees fit. Be aware, Mister Lipwig, that this is *your* Koom Valley, on wheels.'

'And when you get to Quirm,' said Vimes, 'be sure to look for a dwarf called Bashfull Bashfullsson. Very useful and most definitely on the Low King's side.'

'But the line is nowhere near finished, sir!' Moist wailed.

'Mister Lipwig, you know already that it is not your job to tell me what the problems are. It is your job to tell me about the solutions. Do we have an understanding? I am sure that Harry King will have a high-speed locomotive he can spare – one of his Flyers, perhaps?'

'But, my lord, Harry might have a dozen or so locomotives to spare, but it's the laying of the tracks, that's the rub.'

'Mister Lipwig, I want . . . No, I am ordering you to make miracles by all means necessary,' said Vetinari. 'Do I make my point? I am sure I could make it somewhat pointier.'

Moist saluted and with no hint of sarcasm said, 'Exactly, sir! Action this day! Miracles are us, sir!'

And laconically Vetinari said, 'Try to make it yesterday, Mister Lipwig.'

And that, Moist knew, was that, as far as that conversation was concerned.

Drumknott had been busy. Even as Moist was being roused from his bed by the palace guard, messengers had been sent to Harry King and to Simnel's home. By the time Moist arrived at the compound, he found it even busier than it was in the middle of the day. There to greet him in the grey light of early dawn were Harry and Dick. They appeared to be having an argument and Simnel was looking rather unhappy.

'But it's the look of the thing, Dick,' Harry was saying. 'I mean, Iron Girder is wonderful, of course, but I'm sure the Flyers are classier and more suitable for royalty.'

'Sorry, Harry,' Simnel replied. 'I think it might be risky if Iron Girder weren't the engine. Don't ask me why, because I can't explain why, even with my sliding rule, but she is what we need. And to tell thee t'truth, sir, I've shined her up so much, polished her, greased this, checked that, she's fit for any king, or queen, come to that. Oh, the Flyers are good, and reet smart, too, but I'll say it again: my Iron Girder is the best locomotive in an emergency.'

The arguments chased each other through Moist's brain. Vetinari says this has to be top secret, and it would be Iron Girder's first trip beyond the compound in months. Everyone is bound to notice. But we'll be running an unscheduled train, so they're going to notice anyway. And if it's one of the usual Flyers all the regular passengers will want to know why they can't get on it. And there'll be the armed escort from the Watch, that'll really make us stick out a mile. And after all, if you're going to run a special train the loco-motive should be special . . .

'You know what, Harry?' said Moist. 'I think Dick's right about this. There's something about that engine—'

Just then, from Iron Girder, a little way away, there came a perceptible hiss of steam. Even Harry noticed it.

And Simnel said, 'Steam's up, gentlemen. All aboard, those who're going to Quirm. I'm sorry, Mister Lipwig, but his lordship's orders are to send freight trucks only, to distract attention, like. And to tell t'truth it may be the only way we'll get some Watch officers to fit on board. I've to work on that before you get back. Don't worry,' he added hastily, seeing the others' horror, 'it'll be regular carriages hitched up for the return journey.'

'I hope those trucks are full,' said Harry. 'Can't afford to waste the journey when there's goods waiting to go.'

'Well, the front one is presently a bit full of Sergeant Detritus,' said Simnel, and indeed through its open hatch Moist could now make out the form of the troll watchman, patiently hunched against the far wall. 'But yes, we've loaded up the rest right and tight.'

Moist snoozed his way to Quirm, rocked in the cradle of Iron Girder. He was certain she gave a smoother ride than any of the new-fangled Flyers. Everyone said that was silly, but nevertheless, the thought didn't leave him. Somehow the Flyers looked like machinery, but Iron Girder always looked like . . . somebody. And the train spotters all seemed to think the same thing. It was as if she *was* the railway.

The chateau that had been put at the disposal of the Low King while he was in Quirm for the all-important summit had 'ridiculously grand' written all over it.

Moist was greeted at the main entrance by a dwarf who was neatly dressed but notably lacking in the usual weaponry.

'Bashfull Bashfullsson, Mister von Lipwig. I know your face. It's in the papers so often.'

As they hurried inside Bashfull said, 'Please let me, as they say, mark your card, Mister Lipwig. The King is furious. Furious with the rebels and furious with himself for not doing enough at the right time and I dare say he's also furious with me. But me, well, I look to the sky and I say to Tak, "Don't get mad, but when you made us dwarfs you had a bad day and couldn't find anything in the subtlety box." It seems that we'd sooner fight and argue than live.'

Inside the chateau there was a squad of heavily armed dwarfs on guard, heavily armed, that is, being more heavily armed than the average dwarf who, nevertheless, could generally look like a squad all by himself. They scowled at Moist, with the regulation scowl of all guards everywhere, which intimated that you were less than the dust on the dust on their boots, so watch out. Bashfullsson ignored them and led Moist into the Great Hall, which was buzzing with activity.

But then there was the question of *seeing* the Low King. It was a delicate matter, but Moist wasn't going to let courtiers and guards push him around. He knew Rhys Rhysson was a sensible and powerful dwarf, moderate, the kind of person who looks facts in the face, knowing that it's the only way to survive.

Moist waited while Bashfullsson dealt with the protocols, and wondered how many of the glittering company in the hall were actually on the King's side. Suspicion floated in the air like a fine dust, settling on every shoulder. After all, this was the beginning of a clandestine dwarf war. Much better to fight the trolls. You could recognize the trolls as possibly the enemy, but who knew where the traitors were in this chattering throng?

One of the dwarf guards attempted to dispossess Moist of his treasured lockpicks and only let go when Moist had retrieved them using very non-diplomatic language and some clever misdirection. He hadn't actually made use of the lockpicks in years, his tongue generally being more effective at getting into places than some bent pieces of metal ever could be. Nevertheless, he was still fuming and was about to say something non-political when Bashfullsson grabbed him by the arm and took him to see the King.

The King's suite was, surprisingly, at the top of the building. In normal dwarf dwellings, the *lower* a dwarf, the more important he was, and so, Moist surmised, putting the Low King into rooms on the top floor might just be a ruse to thwart any traditionally minded enemies.

Kings don't travel lightly or quietly. There were dwarfish flunkies everywhere alongside the chateau staff, folding things and indeed shovelling things into cases with a sense of panic, as if the bailiffs were coming.

But at last Moist and Bashfullsson were ushered into a small antechamber where the Low King was planning his counter-coup with his inner council. Every so often a clacks arrived and was hurried to the King.

Rhys Rhysson was smaller and slighter than Moist had expected and was surrounded in this cramped room by generals and some of the rest of the circus that has to follow a monarch.

Moist noticed black looks from a few dwarfs, angry at the human trespasser. Bashfullsson bowed to the King as he introduced Moist. 'Mister von Lipwig, your majesty. An envoy of Lord Vetinari.'

'And killer of a number of renegade delvers,' said the King to Moist. 'And not least a bank manager.' Rhys laughed. 'It must be tough in the banking business, Mister Lipwig?'

Moist joined in the little attempt at laughter and said, 'You have no idea, sire; but the most important thing you need to know about me is that I was a crook and a scoundrel and a very clever one.

What better man to run the Royal Bank of Ankh-Morpork and the Mint than a crook? I had the tendencies of a crook and many of the skills of a crook and because I look at things with a crooked eye, metaphorically speaking, I see the opportunities and the problems. I'm very lucky and I have the knack of finding friends easily.'

'But probably not with those delvers, eh?' said the King.

'I was lucky and I survived. I survived and, if I may say so, I wish survival to the Low King and his court.' All right, he thought, that was drawing the long bow and no mistake, but he couldn't avoid it . . . all that armament getting in one another's way, well, with all that milling about something would go wrong sooner or later.

'Mister Lipwig, as you know, I have sudden important business that requires my presence in Uberwald as soon as possible, and at the highest speed. I understand from the clacks I received from Lord Vetinari this morning that you have a plan to get me there. I'm curious to know what that plan involves.'

There were the usual murmurs and glances, but Moist was not going to be intimidated by a bunch of small people who were giving themselves airs. He was never one for protocol – it got in the way and often concealed nasty and dangerous things.

'I'm afraid, sire, that I'm not willing to divulge Lord Vetinari's proposal here. There are too many people in this room, any one of whom could be a traitor!'

Uproar ensued. Moist kept his face blank and totally unmoving until all protestations had been protested.

'I'm not here to be nice, and I have to tell you that, while on this mission, my allegiance is to you and only you, sire. Apart from Mister Bashfullsson here, I don't know *any* of the rest of these dwarfs. The opposition must surely be intelligent enough to make certain they have a sleeper in the palace, funnelling everything back to them.'

He had gone too far, he knew it, but the dwarfs had not impressed him with their security. It was far too stiff . . . all front and pomposity.

'Mister Lipwig, I am the King, surely, and I am still alive because of whom I know and whom I can trust, see. I appreciate your thoroughness in this matter.' The King turned to the dwarf by his side. 'Aeron, some privacy, if you please.'

And the dwarf called Aeron, who seemed to Moist to be a trusted assistant, a dwarf version of Drumknott, cleared the room of hangers-on, leaving only himself, Bashfullsson and a few other obviously senior dwarfs.

'Thank you,' said the King. 'Now, Mister Lipwig, in this small room, I trust everybody. And, boyo, I might just trust you because you are Mister Lipwig and I know your reputation. You're a survivor, quite possibly a plaything of the gods or, perhaps, the most handsome bag of wind that there has ever been. You get away with it, and thus I hope I will too, because more than *our* lives depend on us getting me to Uberwald and the Scone of Stone before those bastards wreck everything I stand for.' He smiled and said, 'I hope that doesn't feel like pressure?'

'Your majesty, pressure is where I start,' said Moist.

There was a noisy party with lots of quaffing and dwarf songs in full swing as the Low King and his commanders left the chateau quietly from the servants' entrance a short hour later. Several coaches had come and gone already that morning and the departure of a few more was unremarkable.

'Tagwen Tagwensson is doing a grand job of playing King today,' Rhys noted to Moist as their carriage swung down the long gravel driveway. 'That song has over a hundred verses. They can keep that up for days!'

When they arrived at the Quirm terminus they were met by the extremely large form of Sergeant Detritus of the Ankh-Morpork City Watch, who was standing guard by Iron Girder, hefting his piecemaker, which had what might be called a wholesale capability.

The Low King's eyes lit up when he recognized the sergeant and he exclaimed, 'Detritus! If you're on board, then perhaps I don't need any other bodyguards.'

This was said laughing, but Moist couldn't help thinking that it might just be true.

'Good to see you, King!' Detritus roared. He looked around sharply and said, 'Dere any grags here? If yes, please line up.'

Behind the King, always present, Aeron was carefully busying himself getting people and weapons on board. He opened the door and quickly ushered Rhys into the gleaming carriage.

Bashfullsson tapped Detritus on the knee. 'I am indeed a grag, sergeant, and lining up as requested. What next?'

Detritus scratched his head. 'But you is okay, Mister Bashfullsson. Der commander knows you, and his lady.'

'Ah, so I'm lining up to get on the train, then?' said the dwarf. 'It's pleasant to meet you again, sergeant, but please remember there are grags and grags.' And he turned to follow Aeron into the carriage.

Once the whole retinue was safely aboard, Moist stood watch while Detritus heaved himself into the guard's van, which gave a tremendous creak and groan; but everything seemed to hold, so with a signal to the footplate Moist scrambled up into the van and they were off.

The train pulled away with the usual jerk of the couplings and as the long journey back to Ankh-Morpork began Moist suddenly realized that he was, as it were, not required on this voyage.

In the coaches the Low King, his bodyguards and councillors huddled together and were speaking very quietly, their thoughts deep in planning. On the footplate, the driver was focused on getting his royal cargo to its destination and was in a world of concentration. You could see it dripping off him like snow; listening to the wheels, listening to the rails, watching the lights, checking the gauges and driving the train in such a positive way that possibly even without Iron Girder herself they might just get there on willpower alone. And the stoker made it clear he had no need of Moist's assistance. So Moist now had nothing to do except sleep and . . . worry *so* much.

If the King was a target, if the grags got to hear that he was on the train, then the train was bound to be a target although, as it happened, Moist hoped they had run some interference.

For his part Moist thought attacks would surely come out in the wilderness, later, on the long lonely haul up to Uberwald. Despite everything he'd said to Lord Vetinari, he knew it was oh so easy to derail a locomotive. The ever diligent Mr Simnel had told Moist that he'd tried it at low speed at the back of the compound in a place where Iron Girder couldn't see, with impressive effects. Once derailed, it required the combined efforts of several trolls and golems over many hours with a clever system of pulleys to get the engine back on the track. If it happened to an engine travelling at speed under full steam . . . And this, Moist thought, is a man who lives by the sliding rule and the sine and cosine, not forgetting the tangent. Moist never challenged Dick's proclamations regarding his sliding rule; he could make the numbers dance and Moist was yet to see him get things wrong. It was like . . . like wizardry, but without the wizards and all their mess.

And indeed, as Dick was finding out, you could even have a girl-friend . . . an intriguing thought that seemed to echo at the back of his mind. And it was common knowledge now that Dick and Harry's niece were, as they say, walking out. He had apparently one night driven Emily around the compound by starlight and that had to mean something, didn't it? And Dick had told Moist, in the voice of somebody having found a strange and attractive new world, that she was very good at handling the fire box, without ever getting her dress dirty. And he'd added, 'I reckon Iron Girder likes her. You never see a smut on her. I come out every time looking like a dust-man and when we've finished she looks like she's one of them ballerinas or something.'

261

But right now there was so much else to think about. This most important of trains was moving its priceless cargo, and Moist knew that the whole business relied on fairly simple things being done properly, at the precise time and in exactly the right way. There were people who made certain there was coal in the coal bunkers along the route and by now he knew how much water would be needed and who would make certain that it would be there when and where it was required. But how did you make certain that the person who made certain actually did these things? It had to be someone's responsibility!

And these tasks seemed to Moist like a great big pyramid whose every stone had to be laid in place before one wheel turned. In some ways it frightened him. For most of his life he had been mostly alone and as for the Bank and the Mint, well, Vetinari had got it right. He did have a knack for finding and keeping people who liked their jobs and were good at them, and since everything was delegated, why, then he could be Moist von Lipwig, a catalyst in the world. And now he could see why people had anxiety attacks, the kind of people who would lock their door and halfway up the garden path would come back to see if they'd locked said door and unlock it to make sure and lock it again then set off up the path only to go through the whole terrible procedure once more.

The fact of the matter was you had to hope and assume that a lot of capable people had done lots of capable things in a capable way, and double-checked them frequently to make sure everything was right. So worrying was stupid, wasn't it? But worrying was never quite like that. It sat like a little goblin on your shoulder and whispered. And suddenly that kind of worried person, in the strange world of mistrust, was now entering the stuff of nightmares, and right now he, Moist von Lipwig, for heaven's sake, was worried, yes, really very worried. What had been left in? What had been left out? I can hear the wheels just down there and I know the journey is going to take four days, at least, not counting breakdowns, dreadful weather and the storms up in the mountains, they can be ferocious, and all this without mentioning some lunatic dwarfs hell-bent on ruining the party for everybody.

It has to be said that this was an inner monologue. Yes, it was an inner monologue's own personal inner monologue, but outside Moist's skin absolute stone-cold certainty reigned: nothing could possibly go wrong. After all, Dick would be dealing with the technicalities, and he was a genius. Not in the same way that Leonard of Quirm was a genius, but, Moist thought loyally, in a reassuring, solid, *Simnel* sort of way. Leonard would probably get distracted halfway through the journey by an idea for using cabbages as fuel, or using the waste from the fire box to grow better cabbages, or painting a masterpiece of a nymph clad in cabbage leaves and coal. But Dick had his flat cap on straight. Vimes would be coming too, and although part of Moist – the part that still thought of coppers as people to avoid even in your best disguise – got the willies when the commander looked him in the eye or any other part of his anatomy, the rest of him was very grateful that Blackboard Monitor Vimes would be on his side if the grags came calling . . .

In fact, Moist was full of little monologues, chasing one another around, but afterwards, because they were *his* monologues, they decided that they would come together again as one whole Moist von Lipwig and would therefore maintain and get through no matter the circumstances.

Everything is going to be mar . . . vell . . . ous, he assured himself. When has it ever not been – you're the lucky Moist von Lipwig! Right in the centre the hypothetical goblin of uncertainty twisted itself into a tiny quivering mush. Moist wished it well, smiled and said goodbye.

Harry King's vast mansion was well protected and a perfect place for a private dinner where the Low King and Vetinari could meet while preparations were being made for the long haul to Uberwald. It was widely considered that Harry's . . . *undertakers* had the jump on your average soldier or policeman when it came to a scrap, because *those* people had been taught to have rules while most of Harry's boys couldn't even spell the word. Any intruder foolish enough to be found lurking in the shrubbery of Harry's extensive estate in the dark and the dripping rain would be pruned in no short order.

Even though this was a private dinner, Effie King was not going to let the side down. She had begun her preparations for the meal with a headache and then moved on to a dither before segueing into an organization of military precision and dimensions, bullying the cooks on the way and frantically looking up such things as what spoon you used with what soup.

Effie genuflected deeply to the Low King as he arrived in her oak-panelled dining room. And Effie was in a more expensive and acceptable version of hog heaven.

'How was your journey, sire? Safe and comfortable?'

The Low King hesitated for a moment. 'It's Euphemia, isn't it?' he said.

Effie was on fire. 'Yes, your majesty, but just Effie to you.'

The King smiled again. 'Very good, and I'm "your majesty" to you, Lady King.'

Effie looked somewhat challenged until the King of the Dwarfs held out his hand and said, 'Actually, you can call me anything you like. I was just trying to make an old dwarf joke, just like myself right now: a fugitive trying to avoid even more dangerous fugitives and reliant on the help of others, such as your noble husband and his friends.'

Moist smiled as the noble penny dropped on Effie.

The King now looked around the other guests. He smiled at Commander Vimes and Lady Sybil and shook hands with Adora Belle who was, Moist thought proudly, a real looker when she wasn't in her work clothes. And from what he could see, she had bought a most attractive and therefore expensive gown for the evening. It was still grey, of course, but with a kind of lustre to it that made it seem almost festive. This was grey letting its hair down. He couldn't possibly argue about it, she earned more than he did.

The King's eyes scouted the room and he continued, 'And Lord Vetinari . . . will be joining us? And Mister Simnel, the technical genius behind your remarkable railway?'

Harry looked around, just as Lord Vetinari stepped forward from the shadows in the room* and got there first and rather more smoothly.

'Your majesty, welcome to Ankh-Morpork. Mister Simnel is overseeing the final preparations for the locomotive that *will* get you back to your home and throne in time. Nothing is being left to chance, I can assure you.'

'Ah, Lord Vetinari – I didn't see you, forgive me,' replied Rhys, and Moist nearly choked on his drink when he continued, 'But I understand there's still some track to lay and bridges that need to be completed.' He paused. 'Rather close to our intended destination, I believe.'

Moist felt the air chill instantly. He quickly scanned the faces of Harry and Vetinari and jumped in – after all, it was what he was there for – 'Excuse me, your majesty, but Mister Simnel has developed a concept called loggysticks, the nature of which is enshrined in the phrase "first things first". Of course, the trick is to know exactly what needs to be first and, right now, since you are many days away from Uberwald, the gangs still have time to complete the last few sections. You will get to Uberwald for the appointed time. I'll stake my life on that.'

---

* At least, that's where Moist assumed he'd come from. Vetinari was one of the greatest students of concealment the Assassins had ever produced, so it could simply have been a shadowy state of mind.

There was a silence that froze the air in the room and Moist counted down to the inevitable comment from a smiling Lord Vetinari.

'Most gratifying, Mister Lipwig, and you have made that promise in front of all of us. Good show! And all good people here with quite excellent memories.'

After that, the first person to speak was Adora Belle, who said, 'Oh, that's definitely my husband, but I'm sure he'll manage it at the last possible minute . . . He always does. And if he can achieve it while riding a white charger he'll be as happy as a clam.'

The King laughed in a rather strange way and said, 'Well, then let's hope that he is not unduly shucked.'

'Your majesty, Mister Lipwig always achieves his goals, I assure you,' said Lord Vetinari, in his best oiled voice. 'I find it amazing and, of course, annoying, but so far he has always succeeded, which is why, therefore, all of his extremities are in their rightful place.'

Everybody present laughed nervously, except Lord Vetinari, who just laughed. The King of the Dwarfs stared at Moist as if seeing him in a new light, and said, 'Is that really true, Mister Lipwig?'

Moist forced his face to go so deadpan that it might have actually been dead. 'Yes, your majesty, everything that ought to be attached still is, isn't that right, Adora Belle?'

His wife didn't say anything. She just looked the look of a wife who was putting up with her husband's funny little ways for which he would suffer in the boudoir later.

After *that*, Effie beamed anxiously and said, in a voice that she considered posh people would use, 'Shall we take our seats for dinner, your majesty, ladies and gentlemen? All the spoons are in their rightful place, I do assure you.'

Conversation around the dinner table, in deference to Effie and the flapping ears of the staff, was . . . nice, and mostly about the new railway and the wonders of what might be achieved with it, and

266

indeed the interesting fact that lots of rich people were buying seaside houses in Quirm now that it was so easy to get there. And there was also another careful conversation about how good the fish and the seafood was becoming now it didn't have to bake in the sunshine, which might have had something to do with the mountainous platter of prawns, monkey clams and unidentified tentacular things sculpted to resemble the lost citadel of Leshp, which Effie had given pride of place in the centre of the table. And this went on in various different ways until dinner was almost over and the staff had left the room, whereupon Vimes gave Rhys a quizzical look, stood up and left the room. He returned a few minutes later, nodded to the Low King and resumed his seat at the table.

'Ladies and gentlemen, preparations for our departures are in place. As I speak, the Low King is departing by fast coach for Uberwald.' And there was something in the way he said that that made Moist think, because the Low King, at that moment, was clearly still in the room shovelling down expensive ice cream.

Sure enough, there was the sound of a coach pulling up outside, stopping for a moment and then driving away, surrounded by well-armed bodyguards.

Back at the table the King licked his spoon in a very regal way and chuckled. 'That should keep those scoundrels busy for a while.' He smiled at Vimes. 'Thank you for your help in this, commander.'

'Think nothing of it,' said Vimes gruffly. 'It's a good idea. And Harry and I have added some embellishments of our own.'

'So who was on that coach, commander?' Moist asked.

'The coach?' Vimes replied. 'This is a very dark night and the King is cloaked and it is almost impossible to see inside, but the dark-accustomed eye might see Sergeant Cheery Littlebottom accompanied by some of my most trusted dwarf officers. Anybody interfering with the coach and its contents will find their life difficult, nay extinct.'

The King coughed before saying to Vimes, 'I remember Sergeant Littlebottom when we met by the Scone of Stone eight years ago. Oh, yes, I remember her.'

'She volunteered for the job, sire,' said Vimes.

'She did, did she?' said the King. 'Well, none of us know what the future holds, but if my backside is still on the Scone when all of this is over then Sergeant Littlebottom and her colleagues will have earned any favours they want from me. A king's gratitude has to be worth something, wouldn't you say, Blackboard Monitor Vimes?'

Vimes smiled as if remembering an old joke and said, 'Well, I hope she does, because she's one of the best officers I've got.'

'How many Cheery Littlebottoms can you afford?' The King looked sombre. 'I'd hate for someone to die, just to see that I don't. Now, if I am to get to Uberwald with all due speed, we should be leaving very soon, yes?'

'Soon, your majesty,' Vimes agreed. 'The rail traffic between here and Sto Lat runs throughout the night. At present it's mostly freight and perishables for the market and the Post Office parcel business, but people are always coming and going at the terminus. Nobody could keep track of everyone. We've set it up so that you'll be just another anonymous traveller on the platform, looking like any one of the Third Class passengers, although, should the need arise, you and your travelling companions would be found to be carrying an inordinately large amount of deadly weaponry. And that, your majesty, includes fangs.

'The Watch is not going to be outdone on this one, sire. If the sh— excrement hits the wossname, nearly every place you go we'll have people watching you. Now, if you and Mister Lipwig will accompany me to the side room over there, we'll make sure that neither of you looks like either of you by the time we've finished.'

Turning to Harry, the commander said, 'Harry, are you sure you can vouch for the discretion of all your people, even those in the kitchens?'

Harry almost saluted. 'Yes, commander. Some of them are scoundrels – well, you know – but they're my kind of scoundrel.'

'Ah, yes,' said the King. 'I'm used to that sort of scoundrel. They are all so very . . . *useful*.'

Moist knew a lot about the tricks of disguise, although he never bothered with makeup as such. Becoming another person was a subtle matter that was probably only understood by those wrinkled old men up in the very high mountains around Oi Dong who knew the secrets of the known universe, one of them being how to kick your enemy's spine all the way out of their body. *They* certainly knew that true camouflage came from within. And, oh yes, an occasional change of clothes was warranted, but mostly Moist just thought about the type of person he wanted to be seen as and it all came into focus. A false nose was definitely a no-no – inevitably, any nose designed to make you look like a stranger would be noticeably strange. And why risk it when his own features were so unmemorable that no one recalled their shape in any case? Of course, trying to look female had some built-in snags, but he'd managed it on a few occasions, back in the bad old days which were, in retrospect, so damn good. And he had lost track of all the clergymen he had been. If there was ever such a thing as redemption, they would have to open a magnum of the stuff for Moist. No, a brewery.

The King's party split up when they arrived at the station. Rhys, now disguised as a rather disorientated, elderly dwarf, was accompanied at a distance by three other disreputable-looking characters, while the rest of his party disposed themselves in small, innocuous-looking groups along the platform.

Bashfull Bashfullsson had gallantly volunteered as another bodyguard, but both Moist and Commander Vimes had considered him too recognizable to other dwarfs, here in his native

Ankh-Morpork, and suggested his special skills could be made better use of elsewhere. The dark clerks, however, had been trained by Vetinari who, as he had so recently proved, could stand in a room full of people without being seen: it was a technique. And there were others. Quite probably overhead. Whatever happened, Commander Vimes was *not* going to have the Low King of the Dwarfs killed on his watch.

Moist sighed as he walked, dragging one leg pitifully, but not too pitifully, to the rear of the train. There he found a station guard berating a well-dressed man who had sat down firmly in the Third Class carriage among sleepy workers with greasy hands and bags of tools, and chimney sweeps with, of course, their sacks of soot, inevitably leaking. Moist was all for the common man, and most especially the common man who could have afforded at least one bar of soap over a lifetime, and possibly didn't spit all the time, great hawking globs of spit, the ones with a personality of their own. And the toff, who reeked and dribbled best brandy, was holding up the train while the guard was dithering, derailed by a haughty voice.

And so Moist put an arm around the wretched man and went straight into his infuriating-drunk routine, complete with explosive belches, a surefire winner guaranteed to work every time. First there was the spittle in the corner of the mouth, and a nasty smell, which Moist was king of, and the conversation in which every word was shredded and mistreated and misapplied unto death while Moist leaned inappropriately and spat and dribbled.

The wretch hurried for the sole First Class compartment at the front of the train after less than a minute. A personal best for Moist, who, still in dribbling and stinking character, staggered and weaved his way to a seat just before the whistle was blown and the train moved in the half-hearted way trains always did as the engine got its act together. He was very proud of it and he'd only used up half of his Boffo's best artificial vomit with lingering smell.

It was a cold night for travelling. The King was on board some-where, but this wasn't the time to show any interest in him. Moist's ragged clothes had been, well, adequate, and everybody in the compartment with the wind whistling underneath them had wrapped themselves up and tried not to exist until the train had reached its destination. Somewhere, he thought, there should be a statue erected to Effie, who had clearly tongue-lashed her husband into making the lower class coaches at least water-proof.*

The leader of the delvers watching one of the main routes out of Ankh-Morpork smiled as the large coach bearing the Low King's insignia came into view. Rain splashed over the coach as the horses galloped hubwards and the leader of the delvers smiled at the rain-drops. How easy it was going to be. He gave the signal to the waiting dwarfs and within minutes they were grabbing harnesses and bridles and bringing the coach to a shuddering halt. He kicked the coach door open.

'Bring out the King and you will not be harmed,' he commanded.

There was silence inside the coach and then he heard a voice say, 'We ain't got no king apart from Harry King and we ain't the ones that are going to get harmed. Consider us as the King Preservation Society, and Sir Harry King don't like his friends being put to any trouble. And you, my son, you are a lot of trouble, but thankfully not as much as we are. Come on, lads!'

The fight was fast and methodical and the coach drove away

---

* The only carriages that were open to the weather were the ones for those extra-large passengers (mostly trolls) who couldn't fit inside anything else, and that was because they were in fact the coal cars. No one minded – trolls were impervious to rain, which helped them cultivate a better quality of lichen in any case, and the coal doubled as a welcome snack during the journey.

with the victors singing and drinking in the storm and the water on the cobbles was tinged with red.

Meanwhile, a few miles away, another group of delvers was having a remarkably similar experience with a remarkably similar coach, which had turned out to contain amongst other horrors a very fierce, very female dwarf in a watchman's helmet . . .

The train pulled in to the station at Sto Lat Junction, and Moist watched as the guard helped a grubby and pitiful old dwarf down from his carriage. The Low King clearly had some skill as an actor. Moist noticed one of the old dwarf's equally decrepit companions in adversity take pity on him and give him a piece of dwarf bread, breaking it in half with his axe. To his horror, Moist saw the King dribbling his thanks to the bread giver.

As he came up to the King, Moist whispered, 'Excellent . . . Where did you get that stink? It's got a life of its own.'

The King put a finger to his lips and said, 'Not me, it leaked from the man in front. I don't think he could have washed for years. But remember, a king has to cope with a lot worse than a little stink.'

There were a few hours to kill before the fast train left Sto Lat for Zemphis, as yet the furthest point hubwards to enjoy a Hygienic Railway service. Getting the Low King out of sight was a priority; even in disguise, there was a risk.

Leaving Simnel and Vimes in charge at the station, Moist and the Low King limped their way outside. Moist looked around for people he knew had to be there because he couldn't see them. Suddenly one of them was right in front of him, so close that they were almost touching. He hadn't seen him until that moment. It was as if he had shot up from below.

'Godfrey, Mister Lipwig – dark clerk. Lord Vetinari has arranged for a safe house to be available to your party. Mister Simnel suggested his mother's house, which isn't far away. We've met the lady and she is a royalist through and through. *Any* royalty, and sensible, too. Nothing to worry about there. Clerk Mavis says the old girl is quick on the uptake and understands the position. She is a good cook and there will be clean sheets.'

Moist looked at the dripping King, who smiled and said, 'It sounds like a gift from Tak on a night like this.'

As they walked the short distance through the rain-drenched and deserted streets to Mrs Simnel's house, Moist was always aware of their escorts because the little hairs on the back of his neck were telling him they were there, showing them the way. Before long, they reached a cheerful little house near the centre of town, the kind that was always referred to as a 'little palace', the kind a lad might buy for his widowed mother so she could be close for doing the shopping.

A discreet knock at the door caused some shuffling within before a lady who could only be Mr Simnel's mother stood in the doorway quietly ushering them inside. Once they were in her small but immaculate house, she paused and looked down at the Low King, then curtsied.

'Thank you so much, my dear Mrs Simnel,' said the King, who had clearly dealt with these things many times before. 'No need for that from the mother of the genius engineer.' And Mrs Simnel was suddenly awash with maternal pride.

'Oh, yes, your majesty. He's a good lad, our Dick. Did you know that when he were quite young he made me an iconograph, caught the imp himself, so 'e did, and trained it with butter. They really like butter, do imps. And it's ever so useful, yes indeed.'

While Clerk Godfrey, on flannel feet, quickly checked the rest of the house, Mrs Simnel turned to Moist and said, 'I know you, too. You're Mister Lipwig. Dick speaks very highly of you. I saw your picture in the paper only yesterday and I've seen our Dick in there, too. Makes an old mum reet proud, so it does. Of course, I don't buy it, the Reverend Amusable comes round and reads the paper to me, what with that tiny print an' all. I don't get around as much these days, but now my lad is in the money he has all kind of food delivered up fresh every day on the train and sees his old mum all right. The other day, ooh, it were a lobster in a bag of ice. I 'ad to go all the way up to t'posh restaurant to find out how to cook it, but it were gradely and toothsome and so much on it there was enough for Mrs Pankweather who's bedbound and can't digest most things, but you should've seen her tooth light up when she saw a plate full of lobster. Well, you 'ave to, after all. Not every elderly lady has a good strong lad to see she's all right.'

Mrs Simnel suddenly looked sombre and said, 'But he sends me money every week *regular*, so much I don't rightly know what to do wi' it, so I give some of it to the poor. You *are* a friend of his, aren't you, Mister Lipwig?'

'Yes, Mrs Simnel,' said Moist. 'You can't imagine how much.'

At this point Clerk Godfrey said, 'We are now going back to the marshalling yard to assist Mister Vimes and other members of the Watch who will be travelling with us on the long haul to Uberwald. Clerks Columbine and Silkworm will remain outside and will escort you back to the station in time to catch the train to Zemphis.' And then he was gone.

Mrs Simnel looked again at the bedraggled King, and said with unconscious informality, 'You look famished, pet. I know it's late but I've got some pease pudding in t'pot . . . not much, but it keeps you going and it'll build up your strength when you most need it.'

As it turned out, Mrs Simnel's pease pudding was the queen of pease puddings and even though the dinner at Harry's had only been a few hours earlier Moist noticed that the King almost sucked it up. When they'd eaten, Mrs Simnel put the lid back on the pot.

'I've got to leave some for my lad,' she said, 'out in all this weather. Mind you, he likes his pease pudding cold.'

And then the King settled into a comfy chair for a snooze. While he slept and Mrs Simnel busied herself clearing the dishes, Moist looked around at the walls and noticed carefully arranged pictures of smiling babies, or was it just one baby taken over and over, because, he thought, at that age all babies look like, well, babies, and only mothers could fathom which one was which. It was amazing.

'My word, Mrs Simnel, what wonderful children,' Moist commented when she returned to wish him goodnight. 'All yours?'

She laughed. 'Oh, dear me, no! Our Dick's my only one, but I were trained as a midwife before I met my late 'usband and you know 'ow it is, I were right good at midwifery and especially when events were going badly.'

And here she looked sternly at Moist and said, 'I'm sure you know what I mean, Mister Lipwig? I only ever lost one because they couldn't find my whereabouts until it were too late. Any road, ever since then people call me out and you know 'ow it is, my lad says I don't have to do it any more, but once you've got a reputation for something it clings. Especially when the young lass is desperate.'

The look of Mrs Simnel was that of the put-upon, but in her eyes pride flashed a fin.

Snoring heavily in the huge armchair, the King turned over. Mrs Simnel adjusted the deep cushions to make him more comfortable and then there was a fleeting stillness as her attention seemed to be caught by something. She sent a quick, surprisingly sharp glance in Moist's direction and gave the cushions a final pat before straightening up and smiling sweetly. The moment, whatever it was, most definitely had passed. Moist's brain was soggy with tiredness, and the natural ability to read tiny signals that had kept him alive on so many occasions had deserted him hours before. Even so, he had to ask.

'Mrs Simnel . . . Is something wrong?'

She cut him short. 'Nay, lad. I were just thinking how strange it is that someone so small and, well, hairy could be . . . a king. But 'appen that's the disguise. I'm sure he'll look reet fine in his crown and glitter when he's back on his scone. Now, you need a bed, my lad.'

Tired though he was, Moist could recognize a deflection tactic, and carried on. 'Mrs Simnel, is there something you're not—'

'Nay, there's nothing, nothing for you to worry about at any rate.'

Moist's thoughts were in a whirl, but then further thoughts were blown away by the sound of the front door being blown open as Dick arrived with water streaming off his gabardine, and greeted his mother. He was carrying so many bundles and boxes that he had to deposit them all in the little hallway where a shiny clock told the time, the days of the week and quite possibly the phase of the moon for that night, but most of all it was there to show the world that Dick Simnel's mother got the very best things he could buy for her. She was in his arms immediately, scattering parcels, but he managed to shake her off, laughing.

Seated in the still warm kitchen of the little house, Dick scoffed the congealed pease pudding while she unpacked some of the parcels.

'That's gradely, our ma! It's blowing up something cruel out there.'

Moist suddenly realized he was dog tired.

Mrs Simnel said, 'I've made up a bed for you, Mister Lipwig. I had made up one for t'King, but he looks comfortable where he is and I don't want to disturb him now. Will you be stopping for the night, our Dick?'

'Sorry, Mother, no, too much to do. We're all on double shifts.'

Mrs Simnel looked at Moist proudly. 'That's my lad. He's a worker, my boy, what with his tiddling stick.'

'That's a sliding ruler, Mother,' Simnel said, grinning at Moist.

'Aye, well,' said the proud parent, 'he's making his way in the world, is my lad, working for that Harry King.' And she went to kiss Dick, who picked her up and kissed her in mid air, and put her back down again, leaving her slightly more wet and greasy than before.

'Oh, Mother,' he said, 'don't make me out to be some kind of saint, I'm just another working man with filthy 'ands. Any road, I 'ave to get going, you know 'ow it is.'

On his way out, Dick looked in at the King and said, 'Is he okay, Mother?'

Moist watched Mrs Simnel's face very carefully.

'He's gradely, lad,' she replied. 'He just needs his sleep, such a shame to wake him up.'

Dick flashed a glance to Moist as his mother said that and seemed to be entertaining a thought and then shrugged like a man who had thought better about it. He handed Moist a parcel of clean clothes for himself and the King and then kissed his mother again.

'You will see to it, won't you, Mother, that they leave in time for the Zemphis express?'

And she did, after a bowl of porridge, hot and sugary, just the kind Adora Belle totally disliked. Moist could feel it sticking to his bones as he and the King, smiling and rejuvenated after their nap, left the haven of Mrs Simnel's little house as the sun began to rise over Sto Lat.

In a cavern somewhere near the gloomy, somewhat twisted metropolis of Slake the grags were discussing the railway menace, and ways of stopping it. They had found an artificer who liked working iron, and since he was a dwarf from Ankh-Morpork he was in a position to explain matters to them.

Sitting nervously in the dimly lit cavern and trying to appear to be very much on the side of the grags while, of course, being on the side of the money, the artificer explained that locomotives are heavy, and derailing them might be best left to when a train was heading through gorges or near the mountains. And he suggested that an alternative would be to deprive the engines of the basic necessities – fuel and water – and then attack them when they were most vulnerable. He had fortuitously come across a map that showed the locations of all the coal bunkers and water cranes and towers, and this he now produced.

'And just supposing we set our sights on stopping a particular train . . . how many people do we need to take down these . . . water cranes?' croaked an anonymous grag in the darkness.

'You'll need plenty of you on this,' said the helpful dwarf. 'The opposition is probably bright enough to realize that you'll be focusing your efforts on disabling the engines, and will have the cranes and bunkers well guarded. Of course,' he added, 'when you're up high in the mountains you have the advantage on 'em.'

The artificer looked hopeful after this, in so far as he could be seen in the dark cavern, and said, 'Well, that's about it, sirs. It's not very difficult, but you know where to contact me if you need me.'

In truth, the cavern was giving him the heebie-jeebies, and he wanted to be out of there as soon as possible. He heard the voice of the leader saying, 'Well done, my friend. Please take this gold as a token of appreciation and, yes, we do know where to find you and every member of your family as well.'

The artificer looked into the heavy leather bag and was delighted. '*Very* kind of you, sirs. I hope to help you again at some time in the future.'

And he went away happy with such big wages for so little real work. The grags didn't know anything! It was like taking money off children, but he kept smiling and said goodbye and had his throat cut in the darkness by a delver before he'd even left the dripping chamber. After all, what grag would hand over gold to an Ankh-Morpork dwarf? To a grag they were all unbelievers.

Moist was aware, as he and the King made their way hurriedly from Mrs Simnel's house back to the station, of the dark clerks keeping an eye on them, invisibly tracking them on either side. Yesterday's clothing had gone, and after a quick wash and brush-up the King had the appearance of a dwarfish businessman while

Moist was scruffier, looking like an engineer hurrying on his way to work.

The cry from the porter announced, 'Shortly to depart from platform one the Altiplano Express, stopping at Big Cabbage for Brassica World and Zemphis for Zemphis Falls. Sleeping compartments at the front of the train. All aboard, ladies and gentlemen!'

Moist whispered to the King, 'You know what to do, sire.'

The King showed his ticket to the guard, who looked at it very carefully before saying gruffly, 'Middle Class, middle of the train.' Moist walked off as fast as he could and didn't look around. Looking around pegged you as a nervous person. You had to rely on instinct alone. Everybody knew what to do.

He had to manoeuvre to get out of the way of crates of chickens and he thought, why are there always crates of chickens? By the sound of it they didn't really want to be there. And now it seemed that chickens were going everywhere. A mother with a child hurried past. A goblin waved to presumably his wife, although it was quite hard to tell with goblins, and Moist glanced at the guard and savoured, just for one moment, the silence before the train came alive.

He embarked via the guard's van and the first person he met was Detritus without his badge and therefore being, well, just another troll. He looked uncomfortable. Behind Detritus Moist found Commander Vimes dressed as a guard, apparently thoroughly enjoying himself, if Moist correctly interpreted his twisted grimace.

Vimes waved a clacks flimsy and said cheerfully, 'The idiots! They tried their tricks while they were still on Ankh-Morpork soil. Poor souls . . . I suppose they thought they were outthinking us, but Cheery and her lads had the measure of them in swift order – Sir Harry's men too by the sound of it – and now both lots are heading for the Tanty where the dark clerks will be engaging them

279

in important discussions. Let's hope the news doesn't get out to the grag command just yet.'

It was going to be a long haul to Zemphis. And after Zemphis they'd be launching on to the new track, which no passenger train had yet travelled. Time enough to worry about that when they got there, Moist told himself firmly. For now disguise was crucial; he must *be* the engineer, the lucky man who got to ride the latest Mark II Flyer every day and *get paid* for it.

As Moist walked up and down the carriages he began to look at the passengers around him. Amongst the normal mix of Ankh-Morporkians and other folk from the Sto Plains and surrounding areas whom he would expect to see on the regular journey to Zemphis, there were some dwarfs, travelling both together and singly. A few he recognized as part of the Low King's entourage; others were, if he was any judge, Ankh-Morpork dwarfs. Mind you, there was more than one kind of Ankh-Morpork dwarf: one sort were *happy* at being Ankh-Morpork citizens, and others seemed to feel grumpy and nervous about their status, not realizing that in Ankh-Morpork nobody paid much attention to what you were – unless you looked wealthy, in which case you would definitely be the centre of attention.

And then there were the people trying a little too hard to present themselves as harmless members of the public. They always stood out and Moist wondered if they knew how obvious they were to the trained eye of the suspicious scoundrel. They were worried and trying desperately not to look worried and nonchalance, real nonchalance, is very difficult to fake. If you didn't have the knack it cried out . . . amateur.

One dwarf in particular had caught Moist's eye as he passed, so he came back a short while later and took the seat opposite. As Moist sat rocking with the rhythm of the train, he sensed some discordance. Not fear, exactly, but the pulse of fear squashed down so heavily that it was almost singing, and in the privacy of Moist's skull the tickertape of suspicion ticked away.

Moist had been clever so far, not staring and, indeed, trying to look like a person who was not trying not to stare, a professional nonchalant, but the dwarf who was under his eyes was sweating. Sooner or later something was going to break.

'Oh, I know who you are!' Moist said suddenly, keeping his voice low. 'You're one of those train spotters, aren't you? I never forget an anorak.'

'Oh, yes, I'm a very keen train spotter, sir,' said the dwarf, keeping his voice level while his beard dripped sweat and his eyes screamed *help.*

'Excellent. So you'd know the top speed of a Flyer, then, would you? No?'

Hardly anyone on the train had looked up as he subtly questioned the dwarf, as subtly as a sledgehammer; it had become an extraordinary* rule of railway etiquette that other passengers' conduct and conversation remained their private business, however obtrusive it might be. The dwarf had visibly jumped in his seat when Moist first engaged him, but he was still grave-faced and, yes, still sweating, so Moist carried on like a friend who wants to borrow money.

'As I said, I never forget an anorak. Taking the long haul to Zemphis, are we?'

The dwarf nodded and said simply, 'Yes.'

'Did you see which engine we've got?' said Moist. 'I tell you what . . . I'm hearing some trunnion rattle. Can you feel it? Maybe she's a new one just out of the yard?'

'Er . . . yes . . . I suppose so . . .' spluttered the wretched dwarf.

As he considered his next move, Moist looked around. Ah, there was another dwarf, further away, surreptitiously watching him

* In that it went against every instinct of a born-and-bred Ankh-Morporkian.

watch the ersatz train spotter. Thinking furiously, he turned his attention back to the sweating dwarf in front of him.

'Hang on, I've seen you before, haven't I, at the gates of the compound, with your little notebook? We all have our little notebooks, buddy, and mine's in my luggage over there and yours is the cleanest anorak I've ever seen. *Real* train spotters get covered in muck and smuts . . . it's their badge of honour to have a greasy anorak. But you, mister, know nothing about trains or train spotting, do you?'

As he said this, he saw the other dwarf leave his seat and start to walk nonchalantly to the next carriage.

'You! Wait here!' Moist barked at the dwarf in front of him as he ran after and jumped on the perambulating dwarf. There were screams of consternation from the other passengers, finally jolted from their careful lack of interest, as Moist rolled off, scrambled to his feet and kicked the dwarf heavily with his plate-layer's boots, the ones with the metal toecaps; an invitation to lie on the ground in agony, even if you were wearing chainmail.

Moist reached up and pulled the communication cord,* hardly visible overhead, and as the train slid to a screeching halt, he shouted to the passengers, 'Nobody gets off this train unless they can fly. We'll soon have company, ladies and gentlemen. This will be something to tell your grandchildren about.'

Reinforcements were already coming from both directions: dark clerks from one and City Watch from the other . . . this particular portion of the City Watch being Commander Vimes, who took one

---

* Some months before, Mr Reg Shoe, travelling in an otherwise empty compartment, had got his fingers trapped when the carriage window shot up unexpectedly fast, and by the time the train reached the terminus he had lost the top joint of one digit. Mr Shoe, being a zombie, though indignant was merely inconvenienced by this accident, but at Effie's insistence Simnel had devised the communication cord: a small rope that ran the length of the train, with a bell attached to either end. If there was a problem, a passenger could pull this rope and the driver or guard, alerted by the bell, would slam on the brakes.

look and said to everyone present, 'Nothing to worry about, ladies and gentlemen. This gentleman hadn't bought a ticket for his journey, and that kind of behaviour makes our railway staff very upset . . .'

A little later, in the guard's van, the nervous young dwarf and his saturnine minder were, amazingly, talking to old Stoneface, who was sitting at the guard's desk and listening intently.

'Now, gentlemen, something is going on here.'

He held up a large, four-sided knife. The weapon really meant business, not just business, but business with ignominy. The young dwarf was being held between two coppers as the commander spoke to him, smiling like a shark.

'This, sir, is what assassins call a roundel, and I must tell you that even the professional killers don't use them. I believe they think it's cruel and has no finesse. Frankly, I think I'll agree about that. And I'm wondering, sir, why you're carrying it on this train?'

Vimes turned to the other dwarf, presently chained to Sergeant Detritus.

'And you, sir. What was your part in all this? We're on a moving vehicle, travelling through wilderness where *anything* could happen. And, you know, anything might happen very soon if I don't get some answers.'

He turned to an officer and said, 'Fred. You and Nobby shackle the young one and drag him somewhere where he can be alone with his thoughts and then I'll continue my little chat with this old feller, who I suspect would very much like to talk to me in a clear, thoughtful, and expansive way, leaving nothing out. You, sir,' and this was to Moist, 'I suggest you go back to your seat. I'll talk to you later.'

Dismissed, and with nothing better to do, Moist resumed his patrol of the carriages. There were long, long miles to Zemphis ahead of them and in some stretches the landscape was so monotonous that another term would have to be devised. To pass the time, he wandered along to the fabled First Class sleeping compartments. Effie had clearly had a hand in these. Whole families in Ankh-Morpork, including aunts and uncles, grannies and granddads and all the kids and possibly their donkey could have slept well in just one of the delightful part bedroom, part drawing rooms.

And when Moist came back to the guard's van after pacing the corridors and gave the not very secret knock, he found the door opened by Nobby Nobbs, a watchman who though technically human (with a certificate to prove it) was so much like a goblin that he had acquired a goblin girlfriend. Adora Belle had met her many times and she had told Moist that Shine of the Rainbow was throwing herself away on Nobby.

'Wotcher, Mister Lipwig. You should have been 'ere when Mister Vimes was interrogating that old suspect. He rolled up his sleeve and the dwarf went mental, and I mean proper mental. He saw that mark, you know, the one on the commander's wrist, and went, well, totally mental, promising absolutely everything. Never seen anyone so scared in all my life and Vimesy hadn't even touched him. He broke, sir, that's the only way I can put it. He broke. I mean, he's had a go at me on occasions, you know, about such things as what I found on the street and was hurrying to give back to their owner and suchlike. Nothing important. But that dwarf . . . it was like he melted, sir. Melted! You wouldn't know Done It Duncan, not being in the Watch, sir, well, the poor bugger owns up to anything just to get a drink and a place to sleep in the cells and maybe a chat and a ham sandwich. But this lawn ornament, he's got it worse.'

Moist looked around. 'Where are they now?'

'In there. And Mister Vimes took the young 'un off somewhere else with Fred.' Nobby pointed towards the far end of the guard's van. 'Mister Lipwig, you know that great idea you had?'

Moist hesitated. 'Help me, Nobby, I have a lot of great ideas.'

'Right, sir – the one about sorting the mail on the train, sir?'

And Moist thought, oh yes, and it would work. But Nobby carried on. 'Well, there's a special carriage on this train. It has shelves and pigeon holes and everything.'

Inside the mail carriage Moist saw the commander and his new little friend, with Fred Colon. Vimes was talking quite cheerfully to the young dwarf and when he saw Moist he gave a quick gesture indicating that he could listen but shouldn't disturb the delicate process. There were no signs of fighting or nastiness of any kind and there were two cups of coffee nestling in the wire pigeon holes. The commander, as soothingly as a mother with a new baby, played a theme that put Moist von Lipwig, confidence trickster, liar, cheat, fraud, swindler and king of slyness, the sort that dripped like the venom of a striking cobra, to shame.

'Oh dear, those grags. Tell me now, which one was it? Come on, help me now.'

'I can't remember.'

'And they did what? Surely not? Oh, it was your chum that we have in the van next door, was it?'

'Well, it might have been, yes.'

Moist wanted to applaud, but the show – if that's what it was – kept on going.

And now, with the strange red snake glistening on his arm, the commander crooned oh so carefully that a grandmother's tea party would appear to be a smash-and-grab raid in comparison. And it finished with a sigh, as the commander said with magnificently sincere anguish, 'Of course, if it was up to me . . . but you see I have to deal with Lord Vetinari and the Low King. I could put in a good word for you, my lad, telling them how helpful you've been . . . Yes, I think I'll do just that, and I thank you for helping me and I can assure you . . .' and here the glowing snake moved as the commander did, 'I can assure you, young man, that no matter what happens to you, nothing will happen to your family. But I don't

285

think I'll be able to persuade people of your innocence if you're caught like this at any future time or, indeed, if you turn out to be lying to me. And now, if you don't mind, I need to talk to your colleague again.'

Moist loved that 'If you don't mind'. As if the fool had a choice. And dark clerks whisked the young dwarf away and came back with the older dwarf, when the careful, methodical interrogation continued, but in a louder voice, considering that this dwarf was much older. The words that Vimes used had more menace in them now; but nevertheless he half suggested that everything would get better if the dwarf in front of him told the commander absolutely everything he knew about the grags and delvers and his fellow conspirators who had been duped into being the ones who got caught and thrown to the Low King's justice.

'You, sir, you'll be sent for trial before the Low King, but, as I said, I'll put in a good word for you. At the next station I'll send a clacks, if your one-time friends haven't burned down the tower.' And *that* made him flinch. Moist had to try hard not to applaud.

'Fred,' said the commander, 'please ask them to bring in this gentleman's accomplice, so that they can enjoy each other's company for the rest of their journey,' and when both dwarfs were in the mail coach under the watchful eye of the dark clerks, Vimes continued.

'Okay,' he said, in the same cheerful tone, 'I'm sorry about the manacles, but we can't have you running away now, can we? And the pair of you must remember – especially you, sir, at your age – it could have been so much worse. I'm afraid to say that it might still turn out that way anyway, but as I said, I'll put in a good word. You'll be looked after until I can arrange for you to be taken off under guard, and if anything jogs your memory don't hesitate to tell them, and I'll see what I can do. But I'm sure you'll agree that it'll be for the safety of all parties, especially your own, if in the meantime you are held in this sealed room where nobody can hurt you. I'll see to it myself that you have regular meals and refreshments.'

He turned to Moist and said, 'A word with you, please, outside.'

Back in the guard's van the commander pulled a cigar from somewhere and lit it in flagrant defiance of every railway law, sat down on a bench and said, 'Mister Lipwig, you look quizzical. Feel free to speak.'

'Well, commander, I'm impressed you did such a number on them. They think that you're their friend, that you want to help them.'

This was met by another puff of smoke.

'But of course I'm their friend,' replied Vimes, straight-faced, 'and I will continue to be their friend, for now. You are a rascal and I am not. Oh yes, I could make their lives impossible, or even worse. The older one you introduced to the railway boot so adroitly, well, he's the brains of this particular outfit, and the little one is what they call a catspaw, an idiot, filled to the brim with lies, exciting lies, telling him that he is doing the work of Tak. I mean, he isn't even a good train spotter.'

Vimes patted his pocket and said, 'And now I have names, oh such names, such wonderful names, and when the facts of life are explained to their owners they'll undoubtedly lead to other names and we shall see the bunny rabbits run. Police work isn't all about kicking down doors, you know, it's about getting to the bottom of things, and once you're right on the bottom you see all the way to the top and the top is what I'm after here! We'll be stopping for coal and water at a place called Cranbury very soon and there should be a clacks tower.'

He smiled. 'I wonder what his lordship will say about my lovely list of names? I reckon he'll go right past acerbic en route to ironic and end up slap bang in sardonic without even taking a breath.' He slapped his pocket again. 'I know some of these, don't I just, all powerful dwarfs, such stalwart defenders of the Low King on the one hand and dealing happily with the grags on the other. Thank you very much, Mister Lipwig, you're a loss to crime prevention, but you recognized the process because you recognize yourself – isn't that right? How useful, so do I. The mark must always think of you as his friend and you yourself must be as a sorrowful yet loving father. The mark's shield from the dreadful darkness outside.'

The commander turned and said, 'Nobby, who's on duty at Big Cabbage station?'

'Sergeant Willard, Mister Vimes.'

Vimes said to Moist, 'That'll do. He's an old copper and he'll have his hurry-up wagon and he'll get them in front of his lordship in no short order. And with them still in shackles, he won't have any problems. You know, I almost feel sorry for them. Grags, delvers, whatever they call themselves, the modus operandi is to find some innocent dwarf with the right connections and let it be known to him or her that if they do not toe the line and do what they are told, then perhaps all of their family will simply disappear into the Gap.'

He smiled and said, 'Come to think of it, that's exactly what I do, but I'm a teddy bear by comparison and on the right side.'

Vimes stood up and waved his arms a bit for the circulation and said, 'And now I think I need to go and see the King about my interesting findings. And don't worry, I'll put in a good word too. You pay attention to people and that's a skill in itself.'

The outside air was permeating the carriages now with the scent of the Sto Plains, which consisted of one scent and that was cabbage or cabbage-like and it was a sad smell, it drooped helplessness. Melancholy. Mind you, the cabbages themselves were excellent, especially the newer varieties.

The town of Big Cabbage, theoretically the last place any sensible person would want to visit, was nevertheless popular throughout the summer because of the attractions of Brassica World and the Cabbage Research Institute, whose students were the first to get a cabbage to a height of five hundred yards propelled entirely by its own juices. Nobody asked why they felt it was necessary to do this, but that was science for you, and, of course, students.

As soon as the train arrived at platform two at Big Cabbage

several watchmen appeared alongside the guard's van. Moist looked on as Commander Vimes passed out the captives he had been so awfully kind to, and watched them whisked away under guard in the hurry-up wagon.

As it disappeared, Vimes said to Moist, 'We have the names and addresses of their families and they'll have bodyguards day and night until this damn thing is over. I know Vetinari will huff and puff about the bill but then whenever doesn't he?'

Right on schedule, the train pulled away from Big Cabbage, leaving the great dirty distant smog of Ankh-Morpork on the horizon far behind them. Moist had a constant feeling that he was going slightly uphill, which was at least moderately the truth. Things were running as they should, people were settling down for the long haul, and that gave him more time to think. Theoretically, he knew the time to worry was when things were going wrong, but his instinct had a tendency to worry when things were just too good to be true and right now a cumulonimbus of worry was again building over his head; the anvil of the gods was just waiting to drop on him. What had he missed? What had he forgotten? No, everything was going to be all right.

There was a bridge ahead, with the usual troll on guard. The troll railway families treated the bridges, shiny and new as they were, as their own. Oh yes, a tunnel to a troll was a delightful walk in the park, but a bridge, your own bridge . . . especially one with toilet facilities, courtesy of Harry King, and enough space to raise a family . . . Trolls, thought Moist . . . Who would have thought it, they keep their bridges sparkling. Indeed, Effie had announced a best-kept bridge contest for the troll bridges throughout the length of the Ankh-Morpork railway, with no fewer than twenty goats for the winner.

To travel by the railway was to see the world changing, as trees, houses, farms, meadows, streams, townships that Moist had never heard of before the railway and barely recalled now – like that one

289

there, Much Come Lately according to the sign – whizzed past at railway speed. But who lived there and what did they do, Moist wondered?

The hamlets of the railway workers intrigued Moist. The wives, noticing that passengers got out of the train at the frequent stops for coal and water and showing a grasp of the mercantile world Lord Vetinari would have applauded, stood ready with clotted cream teas, home-made pies, hot and excellent coffee, and on one memorable occasion a small piglet.

But even this was eclipsed by the wheeze he'd encountered a month back, in the hinterland in deepest Twoshirts, considered by Ankh-Morpork the place that was nowhere. A simple slogan had been put up by two industrious ladies that said, 'We knit nighties for railway sleepers!'. The ladies, knitting away while their husbands were walking the tracks, were building up a small fortune from all those passengers who, like Moist, had laughed and dug deep into their pockets. He loved the fact that if you got your customer laughing then you had their money in your pocket.

There was another sign coming up now and he squinted to see the name on the board and – *whoosh* – he saw they were at Monks Deveril, or had been, since alas the speed of the train had shunted it into the past and – *whoosh* – here came – *whoosh* – Upper Feltwhistle, apparently. But the ever-moving train had passed on and he hungered for sight of the Lower Feltwhistle sign but the train sped past, sending the unexplored townships into oblivion. Strange-sounding places with strange-sounding names living in the moment of the triumphant train.

With a clatter another train passed them on the up line, but where from? And going where? Moist gave up. Too much travelling on the railway could turn you into a philosopher, although, he conceded, not a very good one.

There was another coal and water stop at Seven Bangs. The name meant nothing to Moist and even Vimes shook his head. It was one of those places where people got off the train and disappeared into the hinterland and, presumably, only the tax inspectors and the Post Office knew who lived where. And by the look of Seven Bangs, the tax inspectors would probably take a day off sick rather than go there and possibly the postman, too, if he had bad news to convey, such as overdue tax demands. But nevertheless, the people of Seven Bangs had been joined by four linesmen, with their houses and their families, all cosily close to the line.

Moist chatted with the man who operated the water crane and asked, 'Do you have any trouble sleeping up here with trains going past all the time?'

'Well, bless you, sir, but no, sir, not at all. Oh, it took a little time for us to get acclimatized,' and he giggled like a man using an unusual word for the first time and finding it funny. 'My wife sleeps like a baby and the only time she woke up was last week when the Flyer couldn't get through, and she swears that the silence in the wrong place unsettled her.'

Vimes never seemed to leave the guard's van, except for occasional journeys down the train to talk to the King and his bodyguards, and it was into the guard's van that the clacks flimsies were delivered.

There were always goblins in the guard's van, of course, but it didn't stop at that. You found them everywhere, adjusting screws, oiling, greasing and, well, tinkering and tapping. Moist had asked Simnel about that early on and had been told they greased everything that needed greasing and tapped what needed tapping, and generally stopped things getting out of kilter.

Of course, there was still the smell, but once you got used to it, as Adora Belle had long ago, you never even thought about it. And they ran errands when the train stopped at out-of-the-way places, and collected clacks flimsies for news of everything that might pertain to the journey.

The good old clacks, people called it nowadays. They used to call it unsightly, but now, quite likely, you would ask the clacks what the weather was like ahead of your journey. A little comfort but not necessarily necessary. Nevertheless, once you were bereft of the clacks you thought of yourself as a second-class citizen. Spike was always telling him how enraged clients got about their clacks bills, which were, he considered, not bad in the circumstances; but a kind of ratchet formed in people's minds: here is the new thing and here it is. And yesterday you never thought about it and after today you don't know what you would do without it. That was what the technology was doing. It was your slave but, in a sense, it might be the other way round.

After the excitement of the water crane, Moist was at a loose end and now, by habit, if he felt himself at a loose end he went to the guard's van. Detritus lay asleep on a pile of packing cases near by, snoring, surrounded by all the necessary debris of the place. It seemed that all the travellers who were not passengers treated the guard's van as their home. Possibly the coffee maker was the reason for that. And here was Of the Twilight the Darkness, who made very special coffee. Moist thought about that for a moment, as the grinning goblin handed him a bubbling mug.

'I've got it. You're a shaman, aren't you?'

The goblin's grin was wider. 'Sorry, mister. You is not on the money here. You could call me a shamegog. Unfortunately, dissonance, but can't have everything.'

Moist looked into his coffee and said, 'It smells lovely, but what'll it make me do?'

The shamegog thought for a moment and said, 'It make you wide awake, busy man! Maybe puts hair on chest. Slight tendency to make you piss more often.' Now he gave Moist a sideways look that really only a goblin can achieve and said, 'Guaranteed not to make you killer of dwarfs.' It was really very good coffee. Moist had to give the goblin that.

He peered out of the window. Perhaps it was his imagination, but the Forest of Skund seemed to get blacker the closer they came to it. The forest was worse than the maquis. From what Moist remembered, the trees stood shoulder to shoulder. And if you thought that trees didn't have shoulders, you hadn't been to the Forest of Skund. It was one of those places where the magic hadn't been cleaned out yet. And some of the old fears and fancies still hung around the place. Nobody went in there until they had to, the occasional woodcutter for a bet, perhaps. It was a dark place, staring out across the plain and biding its time. Not a place to go if you didn't want a wizard dropping on your head. If a landscape could growl, that was the Forest of Skund.

Moist took the opportunity to look at the instrumentation in the van. There were two guards on the rota for this journey, and though the train couldn't be driven from here, the guard could at least stop it – a fact worth knowing.

As dusk fell, the sound of Detritus's snoring lessened from somewhere in the vicinity of badgers fighting to the death to a low rumble, which caused the rest of the van to resonate. There was a fascination in watching a chest made of stone move. Not for the first time Moist marvelled: *They are stone and we are told that stone lives*; and once again his thoughts harked back to Iron Girder, and, to his amazement, he stopped worrying: horses, trolls, golems, engines, well, where was the downside?

He looked around him. Apart from the sleeping Detritus the guard's van was for once totally empty. The rest of the train's occupants were settling down for the evening elsewhere, busy with their own affairs; Commander Vimes was making his rounds of the carriages.

Moist moved quickly, no longer able to fight the little devil inside him. After all, he reasoned, he'd waited long enough to do this, and he might not have another chance. It was still light enough. He opened the door of the guard's van, and, gripping the side of the carriage, climbed out, kicked shut the door behind him and clambered on to the top of the train. Once there he scrambled to his feet, and then, throwing caution to the winds, Moist danced on the top of the train, leaping from carriage to carriage, listening to the train's rhythm, moving his body to accommodate it and feeling the engine and the moods of the railway until it seemed that he could understand it. It was a benison, a gift. It was a thing that could be courted but, he expected, it wouldn't allow too much familiarity. It enthralled him and he thought: steam is not to be taken lightly.

Once, he heard a shout of 'Oi!' from below and Moist was no stranger to 'Oi!'. He leaned down and said, 'Moist von Lipwig. I'm doing a little test.' He could hear the 'Oi' voice grumbling, and let it grumble because this was what he had wanted as soon as he had seen the new Flyers.

Flushed with the thrill of the ride, Moist dropped back down into the guard's van, still empty except for the sleeping form of Detritus. He smoothed down his hair and wiped the smuts from his face, and wandered out of the carriage, a smile on his face.

Down the length of the train the lights were going out when Commander Vimes reappeared from his latest sortie and headed for the coffee.

'The King and his council of war are making their plans,' he said. 'Your latest clacks reports and what I hear from let's call them observers on the ground suggest that work on the rails is going ahead reasonably happily.'

He looked slyly at Moist. 'Pretty soon, it seems, Mister Lipwig, you'll have to put your money where your mouth is. Oh, and another thing. Here's a flimsy from your good wife. Even with the news of the Schmaltzberg coup spreading, there appear to have been very few attacks on clacks towers outside Uberwald.'

Taken aback, Moist said, 'Well, that is good news.'

But Vimes just frowned and said, 'Don't get excited. I'd wager that there are still some out there who'd knock over a clacks tower even if they saw Tak on the top of it. That's the trouble, you see. When you've had hatred on your tongue for such a long time, you don't know how to spit it out.'

Moist had made sure, oh bliss, right from the start that he would have a sleeping compartment of his own, but, unlike those in the First Class sleeper carriage, his was more utilitarian and using it was an exercise suited to people who like toying with twisty cubes and other notorious playthings. It had a folding bed, which folded down and hit him on the head, and a washbasin into which his toothbrush would just about fit. But there was a sponge provided, and since he was suitably athletic he made the best of it, ending up if not clean, not any dirtier either. And gods, he was tired, and whatever it was that drove him seriously needed a rest, but the mind was its own worst enemy and the more he tried to get himself lulled by the rhythms of the railway, the more his niggling thoughts seemed to burgeon like a cloud.

They had been lucky so far – only the two grag spies to deal with, and pretty poor spies at that – but sooner or later the rat would surely be out of the bag and the grags would know that Rhys was on board. Simnel's hope seemed to rest on the fact that they would be using Iron Girder by that time. But could she really make a difference, Simnel's little experiment, more used to giving children rides around the yard? I'm sure that when that locomotive of Simnel's first arrived, Moist thought, it was pretty small and I wondered how it could go the distance, even to Sto Lat. But now she seems so powerful. And the way Simnel keeps upgrading her and paying her attention, it's as if something bad would happen if she wasn't the queen of the yard. She never sleeps. There's always that little hiss. That little tinkle of metal. Mechanical susurration, whether or not she is ostensibly running.

Moist thought about whoever it was who had got into the compound to smash her up, who ended up dead, dead, dead. Wild steam from a train that wasn't running. Earth, fire, wind and rain all in one element of speed. And slowly Moist shut down, although a part of him was always listening to the rhythm of the rails, listening in his sleep, like a sailor listening to the sounds of the sea.

As Moist slept, the train barrelled like a very slow meteor through the night, climbing up through the Carrack Mountains. Almost the only light to be seen with the moon under a cloud came from the engine's headlamp and the glow from the furnace when the door was opened to shovel in more coal.

The engine stokers of the Hygienic Railway were a breed apart: taciturn, perennially grumpy, seemingly only willing to talk to the drivers. In the unwritten hierarchy of the footplate the drivers were at the top, of course, and *then* the stokers and after the stokers there would be the wheel-tappers and shunters: lesser beings but acknowledged as useful. At times it appeared that the stokers considered themselves the most important component of the railway, keepers of its soul, as it were. When off duty they all messed together, grumbling, puffing their wretched pipes, and talking to nobody else. But shovelling coal all day built muscles of iron, so the stokers were strong and fit, and sometimes between shifts there were sparring matches with shovels, with the combatants cheered on by their fellows.

In fact, one of the stokers on the train was a bit of a legend, according to the others, although Moist had not come across him yet. Stoker Blake was said to be death on legs if he was aroused. The other stokers were fierce fighters, but it was claimed that none of them ever got to touch Stoker Blake. A stoker's shovel, incorrectly used, was an illustration of Commander Vimes's dictum that a workman's tool used cunningly could give the average watchman a real headache.

And so the stokers laughed and danced as they sparred with their shovels and got drunk – but not when they were going to be on the footplate. They didn't need telling about that.

Tonight, cocooned from the cool wind that flew around the cab,

Stoker Jim said to the train driver, 'Here's your coffee, Mick. Fancy a fry-up?'

Mick nodded without taking his eyes off the track ahead and so Stoker Jim carefully reached out and fried a couple of eggs on the back of his shovel, courtesy of the fiery furnace.

The houses hastily built for the railway workers were close to the water cranes and coal bunkers so that an eye could be kept on the precious coal and water supplies. They were quite small, which put some strain on the accommodation when there were children and grandparents as well, but everyone said that it was twice as good as what might be found in the big city and, after all, you were out in the fresh air, at least in between locomotives.

On this night, Mrs Plumridge, mother of Jack Plumridge the linesman, realized that her chamber pot was overflowing and cussed herself for not emptying it before twilight. She didn't trust the gleaming porcelain in the ablutions. All her life she had gone outside to a designated private spot in the garden, taking care to remember which of her little plots to empty it in this time, and therefore things got rather receptacle-shaped when a dwarf jumped out in front of her, screamed, 'Death to the railway!' and tried to throw something at her.

In response, Mrs Plumridge hefted the chamber pot with a strength you might not have expected from such an old woman who, according to her son, was made out of teak. The pot was very large and remained regrettably very full and the scream woke up all the households near by . . . and when the miscreant delver came back to consciousness he was tied up and en route to Ankh-Morpork for judgement.

The railwaymen and their grannies were no-nonsense people, earthy, you might say, and they didn't even allow the delver to wash himself, and that was a terrible thing in the circumstances.

*

When Moist awoke the following morning, he realized that he was hungry and was pleased to discover that there was breakfast (all-day breakfast it turned out) in the dining carriage.

He found the dining car empty but for Bashfull Bashfullsson and the Low King, sitting chatting like businessmen with a deal to make, taking advantage of the cornucopia.

Quietly, the King welcomed him and said, 'Not seen much of the train so far, Mister Lipwig. Been in a planning session with Bashfullsson and the others since we boarded. Will you join us?'

As Moist sat down, Bashfullsson turned to him as if to an ally. 'I'm trying to get Rhys here to tell us what he's up to.'

The King merely smiled at this. 'I intend to take Schmaltzberg with you, my friend Bashfullsson, and do it with as little bloodshed as possible. Believe me, although it's vexing to remember it, I am the King of my enemies as well as my friends. There's a certain *noblesse oblige*, see. It's a bad king who kills his subjects. I would rather see them humiliated than dead.'

Bashfullsson said, 'Really? After all the things they've done? And the things they've caused to be done? Finding young dwarfs and filling them with excitement and idiotic revelations . . .'

'I have names,' said the King. 'Names of leaders, names of hangers-on. Oh yes, there will be a reckoning. Not an auto-da-fé.'

'I fear you were too understanding with them last time, sire,' Bashfullsson said, picking his words carefully. 'Sad to say, but I've come to the conclusion that if you keep turning the other cheek they'll go on slapping you in the face. I think there's nothing for it but to go in, cut out and have done. No point in knocking politely this time, saying can I have the Scone of Stone back, please.'

To Moist's surprise, the King said, 'However much we disdain the word "politics", one of its most useful aspects is the stopping of bloodshed. Oh yes, bloodshed there will be. But the generations stream away and people change and things thought of as totally impossible suddenly turn out to be everyday. Nay, essential. Just like the railway is becoming, see. Apropos of that, Mister Lipwig, how *is* the railway progressing? How are your loggysticks going?'

'Copacetic, sire. That's an engineer term meaning all satisfactory.'

The King gave Moist a look. It wasn't by the standard of looks a nasty one, but it was after all a King's look, and the gaze of the King was subtly quizzical and testing.

'We shall see, boyo, we shall see.'

And after breakfast, there was nothing for it but to watch the mountain scenery flow past as if on some endless winding belt: trees, rocks, more trees, bigger rocks, trees again, what was possibly a clearing where lumbermen were working, brief darkness as they reached a rock big enough to require a tunnel, and so on, and yet, Moist thought, behind all those trees and all those rocks and crags, there are homesteads and small villages that we don't know about and so one day we will have to have a stop here . . . here . . . and here. And then one day, some kid from the settlement high up in that last lot of rocks will catch the train and end up in Ankh-Morpork, full of hope, and why not? Station by station we are changing the world. And he allowed himself a little glow of pride.

Apart from the Falls,* the only place that was of any significance in Zemphis was Downsized Abbey. It was a ruin now, the monks long gone; these days it was more of a souk, a medina, a heaving bazaar which reminded Moist of the Shades of Ankh-Morpork on their holidays. Nothing was still. Silence was a rare blessing. And everyone was a trader and it seemed that sooner or later everything and everyone could be bought and sold. And, if necessary, disappeared.

Of the trading routes in Zemphis, the Aglet Road stood out, as caravans of camels arrived on their way to bring the people of the Plains the tiny little things on the ends of their shoelaces without

* Moist had seen the Falls before and that's just what they were . . . falls. Pretty good falls by the standard of falls, but once you'd looked at them for a few minutes undoubtedly someone would say: 'Where can we get a coffee around here?'

which civilized life would be unbearable and quite dangerous. There were spices from Klatch*, materials from the Counterweight Continent which had arrived by slow barge, other mysterious delicacies, and unfortunately many ways to become very happy in a short space of time and stone dead shortly afterwards.

Alongside the legitimate goods traded at the front of the stalls, without doubt there was some contraband, as many traders luxuriated in the semi-lawless landscape. Cages of undomesticated imps were available in the back rooms of some more unscrupulous shops, and after dark the occasional camel slipped in or out of the town carrying barrels of crude treacle.

And even though most sensible people wishing to hang on to their personal possessions, or indeed their lives, would follow the advice of those who had been there and give it a wide berth, some possibly foolhardy tourists did come to Zemphis on their way to see the Paps of Scilla, a jagged mountain range which allowed the determined mountaineer an absolute smorgasbord of ways to be found upside down above a crevasse and hanging by one leg over white water that acted like the mother of all grinders. There were eight peaks in all, sharp and unforgiving, and if there were such a thing as the good ambushing guide it would be right up there with the winners.

Contemplating the Paps from a seat conveniently placed by the burghers of Zemphis as a lookout point for those admiring the view, Moist reflected that shortly their train would have to travel through those peaks. They didn't look so bad on the map, but up close and personal they were awesome. Scilla must have been very proud eight times over.

A mist hung over the greenery clinging to the steep foothills of the Paps. The terrain looked impassable for a train, but Simnel's sliding-rule boys had found a suitable way through. Track had been

---

* And if you knew where to ask, the fabled Klatchian migratory bog truffle, which despite resembling the Klatchian bog toad in both taste and appearance was extremely rare and therefore a delicacy.

laid and Moist knew that they'd had trolls hanging around there all week, keeping guard.

Just then, there was a shout from Commander Vimes. 'Lipwig! Drop!'

Moist dropped, while whatever the commander had seen scythed overhead, and he was just picking himself up when Vimes tackled him back down to the ground as the missile whistled round for another slice before finally dropping somewhere near their feet.

'And there you have it,' said Vimes. 'Really nasty fellows, delvers, but you've got to admire their workmanship.'

Moist, still at ground level, said, as if it mattered, 'Was it really them?'

'Quite likely, but there are other nuisances in these hills. You must know that where there are tourists there are also people eager for their dollars. Don't touch it!'

Moist's hand flew back.

'It's a boomerang,' said Vimes. 'You find something like this all over the world. You have to wave it carefully and suddenly your opponent gets it in the back. I've heard that there's a lad in Fourecks who can throw a boomerang with such precision that it can get the morning paper and come back with it.'

Moist gave the commander a look of disbelief.

'Well, that's what they say, and you know those boys from Fourecks, they love to draw a long bow,' Vimes continued, picking up the boomerang gingerly with a handkerchief. He sniffed it, grimaced and said, 'The stuff the grags have put on this one might not kill you but you'll wish that it had for a day or two, if you're lucky. I'm going to have to talk to Vetinari about this place. They've got *something* like a government here, but their policing might just be adequate in a kindergarten. They're not exactly bent, just not organized in the right way. Good grief, I could even send Nobby up here and the quality of the policing would go comparatively sky high.'

'Surely Vetinari's remit doesn't stretch all the way out here? And you're well out of your jurisdiction, aren't you?'

To Moist's amazement Vimes laughed, and said, 'I couldn't speak for Vetinari, but we all know he has his . . . ways and his means. I think he allows this place to exist so that it doesn't exist in Ankh-Morpork. And as for my jurisdiction, I wouldn't be surprised if there are a number of people in this place who'd like to see some law in the streets. So if that were the case, well, it might be my duty to assist. But not today.'

He patted Moist on the shoulder and said, 'Mister Lipwig, I'm sure there've been times in your life when you've seen a wonderful opportunity to steal something valuable and you've decided for various reasons not to? Well, I feel as you would then. This place is a sink. Who knows what dreadful things are happening behind closed doors.' He shrugged and went on, 'But you can't kick down every door in the universe. And we have more pressing matters to attend to.'

Moist accepted this sad explanation and after a fruitless hunt around for their assailant they turned their backs on the Paps to head back to the station. As they left the lookout point, they heard a train whistle in the distance. Far away, climbing into Zemphis on the main line from the Plains, there was a streak of scintillating sunlight with a trail of steam.

Vimes looked at Moist and said, 'What the hell is that? There isn't another train due today, is there?'

'Well, Dick said he was polishing up Iron Girder for the big event, and before we left he was talking as if his favourite loco-motive had been getting a complete overhaul. That must be her.'

In fact, it wasn't just an overhaul. When Moist had shown Simnel the micromail he had received as spoils of the battle with the dwarfs at the Quirm railhead, the young engineer had smiled and said, 'Aye, I know what the secret is here. This is a metal stronger than iron, malleable and half its weight, and it never rusts. Its ore is rare but it's the base of a new alloy I've made. I call it sorortanium, which Mister Thunderbolt says means the sister of iron. It's stronger even than steel! What boilers I could make with it if only I could get 'old of enough of the stuff! Thank you. It's amazing and I know just what to do with it.'

As they watched the astonishing locomotive dealing with the steep haul into Zemphis, Moist noticed that the engine appeared to shrug off the load behind her. The Flyer they had come in on earlier had been creaking as it chugged up the last steep haul into Zemphis. This new train didn't even seem to notice the gradient.

Vimes smacked his head and said, 'Is that really Iron Girder? Last I saw of Iron Girder, she was providing a playground entertainment for grown-ups. If that's Iron Girder,' he said, pointing at the shimmering apparition, 'surely she's grown?'

'It *is* Iron Girder,' said Moist. 'Dick spends all his time tinkering with her, over and over again, improving her at every turn and opportunity. And at the end, well, she's still Iron Girder. She'll always be Iron Girder.'

'But she's so easily spotted, all that shining . . . People are going to see her coming for miles! No chance of an inconspicuous departure, then!'

'I know,' said Moist. 'But since you can *hear* her coming for miles, Dick said it won't make any difference. Everyone'll know we're coming.' Though the silver carapace in fact could make a significant difference in other ways, he thought.

'If you please, *ah grag nun**, we have lost track of two agents on one of the trains,' said the acolyte. 'Alas, we are no longer in touch with them.'

The grag commander looked up. 'Ah-ha!' he said. 'Where were they when we last heard from them?'

'On the regular service from Sto Lat to Zemphis. But they failed

* Dwarfish, trans.: my lord.

to report at Big Cabbage or earlier as the train passed through Cranbury.'

'Are you certain?'

The acolyte jumped. 'Well, my lord, we are in the dark, but I think so ...'

'In that case,' said the grag, 'make it known that we are no longer bothering with the other routes. Our ... package must have been on that train to Zemphis. And from there ... The Paps await, and they take no prisoners! They, my friend, are coming to us. And the creatures that live in the Paps will be our allies! It's all about the railway now, and we know that it is in the compass of our agents to stop those blasted wheels turning. Be mindful of bridges, however. The enemy favours the dreadful stone people who love to guard them. And surely tunnels can also be made to fail ... This wretched technology contains the seeds of fallibility.'

'Yes, *grag nun*, we know that the locomotive has to stop frequently for coal and water. Deprive it of either and there is no locomotive, just a lump of old iron. So, the coal bunkers and, yes, water cranes ... There will be guards, of course, but they should be easy to overcome when stationary.'

The chief grag returned to his study of the words of Tak as annotated by Grag Hamcrusher.

'Let me know when the deed is done.'

Down at the Zemphis terminus, Iron Girder looked even more spectacular up close. Dick Simnel was dressed smartly and grinning proudly as he showed off the glittering engine and all the dials and gauges on the footplate. Seeing Dick wearing clothes that had no grease on them was astonishing, like seeing a lion without a mane.

Along with Cheery Littlebottom and other members of the City Watch who had been summoned by Commander Vimes, Moist was surprised to see the cheerful and homely face of Constable Bluejohn, the largest troll on the force. Bluejohn, whom even

Detritus described as 'a big boy', was by nature as gentle as a breeze and wouldn't hurt a fly – at least not on purpose, although he could quite possibly tear a lion in half with his bare hands if needed. Nevertheless the sight of him on the scene of any fracas was an invitation to run a marathon in the other direction rather than face the megalith. He lived in a reinforced house somewhere in Sunink, a little town inadvisably nestling in the outskirts of Ankh-Morpork. They said that the sound of Bluejohn walking to work was better than an alarm clock.

Vimes marched off down the platform to greet the new arrivals. Cheery was looking very cheerful, as cheerful as any decoy could be who had been the winner of a battle and had come out more or less unscathed, except for a small scar which you had to have, didn't you, or no one would believe you.

The tour of the footplate finished, Simnel turned to Moist. 'According to our schedule, we ought to be going.' He blew his whistle and shouted down the platform, 'All aboard!'

There was no way of avoiding considerable attention as the King's party assembled to board the armoured carriages behind Iron Girder. The engine herself was spectacular and her passengers were unusual even for a city like Zemphis. There were the dwarfs: the Low King and his bodyguards, Aeron his secretary and Bashfull Bashfullsson; there were suspiciously deep shadows that suggested the continued presence of dark clerks; there were several specialist members of the Watch;* there were the goblins, who scrambled into the guard's van being coupled on at the rear; and just in front of the van was a flatbed carrying Constable Bluejohn along with equipment and baggage too bulky for the guard's van.

Iron Girder was fully in steam again now and the vapour surrounded everybody. Vimes went with the engineers as they

---

* Which didn't include Corporal Nobby Nobbs or Sergeant Colon, who were not precisely special but, as Moist knew, curiously useful, which was why Vimes put up with them.

walked right around the train for a final check. Then came the scream of the whistle and the little shunting dance that Iron Girder did before gaining speed. With someone staring from every carriage window, the special express train to Uberwald started to show what it could do.

The story told locally about the Paps of Scilla was that they were formed when one huge mountain fell apart, leaving a treacherous network of broken caverns – some full of water, always overflowing – topped by the eight forbidding peaks, which seemed to hang in the moisture-laden air, surrounded by rainbows. After the boomerang incident in Zemphis, Moist wasn't very keen on seeing the Paps up close and personal, but Simnel's surveyors had excelled themselves. The railway track insinuated itself up through the craggy gaps so that the train climbed majestically higher and higher, leaving the city of Zemphis and the heat shimmer of the sierra far below.

Halfway towards the gloom of the pass between the tallest peaks, the train emerged from a large natural tunnel into another kaleidoscope of rainbows, which were distracting even when people weren't throwing things at your head.

Without warning, a boulder smashed down in front of the train and rolled across the tracks, to shatter in the opposite gully. Then there was another crash from the rear. The train shuddered horribly, and carried on.

Moist looked up and saw dwarfs perched on the craggy cliffs on each side of the canyon, levering boulders down on to the train. Commander Vimes could be heard cursing and shouting orders down the carriages, his words drowned out as yet larger boulders fell, raining down on the locomotive, which was moving slowly forward like an old lady testing the water.

Surely, Moist thought, this is the end. Even if the tracks ahead remain undamaged, no normal engine could withstand this bombardment. But then he realized that Iron Girder, slowly and methodically, was actually steaming on despite the boulders continuing to pound the train.

Moist couldn't stop himself. He shouted to anyone who would listen, 'They're bouncing off! It's the sorortanium, it takes the punishment and throws it right back!'

Meanwhile, at the rear of the train, Constable Bluejohn, standing on his flatbed gently rocking with the motion, thundered a troll threat, reached out and plucked a miscreant from his foothold unwisely close to the track. When he was joined by Detritus, the assailants soon discovered that aiming boulders at the trolls was a fool's errand. The lads, who were quite literally in their element, just grabbed them and tossed them back with interest.

Looking out of a broken window, Moist saw a small swarm of goblins leave the train and at first he thought, ha! Trust the buggers to run away, and then he mentally corrected himself: that was storybook thinking and with clearer eyesight and a bit of understanding he realized that the goblins were scrambling up to the delvers on the rocks and beating the shit out of them by diving into the multiple layers of dwarf clothing. The delvers discovered all too rapidly that trying to fight while a busy goblin was in your underwear was very bad for the concentration.

Of the Twilight the Darkness suddenly appeared at Moist's elbow. He was wearing a helmet that was far too big for him and spun around on his head. He pushed one arm into the greasy nest he called a jacket and struck a pose.

'Marvellous, ain't they? Always going for the gonads.'

There were screams, sometimes high-pitched, as the delvers lost their hold and fell down either under the train or into the water, still fighting the speedy goblins.

As Iron Girder steadfastly steamed on round the next bend, she and her coal tender came into Moist's field of vision and he was horrified to see that a couple of delvers had gained a foothold on the tender. They were being held at bay by a soot-blackened stoker

307

who was valiantly protecting access to the footplate by wielding his shovel to deadly effect. Moist caught a glimpse between the chaos of fighting bodies of the stoker dispatching one of the delvers, kicking him over the side. A massive blow with the shovel dealt with the other dwarf, and the stoker dropped out of sight. His sheer efficiency had been vaguely disturbing. Perhaps that's the legendary Stoker Blake, Moist thought, and then ducked back inside as another boulder crashed past.

Finally the bombardment ceased and Moist made his way down the train. He found the Low King in one of the armoured carriages with Bashfullsson and the rest of his party. There was blood on the King's beard.

'The foe is either fleeing or dead,' the King said. 'The wounded will be taken aboard under lock and key and undoubtedly the good commander will have them talking to him as if they were the best of friends. He has a knack for that sort of thing.'

A while later Moist went into the guard's van, where Commander Vimes was having little chats to grags and their fellow travellers. He was speaking in his very low, *understanding* voice.

'I do understand your position. It's such a shame, especially since the ones that started it all are likely to get away into the darkness.'

And yet again Moist was impressed. The grizzled commander was all honey as he continued, 'Of course, as a friend, you might give me certain names. I like collecting names, they sing to me.'

And Moist thought, they have the honey, here comes the sting.

Cheerfully, Vimes took names like a guardian uncle, while in various corners of the van people were being bandaged, cleaned and fed.

And so, battered but triumphant, Iron Girder blew her whistle and gently got up to speed on the track out of the Paps towards Uberwald with goblins everywhere: panel-beating, tidying up, greasing, bending and cleaning and almost rebuilding her on the run, as it were, and Moist noticed that at no point did Iron Girder turn them into a pink haze with live steam. The queen of loco-motion valued her courtiers.

Moist had lost all track of time after the excitement of the ambush, but what he thought must be teatime refreshment was interrupted by the squealing of brakes followed by a jerk that caused crockery to scatter all over the floor as the driver leaned on his emergency brake lever, which did little more than pit screaming metal against metal. And then the train came to an abrupt stop, overturning any-thing that was left upright, followed by the voice of Bluejohn from the rear of the train saying, 'I reckon it needed pullin'. Sorry if I was wrong.'

Moist hurried towards the troll's flatbed. 'You appear to have stopped the train all by yourself,' he said, and waited. You waited a lot when you were talking to Bluejohn.

And at last when Bluejohn had assembled his words to his satisfaction he said, 'Oh, sorry, Mister Lipwig, if I broke anythin' take it outta my wages if you like.'

Moist said, 'That won't be necessary.' He leaned out to look down the track towards the front of the train. Simnel had jumped from the footplate to investigate.

'It's a load of kids!' he shouted back.

Moist jumped down on to the track and ran towards Simnel.

'Leave it to me, Dick, I can handle this,' he said as he reached the engine. In the fading light he could see some children on the track a short way ahead, who, it appeared, had flagged down the train with their pinafores.

The eldest of the children was female and well dressed and almost in tears. She said, 'There's a landslide, mister.'

'Where?'

'Round the next bend, sir,' gasped the girl.

And sure enough, when Moist strode along the track and looked into the gloom beyond, he saw a load of old timbers and rocks surrounded by other debris. And then the situation dawned on him. He carefully set his face like thunder and said, 'What's your name, young lady?'

'Edith, sir,' she simpered, but not properly, and he could tell that she wasn't used to a life of crime.

Moist beckoned the girl to come closer. 'Edith, pardon me for being suspicious, but my instincts tell me that your charming little scheme was devised so that you brave young people could save the train from derailing and then be heroes, am I right?'

The girl and her smaller chums looked miserable, but the scoundrel in Moist urged him to say, 'Well, it's an ingenious idea, but if Lord Vetinari were to hear about this you'd be having the kitten treatment.'

And the girl smiled and said, 'Oh, that's nice. I like kittens.'

'I dare say you do, but I don't think you'd like Cedric who comes with them . . . Now, I admire the resourcefulness of your little plot, but people could have been hurt.' He raised his voice. 'Can you imagine a railway accident? The screaming of the rails and the people inside and the explosion that scythes the countryside around when the boiler bursts? And you, little girl, and your little friends, would have done all that. Killed a trainload of people.'

He had to stop there because the girl looked like death. And, if his instincts were right, somewhat damp around the legs, not weeping for effect this time but traumatized, her face white.

Moist lowered his voice and said, 'Yes, you've seen it in your head now, and probably, when you think about it again, you'll remember that you very nearly killed lots of people.'

Edith said in a small voice, 'I'm really very sorry, it won't happen again.'

Moist said, 'Actually, it hasn't happened once. Still, I'd like you to see to it that it *doesn't* happen around here or anywhere else. Have I made my message clear?'

Damp and scared, Edith managed a weak, 'Yes, sir.' And Moist recognized true contrition.

He looked into her hopeful face and said, 'I'll square this with the engine driver, but if I was you I'd get my pencil and turn any clever ideas you have like this into a book or two. Those penny dreadfuls are all the rage in the railway bookshops. I hear there's money in it, and you won't meet Cedric that way. Oh, and don't keep waving your pinafores at people. It could give quite the wrong idea in the dark. Now, where do you live, young lady? I haven't seen any settlements round here, it's all woodland.'

She curtsied. She actually curtsied. And still red-eyed, she said, 'We live in the railway houses, just back by the water crane and coal bunker.'

'And is your father likely to be at home?'

The girl went white again but gamely managed, 'Yes, sir, if you please, sir.'

'In that case, while the gentlemen back there are settling things down, I'd like to see him, please.'

And uncertainly Edith led him to, yes, the railway houses and introduced Moist to a burly but cheerful-looking man who was sitting at a table devouring bread and cheese with half a pint of beer in his hand.

'This is my dad.'

The man put down a large slab of cheese and said, 'Can't shake hands, sir, I'm all over cheese, apart from what's not all over grease. Nesmith is the name.'

'Well, Mister Nesmith, perhaps your children might go off and play while I have a little chat with you.'

When Edith and the others had made themselves scarce at the speed of sound, Moist said, 'You must have heard the squealing?'

'Oh, yessir, I did, and our Jake and Humphrey were sent off to see what was going on, what with me just home after a long shift.'

'Well, Mister Nesmith, I congratulate you for your clean and

311

well-spoken children, but I'm sorry to say they came very close to at least disabling the new express to Uberwald.'

Nesmith's face went grey as he contemplated a future with no work and no pension and quite probably a criminal record. Greasy tears flowed out of his eyes and he said, 'Anyone hurt, sir? If anyone's hurt I'll tan their hides.'

'Some broken crockery, and there's work to be done to get the track cleared before we can leave.'

The big round face was contorted. 'I can help there, sir, I can help, but I'll tan their hides for them, you see if I don't.'

'No, you will not, Mister Nesmith, I'll see you pay for it if you do, indeed I will. Look, they could have caused a terrible accident, but the important thing is that they didn't. They wanted to appear brave, as far as I can see, and you can't blame kids for that. However, the railway isn't a playground. Do you understand me, Mister Nesmith? Now, if I were you I'd get out my jim crow, off shift or not, and help clear the rails. Oh, and treasure your eldest daughter: you might be grateful for her imagination one day.'

Ohulan Cutash beckoned. Moist knew it as a likeable kind of place: a little market town with the usual hinterland of farmers and lumberjacks. Some mining too, dwarfs and humans quite often these days working on the same mine and even the same seams. It was big enough to have a mayor and sensible enough to have a very good tavern called the Fiddler's Riddle. And apparently it was a place where the current unpleasantness had not yet reached.

What Moist hadn't expected to find, as they pulled up to the platform just past midnight, was the brass band and the flags and the Morris dancing and the fun-fair, which it appeared had been organized to welcome the first proper train to arrive at the newly constructed station and had been going on for hours.

And as soon as Iron Girder came to a stop with her last hiss, Mr Skiller, the landlord of the Fiddler's Riddle, who turned out also to

312

be the town mayor, began an address offering the freedom of his little town to everyone on the train. Although of course it wasn't a little town, oh indeed not, to its mayor. It was chasing Ankh-Morpork. A little part of Moist's brain laid a bet with itself that very shortly the words 'on the map' were going to be uttered.

And indeed, the mayor, large and florid as a proper mayor should be, said as Moist stepped down, minding the gap, 'This will put Ohulan Cutash on the map and no mistake. We're already breaking ground for a much bigger tavern with facilities.' He looked at Moist solemnly and said, 'You have to have facilities, these days, you know. We paid for our own clacks tower. We're very modern here, that's for sure.'

Moist looked around at the cobbled town square that lay a short distance from the platform. It would have been better if it hadn't been the middle of the night, but the mayor saw no problem with this and cheerfully pointed out to the now clustering passengers the locations of the wonderful things they would be able to see when it was daylight.

And it nearly broke Moist's heart to say to the man, 'I'm afraid we have to go very soon. Schedules, you know.'

And indeed, he could see the water crane pumping and could hear the rattle of the coal being delivered to the engine, but nothing could stop the mayor in his rampant hospitality.

'But we've arranged for a mayoral banquet.'

'Ah . . . will you excuse me for a moment, mister mayor?'

Moist had a private word with Simnel about arrangements for the next leg of the journey and then with Vimes, who nodded and said quietly, 'Sensible. I wouldn't mind eating off a plate that wasn't rattling. There's no harm in pandering to a little civic pride. The mayor is a decent cove and they've got a Watch of sorts. Two watch-men, not too bad in the circumstances, and I know that because I trained them.'

Moist came back to the reception committee, put his arm

313

around the ebullient red-faced mayor and said, 'Well, sir, I'm sure we can spare the time for a modest banquet before the dreadful pressures of the timetable force us onwards.'

They left Simnel at the station with his fellow engineers to await the arrival of the back-up Flyer, which had left Zemphis a few hours after Iron Girder. The King and Aeron remained ensconced on the train, safely guarded in the armoured carriage, busy with paperwork and plans for their arrival in Uberwald. The rest of the party followed the mayor across the square to his hostelry.

The town really had tried. Something about the mayor's conviction that the world revolved around their town, or would do if it ever came there, had dribbled into the minds of his ratepayers, who now set to warming up marvellous dishes they had expected to be serving several hours before. And were very understanding, especially after Moist's description of the fight along the Paps. Admittedly he had put a certain amount of shine on the episode; surely that was what shine was for? And it permeated, even into the consciousness of those who had travelled, and at one point Of the Twilight the Darkness actually stood up and made a bow.

And Moist couldn't help himself and pointed at the goblin, saying, 'Of the Twilight the Darkness and his gallant fellows fought alongside Commander Vimes, with great courage.'

And then Moist glanced at the commander, who puffed his cigar and said, 'Excellent fighters, to a goblin.'

'Oh, we like goblins,' said the mayor. 'They run our clacks tower. And do you know, the snail infestation in my Porraceous Sprouter patch has completely gone since they moved in.'

And there was another toast to the clacks at this point with a side order of goblins. By the time they had all processed back to Iron Girder, she had been covered with petals by the virgins of the town.* The Flyer had been and gone some time before, with its

---

* At least they said they were virgins. There certainly were petals.

crew of engineers supplemented by Cheery Littlebottom – once more playing decoy – and other good fighters. It was even now on the track to Slake, acting as a pathfinder for Iron Girder to confuse the enemy.

As Iron Girder steamed out of Ohulan Cutash, most people headed off to sleep. Moist had loaned the sleeping compartment assigned to him to two of those wounded in the battle and was now bunking down in the guard's van, comfortable enough when you were dog-tired and Detritus wasn't snoring. All Moist's life he'd managed to find a way of sleeping in just about every circumstance and, besides, the guard's van was somehow the hub of the train; and although he didn't know how he did it, he always managed to sleep with half of one ear open. And now he savoured the familiar sounds of the journey, the rocking soothing him right up until somewhere down the line when he was catapulted into the real world by the screech once more of the locomotive's wheels in distress, and the squealing of brakes in torment.

It was still dark outside. Moist drowsily stumbled across the flatbed as doors were being opened and feet were running in the carriage ahead and reached the armoured compartment of the King. It was empty.

There was a dwarf guard, who said, 'The King went to the footplate.' The dwarf looked ashamed. 'I tried to persuade him to let me go with him, but what can you do? He is the King.'

Moist said, 'Don't worry, just keep this station. I'll go and see what's happening.'

There was a drill for this, he knew, and where *was* the King? That was the trouble with royalty. However decent they were, and understanding, they were also likely to think that such things as security arrangements were for other people.

Frantically searching, Moist finally dropped down on to the track and ran along to the engine, where he found the King talking to Dick Simnel on the footplate and getting covered in smuts.

Pale flames were visible ahead on the track and Simnel's expression was grave.

'It were just as well the King were 'ere because the decoy Flyer has been derailed ahead of us and so would we 'ave been if it weren't for 'im. He can see in t'dark!'

'Ah, Commander Vimes,' said the King to Vimes, who had arrived at speed. 'You should know about the dark-accustomed eye if any human does. There's a long straight ahead and Dick hadn't seen the derailment, but I did, just in time. Now, there may be injured people up there.'

And then the King was running towards the flames, adopting the traditional dwarf strategy of running at the enemy with as much weaponry as you could swing. But Vimes caught up with him and rolled him to the ground just as an explosion rattled the trees and bounced off the mountains. The Flyer's boiler had blown up. Ahead of them now was just a warm mist and the occasional clink of stricken metal.

Vimes got the King upright and said, 'Apologies for the lèse-majesté – though you must know that we Vimeses have gone a lot further than that in the past. You should have listened. The whole deal for the crew of the decoy Flyer was to run away as fast as possible if attacked, but not before making sure that the emergency bung in the boiler was strapped right down.'

'Ah, yes, Blackboard Monitor, how easily we revert to type in an emergency. I'm sorry to have put you to extra trouble.'

'That'll teach the buggers a lesson,' said Dick, panting as he caught up with them. 'They'll think twice about messing with one of my engines again.'

The crew of the Flyer were up a little gully, into which they had dived for shelter. It had once been home to frogs. Regrettably, it still was, and several of the designated bodyguards rose from the little swamp with nothing more than torn clothing and a lot of mud, some of which was hopping, but Cheery Littlebottom was as cheery as her name suggested.

There seemed to be no grags, but even as Moist looked around, an arm dropped out of a tree, still holding a club in an iron grip. And hereabouts, if you cared to look, and frankly nobody cared to do so but did nonetheless, there were several signs that grags and delvers and many others of the dark underworld had passed away in this spot, resting at peace and, thanks to the exploding boiler, in pieces.

Detritus appeared out of the gloom, saying, 'One or two of dem was still out dere. Not any more.' He slammed down a breastplate with a resounding clang.

'You all right, lads?' said Simnel to the engineers. 'Shame about the Flyer. It hurts, killing a locomotive, and it means we've not got either a pathfinder or a back-up engine no more. We need to clear the track now, then we'll pick up the scrap when we come back, to go towards a new Flyer. After all, we're getting reet good at building these things. But any bits of micromail you find, like this here' – he pointed at the arm holding the axe – 'I'll have now, mind, call it tit for tat. It'll be another trophy for Iron Girder.'

In the grey light of dawn the trolls made quick work of clearing the track ahead. As Moist watched, he suddenly saw creatures moving in the shadows, and then a sad little voice in the vicinity of his foot said, 'Please don't hurt us, please! We live here, we're gnomes, we're cobblers, it's what we do in these woods. We make charcoal and other things for sale, turned wood, excellent wooden furniture, and we try not to be in anyone's way, but the dwarfs have been marching and we think the bad times are coming again and we're scared.'

There was a sigh, then the voice went on, 'You must know it's the little people who're the last to be thought of when great tribes go to

317

war. My name is Slam, I'm the speaker for all the rest who are in hiding in these hills because we know how to hide. It's a skill we've perfected over the years. May we be of assistance?'

'Gnomes!' said the King at Moist's side. 'I haven't heard of them for ages. There used to be a lot of them once upon a time.'

And Moist thought, yes, these are the little people who get trodden on and left behind like the goblins! If they had a cheeky champion like Of the Twilight the Darkness, or Tears of the Mushroom and her wonderful harp, they'd become known gnomes. But the face of Slam suggested to him that the gnomes had been through the mill and come out as a very fine grist, and had been content to slip into obscurity and somehow were now drifting into a kind of sad oblivion.

He realized that the King was staring at the spokesgnome. Rhys said, 'I knew you were around here, in the forests. What can I do for you?'

'You could leave us alone, your majesty. Your absence. That's what everybody needs. To be left alone. Left alone to get on with their lives and, indeed,' said the little gnome more sharply, 'to be allowed to live at all.'

The King stepped back along the track and put one hand on Iron Girder, still spluttering and steaming, and, like somebody taking an oath, which he possibly was, said, 'I've known of you people since my childhood and right now, boyo, you may live as you like in these woodlands, and I'll be the first to defend your right to do so.'

He looked around at the rest of the crew and said, 'We must continue. There're still a lot of miles between here and Uberwald.'

Dick, who had been in an urgent conversation with Wally by the water tender, grimaced. 'I'm sorry, your majesty, but we've got a problem. There were a depot here for coal and water, but it's been smashed, and the grags have smashed the water crane and emptied t'water. We've still got t'coal, but we've barely got enough water to get to t'next depot. The engine can't run without water. We need to refill t'tank.' He paused. 'Come to think of it, where are t'railway folk? The way I reckoned the schedules, there should have been people 'ere all ready and waiting for us.'

Slam cleared his throat. 'We heard noises . . . People fighting . . .'

Moist looked at Vimes meaningfully and the commander said, 'Detritus? Think you could find them?'

The watchman saluted with a thud. 'Me an' Bluejohn will go lookin'. We are good at findin' humans. 's a troll fing. We'll find dem. Dead or alive.'

The two trolls headed into the undergrowth and Moist was sensitive to the fact that a large amount of firepower had gone with them. The commander looked grim.

The little gnome by Moist's feet tugged at his trouser leg to get attention. 'We can help with the water,' he said. 'There's a good spring behind the rise, and there's hundreds of us and it's not far and we make excellent buckets and I reckon we can fill your tanks in an hour or so.'

And they did.

Slam brought out a whistle from his jacket and blew it, and about a hundred replicas of the little gnome appeared. Not walked up, not came out of the sky, not came out of the earth. Simply appeared, each one carrying two buckets. It was evident that, small as they were, the gnomes were tough. Simnel watched them dashing away to the tender and back again, looking very carefully at their boots, massive things.

'Ey up, mister gnome, do you make them boots? I'm not being funny . . . but they are the biggest boots I've ever seen on such little folk. And, you know, with all the walking on t'lines and cinders and all, our boots wear out too damn quickly. I mean, look at these. Worn in all weathers. You said you were cobblers. Can you work metal an' all? Because if you can, what we really need are lads who can make heavy boots for t'railway workers. I'd be dead

319

chuffed if you could. Boots for lads on t'permanent way've got to be permanent boots.'

Slam beamed. 'If someone could send us the specifications as soon as possible we'll send a sample. And, for your interest, mister engineer, we are not little folk. We are big on the inside.'

He was interrupted by Detritus coming through the under-growth like a creature from the dawn of time, followed by Bluejohn in his role as heavy weapon. Bluejohn carefully put down two corpses and a mangled water crane.

Rhys Rhysson swore when he saw the corpses and young Simnel wept, but it was now fully morning, and time was passing. After a quick consultation with Commander Vimes and the Low King, the decision was made to leave. As everyone reboarded the train, Moist and Simnel said farewell to the gnomes.

'Please look after this place and give these gentlemen a decent burial, with a stone,' said the red-eyed Simnel. 'And if possible can you do owt wi' t'water crane?'

Slam beamed again. 'It's only metal. Didn't I mention that we're tinkers as well? We can definitely fix it for you.'

'Well then,' said Moist, 'you and your people are now working for the railway and that means you are working for Harry King and Sir Harry doesn't like anything bad to happen to his employees, oh my word yes. You'll see trains a lot in the future and I think you'll find your lives considerably more busy. I'll send a clacks to Sir Harry about remuneration.'

'What's remuneration?' said the little tinker.

Moist said, 'You'll find out.'

As Iron Girder struck out for Slake, the gnomes lined up and waved tiny little handkerchiefs until long after the train was out of sight.

Fishing for carp in Lake Overshot that afternoon, Mr Geoffrey Indigo was quietly surprised when the water in the lake simply disappeared in a certain amount of bubbling, leaving some gasping fish, startled frogs and a rather attractive nymph, who was very angry and spat at him as if it was his fault. But the man who had written that well-known book *Out with my Flies in All Weathers* kept his calm and made a note to mention this phenomenon at the next meeting of the Overshot Fishing Society.

As he meticulously cleaned his gear and generally tidied up, he heard a liquid noise and was surprised for a second time to see that the hole in the landscape was now refilling with water. He watched amazed as the nymph spat at him again, leaving him feeling somewhat wronged. And on the way home, squelching a little, he wondered if anyone would believe him.

When he told his wife later about the strange day, she snorted.

'Geoffrey, you really shouldn't take your brandy flask with you!'

'I didn't take it with me,' he protested. 'It's still on the sideboard, where it always is!'

'Then just don't tell anybody,' his wife concluded. 'People will think you're strange and we can't have that.'

Geoffrey, the least strange person in the world, except possibly when it came to talking about fish, decided not to say anything. After all, you didn't want to become a laughing stock . . .

Moist was starting to worry about Dick Simnel and his band of overworked engineers. What sleep they got was in sleeping bags, curled up on carriage seats, eating but not eating well, just driven by their watches and their desire to keep the train going. If you met them away from the cab, their conversation was about gears and wheels and timings, but it was clear to Moist that they were frazzled after days of living on the footplate and wrestling their locomotives through various little tantrums.

And so he confronted Mr Simnel, saying, 'Surely we can afford to slacken pace a little and let you and your lads get your heads down for a bit? As far as I can see, we're well on schedule.'

And he detected in Dick's eyes not madness but something else more subtle. He was sure it had no name. It seemed to be a sort of hunger for anything that was new and above all for proving that something could be refined to the point of perfection and kept there. In the goblins this was endemic, although it didn't seem to do *them* much harm. Humans, apparently, were another matter.

'People are going to die if we push them any further,' he said to Dick. 'You lot would rather work than sleep! I swear, sometimes you seem to be as mechanical as Iron Girder, and that's not right, you have to . . . chill, get laid back before you are laid-back and laid down for ever.'

To Moist's amazement, Dick suddenly ripped out at him like a lion. He could almost hear the growl.

'Who are you to talk, Mister Moist? What have you made, built, fretted over? I see none of your fingernails are torn and you can talk well in a fancy way, but what is it you've made? What is it you are?'

'Me, Dick? Well, now I come to look at it I'm the grease that turns the wheels and changes minds and moves the world along. Or you might say that I'm a kind of a cook, but it is a special kind of cookery. It's a bit like the sliding rule; you just move things about at the right time and you get the answer you need. In short, Dick, I make things happen, and that includes your railway.'

The young man swayed in front of him and Moist's tone became gentle. 'And I now see that part of my job is to tell you that you need some rest. You've run out of steam, Dick. Look, we're well on the way to Uberwald now, and while it's daylight and we're out of the mountains it's going to be the least risky time to run with minimum crew. We're all going to need our wits about us when we get near the Pass. Surely you can take some rest?'

Simnel blinked as if he'd not seen Moist the first time, and said, 'Yes, you're right.'

And Moist could hear the slurring in the young man's speech, caught him before he fell and dragged him into a sleeping compartment, put him to bed and noted that the engineer didn't so much fall asleep as somehow flow into it. And that job done, he went to the guard's van where Vimes was drinking coffee and carefully going through the paperwork relating to the captive delvers, who in the pinch sang like most canaries.

'Commander Vimes, can you help me a moment?'

'Problem, Mister Lipwig?'

'The lads are working all the time and they seem to think it's the badge of a man never to go to sleep.'

'I have to teach that to young coppers. Treasure a night's rest, I always say. Take a nap whenever you can.'

'Very good,' said Moist. 'Now look at them here. Still working on the sliding rules and fretting themselves because they've spent too much time trying to put one over on the universe.'

'It seems like that,' said Vimes, getting up.

Together they wandered along the train forcing the engineers to at least lie down in their bunks or face the wrath of Sir Harry King. And in a few cases Moist suggested Of the Twilight the Darkness should dose them with one of his harmless little potions. Not all of them, of course, in case there was an emergency. You never knew when you might need an engineer.

In his cell Albrecht Albrechtson had had plenty of time to consider Ardent's tactics. Ardent was a mere stripling youth,* but was already revealed as a manipulative chancer, seeking advancement come what may and by any means he deemed necessary. He wormed his way into everything and in that sentence Albrecht thought the important word was 'worm'.

Being Ardent's prisoner was galling. The food was good and drink likewise, even if the small beer was smaller than than he'd have liked. He was allowed some of his books, too, apart from those

---

* A dwarf is not thought of as a youth until he is in his fifties.

Ardent considered un-dwarfish – a terminology that told you everything about the arrogant young upstart, still wet behind the helmet, who was no doubt keen to get his paws on the whole of Schmaltzberg, 'un-dwarfish' fat mines and all.

And in his little dungeon Albrechtson had to endure Ardent's self-serving philosophy about the role of the Low King. What insolence! Lecturing *him*, the foremost scholar on the subject. But it didn't do to get angry, at least not yet. Anger was a weapon to be honed and treasured and used only at the moment yielding most premium. And that thought was followed by a noise on the stone stairs as the pompous fool came again to get him to change his mind.

Of course, Ardent would begin as if he was just an old friend coming to chew the rat, but as he talked, Albrechtson would glimpse the coils of a decent mind unfolding. After all, he was opposing his sovereign, something not done lightly, if ever. Ardent had to be aware of the penalty for those who took up arms against the Low King. Despite everything, there must have been a good mind there, one which could have been useful to dwarfkind as a whole and might yet be useful, even if right now it couldn't tell pyrites from gold. It was no secret that the most highly balanced minds sometimes, well, overbalanced.

The key turned in the lock. There was Ardent, and his expression seriously frightened his erstwhile mentor. You needed to be mature to sense this sort of thing but you could tell in a person's eyes if they were being driven by an idea. They had a clammy look about them, and so did Ardent.

Nevertheless, Albrechtson laid down his pen and said in a calm voice, 'So kind of you to come and see me. I understand the King will be here shortly, courtesy of the train. Won't that be nice?'

There was a little bloom of spittle on one side of Ardent's face and he snapped, 'You can't possibly know that!'

Albrechtson sat back convivially and said, 'It's probably true that I taught you all you know, young dwarf, but I did not teach you all *I* know. I have some skills that I didn't impart.'

'Then they must include guesswork. *I* hold the key to information in Schmaltzberg. No clacks towers are standing.'

'Oh yes, so I hear.'

'Rhys Rhysson is betraying all that is dwarfish. And for the sake of our species you surely know that I must take the Scone of Stone. The majority of the dwarfs here are behind me.'

Albrechtson twiddled a pen in his fingers and said, 'Possibly in order not to have to look at your face, Ardent. You're shaken and the courage of your convictions will see you convicted, the moment the King steps into Schmaltzberg. From what I know of Rhys Rhysson, he *may* be merciful.'

'Yes, I thought you'd say something like that, but the deed is done.'

Albrechtson looked stunned. 'You have actually taken the Scone?'

For a moment Ardent looked foxed. 'Not as such . . . Everything is in place. It only needs me to take the final step and Rhys Rhysson can have a retirement somewhere out of the way, like back in Llamedos.'

'Then do it now. Go on. There's nothing to stop you, is there? But the Low King is elected, isn't he? How certain are you? How certain are you that all your fellow travellers are stalwart? Because I'm absolutely certain that many of them are not. Oh yes, they fawn on you and promise a lot, but as the train comes closer and we hear the whistle of change blowing, I think you'll find that suddenly they have other engagements and recall never talking to you about the Scone of Stone. That's happening now, and you don't know it.'

It was unfair really. Ardent said, 'I invite you to remember that you're locked in here and I have the only key.'

'Yes. And of the two of us you are the only one sweating. You'll be surprised at what I know. How many clacks towers have come back out of the ground like mushrooms? And I know what the Ankh-Morpork dwarfs are saying. You want to know? They say "Why don't we have the Scone of Stone in Ankh-Morpork? After all, there are more dwarfs in Ankh-Morpork than there are in Schmaltzberg."'

'You would countenance our Scone in that wretched place?'

'Of course not. But neither will I see you on the Scone of Stone. Your grags are losing their followers, not just because of the clacks towers and not because of Ankh-Morpork but because new generations arise and think what's all this about – how could our parents be so stupid? And you can't stop people any more than you could stop the train.'

Albrechtson was almost sorry for Ardent now. You could live in denial for a long time, but, like a snake, it doubles back and strikes.

'You should face facts, Albrecht Albrechtson. You will be amazed at my support. Dwarfs must remain dwarfs, not simulacrums of humans. To follow Rhys Rhysson is to become *d'rkza*, a half-dwarf, less than that even.'

'No, it is your kind of thinking that makes dwarfs small, wrapped up in themselves: declaring that any tiny change in what is thought to be dwarf is somehow sacrilege. I can remember the days when even talking to a human was forbidden by idiots such as you. And now you have to understand it's not about the dwarfs, or the humans, or the trolls, it's about the people, and that's where the troublesome Lord Vetinari wins the game. In Ankh-Morpork you can be whoever you want to be and sometimes people laugh and sometimes they clap, and mostly and beautifully, they don't really care. Do you understand this? Dwarfs now have seen liberty. And that's heady stuff.'

Ardent almost spat and said, 'You say that when you're known to be one of the biggest traditionalists in all the mines?'

'I still am. And most of our traditions were to keep us safe, just in the way that the grags in their great, heavy clothing exploded the firedamp so that we wouldn't be burned alive. The rules of the mine. They learned the hard way and the traditions are there for a purpose; they work. But somehow, you and the others don't realize that outside the caverns the world is different. Oh, I keep the special days and knock twice on every door and follow all the tenets of Tak. And why? Because they bring us together, as did the clacks towers until your blessed delvers started to burn them. Burning words dying in the sky! Is that to be the legacy of the dwarfs?'

He stopped. Ardent had gone pale and seemed to be shivering. But then his eyes blazed, and he snarled, 'You won't be driven, Albrecht, and nor will I. Train or no train. It'll never get here anyway. The world is not ready for locomotion.'

He glared at Albrecht, who said, 'Yes, of course it isn't. But what you don't understand is that the world wasn't ready for the clacks but now it screams if they are burned down. And I believe that locomotion has not finished with us yet.'

The response was the slamming of the door and the turning of the key. And now the fool had locked him in for the night, just where he wanted to be.

There were guards, Albrecht knew, but like guards everywhere they tended to slumber or go off somewhere to smoke a pipe during the long hours of the night, and in any case very few of them came near to this particular dungeon since sensible guards didn't want to upset someone like Albrecht. Even if you thought you were on the right side, you never *knew* who the winner would be and in those circumstances smaller fry might be the ones to get fried . . .

After a while, Albrecht picked up the little spoon with which he had eaten his meal and there was the subtle scratching of rock dust which led to the appearance of a goblin, who grinned at him in the gloom.

'Here you are, squire, here's clacks flimsies, fresh from

Commander Vimes. And bottle of oil for lamp. Oh, and toothpaste you asks for. Have been told to tell you that train is moving like no one business. Sure to be here on schedule.'

It was a kind of therapy to hear of the inevitable approach of the famous Iron Girder, day after day.

The aroma of a goblin, Albrecht thought, seemed to be a metaphysical one. After the initial shock, you had to wonder if the goblin smell was somehow arriving inside your head as much as through your nostrils. It wasn't even all that bad. It had the savour of old sculleries and southernwood.

He took the packages and scanned the flimsies with the speed of a dwarf who had learned to assimilate the written word quickly. And he spoke with interest to the young goblin, a caste he had hitherto dismissed as a waste of space at best and a nuisance otherwise, but they seemed to be more level-headed than most of his fellow dwarfs, especially that fool Ardent, and it was amazing how they could get about in the darkness of Schmaltzberg and make use of every rat hole before making use of the rat.

And this one waited patiently while Albrecht sorted out some flimsies of his own to go back to the locomotive. And then the old dwarf did something else that surprised him.

He said: 'What's your name, young goblin? And may I beg your pardon for not enquiring earlier? Please forgive an old dwarf who hasn't kept up with the times.'

The goblin looked stunned and said, 'Well, guv, if it don't hurt anything, I am The Rattle of the Wheels. Railwaymen friends is calling me Rat for short name. That makes oldies very annoy.'

Albrecht held out a hand. The Rattle of the Wheels stepped back and then came forward sheepishly.

'Nice to meet you, Rattle of the Wheels. Have you any family?'

'Yes, your worship. My mother is Of the Happiness the Heart, father is Of the Sky the Rim and small brother is Of the Water the Crane.'

And after a moment the goblin said, 'Actually, sir, you can stop holding my hand.'

'Oh, yes. I suppose that my name should be Of the Moment the Stupefied. Good luck to you and your family. You know, in a way I'm jealous of you. And now I've finished my work for the day I'd like you to take my paperwork, such as it is, and hide it somewhere around here where no dwarf is going to look.'

'We cleans toilets, sir. Knows plenty-many places that not visited. Same time tomorrow?'

The handshake fulfilled, the goblin disappeared into a hole that even a rat might find difficult to get into. And as the sounds of the goblin scrabbling through the hole faded away, Albrecht thought, I would *never* have done that before. What a fool I was.

Miss Gwendolyn Avery of Schmarm awoke in the middle of the night to the shaking and rattle of the multiple bottles of age-defying unguents on her dresser. And then she realized that the whole house was shaking to a rhythmic thudding.

When she described this episode in dramatic tones to her friend Daphne the following morning, she said that it was like the sound of a lot of men marching past. She put it down to the cherry brandy she had had before going to bed whilst Daphne, knowing Gwendolyn's regrettable spinster status, put it down to wishful thinking.

The Slake ranges were half tundra, half desert, mostly windswept. In short, a fossil of a landscape where nothing generally grew but stumbleweed,* and the occasional gregarious pine, the nuts of which were said to be an antidote to melancholy.

There was water, oh yes, but mostly underground, and

---

* Stumbleweed is like tumbleweed, but less athletic. This tells you everything you need to know about Slake.

prospectors and rock hounds were said to send down buckets to dredge water from the depths of the caves.

It was slightly easier to find water on the uplands hubwards of the tundra, where there were icy streams courtesy of the Everwind glacier, making it possible to raise goats there. And so goats were what young Knut's family had bred and milked and minded down the centuries. And when the goats were eating what passed as grass on these highlands, he would sleep and dream of not chasing goats over a near-barren landscape. He had liked it at first but he was growing older and something was telling him that there was a better life than watching goats eat their lunch . . . once, twice and sometimes thrice. Sometimes the faces they made were an entertainment and sometimes he laughed. And yet a yearning in him told him that goats were not enough.

And so it was, when the long sound echoed across the tundra, that he hurried to see what was making the wonderful noise and saw a shining streak snaking its way over the landscape in the early morning light; and it was heading his way. He wondered if it was anything to do with the strange bars of metal laid carefully on the tundra below by the gangs of men some weeks before. He had run errands for them and sold them his mother's cheese, but he couldn't really understand what it was they were doing and since the goats stepped carefully over the metal strips without harm he had given up wondering. But as far as he could make out from what the men had said, it was all for a wondrous thing that could go around the world on a flash of steam, and now he wanted to know more about this singing beast coming over the tundra, occasionally spitting fire.

Knut scrambled down off the hillside to where the air was warmer, leaving the goats, and ultimately traced the noise to a kind of big shed. And just as he got to it, the creature, carrying people inside it, broke out of the shed and hurtled away along the metal rails. He watched it until it had entirely disappeared. And later some of the townspeople told him it was what they called a 'locomotive', and in his heart the yearning started and began by degrees to grow. Yes, there truly were other things than goats.

Having spent a long afternoon and evening alert for anything untoward while Simnel and his lads lay dead to the world, Moist in his turn had slept soundly all night and now dozed right through the morning, rocked by the motion of the train as she steamed on from Slake across the valley of the Smarl, dreaming of the bridge over the gorge at the Wilinus Pass, never a picnic at any time, that was looming up fast like a tax demand.

Anything could happen before they entered that dry-land maelstrom of sliding rocks, falling rocks and, well, rocks full of bandits of all disciplines. To coin a term that might fit the circumstances: it was like running a gauntlet with no shoes – a gauntlet full of rocks. And even pebbles had bad attitudes at that altitude. Moist winced at the thought of the place.

The train hurtled on through the vast landscape. A huge amount of space, oh yes, but not many towns, just the occasional settlement. There was so much space everywhere and Iron Girder ate it up like a tiger, attacking the horizon as if it were an affront, stopping only if it was known that water and coal were available. You could never have too much of either.

By the middle of the day, the mountain ranges of Uberwald were getting closer and the air was getting colder and Iron Girder's pace had settled to a steady climb through the foothills towards their destination.

Lonely goatherds could be seen on the trackside, and amongst the people staring at this new mechanism there was a definite outbreak of dirndls. In every township they passed people were ready for them with flags and, above all, with bands that wheezed and oompah'd as the crowds cheered Iron Girder on her way. And, yes, as the train came past slowly and carefully you had to watch out for the little boys running after her, following the dream. It was a sight to yodel for.

And now Moist noticed that Simnel was looking increasingly worried and took the opportunity of one of the engineer's rare breaks from the footplate to speak to him privately.

'Dick, Iron Girder is the best locomotive you've ever built, right?'

Simnel wiped his hands on a rag that had already seen too many greasy hands and said, 'She surely is, Mister Lipwig, we all know that, but it's not Iron Girder I'm fretting about. It's that bridge over t'gorge. We've done everything we can, but we need more time. There's no way the bridge will hold with all the weight of the train an' all.'

'Well now,' said Moist, 'you have the loggysticks and the knowledge of the weights and the stresses and all the other sliding rule business and that's telling you one thing, but I'm telling you now that if the bridge is still not secure when we get there I propose that Iron Girder will fly across the gorge with you and me on the footplate. You might call it a sleight of hand, even a trick, but we *will* fly.'

The engineer looked like a man who has been challenged to guess under which thimble the pea is, and knows deep in his boots that it will never, ever be the one he selects.

'Mister Lipwig, are you talking about magic here? I'm an engineer, I am. We don't 'old wi' magic.'

And suddenly Moist's voice was as smooth as treacle. 'Actually, Mister Simnel, I think you're wrong in that. You believe in the sunshine, although you don't know how it does it. And since we're on or near the subject, have you ever wondered what the Turtle stands on?'

Dick was cornered and said, 'Ee, well, that's different. That's just how things are meant to be.'

'Pardon me, my friend, but you don't know that. Nevertheless you go to bed at night quite happy in the belief that the world will still be there when you get up in the morning.'

Once again, Dick tried to get a grip on the proceedings, still wearing the look of a man certain that whichever thimble was going to be picked up it wouldn't be his. A given in the scheme of things.

'So we're talking about wizards, then, Mister Lipwig?'

'Well . . . magic,' said Moist. 'Everything is magic when you don't know what it is. Your sliding rule is a magic wand to most people. And I know some kinds of magic. And so I'll ask you, Dick, have I ever let you down in any way during our time on Harry King's business?'

'Oh no, Mister Lipwig,' said Simnel, almost affronted. 'I see you as what my old granny called full of fizz.'

Moist caught the fizz in the air and juggled it.

'There you are, Dick. I believe you when you say that the numbers on the sliding rule are telling you things. In return I'd like some trust from you. No, please don't use your sliding rule for this. It's the wrong tool for the job. I know something . . . Not exactly magic, but extremely solid . . . and with what I have in mind, by the time we get to the bridge you'll think we're riding through the air.'

Simnel once again looked as if he was about to cry. 'But why won't you tell me?'

'I could,' said Moist, 'but Lord Vetinari would have me dead.'

'Eee! We can't 'ave that, Mister Lipwig,' said Simnel, shocked.

Moist put an arm round Simnel and said, 'Dick, you can perform miracles, but I propose to give the world a spectacle that'll be remembered for a very long time.'

'Eh up, Mister Lipwig. I'm just an engineer.'

'Not just an engineer, Dick: *the* engineer.'

And as Simnel cherished that thought he smiled nervously and said, 'But 'ow? There just isn't enough time and there aren't enough men, neither. Harry King has brought out all his 'eavy-duty workers from the city and the plains and so I don't know where you'll get more support from.'

'Well,' said Moist, 'I'll have to be like Iron Girder. I'll just whistle.'

Simnel laughed nervously. 'Ee, Mister Lipwig, you're a sharp one!'

'Good,' said Moist, with a confidence he wasn't entirely feeling. 'We should be ready by dusk.'

Just then Iron Girder let loose a little bit of steam and Moist wondered if it was a good omen, or possibly a bad one, but it seemed to him to be an omen anyway, and that was enough.

That afternoon, in an attempt to distract his thoughts, Moist decided to tackle something that had been niggling at the back of his mind ever since they had left Sto Lat. And for that he needed to talk to Aeron.

The King's secretary was slim for a dwarf, almost nimble and quick, and decidedly ubiquitous, his long beard following him like a banner as he went about on the King's business. He carried a sword, not traditionally a dwarf weapon, and had acquitted himself well during the attack on the train at the Paps of Scilla.

Choosing his moment carefully, Moist waylaid Aeron in a place where they could talk privately.

'Mister Secretary, I have to ask whether all is quite as it seems with the Low King.'

Aeron's eyes narrowed and his hand went to the hilt of his sword. 'Of course it is. What a ridiculous question. Treacherous, too!'

Moist put his hand out placatingly. 'Look, you know I'm on your side! I have to ask because of something I saw at Mrs Simnel's house.'

Aeron looked startled and said, 'I believe the side you're on is your own, sir, and whatever you think you saw it's certainly no business of yours.'

'Indeed it is, my friend,' Moist replied. 'The gods, for my sins, gave me a nose for scenting when the metaphorical shit is about to hit the windmill, and I want to be prepared.'

Aeron stood frozen, and without looking directly at Moist he said, 'Your perspicacity does you credit, Mister Lipwig. Your silence even more!'

'Oh, come on. There's something going on here and I'm not in on it. Don't force me to draw my own conclusions. I do have a very big pencil.'

But Aeron clearly had nothing further to say. The appearance of a couple of engineers at the end of the carriage provided the excuse he needed for bringing the conversation to an abrupt close. He turned on his heel and marched smartly off down the corridor, leaving Moist with every suspicious nerve in his body jangling.

An hour or so later, a knock at the entrance to the guard's van heralded the King's secretary, who this time smiled strangely and said, 'The King would like to grant you an audience, Mister Lipwig.' And he smiled again and said, 'And that, I'm sure you're aware, means at once.'

The King was sitting at a little table doing paperwork when Moist arrived, and beckoned him towards another chair in the carriage, saying, 'Mister Lipwig, I understand that following our visit to Mister Simnel's mother, you appear to be under the impression that I may be . . . hiding something. Is that the case, boyo?'

The King looked at Moist with a stern glare, almost as if daring him to utter what he was thinking.

'Well, she does have a lot of . . . feminine insight . . .' Moist let the rest of the sentence tail away and watched carefully.

The King sighed and looked at Aeron, who was standing on guard by the door. Rhys nodded and then turned back to Moist.

'Mister Lipwig, I'm sure you are aware that the sex of dwarfs is often a well-kept secret and there have been times when even to enquire about the sex of another dwarf was considered a terrible thing. I am the Low King of the Dwarfs, but if I can get to what I might call the bottom line, I am also female.'

And there it was. This was the thing that had been niggling at the back of his mind ever since Mrs Simnel had started making the sleeping King – *Queen* now, he reminded himself – comfortable back in Sto Lat. He coughed and said, 'Well, nobody's perfect, your majesty. And to tell you the truth, I think I've known for some time. I'm good at putting rumours, suspicions and instinct together and getting the right result, because I'm a scoundrel. I expect Lord Vetinari has warned you about me. You could say that I'm Lord Vetinari's scoundrel.'

'As if *he* needs one!'

'Scoundrels take a different look at people, just to get the measure of them: the way they walk, the way they talk, the way they sit. All the little details left unsaid in the wrong place.'

The Queen was silent for a moment and said, 'A *real* scoundrel?'

'Yes, m'lady, I would say one of the best, possibly *the* best,' said Moist. 'But these days you might say that I'm tamed and at heel, which means I'm a very trustworthy scoundrel.'

'At Vetinari's heel? You poor boy.'

And now the Queen looked as if something worrying had been chased away and she said, 'You must know, Mister Lipwig, there are only very few people who are aware of my secret and they are trusted. One of them is Lady Margolotta and another, of course, is Lord Vetinari.

'It has always seemed to me that the attitude of dwarfs when it comes to gender is curdling us. Dwarfs, we keep insisting, must be *seen* to be male – and what does it say about a species if they can't look their own mothers in the face? We live a stupid lie and play a stupid game and I don't want this state of affairs to continue. I am indeed the Low Queen, Mister Lipwig, and I thank you for your silence at this time.'

The Queen appeared as innocent as one of those mountains which year after year do nothing very much but smoke a little, and then one day end up causing a whole civilization to become an art installation.

336

'Mrs Simnel is a nice lady,' she continued, 'although perhaps not as discreet as she thought . . . Of course, I know I can depend on you to treat my secret as if it were your own. I'm sure Lord Vetinari would be upset if you didn't do so.'

Moist polished his best reassuring smile to sparkling. 'As I told you, ma'am, I'm a born scoundrel, so I've learned to be very, very discreet for the sake of keeping my own neck safe from people who take a dim view of scoundrelhood. And as for Mrs Simnel, she knew all about the secret of steam and never told anyone about it.'

The Queen stroked her beard and said, 'For a proud mother that must have been testing indeed . . . Very well, Mister Scoundrel, I will have faith in you both. And now I can see that Aeron is becoming restive, so I'd better return to my paperwork.' She sent what Moist would swear was a teasing glance in her secretary's direction.

Moist, for whom it was second nature to watch and listen carefully – most particularly to what was not said – now felt he knew another secret, a secret as yet unacknowledged. The Queen and her secretary were, without doubt, lovers. Possibly you had to be married to notice this fact, but their body language shone through.

A meaning cough from Aeron recalled his attention. The secretary was holding the door open for him, in a clear signal that the audience was over. As Moist stepped out past him Aeron said, 'Thank you, Mister Lipwig . . . From both of us.'

Before he set off back to the guard's van, Moist stood for a while letting the revelations settle. The King being a Queen was looming in his mind. Oh yes, everybody knew that dwarf women looked very much like the dwarf men, beards and all, even Cheery Littlebottom – an Ankh-Morpork dwarf if ever there was one and a strict feminist; although she was adamant that beyond the beards dwarf females were not the same as dwarf men. And since she was now very big, as it were, in the Watch, her insistence on chainmail skirts and subtly altered breastplates didn't matter too much, but the Queen—? What would happen if the Queen declared it! It would be *iacta alea est* in spades! And there would be no going back from that.

Aeron had now disappeared back into the Queen's armoured coach, and Moist was left listening to the rattling of the train. The future, he thought, was going to be . . . incredibly interesting.

The everlasting fog that filled the vertiginous gorge created deep swirling shadows in the fading light as they approached the final bridge before the Wilinus Pass. And the fog itself seemed to be alive as it moved and twisted, leaving the watchers with the feeling that they were teetering at the edge of the world.

The far side of the bridge was barely visible as Simnel stood in earnest conversation with the head engineer in charge of the bridge works. A bit of darkness in the fog near Moist turned out to be Commander Vimes, grinning.

'A rickety bridge, a heavy train, a terrifying drop to certain death below, with a pressing deadline and no back-up plan?' said Vimes. 'You must be in your element, Mister Lipwig. I'm told the engineers say it can't be done. Are you really planning to risk the Low King and the future peace of this region on one throw of the dice?'

Behind them an engineer said, 'I wouldn't travel over that for a pension.'

As Rhys and Aeron joined them, the creaks and groans of the ancient bridge structure intensified, and seemed almost alive, like some demon daring them to chance their fate. The less fanciful of the engineers might talk of natural movement caused by the drop in temperature as night approached, but it was hard to ignore the ominous atmosphere of the place which was almost . . . eldritch.

Then Iron Girder snorted steam, panting like a dog ready to be unleashed. Moist took a deep breath, stuck his fingers into his jacket and smiled with a confidence which had blossomed just a second before when he had finally heard the subtle sound he had been waiting for.

'It's a little-known fact, my friends, that these fogs have remarkable solidity. Allow me to demonstrate.'

He stepped off the edge of the cliff beside the track and stood there with the fog swirling around his ankles. He heard gasps from behind. He turned and faced his fellow travellers with a huge grin and a silent sigh of relief before stepping back on to what might be called solid ground.

'You see. Would you like me to run to the other side and back again while this mystical phenomenon continues, as I believe it will, or shall we all go over now, while the time is ripe?'

'D'you mind if I try?' said Vimes.

There was a *twinkle* and Moist said, 'By all means, commander.'

And Vimes disappeared into the swirling fog, lighting his cigar, saying, 'Just like standing on a pavement. Amazing. I suggest you make steam, Mister Simnel! I'm in some doubt about how long such a, as you say, mystical phenomenon will last. So I think alacrity is our motto here, gentlemen.'

Simnel, resisting the natural temptation of a scientist to examine the phenomenon more closely, looked around and said, 'Oh aye. All aboard, everybody!' And after a moment, he added, 'Quickly . . . please.'

Moist looked at Simnel and said, 'Do you now believe, Dick?'

'Yes, Mister Lipwig.'

'But do you *really* believe?'

'I surely do, Mister Lipwig! I believe in the sliding rule, the cosine and the tangent and even when the quaderatics give me gyp, yes, I still believe. Iron Girder is my machine, I built 'er, every last rivet carefully forged by 'and. And I reckon if I could bolt rails on to the sky, Iron Girder would take us to t'moon.'

Moist whistled and heard a signal from below. He raised his voice and said, 'Forward, please, Mister Simnel!' And immediately there was the familiar chugging sound of a train anxious to be travelling and getting up steam. Moist loved the moment as the power built up slowly and by degrees until there was a rolling thunder, taking charge of the universe, and they were moving into the villainous fog and on to the bridge.

It was difficult to see anything from the footplate, but Moist could just make out Simnel's white face as the vibrations and swaying intensified. Despite Moist's dramatic demonstration earlier, he could tell that Simnel and his crew were terrified and even he began to doubt whether the bridge would in fact hold under the pressure. And then the vibrations suddenly ceased and there was a strange sensation as Iron Girder left the rails and she flew.

Down below, the fog curled into even stranger shapes, spiralling vortices, stirred up by the passage of the train, and after a strangled few minutes there was a thump of wheels on rails as Iron Girder consented to exchange flight for the sensible permanent way once more and then Dick blew the whistle and kept blowing, and she was bowling along again as if nothing uncanny, mystic or even eldritch had happened.

It wasn't until Moist found time to himself after all the back-slapping he had received that the enormity of what he had done hit him like a jack-hammer: a whole train under steam, full of passengers! And a king apparently flying through thin air! And he sweated again as the next thought said, 'So many things could have gone wrong.' In fact so many things *could* have gone wrong and he began to feel certain that history might just slam backwards to ensure that they did. And the sweat ran down his whole body but he wouldn't have been Moist if he couldn't recover from this sort of thing. Just as long as Vetinari *never* got to hear about it.

The thought of Vetinari was still proving hard to banish later that evening when Moist finally bunked down in the guard's van. As the motion of the train lulled him into a tired and relieved doze, an image of the Patrician swam into Moist's mind. He shuddered at the recollection of his recent encounter. Vetinari had been at his desk reading reports of what looked suspiciously to Moist like other people's clacks messages.* He had frowned when he saw Moist and said, 'Well now, Mister Lipwig, is the train already cleared for Uberwald, by any chance?'

Moist had assumed an expression that would not have deceived a child, which was, of course, part of the game. 'Not *quite* yet, my lord, but I think the prospects are getting rosier by the hour.'

'Long-winded. Very long-winded indeed. Come to the point, if such a thing exists, please? After all, I *do* have matters of state to deal with.'

'Well, sir, I'm sure you recall, we have buried within the city limits a number of very ancient golems, and you vowed that they would only be deployed in the event of a threat to national security, and right now I think I could use several dozen of them, sir, that is of course if you don't mind?'

'Mister Lipwig, you surely try my patience. I'm quite well aware that both you and your wife have the tools that would allow you to enter said vault and, indeed, give said golems instructions, but nevertheless I strictly forbid you to try anything of the sort. This has to do with the railway, I am assuming.'

'Yes, my lord, a minor little problem on the train to success, as it were.'

'Let me make myself entirely clear. If I find any evidence that you have removed city golems from their proper place and moreover have taken them outside the city limits, you will be thrown to the kittens. Is that understood?'

Vetinari's expression was as flat and impenetrable and as placid

---

* Although this accusation has never been levelled by anybody at his lordship, which is to say, none have been found.

as a sea of pitch, and Moist had bowed and said, 'I assure you, sir, no such evidence will ever be found.' While overhead, the words 'If I find' floated like a sly invitation.

Uncomfortably alert again, with Vetinari's voice echoing in his head, Moist drew out the clacks flimsy he'd had from Adora Belle about the progress of the golems. He tore it up and threw the pieces out of the nearest window, from where he watched them disappear in the wake of the wonderful train.

From the gloom of the guard's van behind him someone coughed, pointedly. Vimes emerged with a little smile and said, 'Plausible deniability, eh, Mister Lipwig? But well done, anyway. Just between ourselves: those golems that'll never be used . . . What do you suppose they're doing right now?'

Moist opened his mouth to deny all knowledge of the golems, then thought better of it. Something in Vimes's eyes dared him to try. 'Digging their way back home, I trust,' he said. 'Rather more easily since they tunnelled their way up here in the first place.'

And in the distance behind the train, the rickety bridge was falling bit by bit into the valley in a curious kind of mechanical ballet. It would be some time before it could be used again, thought Moist – but now we've got Rhys this far we can throw everything into getting this damn bridge built properly.

And a few hours later, as the golems tunnelled under his tavern, the Grosszügig Stein, Herr Muckenfuss noticed the floor dancing and every glass and stein in the building shook rapidly. Plump though he was, he scooped up every falling stein and glass with great determination until there was a sudden settling in the air and the tavern was eerily silent. He looked at Herr Bummel, his solitary customer, who stared at the dregs in his stein of the new cask of Old Blonk they had been sampling before whispering in impressed tones, 'I think I'll have the same again.'

As Bonk came ever closer and the horizon was now eaten by the mountains – looming outlines visible against the night sky, steep slopes occasionally catching the moonlight – Commander Vimes called a council of war in the guard's van, the centre of operations. With the experience of the attacks at the Paps and the destruction of the Flyer to draw upon, careful plans were laid for the defence of the train and the King.

'Well now, look around, all of you. What you see is canyons and trees. If I was a grag I'd probably see this next stretch as my last available opportunity to derail Iron Girder.'

Vimes's face was grim as he outlined his proposals and Rhys nodded his approval, interrupting now and then to add a refinement.

'We must also take care of attacks from above,' the commander continued. 'As we've seen, Iron Girder is well protected. She has her corsets on now, thanks to Dick's new alloy, but we might have to fight on top of the carriages. I see you grin, Mister Lipwig. So, smart boy, if that happens I invite you to join me and the others on the roof when the time comes. Are you game, sir? It's likely to be very dangerous up there.'

The inner Moist patted himself on the back as he thought of his illicit adventure on top of the Flyer. He could dance on the train, jump and spin and twirl, because he had the measure of the moods of every part of the train.

'I've wanted to do something like this ever since I saw my first locomotive, commander,' he said to Commander Vimes.

'Yes,' said Vimes, 'that's what I'm afraid of. So I must tell you that we work as a team or we become separate corpses.' He pointed at the trees towering overhead in the deep cutting they were travelling through. 'There is very little space in this damn cutting. Trees? Nothing but stiff weeds – remember that!'

'I'm sure we could do it,' said Moist. 'Why not bring Detritus up top as well?'

343

'No, he's good on the ground, but he isn't limber. Anyway, with Detritus on top of it I'm afraid the roof would pretty soon become the floor.'

The commander looked around and said, 'The rest of you know your stations. Remember, we're on this train to get the King back again. Guard him! Don't bother about us on top.'

When he could speak to Vimes with nobody else listening, Moist said, 'I know the rhythm of the train, but I'm no fighter, commander. Why choose me?'

'Because, Mister Lipwig, you'd pay a king's ransom in order to say that you fought on the roof of a train and I've seen you, you're a bastard in close combat, worse than Nobby and he tends to bite their knees. I saw the corpses of the grags from that incident at the Quirm railhead. You can fight, if only in terror, but it's true that the coward can often be the best fighter of all.'

As the sky grew pallid in the pre-dawn, the atmosphere on the train changed. The whole crew knew that they were now heading at top speed right into unfriendly territory. On every crag in the mountains of Uberwald you could see the lights of the Igors twinkling and wobbling in the darkness of the canyons, and green lightning flashed from gargoyle to gargoyle like spectres.

Moist had generally always kept away from the place. You got the occasional werewolf or zombie in Ankh-Morpork, of course, but in Uberwald they were commonplace. This was their place, with their rules – and that included the black ribboners, the slightly weird types who had sworn to shun the temptation to drink people's blood and similar . . . But they were still weird, possibly even more so, drinking only cocoa and marching with banners and drums on every possible occasion. Arguably that was better than being taken to the crossroads and staked . . . again. The hand of Lady Margolotta was visible everywhere, and Moist knew that where you found her hand you would also find the hand of Vetinari.

But now there was menace in the air. Although Moist was, in fact, okay with menace, it was the thought of dying that was uppermost in his mind, and his little internal demon was shouting, 'Hahaha! Remember that a life without danger is a life not worth living!' And valiantly he stood by that assertion . . . though quite frankly he would rather have been standing on a beach in Quirm, if possible eating one of those really nice ice creams they made with a wafer-thin cone that crunched so beautifully as you bit into it. With strawberry sauce. And sprinkles.

Moist stood in the middle of the guard's van letting his body understand the motions of the train. He rocked when it rolled and concentrated on staying upright. After all, he reasoned, if there was going to be a fight then your legs had to know what was waiting for them. Vimes was puzzled about what he was doing, but when Moist tried to explain, the commander snorted in derision.

'In general, Mister Lipwig, I try to disable those who're trying to do the same to me as quickly as I can. It's a simple little approach. Not very complicated, but it helps me stay alive . . . that and the understanding that almost everything has a groin and every foot has a boot.'

The sound of metal and stone bouncing off the carriages came as a relief. Like an expected shoe dropping.

The train was travelling through a cutting that had once been used by wagons, and Iron Girder almost touched the rocky sides as she passed through at less than half speed. The guard's van was in a state of siege and only later did Moist learn that grags had swung down from the sides of the cutting.

An unfortunate few dwarfs had landed on Bluejohn's flatbed and while the biggest officer of the City Watch was at heart a pussycat, two grags trying to hack lumps out of him was clearly causing him to become somewhat acerbic and so the pussycat was now fighting like a lion. He hurled curses in trollish which actually shone red in the air as they were cast.

Quelling his nerves, Moist grabbed a jim crow and opened the trap door on to the roof of the guard's van, to the initial amazement of the grag who had been trying to force his way in. But any sense of achievement the dwarf might have felt was knocked away by the vicious metal bar hitting his jaw with a satisfactory clang.

Moist wasn't surprised to hear Commander Vimes scrambling up after him. And now, surrounded by grags in a state of disarray, Vimes tore off his shirt and as other dwarfs approached him Moist saw them suddenly realize that their futures were in the hands of the legendary Blackboard Monitor. Once freed, the brilliant scar on the commander's wrist was almost throbbing in the half-light. The grags stared at it and that was the first of their many mistakes, because the commander went, as they say in Ankh-Morpork, totally librarian on them.

As Vimes charged towards the far end of the van he smacked away one distraught grag so that he landed on top of another, making it look almost balletic as they twisted and fell on to the rails below. And now the goblins joined in to make the grags' day just a little bit more interesting: goblins in your armour was definitely *not* an aid to fighting.

The trap door and an adjoining panel had been torn away from the top of the guard's van and, while battling a particularly ferocious dwarf,* Moist saw Detritus levelling his enormous crossbow through the hole and heard the troll shout, 'Piece Maker!', a signal to anyone of sense to take extreme cover immediately. The darts that the piecemaker fired were hardwood and therefore horribly dangerous. And if Detritus was really feeling fit, the weapon spat the wood so fast that the darts ignited as they flew. Not metal, only wood, but wood going so incredibly fast that it splintered into a thousand more darts all travelling at terrible speed.

When the thunder had died away, Detritus yelled up to him,

---

* The way that Moist fought was erratic, since he took the view that if you didn't know what you were going to do next, neither would the enemy. After all, it was a mêlée and nobody owns a mêlée. You might as well try to control a hurricane.

'Hey, Mister Lipwig! Dis van is goin' backwards! Der gritsuckers knew jus' where to take der engine off!'

Moist turned and saw, to his horror, Iron Girder pulling away at speed from the now stranded guard's van. He looked down at Bluejohn who was holding a grag in each hand and there was screaming as he banged their heads together and tossed them into the darkness between the tracks.

'We're going backwards, Bluejohn!' yelled Moist. 'Take us forward, could you!'

There was a jerk as Bluejohn stopped the guard's van dead, quite possibly with his feet, and Moist jumped down on to the shuddering flatbed.

'Nice work, Mister Bluejohn. Now get out that thing Mister Simnel's lads made for you, please.'

In his curiously childish voice, Bluejohn said, 'Oh yes, Mister Lipwig, I can do dat and I can tow der guard's van as well.'

Vimes dropped down from the roof where he had been making life difficult for the grags on top – who were now essentially on the bottom – shouting 'What the hell's going on! Why've we stopped and where's the rest of the train?!'

'Those buggers have uncoupled us!' yelled Moist. 'But it's no problem ... there's a handcar on Bluejohn's flatbed ... for emergencies!' And, indeed, when the pedals of the handcar started to turn, the guard's van accelerated and shot like an arrow towards the disappearing Iron Girder.

Bluejohn's big face was aglow as he pedalled like, well, Bluejohn, because nobody else could have made that flatbed fly along the rails. It rattled and screeched and complained, but the troll's huge feet oscillated up and down in a blur and the inner demon of Moist von Lipwig whispered to himself, 'A little treadle machine to help somebody travel fast? Might be an idea to remember that.'

The whistle of Iron Girder echoed around the canyons, and Vimes shouted, 'Get me up close to that train, officer!'

347

Trolls don't sweat as such. A kind of blooming takes place instead. Bluejohn grunted, 'Gettin' a bit outta puff now, commander . . . but I'll do my best.'

Bluejohn's handcar, still dragging the guard's van, including the recumbent grags, slammed into the last carriage, and before it bounced away again he reached forward and grabbed a buffer in each hand. Immediately Vimes flew like a demon, running across Bluejohn's ample back and into the besieged carriage. Moist followed as best he could. Grags and delvers were everywhere, still trying to get into the armoured carriage ahead, and then it was just a matter of who was friend and who was foe, and there were far fewer friends, making it very easy to spot the foes.

'Come on, lads! No speeches, you sons of mothers!' Vimes shouted back to the others in the guard's van. 'You know who the enemy is and you know what to do . . . Get them before they get you and don't let them get anywhere near the King! I'm heading up on the roof!'

Up on the swaying roof of the armoured carriage, Vimes quickly started to take his toll on the enemy, who were swinging down from the canyon walls on to the moving train. Unhappily for the attacking dwarfs, the problem with swinging down was that the defender on the train could easily judge where you were going to land, which was precisely the place you then got hit mightily with a jim crow. While Moist and Vimes, well accustomed to the motion of the train, could keep their feet, the dwarfs, even with their low centre of gravity, simply couldn't fight on the rocking and rolling carriages, and the two men were able to knock them down like skittles. Moist couldn't help feeling sorry for them. Idiots with a cause and it had been such a stupid cause to begin with.

And as he was watching Vimes fend off an attack from two of the buggers, there came a blow out of the darkness that knocked Moist on to his back, taking the wind out of him. He looked up into the face of madness. That special kind of madness warped by idealism. The madness that gloats – which, in these circumstances, was a bad idea. The grag swung his axe, but with reactions born out of terror Moist managed to roll as the mighty blade struck the roof beside him, splintering the wood where his head had just been. The grag lifted the axe once again and Moist thought, well, this is it, then . . . a life without danger is a life not worth living . . . Maybe the next one'll be even better . . .

And then he saw it and grinned: the entrance to the tunnel. And so he winked, as only Moist von Lipwig could wink, and said, 'Goodbye.'

Sparks rained down and it took him a moment to realize what had happened. Or, indeed, what unfortunately had not happened. The tunnel was just too capacious – the grag had not been shortened as expected and his axe was scraping along the roof, making a rather impressive fountain of sparks in its wake, illuminating the scene just enough for Moist to kick up and find his target, hoping against hope that *this* dwarf wasn't a female. And fortunately luck was with him and therefore regrettably not with the grag, who dropped his axe, clutched at his groin and unceremoniously fell from the carriage on to the tracks below.

As the train emerged from the tunnel, it came to a grinding stop. Moist scrambled to his feet and clambered back down across the flatbed to find out what had happened to the rest of the gang. He was relieved to discover the crew of the guard's van all more or less unharmed, including Of the Twilight the Darkness and his group of goblins, Fred Colon, Nobby Nobbs, Cheery Littlebottom, Detritus and Bluejohn, who was still hanging on to the last carriage, keeping the train together. There were also a few rather bewildered engineers and train drivers, some of whom had been trying to catch up with their sleep when the attack came but had apparently done their best.

Moist hadn't noticed Nobby and Colon in the mêlée but decided that he would not be surprised to hear that they had acquitted themselves with great derring-do and, of course, it was such a pity that it would turn out everyone else had been too busy to see them doing it. Even so, looking around the few groaning grags still on the train, Moist acknowledged that Nobby and Colon, if given no alternative, could fight like tigers, especially tigers with the nasty weaponry of the streets where anything went and wherever it went it could be very, very painful. Colon, in particular, was master of the underhand, and some of the groaning was familiar to Moist as the famous Ankh-Morpork lullaby.

Moist never thought of himself as a leader of men, so he delegated in circumstances such as these. The chore of marshalling went to Fred Colon, known to all for his excellent shouty voice that turned his face an unusual shade of puce and was expelled at a volume that even Iron Girder would have envied.

Such grags as were alive or weren't definitely dead were trussed up before being taken to the guard's van, where, Moist suspected, Commander Vimes would have a little talk with them about this and that and names and places and who and when and what dreadful manners they had. Lovely.

And now a figure leaned out of the armoured carriage. It was Aeron.

'The King is safe! Thank you all! Iron Girder came in for a hammering but the grags that managed to get on to the footplate were shown the furnace by Stoker Blake.' Moist winced at that. He had been close to the furnace a great many times when it had been opened by the stoker and it was instant suntan time, but if you were standing in the wrong place at the critical moment it was instant fiery death.

The journey onward, with the couplings once more in place, was altogether a sombre ride, for the victors as well as for the surviving dwarfs awaiting their dreaded conversation with the Blackboard Monitor who, it was believed, could cause you and your family never to have existed. Rubbed away, as it were, in the chalk dust of the blackboard.

*

A little later Iron Girder gently kissed the buffers at the Bonk railhead, and the first person to step down on to the hastily erected platform was Rhys Rhysson. He was greeted by a very large and extremely agitated rotund man, who had the word 'burgomaster' stamped firmly into his demeanour. He was sweating cobs and a fat man can sweat just as much as an engine. He genuflected to the King, an achievement considering his shape which was, not to put too fine a point on it, a globe.

'Welcome back, sire,' he said, panting. 'The humans of Bonk have always had a good relationship with your countrymen and I sincerely hope that this amicable arrangement is going to continue.'

This invitation was uttered at a very high speed and Moist saw it for what it was: a plea saying, please don't hurt us, we are fairly decent people and have always accepted your highness's claim to the Scone of Stone. The unsaid codicil being, please don't hurt us and above all, don't interfere with the running of our mercantile activities. Please. Please?

Rhys gripped the proffered and rather sweaty hand and said, 'I'm so sorry if you have been inconvenienced by the recent unpleasantness, Humphrey.' A gesture which left the burgomaster all smiles.

'Oh, it wasn't too bad, Your Majesty. It was a bit of a nuisance when you . . . I mean the others started knocking down the clacks and all that. But you know how it is, it's like a family squabble in the house next door where you know it's not your business so you're ready with tea, sympathy and possibly bandages and medicaments. And next time you meet the couple next door you don't look too hard and mind your business and are still friends on the morrow.

'And anyway, her ladyship got involved, and once she'd made a couple of examples . . . Well, thank goodness, we had our clacks back. She's firm but fair is Lady Margolotta, and remarkably swift.'

The sweating Humphrey knew full well he was talking about the most influential vampire in the world whilst at the same time giving her the appearance of an elderly lady who only had to bang her walking stick on the floor to get total respect.

'Of course all families have their ups and downs,' Humphrey continued, 'those little spats so easily started and so quickly left behind with no real damage done.'

Behind the burgomaster the train was unloading its passengers while Iron Girder occasionally hissed or spat in the way a loco-motive has of making it clear it is not entirely quiescent.

Moist could hear Vimes debriefing Captain Sally von Humpeding, the Watch's only vampire member, who had been seconded to the Bonk Watch. They came over to report.

'Sally tells me that even though all communication from within Schmaltzberg has been cut off, reports have been reaching the Watch that all is not well with the conspirators,' said Vimes. He looked to Sally for confirmation.

'Yes,' she said, 'our sources indicate that the grag known as Ardent—'

She was interrupted by a snort of rage from Rhys and a rattle of axes from his assembled compatriots.

'Him again!' snarled Rhys.

'Yes,' said Sally. 'Him and a few others we'd been trying to locate after the massacre in Quirm. Well, it seems that Ardent and his followers are losing support; they're not having it all their way. There is unrest—'

'Good,' said Rhys. 'We can use that.'

'And Albrechtson?' asked Aeron.

'Well,' Sally smiled, showing a hint of fang, this being the most appropriate place in the world to let them get some air. 'Well. And loyal to you, sire.'

A rather smart goblin messenger insinuated his way through the crowd and passed a message to Sally, who read it. 'Ah,' she said. 'It's a message from Albrechtson. It seems the opposition know you've arrived, sire. Albrechtson would like you to know that he's being well treated and has been able to follow the progress of Iron Girder, thanks to the goblins.'

Rhys turned and looked at Simnel and Moist and said, 'Thank you, and Sir Harry, for getting me here safely. And Iron Girder, too. At the appropriate time you will know my generosity and I'd like to talk to you further. But do excuse me. I have a kingdom to reclaim.'

Addressing the company of dwarfs now fully assembled on the platform and armed to the teeth, he proclaimed, 'Let it be known that the Low King has arrived and will take his place on the Scone of Stone. Anyone wishing to deny him that trivial pleasure should be prepared to back up their coherent and well-founded objections with weaponry. It really is quite as simple as that. This message will be carried into Schmaltzberg by Bashfull Bashfullsson, a highly respected and knowledgeable dwarf known to all, accompanied by my trusted secretary, Aeron. We should also include Commander Vimes, the Blackboard Monitor, and one-time Ambassador, to see fair play. Remember that at all times tampering with the King's Messengers is a matter of treason. Be aware, I'm not going to be a nanny about this. Insurgent dwarfs will get their just deserts.'

The sound of Vimes loudly lighting his cigar broke the silence.

'Let the others go first, I'll go along in a minute or two,' he said.

Moist, of course, hadn't been at Koom Valley but right now he wondered if he was about to see the ghost of Koom Valley's second incarnation – except it would be dwarf against dwarf. He wanted to shout out 'This is nuts!', and realized that in fact he had said it aloud.

To his surprise, the King said, 'Certainly so, Mister Lipwig. It beggars all reason, doesn't it? But sooner or later there comes a time when you have to take names and crack skulls. I'm sorry, it's at the other end of the spectrum from the little chat and it's what happens when reason no longer holds sway.'

'But you're all dwarfs. What can you possibly achieve?' groaned

Moist, who for the rest of his life would always remember the tone of the King's voice . . .

'Tomorrow. That, Mister Lipwig, is what we can achieve. *Tomorrow.*'

The arrival of the messengers sent an immediate buzz around the multiple caverns of Schmaltzberg, somehow the centre of the galaxy when it came to hubbub of all sizes and rumour mills that turned faster than the mills of the gods. Rumour flowed like quicksilver. The phenomenon might be called the dwarf clacks were it not for the fact that the clacks didn't scramble the messages on a whim, thought Moist as he followed Rhys and the main band of dwarfs down into the honeycomb that was Schmaltzberg. The myriad noises flowing up from below through every tunnel and cavern were merging into a kind of audible mist or, he thought, fog. It simmered around the earlobe. The terrible sounds and confusions of war.

But now individual sounds were getting through. Raised voices, screams and the clatter of weaponry, punctuated with the occasional yell and dwarfish curses, which are known to have a life all of their very own. Further down, they came across Aeron, who was waiting with blood dripping from his sword. He noticed Moist's look and shrugged.

'There was a grag. He fought hard but would not submit, preferring death to ignominy . . . and so I accommodated him.' That last phrase contained more emphasis than Moist had heard for a very long time. Aeron turned to Rhys and reported.

'There have been certain clashes of opinion, your majesty,' he said, pointing to several dwarfs being treated in what would have been an impromptu field hospital had it been in a field.

Swords, hammers and axes were being deployed below as the King carried on marching, until they came to what must be the great hall, the largest cavern of them all.

As they passed through the portal, Moist came to a halt, trying to get a grip on this subterranean landscape, lit by the enormous chandeliers of dribbling candles along with cressets and great vats of squirming vurms* writhing in the corners; so there was light, he thought, but a strange light that was somehow negotiating with the eyes. You could see but what you saw was the darkness.

'Well, it's not a war any more,' said Vimes, suddenly there beside him. 'And not too many serious outcomes, except for the grags. That's dwarf-on-dwarf war: a hell of a lot of shouting and accusing and spitting, a lot like cats really, but that's dwarfs for you. They're not that stupid. Bags of bravado and sabre-rattling, but no one really wants to get hurt. You fight hoping for a small wound that looks good afterwards. Something to show the grandchildren, but really, when it comes to it, dwarf against dwarf, it generally settles down.'

Vimes puffed his cigar and continued, 'Mind you, if it were dwarf against troll this place would be running with blood. On the whole, it's like the taverns in Ankh-Morpork on a Saturday night. Everyone is full of gumption and pissy bravery and beer. Much too much beer. And then afterwards it's just a lot of groaning until they see the light.'

In fact, what Moist could see near by was dwarfs in small groups, some of them bandaged, in positions which suggested that war as such, if not over, had been set aside for a breather and maybe a decent quaff. And younger dwarfs were going between the hurt and wounded with flagons. And one by one the dwarfs got up, shook hands with the nearest dwarf and walked haphazardly to the next group, where perhaps they would sit and chat and make up stories

---

* Vurms are somewhat like glow worms, but with a stink that illumines. They can be found in deep dark places, where they subsist on the effluvia of any creatures that may arrive there. They are very useful to tomb raiders and others of that kidney – who in turn are often very useful to the vurms, especially their kidneys.

of near misses and clever parries and similar boozy boastings. Little by little, dwarf normality was flowing through Schmaltzberg once again.

'Pissed as farts,' said Vimes. 'But at the bottom, not bad, just susceptible to rabble rousers.' He sighed again. 'Maybe this time they'll have learned. And on that day Nobby Nobbs will be a shining hero!'

And that was all it took? Moist found himself wondering. After all the adrenalin of the train journey, the ambushes, the attacks . . . the bridge . . . the sleepless nights . . . expecting at every turn to hear the swish of a scythe and to find that this time his luck really had run out . . . and then Rhys gave a fine speech and just walked in and took back the kingdom?

'I was expecting them to put up more of a fight,' he said. 'You know, more of a glorious battle that would become the stuff of legends.'

'That's a very foolish thing to say, Mister Lipwig,' said Vimes. There's nothing "glorious" about times like this . . . People have died, not necessarily good people and not too many, but nevertheless the face you wear on a battlefield should be a solemn one until the time when things are cleaned up and the real world drips its way in.'

Moist felt the shame welling up from his boots and said, 'Commander, I stand abashed, quite sincerely.'

And instantly Vimes's face was eyeballing his and the commander exclaimed, 'Really? It seems it's not just the railway breaking new ground here!'

For once short of a ready reply, Moist turned to see what had become of Rhys and his party.

Rhys Rhysson had entered the cavern at a run. He headed straight for its centre, where stood the Scone of Stone. Now he looked around and demanded, 'Where is Ardent? I want him brought here, and as many of his followers as still remain. Though doubtless most have run: this place is full of exits.'

Bashfull Bashfullsson shouted, 'I have the scoundrel here, sire!'

The assembly of dwarfs went into the usual seemingly endless dwarfish hubbub, followed by a deep intake of breath from all concerned when Ardent was brought forward. His expression Moist couldn't read. But Moist, the man for atmospheres, could tell that Ardent was already somewhere beyond sanity, whilst Rhys seemed as cool and calm as ever, however fearful he might have been on the inside. And Moist would have wagered the mint that the King wasn't actually fearful at all. There was something in his demeanour that suggested an absolute assurance that this day was his (or indeed, *hers*, as he finally allowed the thought to creep back into his consciousness).

Sitting on the hallowed Scone of Stone with Ardent in front of him, Rhys said, 'You were dealt with mercifully after the Koom Valley Accord and still you thought it was right to try to take this kingdom from me. You encouraged those who tortured families to get their own way. What would people think of me if I had even a most minute inclination to treat you kindly? You are clever and many dwarfs speak highly of you, but your cleverness has been used to undermine my rule and make dwarfs appear to be vicious and stupid criminals in the eyes of all other species. What have you to say, in front of me and your kin?'

Ardent was silent.

'Very well,' said the King. 'No answer. You leave me no alternative. In times gone by a dwarf king would execute someone like you as a matter of course.'

And then there was the sound of metal and the King stood up, axe in hand. At last the light of terror passed across Ardent's face.

The King said, 'Oh, I see. Then perhaps as I am . . . you know . . . a modernizer, as you always say with a sneer, perhaps I'll deal with you as a modernizer should. Therefore, you will go on trial. And I shall see to it that among the jury there will be the families of those the grags tortured and those surviving guests of the wedding in Llamedos and all the others whose lives have been unnecessarily troubled by your existence in this world. They may be merciful and I will accept their verdict.'

Ardent remained silent and the King said, 'Take him away in chains but keep him alive, if only as a reminder for me that being a King is not an easy job.'

As Ardent was led away to much applause Rhys turned to the assembled dwarfs. 'Now I suggest someone goes and brings me my friend Albrecht Albrechtson who, to our shame, has been shackled and stuffed into a dungeon. Then perhaps the people delegated to go and let him out might hand him a flagon of brandy and, if practicable, run away. He has a piquant sense of humour.'

Rhys sat down again on the Scone of Stone and said, in tones that echoed around the cavern, 'It is usual at this time for me to say "my fellow dwarfs" . . .' There was a sucking feeling in the air as the King went on, 'but today I'll say "ladies and gentlemen dwarfs" . . . I am here not only to reclaim *my* Scone of Stone, which over the years has seen many important and notable buttocks sitting on it. I wonder, how many of those buttocks down the years were female?'

The sharp intake of breath by the whole gathering now seemed to draw all the air out of the place as the Low King continued.

'Hear me out! It is well known that the gender of a dwarf is entirely their secret unless they decide otherwise. And I recall that in Ankh-Morpork, a few years ago, there was a fashion show for dwarfs only. I was there, incognito, and I recognized a few of you, quite possibly purchasing for use in the privacy of your own home? Shatta made a lot of money that day and I understand that Madame Sharn wants to open a new shop here. Here in Schmaltzberg! Does this thought frighten anybody? In these days, I think not. And all I am doing now, my friends, is to introduce to you something important: it is the truth! You know . . . that thing which remains when all the lies have been burned away. And now I will tell you that I have decided to no longer be your King!'

There was an extra hubbub of indrawn breaths and sotto voce speculation from the populace at large, with all eyes focused on the King. The magic was broken or possibly enhanced by the tiny sound of a match being struck by Commander Vimes. And the fat cigar glowed like a beacon. Vimes smiled and nodded at the King, and in that moment Moist realized that Vimes had probably always known, or at least since the famous adventure several years before when he was Ambassador to Rhys's election as Low King.

There was a disturbance as the crowd parted to allow the venerable Albrecht Albrechtson to make his way to stand by the Low King, who greeted him warmly in the traditional dwarf manner of butting helmets.*

'Welcome, old friend. I'm sorry that you have been . . . inconvenienced by my absence. Those responsible will pay for that,' he said in a loud voice, glaring at the crowd. Then more quietly to Albrecht, Rhys said, 'You've arrived at a good moment. I'm in the middle of making an announcement.'

'So I heard,' said Albrechtson. 'What are you doing? You don't have to stand down. You won.'

The Low King laughed. 'Stand down? Oh, I don't think so, boyo. You'll see.'

Turning back to the crowd, Rhys took a deep breath and said, 'This will be surprising news to many of my subjects, but I am female, just like your mothers were, and therefore am in truth your Queen!'

---

* A part of dwarf etiquette that outsiders find near impossible to master, the traditional helmet butt is a little less vigorous than the manoeuvre known on the tougher streets of Ankh-Morpork as the 'Shamlegger Kiss', but it must also not be so gentle as to imply that either the giver or the receiver is a sissy.

There it was again. The famous dwarf intake of breath. Even Albrechtson seemed startled. Moist looked at Aeron and noticed the dwarf's mailed fist was resting, oh so lightly, on his sword. Bashfullsson was standing right behind Albrechtson, watching him closely. Next to Moist, Vimes carefully laid down his glowing cigar on a rock ledge and tensed. This could be very interesting, Moist thought.

'And if you think your Queen is not as good a ruler as your King, do you really believe your mother was inferior to your father?' The Queen laughed. 'I see embarrassment among all of you. That's good. The thing about being embarrassed is that sooner or later you aren't, but you remember that you were.'

There was a noticeable shift in atmosphere as the Queen carried on, saying, 'I have seen that in warm breasts there is a truth which is not to be denied, but we dwarfs seem to deny everything, building little worlds inside a big one. And one might ask what we are trying to escape from – unless it is ourselves. We are dwarfs, yes, but we could be better than our dwarf ancestors stuck in their holes.'

When she had finished the Queen looked around at the assembled dwarfs and said, 'Well? No dwarf man enough to challenge me?'

Several eyes turned to Albrechtson, who looked thoughtful but did not move. Bashfullsson relaxed his stance.

And suddenly the Queen's finger was pointing and she said, 'Shod Orebreaker, I always thought of you as a level-headed dwarf with your head screwed on, although possibly against the thread.'

And Moist felt the exultation of those who hadn't been the one facing the finger and the misery of Shod Orebreaker, and he wondered: had the Low Queen's voice changed, or had it always been like that? She hadn't threatened, but a visible threat was in the air. She had them in her hand, and she was squeezing, and the dwarf stepped backwards as she pointed at him and she said, 'Where are your grags now, Shod Orebreaker?'

The said Shod became a picture of panic. 'Not my grags, my Queen!'

This was possibly because Aeron had passed the Queen a thick file. The Queen licked a finger and riffled through the pages, looked down and said, 'Really? Then I must have been misinformed.'

She turned to the rest of the dwarfs and said, 'I wonder if I have been misinformed about all of you?'

But the assembled company was watching the flicking pages, trying not to crane to see whether their name was on the list . . . It was laughable. She had them by the short and curlies, and she said, 'Strange, isn't it, that when the chips are down they take other chips with them. If anyone wants to test my claim then let them step forward now!'

There were murmurings, dwarfs turning round to other dwarfs and the traditional aforesaid hubbub of such occasions and then there was a hush as Albrechtson spoke.

'My queen,' he said, and the hubbub bubbled. It was the unexpected moment: the great defender of all that was dwarfish now having a stocktaking of his thoughts. 'My queen, we, fortuitously, live and so we should learn. I have always considered myself knowledgeable, a true scholar of the ways of Tak, but the past days have shown me that even I have lessons to learn. In my little dungeon, I heard my ways changing and understood the meaning of humility. In fact, I am prepared to admit before you all that some of those lessons were taught me by a goblin a fraction of my age, whom I am proud to call my friend.'

Moist saw that the old dwarf was crying. Albrechtson hesitated, then shouted, 'Tak save the Queen! And I will fight anyone who says otherwise.' And Moist thought, Oh blast, it's all going to start over again.

But the assembled dwarfs made no move to take Albrechtson up on his challenge. The sea of faces in the hall looked universally stunned, as if someone had announced that gold was, to be honest, not that interesting after all.

The Queen gracefully thanked Albrechtson, then pulled herself up and said, 'I am well aware that many of you have financed the grags and their entourage and I know the names, yes, indeed I know the names of those who'd kill for a curdled thesis. In the fullness of time there will be no redemption for them. We were generous after the mess of Koom Valley and those were the stupid days, but if the grags and their friends think they can take my Scone from me they will know me for what I am. Your Queen. I believe all of you will have heard of Queen Ynci of Lancre, yes? Well, I consider her my role model, but right now I'm looking for peace for all the world and specifically for myself and my child.'

And in the thundering susurration that followed this there was one dwarf suddenly standing next to the Queen. It was Aeron, and he drew his sword, not against anyone in particular, but nevertheless very ready to defend his wife and his unborn child.

Over the uproar the Queen said, 'And is there anyone here now who doubts that I am the Queen by right? It seems to me our ancestors thought their mothers were inferior. Well, as I say, I am soon to be a mother, so which of you gentlemen would like to try and take my Scone from me?'

Moist looked around. There were no takers. The Queen looked dangerous to touch and she didn't even have a weapon in her hands. It had to be game, set and whole boxful of matches.

'Very well,' the Low Queen of the dwarfs concluded. 'There will be a feast for all who come with goodwill and there will, of course, be much quaffing.' She smiled and added, 'That includes cocktails, for those who like them. Believe me, the world is upside down, as it was meant to be. Praise Tak! And praise Iron Girder and all those who built her, fed her and polished her.'

*

'Ardent was on a hiding to nowhere,' said Albrecht at the banquet later that day. 'People broke away to avoid the inevitable. You're right, your majesty. We forgot what it was to be true dwarfs, but then people were getting hurt! There were too many threats against decent dwarfs. The little bits of mercury flow together and in the end his support turned out to be built of sand.'

Vimes gazed around from his place as honoured guest at the low table and said, 'Look at them there, the world has indeed turned upside down. There will be grumbling, but what are you dwarfs without grumbling?'

Albrecht snorted and said, 'There should have been more of a reckoning.'

'Oh, really?' said the Queen. 'I don't intend to start my new life with a bloodbath. Justice will be done. Everyone knows who the main players are, we always have done. We have names, depositions. It's a small world for dwarfs, with nowhere else to hide, and, frankly, the work is almost completed. The deep-down grags behind this lost a lot of their best fighters attacking Iron Girder on her peregrination across the landscape.

'What a voyage that was! And the wonderful discovery of loggy-sticks. The train is the future; bringing people closer together. Think about it. People *run* to see the train go past. Why? Because it's heading to the future or coming from the past. Personally, I very much want the future and I want to see to it that dwarfs are part of that future, if it's not too late.'

Vimes smiled and said, 'Well, your majesty, you have the oppor-tunity right now. I understand from young Simnel that the bridge at Wilinus will take several months to be repaired and strengthened sufficiently to be able to take the weight of a fully loaded train. That means that Iron Girder and her carriages will be stranded here until the line is rebuilt.'

He looked down the table to where Moist was in earnest conver-

363

sation with Bashfullsson. 'Mister von Lipwig will no doubt be happy to advise on the . . . commercial opportunities.'

Rhys smiled. 'Ah yes, I'm familiar with Mister von Lipwig's reputation, and have been impressed with his, ah, capabilities. However, I think it might be advisable to summon our lawyer, Mr Thunderbolt, to ensure that all is done fair and square, see.'

Vimes laughed. 'Very wise.'

'And no doubt there will be a need for workers to help with construction?' enquired the Queen. 'The young ones, in particular, who may not be so interested in staying in the mines, but nevertheless want a good solid job with plenty of metal and hammering involved? We are still dwarfs, after all.'

Afterwards the Queen walked among her quite possibly loyal subjects and it was a grand perambulation, with little outbreaks of mail skirts and elaborately coiffed beards amongst certain of the dwarfs rushing shyly over to assure her of their fealty. As Vimes said afterwards, for that day at least she had won hands down, especially since a great many of the dwarfs she was talking to were already openly declaring themselves females who had been waiting for this moment for a very long time.

The evening before they were to leave Bonk, Moist wandered down to the railhead, idly pondering recent events. Well, he thought, the world has seen the footplate of Iron Girder and the Queen has been given her crown back and according to Commander Vimes the worst of the grags are either dead or behind bars.

At the makeshift station Iron Girder was being guarded by Nobby Nobbs and Fred Colon, who were both sound asleep. Iron Girder, however, wasn't, although the kettle was barely simmering after a long day giving rides to the locals up and down the single track.

Moist tiptoed to the empty footplate and whispered, 'What are you, Iron Girder?' There was a moment of silence, then a shimmer as the wisps of steam drifted up into the night air above the loco-motive and a voice breathed into his brain, soft and warm and somehow damp.

'My, oh my, Mister Lipwig, you are the smart one, just as they say. I am me. I am Iron Girder. But all it takes is for people to believe and I am no longer just an artefact put together by clever engineers. I am an idea, a something made of nothing, whose time has come to be. Some even call me "goddess".'

Moist's fleeting thought about traditional representations of goddesses in diaphanous nighties with maybe an urn or two was banished as the voice continued a little more sharply.

'Am I not beautiful? And I tell you, my children will be even better! More sleek and more handsome and more powerful! Even now Mister Simnel is making my children for me. In time I will become ubiquitous, part of the landscape which is ennobled by my fleeting passage. I hear the worship every day that tells me that I am power personified and those who think to oppose me and put out my fire will find themselves thwarted, and swiftly. I, Mister Lipwig, I will rule on the up line and I will rule on the down line.'

In the twilight Moist saw a skinny figure walk up to Iron Girder. Dick Simnel shut down some hissing mechanism or other and the voice, the beautiful voice, was silenced.

'Aye, she's gradely all right! Come to see her for the last time before we head back to the city, have you? I can't blame you. Everyone's been wanting to see 'er, and I won't lie, Mister Lipwig, it's a wrench to leave her behind, for all she's got good work to do 'ere. Iron Girder, she's turned out to be a great lass. She was the power and she was 'arnessed, by gum. Oh, yes! 'arnessed by the sine and the cosine, and even the tangent had its little 'and in there somewhere! But not least she was tamed by my sliding rule.'

Dick grinned at Moist and continued. 'People see Iron Girder and they're gobsmacked by what can be done with mathematics! Don't you go thinking she'll burn you with living steam because she won't. I've seen to it that she won't. She'll always be my favourite engine, Mister Lipwig, the queen of them all. She lives. How could anyone say she doesn't?'

Moist looked around and saw that they were surrounded by goblins sitting quietly in a big circle like worshippers at the shrine, and once again Dick Simnel said, 'Power, Mister Lipwig, power under control.'

Moist was seldom speechless, but this time all he could say was, 'Good luck with that, Mister Simnel. Good luck.'

And the driver made his magic and the fire box opened and spilled dancing red shadows all around the footplate. And then came the rattle and jerk as Iron Girder took the strain and breathed steam for one more turn around the track as the goblins whooped and cackled and scrambled up her sides. And then came the first chuff and the second chuff and then the chuff bucket overflowed as Iron Girder escaped the pull of friction and gravity and flew along the rails.

Dick Simnel lit his pipe from a hot coal and said to the night, 'Aye, gradely.'

When Drumknott entered the Oblong Office a few days later there was a familiarity to the silence, interrupted only by the scratch of a pencil as the austere figure behind the desk filled in a word on that day's crossword. Drumknott coughed.

'Yes?'

The face of the Patrician was forbidding. An eyebrow shifted quizzically, a characteristic known and feared by many. Drumknott smiled.

'Many congratulations! You have that expression down to a T and the accent never faltered. And, of course, the frown! You've always been very good at the frown. Quite frankly, if he was standing next to you I wouldn't know whom from which.'

Suddenly the face of the Patrician disappeared, leaving only Charlie the Clown in Lord Vetinari's clothes, looking embarrassed.

'It wasn't very difficult, Mister Drumknott, with you giving me those little signs and everything.'

'Oh no,' said Drumknott. 'Your performance was perfect. You've impersonated his lordship for two weeks and not put a foot wrong! But now to business. The sum we agreed will be deposited in your special account at the Royal Bank tomorrow.' Drumknott smiled again and said, like a cheerful uncle, 'How is your wife these days, Charlie?'

'Oh, Henrietta's fine, Mister Drumknott, thank you for asking.'

'And your little boy – Rupert? He must be out of school now, yes?'

Charlie laughed uncertainly and said, 'Not so little, sir, he's growing up like a weed and wants to be an engine driver.'

And Drumknott said, 'Well now, Charlie, you already have enough money to put him through a trade anywhere in the city and give your daughter a dowry fit for a queen. And, of course, you're still in the same house? Excellent!'

'Oh, yessir, and thanks to you we've got much better bedrooms for the kids now and are saving up for a granny flat for when we can afford a granny. And Henrietta is overjoyed at the amount of money I'm bringing in these days and can even afford to get her hair cut at Mister Fornacite's, just like the posh ladies do. She's over the moon about it.' He grunted and said, 'I don't earn that much from the puppet shows and clowning business.'

And now Drumknott beamed once again and said, 'I'm sure his lordship will be glad to hear that your family is so happy and . . . alive. Long may it continue. I'll be recommending to him that you could be promoted, as it were, to higher things. And now, since his lordship is expected back within the hour, if you don't mind I'll take you out through the back door. We really don't want to see two Vetinaris in one place, do we?'

Charlie went almost white and said, 'Oh, no sir, we don't want that.'

'Well, we shan't, shall we,' said Drumknott. 'Off you go and I'll lock the door behind you.'

When Charlie had disappeared, happy but in haste, Drumknott, after a moment's thought, said to Dark Clerk Ishmael, 'I'm sure his lordship will want to know that we've checked the location of this Mister Fornacite's salon and the school that our friend's children go to. Is it the same as last year?'

And the clerk replied, 'Yes, it is, sir, I checked again the other day.' 'Well done.'

As his lordship had pointed out: 'If you take enough precautions, you never need to take precautions.' It was just a matter of making sure that Charlie didn't get . . . well, creative about his future.

Never had Moist been more happy to see his front door than when he got home and his wife opened it before he did, saying, 'Oh, it's you. Not dead? Good. How did it go?'

'Pretty well. The golems were incredible. Sad that we've had to leave Iron Girder there until the bridge is repaired. Still, we've got so many of Harry's golems and workers on it now it's not going to be long before Vetinari can have a special train of his own, if he likes.'

'To make sure relationships between Uberwald and Ankh-Morpork proceed in a . . . cordial fashion, no doubt,' said his wife with a smile.

Behind him, Of the Twilight the Darkness said, 'Already Uberwald goblins giving themselves railway name. Speaks funny, those ones, but quick clever, like all goblin.'

'Yes,' said Adora Belle, 'that reminds me. We got reports while you were away from clacksmen along the road from the Shires about some rather odd occurrences. Strange rumblings, steam coming out of molehills, that sort of thing. You wouldn't know anything about that, would you?'

Of the Twilight the Darkness reassembled his features into the closest approximation of innocence that a goblin can muster. 'No ideas, missus. Steaming molehill? Maybe cow eat bad grass. Course, maaany goblin interest in steaming things. Some even practises own little engine. Educational! Clever goblins.'

It was clearly a conversation for another day. Moist headed for the fluffy pillows with a grateful sigh. 'I'll have a rest and tomorrow I'll dally with the Bank. There must be some paperwork for me to sign. It would be nice to have a simple job for a while.'

Adora Belle snorted. 'How long would that be?'

Moist hesitated. 'Maybe a fortnight? There might be a *lot* of paperwork.'

'Yes, and you won't do it,' said Adora Belle. 'You know Mister Bent keeps everything shipshape. All you have to do is go around being friendly to everybody.'

'And nobody's trying to kill me, Spike.'

And Adora Belle said, 'We can but hope.'

At breakfast, Lady Sybil said to her husband, 'It sounds quite an adventure, Sam. I hear the Queen has changed her name to Blodwen. It means "fair flower" in Llamedos. Isn't that nice? I must write to her.'

'She'll like that,' said Vimes, whose wife's capacity to remain in touch with everybody she had ever met was well known and sometimes quite useful. Especially in political circumstances. The commander looked down at his muesli and said, 'You know, that Lipwig character isn't quite as bad as I thought. Acts like a scoundrel, but reasonably helpful when the chips are down. Mind you, I'm not going to tell him so.'

He pushed the healthy fibre around his bowl, wistfully recalling the stoker's fry-ups. 'But he does like being the centre of attention, of course.'

'Yes, some men are like that, dear.'

Lady Sybil was silent for a moment, then said, 'Sam, I know you're going to be busy what with the backlog and everything, but can I ask a favour?'

'Anything, dear.'

'When they have the line to Uberwald running, I'd love to go to visit the Queen, and most of all I'd like a holiday by the train. And Young Sam's mad about trains, you know. He's nearly filled up his first notebook already.'

'Well,' said Vimes, 'you know if I have a holiday I walk into a crime.'

Lady Sybil finished her egg and said, 'Jolly good, dear, you'll like that.'

Harry King was not entirely surprised when Drumknott arrived at the compound the following day and said, 'His lordship commands you and Lady King to present yourselves to him within the hour.' And the secretary winked uncharacteristically at Harry, and his wife when he told her was, according to her, all of a tizzy at the news.

'The palace in one hour! How can a girl look her best inside an hour?'

'Come on, Duchess,' said Harry. 'You look a treat as always and getting younger every day.'

'Oh, you teaser, Harry King!'

But Harry said, 'The coach is here and clean as a whistle and his lordship believes that punctuality is the politeness of Princes and that applies to you, too, young Emily. I expect your boy wouldn't want you to be late. That's not the railway . . . way.'

Harry hadn't told his wife what to expect, preferring to keep it as a surprise, and so as the coach arrived at the palace, his wife nearly had another tizzy to contend with because there were the great and good of Ankh-Morpork, and presumably some of the silly and nasty as well, just to see Harry King being turned into a Lord. *Lord King of the Permanent Way*. And in the wonderful ceremony that followed, Lord Harry's old Dutch did indeed become a Duchess.

Dick Simnel was made a knight, and a master engineer too, courtesy of the Chief Mining Engineer himself, and now stood hand in hand with the beaming Emily. Commander Vimes, resplendent in his ceremonial pantaloons and looking furious about them, was already burdened with every title it was his lordship's pleasure to bestow, but was given another medal anyway, struck in sorortanium and featuring Iron Girder herself. In fact there was a medal for every watchman who had been on the train, and every crew member, goblins included.

Later, there came the inevitable interview in the Oblong Office with Drumknott at a side table taking notes.

'I understand, Mister Lipwig,' said the Patrician, surveying the city below them from the window, 'that there were some remarkable events along the journey.'

Moist kept a straight face but around his neck he felt the prickle of a phantom noose.

The Patrician continued. 'A fog which became conveniently solid, a train which apparently flew across a gorge, and I'm still getting reports of subterranean phenomena all the way from the city to Bonk. The Archchancellor has assured me that no magic was involved in any of these events. You will recall, I am sure, Mister von Lipwig, that I expressly forbade the use of the buried golems in the railway enterprise, and that any evidence of their use would send you to the kittens?' He moved towards the fire, which was getting low in the grate, and gave it a prod with the poker – rather too pointedly, Moist thought.

'Excuse me, my lord, but did you find any such evidence?'

Vetinari turned to his secretary. 'Did we find any evidence, Drumknott?'

Drumknott looked at Moist. 'No, sir, we did not.'

'Well then, there is nothing more to say,' said the Patrician. 'After all, strange and inexplicable things turn up around here almost every week.'

Drumknott cleared his throat. 'Yes, sir. There was that fall of pianos in the Fish Market last week. It's just a part of being Ankh-Morpork.'

'Indeed, we are no strangers to strangeness. And frankly some things can be written down as phenomena without cause or issue,' said Vetinari, looking as benevolent as it was possible to do whilst holding a red-hot poker, and whilst being Vetinari.

'Incidentally, Mister Lipwig, your prowess in that fight on the train was excellent! Of course you needed a *little* assistance.'

Moist looked up at the Patrician, silhouetted by the flames behind him, and inside his head there was the horrible tinkle of a penny dropping. He gulped.

'You! You were Stoker Blake! That's impossible!'

'Really?' said the Patrician. 'As impossible as a train travelling on free air? Do you not believe that I could throw coal into the fire box? After all, what is that compared to dealing with Ankh-Morpork with its myriad demanding problems every day? I assure you of this, Mister Lipwig, I am a man of many talents and you should hope never to encounter some of them. Compared with them, Stoker Blake was a mere babe in arms.'

'What,' said Moist, 'fighting with shovels?'

'Dear dear, Mister Lipwig, you *are* easily impressed. You surely remember that I was schooled in the Assassins' Guild. After that experience, my predecessor on the footplate, Killer John Wagstaff, was, as they say, a pussycat in comparison. Indeed, I enjoyed my life as Mister Blake and all the new little skills it has taught me. Excellent implement, the shovel. And as for the other stokers, I think I made friends there, yes, there was a certain camaraderie among us. All said, a little holiday from the weighty business of the city, and I dare say I might be predisposed to travel on the footplate again when the mood takes me.'

'But why?'

'Why, Mister Lipwig? You of all people ask me why? The man who danced on the train roof, the man who actually looks for trouble if it appears to be the kind of trouble which is associated with the term derring-do? Though in your case a few more derring-don'ts might be a good idea. Sometimes, Mister Lipwig, the young you that you lost many years ago comes back and taps you on the shoulder and says, "This is the moment when civilization does not matter, when rules no longer hold sway. You have given the world all you can give and now it's the time that is just for you, the chance to go for broke in the last hurrah. Hurrah!"

Vetinari swung the poker against the fender, causing sparks to dance in the fireplace. He looked at the sparks and in whiplash fashion turned to Moist and said, 'And if you, Mister Lipwig, ever tell anyone else about this, Mister Trooper will be very glad to see you again. Do we have an understanding? Excellent.'

As if anyone would believe him if he did breathe a word about it! Moist was finding it hard enough to credit from the man's own lips. Then as he tried to process what he had been told, the Patrician's words about his own prowess sparked a renewed sense of grievance.

'You've given everyone else on that train a medal, even Nobby Nobbs. Is there nothing for me, then, my lord?'

There was a pause and Vetinari said, 'Oh, there is, Mister Lipwig, there is, and it's something wonderful: it's the precious gift of staying alive.'

And later, when he came to think about it, Moist thought that was, well, on the whole a good deal and, after all, he had *danced on the speeding locomotive.* That was living, all right!

*

373

A few weeks later, Drumknott persuaded Lord Vetinari to accompany him to the area behind the palace where a jungle of drain pipes emptied and several mismatched sheds, washhouses and lean-tos housed some of the necessary functions without which a modern palace could not operate.*

There was a young goblin waiting there, rather nervous, clasping what looked like two wheels held together by not very much. The wheels were spinning.

Drumknott cleared his throat. 'Show his lordship your new invention, Mister Of the Wheel the Spoke.'

Vetinari's face was unmoving as he watched the goblin put a leg over his creation and pedal the little machine around the washerwomen, who threw up their arms saying things like 'Oh my! Whatever next?'

And the oldest washerwoman said, 'I reckon you could have a young lady on the pillion behind you.'

Lord Vetinari said, 'You're going to want one of these, aren't you, Drumknott?'

'Well sir,' said Drumknott, 'this is not a mechanism, really. All it does is simply extend the parts of the body and look, no steam, no soot, just sweat.'

'Interesting,' said the Patrician. 'One man, his own motor.'

When the goblin eventually stopped in front of Lord Vetinari, he looked imploringly at Drumknott, who waited patiently for his master to decide.

Vetinari finally did smile and said, 'A remarkable *velocipede*, Mister Of the Wheel the Spoke. I do believe that Leonard of Quirm had a similar idea, but now we are in a world of motion, I see no problem here. It appears that every man could be his own horse. I commend you. May I suggest, young goblin, that you take your prototype along to Commander Vimes. An instrument that

* Frankly most palaces are just like this. Their backsides do not bear looking at.

doubles one's speed ought to be very useful to a hurrying watch-man, or, indeed, an insufficiently hurrying one. Mister Drumknott, please write a note to the commander and I will sign it. After all, some of them could do with the exercise. And if I were you, sir,' he added to the goblin, 'I would make an appointment with a certain troll lawyer called Thunderbolt and do what he tells you.

'The world is changing and it needs its shepherds and sometimes its butchers. And in this case, I'm its shepherd. Your enterprise has been noted. And all that anyone can say now is: What next? What little thing will change the world because the little tinkers carried on tinkering?'

Acknowledgements

I was assisted in writing *Raising Steam* by the boiler-suited gentlemen of the Watercress Line in Hampshire, who showed me – well, they showed me everything, including their workshops, the footplate and the fire box of a travelling locomotive and, wonder of wonders, the signal box: a treasure in mahogany and brass. Champion!

And, of course, my grateful thanks go to Rob for keeping the whole show on the rails, and to my editor, Philippa Dickinson, who supplied advice and flapjacks and, above all, patience.